Next Year in Jerusalem

By L. D. Bergsgaard

First published by Dog Ear Publishing
4010 W. 86th Street, Ste H
Indianapolis, IN 46268
www.dogearpublishing.net

ISBN: 978-145750-517-1

This book is printed on acid-free paper.

This book is a work of fiction. Places, events, and situations in this book are purely fictional and any resemblance to actual persons, living or dead, is coincidental.

Printed in the United States of America

Dedicated

To my wife, Donna, who has given loving encouragement and expert editing.

To my two beautiful daughters, Anne and Kate.

Acknowledgements

Thanks to my brother, Professor Mike Bergsgaard, who read the first manuscript and gently told me a little rewrite would help - three years later, I finished the edits.

Thanks to Todd Taylor, special agent (retired) who kindly read the manuscript and diplomatically said he didn't like the ending. I rewrote the entire book.

Prologue

HAD THE SAUDI KNOWN THIS was the last time he would be intimate with his wife – number three – he might have lingered long in her arms. He lay naked, his lanky frame stretching the boundaries of the bed until his feet dangled over the end. The man's eyes fixed on his feet, missing a few toes, scarred and still calloused from exhausting travel through the Afghanistan mountains. His gaze moved up to the scar, never properly stitched, running from his ankle to his knee. The American Special Forces gave him that gift. And that was how he saw it – a gift to act as a reminder every day of his hatred of the Americans.

A cool breeze passed through the open window along with the moonlight as the Saudi's thoughts drifted to the day the gift was given. He was stirred that morning by bombs exploding in the distance – a clear warning that troops would follow. Scouts from nearby summits reported local Afghan forces mounting attacks from below although the scouts reported it was a half-hearted effort. Mostly they shot mortar shells into the rocky crags, fired their AK-47s indiscriminately, and screamed insults into the wind blowing up the mountain side.

It was the thumping beat of the helicopter rotor blades that caused more concern that day. The bombing had stopped. The local forces advanced maybe a hundred meters, however the thump-thump-thump of the Blackhawk helicopters meant it was time to move. The Saudi and his small band scattered from the protection of the caves and scurried over the rugged mounts towards Pakistan. The armed force had nearly escaped when American helicopters appeared on the horizon and blocked their exit. Machine guns, fired by soldiers from open doors, raced towards his party and twice pieces of metal ricocheted off rocks and tore into his legs. Then the helicopters left as quickly as they had appeared.

The sounds of the rotors beating the air never left the Saudi's mind. Never did the relentless ratatat-tat of machine gun fire pouring a rain of hot lead down upon him. His sleep was restless and often resulted in waking suddenly drenched in sweat and screaming. Tonight was different. Tonight satiated by the exhaustion of his lust, he slept sound.

For maybe an hour, the Saudi enjoyed peace and the sleep of a contented baby. Then the helicopters came back, the rotors making music accompanied by machine gun fire – a symphony of war. The dream always came back. The Saudi sat up in bed, his torso dripping with perspiration. Intruders burst through the closed door shouting commands, in English. American Special Forces, the name rushed through his mind. This was no dream. He threw his long arms into the air. The shots were silenced and true to the aim of the Seals. bin Laden crumbled, naked, in a pool of blood.

....

News of his death reached the White House about the same time Omar and al Thani heard from the look-outs across the street from the bin Laden compound. It was welcome news to Omar who recognized the death as a clearing of the playing field – the first move in the Council's plot to unite the Islamic nations. al Thani, while he, too, knew this was necessary, he mourned the death of his old friend and knew he would have to bear the burden of guilt, for a lifetime, of being the Judas amongst the disciples.

Thursday, October 4th

Chaman, Pakistan

THROUGH THE RIFLE SCOPE, ALEX Stone watched a squat, bearded man dressed in a flowing white outer garment crawl from the dinged and dusty SUV. Stone moved the fine crosshairs to the man's left ear. "Like the snitch said, Ali's wear'n the scarlet velvet kufi," Stone whispered to his partners, although there was no need for hushed tones. "The little rat's earned his money."

"Only two bodyguards," Rooster reported as he watched the party of three men leave the gray Hilux SUV. A couple of burly robed men shuffled across the rocky and rutted roadway on either side of Ali headed towards a tiny mud brick home. A small dust whirlwind briefly obliterated the lone oil lamp that burned dimly in the single wood framed window facing the street. The shorter of the two bodyguards slumped on the dirty gray wooden bench, an aged AK-47 balanced on his lap. The other, who stood as tall as a camel's ass, also lugged a tired looking rifle held together with duct tape, entered ahead of the rotund Arab. The driver moved the Hilux to the south and waited out of sight.

Ali's wife's house was located outside the legal limits of Chaman some ten kilometers east in a little settlement that didn't merit a name. Everyone who lived there or needed to travel there knew where it was and that was enough. They had few visitors. Alex and his team had easily located the house from a handwritten map drawn by the informant plus a little help from enlarged satellite photographs.

On Monday, Alex and his partners slipped across the Afghan/ Pakistan border in a beat-up but reliable white Land Rover. They received a bit of guidance from the CIA officer who pointed them towards holes in a vast region of unprotected border where only the gun ruled. Guns, testicles, and a fist full of cash would be all they needed.

Rooster found the residence of the target's wife. Across the road, he rented an upstairs room from an elderly couple who charged only a few dollars. Rooster had dropped ample hints that they were Taliban and not to be disturbed. The others arrived in the dark and settled in unnoticed except for the rats scurrying in their wake.

On the second day, it became evident that real Taliban were about. Early one morning, they saw two Taliban bullies whipping a lone woman with canes. The room overlooked the street offering an unobstructed view of the front entrance. They only ventured out when the sun dropped below the desert floor and then rarely. The plan to snatch Ali unfolded as they watched the pattern of activities on the rocky street below. As it turned out, there wasn't much activity - so the plan was most simple.

Their room was square, ten by ten. The walls, floor and ceiling were clay, dirty clay with no decorations or ornaments. Tattered red and black woven rugs lay on the stained and dusty floor offering the only place to sleep. It didn't matter that the place was beyond austere, at least there were two windows with a view – a view worth a couple hundred thousand, U.S. The windows were simply thick clear plastic, filthy plastic, stapled to a rough wooden frame. Rooster set about to clean the plastic, however, Stone stopped him pointing out that the dirt provided better cover for the watchers.

They ate MREs, slept, and relieved themselves in a six gallon bucket that leaked in two places despite the duct tape applied liberally to the holes. After being cooped up in the hot upstairs room they were growing tired of each other and the smell. No one complained, except Lee, whose asthma was aggravated by the four inches of dust in the room. He took it in stride, although they had come to the point where they wanted an end to the grand scheme regardless of outcome just for some relief of the mundane.

Although they seldom left the room, being bearded, sun-baked, and dressed in gray kurta shirts and white wool dish dashas they were comfortable moving in the evening hours on the narrow alleyways. There were no street lights so there was little chance they would be compromised. They each carried an AK-47 and the few locals who saw them assumed they were Taliban fighters and kept their distance. They scouted potential threats and escape routes. They were pleased to find that there were no soldiers, or police – like a lion at a watering hole, the Taliban kept their prey at bay.

A day ago, Lee stashed the Land Rover in the next village, a few klicks down the road with the informant's relatives. They found that for a few dollars they could have the cooperation of anyone. That being said, Stone reminded them that they weren't buying loyalty and no one could be trusted. Only by instilling fear and capitalizing on greed could they stay for a few days with a modicum of secrecy.

Alex looked at his watch, for the umpteenth time, and twisted the band once around his wrist. A few hours passed since Ali had arrived. The pleasures of the flesh were not to be rushed. Alex rolled back from the window for a moment to grab a plastic bottle of water. When he returned, he saw the larger bodyguard step halfway outside the doorway and wave to the driver.

"Get going," Alex ordered. He looked at his watch and then twisted it once around his wrist.

Rooster and Lee left quickly, radio earpieces hidden under their pakals. They hustled thirty meters to the north to where they had hidden a rusty VW bus they had stolen in Chaman on Wednesday night.

Alex kept watch on the house while Jake shouldered his weapon, a .308 Patriot Sniper rifle. It was equipped with a silencer to dampen the report. Jake took time to nestle the rifle into the small sandbags. Once on the scope, he would not move – so he might as well find comfort from the get-go.

"We are moving down Shami Street and are 30 seconds out," Rooster told Alex over the radio.

"Copy, I'm en route to meet you at block's end." Alex turned away from the window to face Jake. "You ready?"

"Yes, sir." Jake put the crosshairs on the doorway across the street. Focused so intensely, he'd become vulnerable from behind – an observation that worried Alex as he left his partner's side.

Three steps at a time, Alex loped down the dark covered stairway which attached to the back of the house and ran northward. It was a relief just to get into the cool evening air. The sun had set and thick cumulus clouds obscured the moonlight. Alex welcomed the darkness.

It gave his team better cover. On the other hand, it afforded their enemy, which was everyone, the same protection.

The rusty van had slowed its southbound movement as the side door opened and Alex piled in. Lee rounded the corner and moved ahead to within 30 meters of the door. Even at this short distance, the visibility was poor as a stiff wind rolled dust down the street, sometimes swirling in mini-tornadoes.

The three in the van listened intently to Jake's transmissions. Calls from the nearby minarets summoned the local Muslims, which was everybody, to prayer.

"Doors open," Jake called out over the radio, in a voice loud enough to be heard over the call to prayer.

"The driver is pulling up across the street."

"The second bodyguard is out, looking around."

Lee eased the clutch and slowly pulled ahead. He fingered his rosary, ever so slowly.

"Ali's out with second bodyguard."

"GO!" Jake shouted into the radio microphone.

Lee moved the van ahead the remaining few meters, coming to rest between Ali's car and the doorway.

Alex slammed open the van's side door in front of Ali and the two bodyguards. Ali looked wide-eyed at Alex and Rooster, each with a suppressed MP-5 Kurtz leveled at the bodyguards. Blood and brains rained on Ali as Jake's .308 rounds dropped the two in less than three seconds. Ali turned to run back to the house.

Behind the steering wheel, Lee put his front sights on the chauffeur's nose - a big target. Four times Lee fired his suppressed CZ Kadeti .22 cal. pistol through the Hilux Vigo's window driving four hollow point bullets into the driver's skull. The soon to be dead driver's right foot reacted to the first shot, pushing the accelerator through the floor board and sending the Hilux careening down the dusty road into men walking to the mosque.

"*Taa'la maei!*" Rooster shouted at Ali.

Alex and Rooster reached Ali in two steps, hoisted him off his feet, one by his hair and the other by his ass-end, and tossed him through the open side door. When he slammed into the back of the driver's seat, he separated his shoulder. Ali screamed as Rooster crouched on his back and pushed his face into the pile of rugs. Alex pulled a syringe from the top of his ear where it had rested like an accountant's pencil and jabbed the 33 gauge needle into Ali's flabby arm. He fell quiet.

As the minaret's tinny loudspeaker also fell silent, the job was completed and the team sped away with their target. The entire operation spanned less than ten seconds. After the informant's share that was about $25,000.00 per second.

For a few moments Jake remained at his second story window to provide cover for the team's departure. Seeing no threat, he too left the house racing down the steps and made his escape on a waiting Suzuki Hayabusa motorcycle. The cool evening air racing pass his bare head accompanied by the adrenaline rush made Jake feel so alive and so invincible. It was better than sex, which may be why Jake had no regrets having left the last wife for the wilds of Afghanistan. Full throttle, he popped a wheelie and sped off to join the others at the hidden Land Rover.

Friday, October 5th

The Alhambra
Andalusia, Spain

IN PANIC, ELEVEN MEN RUSHED from eleven nations to The Alhambra – built in the 1300's as a Spanish fortress and residence for Muslim conquerors of Christendom. Its tall fortified stone walls are flanked by 13 towers and the Darro River cuts a deep ravine to the north. The red clay buildings are set on a hilltop surrounded by luxuriant woods. The sun beat down on the walls drawing the night's dew into the air creating a thin veil of fog around the castle – a remarkably fitting location to launch a new Islamic conquest.

Omar, the Egyptian, arrived late. When he joined the ten others at the long marble table, they were engaged in animated debate. Their loud chatter echoed against the stone walls. The Egyptian was a tall, angular middle-aged man. Handsome, if not regal in his appearance, he dressed in a traditional long white outer robe and checked headdress. He nearly floated across the room and assumed his place at the head of the table. He carried a mystic, perhaps as his grandfather claimed, they truly came from the linage of the pharaohs. Omar's presence brought silence to the room as they waited for him to speak at this hastily called meeting.

The room was enormous, thirty-foot ceilings with wrought iron chandeliers hanging just above the long table where the men sat. The walls of stone were cool to the touch and kept the room as such even in the warmest of days. Barred windows, twenty feet off the floor allowed the sunshine to enter and it danced on the stained glass lamps.

"Ali Shah Masood has been taken prisoner. By whom I do not know. He was visiting his wife in Chaman. As he left her house, his bodyguards were assassinated and he was grabbed by men driving a van. At least that is what one neighbor told the wife. We must presume they were CIA and that he will be tortured. You all know what this means…Ali knows many of our plans," Omar said, pausing to lick his lips.

"This is a disaster!" Abdul Hakeen Faza Mahmood, the Pakistani interrupted.

"He was warned to take more precautions!" protested Jabir bin Ahmed, the representative from Yemen.

"Someone inside the organization must have informed on him," Mahmood added.

The men were chattering and clucking like hens cornered by cur dogs. It was most irritating to see them succumb to fear so easily – at this first crisis. Omar wondered if these men, so carefully selected, would be up to the task.

"Quiet," Omar shouted. It echoed in the room, "Quiet, Quiet, Quiet." He paused to regain his composure. In a nervous gesture, his tongue darted through his parted lips, in a serpent-like manner. "We all know this is a problem we must address immediately. We must find him and put a merciful end to his life. He isn't in Pakistan; I am assured by Pakistani government officials in direct contact with the CIA. He was likely moved to Afghanistan. We have people close to the Americans making inquiries. We will find him." Omar understated just how close his people were to the Americans.

"We must move our timetable forward. If the CIA breaks Ali, our years of preparation will be for naught. We must not fail in Allah's work on earth," Omar said.

"Ala Qukbar!"

"Ala Qukbar!"

Friday, October 5th

Charikar, Afghanistan

LIKE MEAT CUTTERS ON THE slaughter floor, Rooster and Jake threw the carcass of the fully clothed Ali under the cold water shower to wash away the thin crust of blood and tissue that had once been his bodyguards. Alex yelled sternly at the two, reminding them of the value of a breathing Ali and the worthlessness of a dead man. Still suffering from shock as much as from the Nembutal they had administered for the ride back to Afghanistan, he was barely conscious. As he lay in a widening swirling pink puddle, they cut his blood soaked white disha dasha from him, leaving him naked under the showerhead. His pale flabby body resembled a beached whale.

"Get him a jumpsuit," the ramrod straight Colonel O'Neil ordered as he and Alex looked through the doorway of the shower room. The colonel compared a faded photo of Ali Shah Masood which the C.I.A. had provided to the bare-assed man before him. "Appears you are in the money, Commander," the colonel said addressing Alex by his former naval rank. "How'd you find him?"

"An informant that Rooster had cultivated – a Taliban with a taste for whores and whiskey, go figure."

"Where'd you find him?"

"You don't want to know that."

Alex Stone was a slight man. 'Scrawny' was how the Navy drill instructors referred to him. 'Wiry' was how he preferred to think of himself. He'd fancied himself a ladies' man, although his latest assignment left him little time for that. He wore his blond hair cut high and tight and kept it covered. While it made him uncomfortable, he grew his facial hair long as was the local custom and kept it colored dark. He could do nothing to hide his bright blue eyes.

Stone had retired from the Navy at age 41 and signed on with Blackstone. He and his crew were stationed in Afghanistan to function as a quick response team providing heavy firepower in critical situations.

None of these fighters had the personality to finesse egotistical officials who were being provided protection. They remained in the shadows, only seconds away to provide a quick and usually deadly resolution to any threat while the protectee was whisked away to safety.

"We'll take him to MI Corp. Sergeant, get him up and dressed."

"Speak'n a money, Colonel, I assume you'll be in contact with the CIA?" Alex asked.

"Already done, Commander, they told me the cash is on the way as soon as I verified his identity."

"Get your fat ass up." The stocky sergeant violently jerked Ali to his feet and with the assistance of Rooster dressed him in an olive drab jumpsuit. He covered Ali's head with a rough burlap bag, tied his hands behind his back with nylon straps and pushed him into the commons of the concrete block bunker that the Blackstone men called home.

Each common area housed four men in a cluster all of which led to the shared bath and shower. The quarters, shaped like a pentagon, had been built with no regard for style just a need to quickly put a roof over their heads. The local builder had made windows in the block structure which the mercenaries promptly filled with sandbags. The tin roof was covered with a layer of sandbags and more tin and more sandbags to protect from mortar attacks. If there is one natural resource Afghanistan has it's a lot of sand. Outside the entire building was protected by three rows of concertina wire, more sandbags, and some claymore mines traded for whiskey which the American soldiers couldn't get into the country, but the Blackstone mercenaries smuggled in on diplomatic flights. They'd found that whiskey and cigarettes went further than cash with those soldiers who never knew if they'd live long enough to enjoy the cash. With the liquor and smokes there was no doubt.

"Let's go," the colonel barked and then led the three MPs and Ali to the waiting Humvee. They pushed him through the open rear door and left, wheels spinning, in a cloud of dust.

Rooster poked his linen wrapped head through the front doorway of the living quarters, "Alex, some Afghani is waiting outside the wire with his donkey and wants to know if we need more firewood."

“Buy all he has, we need to start to stockpile for the cold season before the price shoots up. Jake, you go with Rooster and keep the M-60 on the dude. The donkey could be constipated with explosives.”

“He says he has hashish or opium if we would like, you know what I mean?”

“We don’t like. Tell him the wood will do. Don’t let him through the wire in case he’s got a bomb under that wood. Tell him to unload the wood outside the wire and we’ll carry it in ourselves. Hurry, it will be dark soon.” Alex looked at his watch and turned the band once around his wrist.

Jake, M-60 over his shoulder, hustled out to provide cover for Lee and Rooster as they packed the firewood into the compound. He was so large, he made the machine gun look like a child’s toy. Jake had been a sniper, first with LAPD and later with the U.S. Secret Service. He signed on with Blackstone on his 50th birthday. More excitement, more adrenaline was what motivated Jake to become a mercenary instead of a pensioner. Besides, he had nothing holding him back… he had lost all of his personal relationships including his wife when he chose duty with the Secret Service.

Before the local man departed, Alex shouted from the doorway. “Rooster, if he can get us a goat or lambs for Sunday tell him to come back otherwise he can piss off. And I want the goat at the end of a rope, alive. I don’t what to buy some poisoned or rotten meat.”

Friday, October 5th

Federal Court House
Minneapolis, Minnesota

HALF-WAY AROUND THE WORLD A clap of thunder unleashed from the heavens as Special Agent Martini stepped out of his black Dodge Durango. The agent might have remained home in bed had he known he was on a collision course with Stone, Ali, and Omar, and the creation of a new world order – something none of them could have anticipated.

He despised umbrellas, thought them best left for women and sissies, although as he ran towards the courthouse in a downpour he reconsidered that position. He slowed as he reached the mounds of earth – reminiscent of Chippewa burial mounds – with huge granite gnome-like figures placed in the front of the courthouse to prevent another Oklahoma City-style bombing. He could not help but tread lightly over the sidewalk which was designed to give way to the weight of a five-ton truck. He thought that perhaps his own weight, which was not much, may be the final straw and he would trigger the collapse into who knows where. Three women, dressed in suits, and carrying umbrellas beat him to the door. While they lowered their umbrellas, he held the heavy glass door opened for them. Each woman shook their silky sticks at his feet, leaving his shoes tops beaded with water.

As he entered the courthouse he brushed the rain from his shoulders and then badged his way past the metal detectors manned by the Blue Coats, so named by the ill-fitting blue blazers they wore. They were mostly retired police officers with protruding paunches who delighted in making defense attorneys all but strip naked to clear their checkpoint. Revenge best served cold. He elbowed the nearest guard, a man who had trained him in. "I think you ought to give the dark-haired one a closer look. I see some bulges that would bear further scrutiny." The guard chuckled and waved a brunette through the metal detector. The buzzer sounded and the red light flashed. Martini, wearing a mischievous grin, continued to the elevator.

He was early enough for the judicial hearing to make his way to the rest room and dry off. He looked into the mirror, wiped the rain water from his head, straightened his blue and gray striped tie and fixed his starched white shirt collar. As always he was disappointed to see his hair had turned so gray and his faced had wrinkled. When the hell did that happen, he asked himself again. He was a thin but muscular man, almost too small to become a police officer back when they had height requirements. Gossips said he had lifts in his shoes when he took his police physical. While he wasn't going to get into the movies on his looks, he was handsome enough, at least he thought so.

By 10:00 a.m., Special Agent Martini was on the stand as the only witness in this hearing. The Assistant United States Attorney walked him through his testimony before the federal magistrate. Within 20 minutes they had established a record of facts that should lead the judge to conclude the defendant had violated the law and should certainly go to trial on his way to jail. In the good-old-days it would have been enough to hang the fellow. The defendant was charged with conspiracy to kill a federal agent who happened to be investigating his membership in a neo-Nazi group suspected of trafficking in machine guns and explosives.

Next, it was the defense attorney's turn on stage. The bald man with the pencil thin mustache rose and struck his best theatrical pose which was wasted on the seasoned judge. He stepped towards the witness closing the gap and moving in for the kill. His polished head sent light reflecting into Martini's eyes as he made the rush to the stand. He pointed his pale index finger at the witness, "Agent, prior to your first meeting with my client on September 30th, had you known him?"

"No."

"So you knew nothing of him as a person?"

"That's right."

"So, when and how did you first hear of my client?"

"As I already testified, I received a telephone call from a confidential reliable informant on the 30th."

"What time of day was this call and was it to your cell phone?"

"It was to my cell phone and it was at 5:36 p.m."

"And where were you when you got this urgent call?"

"I was at Finnegan's Irish Pub in St. Paul."

"Had you been drinking?"

"I was at the Pub so I believe it would be reasonable to conclude I may have sipped on a beer."

"And what did the informant tell you?" He rubbed his chin and executed a spin on his heels away from the bench. He reached for some papers on the table as if they held some weighty surprise evidence that would crush the agent and prove him a liar.

"The informant told me he was drinking with the defendant at Jimmy's Bar and that the defendant, your client, was asking the informant if he knew anyone who would kill this woman."

"So while you were 'sipping on your beer,' this informant who had been drinking at the bar, calls and tells you someone wants to kill someone. What did you do next?"

"As I already testified, I told the informant to stay with the defendant and I would meet them both at Jimmy's in an hour. I asked a couple of agents who were with me to cover me and we all drove to the meeting."

"Had these other agents been drinking also?"

"I think that would be safe to presume."

"There's no room to presume Agent – yes or no?" The attorney threw his arms high into the air as if personally insulted by a presumption the agent knew better than to utter.

"Yes."

"Were you all armed... carrying firearms?"

"Of course." Agent Martini moved a little further from the back of the chair.

"So the three of you who had been drinking and were armed all drove over to the bar to meet your informant and someone that he claimed was intent on murder, is that true?"

"Yes."

"When you got to Jimmy's did you resume drinking alcohol?" He swept his hand towards the witness.

"Yes."

"Were the others also drinking?"

"Yes."

"You testified earlier that the snitch introduced you to my client and my client told you he wanted this woman killed. Is that correct?"

"Substantially, at first he didn't identify the intended victim as an agent. He just said there was this gal that was giving him and his friends a hard time. The longer we talked, it became apparent that the woman that he wanted dead was a federal agent."

"How drunk was my client when you claim to have had this conversation with him?"

"He was under the influence...."

The attorney interrupted and directed his comments to the judge. He rolled his bulging eyes. "So, as I understand the situation, three drunken armed cops drive halfway across town to meet a drunken snitch who introduces the drunken cops to my client who is intoxicated and now he sits accused of conspiracy to kill a federal agent? I have no more questions." He executed another spin on his heels and returned to his chair. He was a theater major at a state college before he wiggled his way into law school.

The Assistant U.S. Attorney stood, paused, straightened his suit coat and began redirect. "Agent, were you or any of the other agents intoxicated that night?"

"No sir, we each had maybe half a beer at Finnegan's when I got the call and I had another at Jimmy's while my cover-guys drank cokes."

"Was the informant intoxicated?"

"He is a recovering alcoholic who doesn't drink."

"Were you concerned that the defendant was too inebriated to make a conscious decision to hire you to kill this agent?"

"Yes." Martini sat back in his chair and uncrossed his legs.

"What, if anything, did you do to address this concern?"

Martini looked at the judge. "I listened to the defendant rant about wanting her dead, how he intended to get even and her put out of her misery as he called it. He wanted her to suffer and wanted her sexually assaulted. I agreed to do the job and we exchanged telephone numbers and I left the bar."

"If you thought he was drunk, why did you agree to be hired to kill this agent?"

"I wanted him to lock onto me as his hired gun. If I had just walked away that very night he may have gotten someone beyond our control to do the deed."

"Just for the record again, what steps did you take to assure yourself that the defendant wanted her dead?"

"I met with the defendant three more times, each in the early morning hours over coffee at a restaurant. All of the meetings were recorded both audio and video. We went over the details of how he wanted her murdered. He wanted me to torture her, rape her, and let her know it was from him. When I was finished, the defendant wanted a slow, painful death. He left that up to me. He gave me maps, photos, and personal information pertaining to the agent. He or his friends had done a lot of background on the target. They knew where she lived, what she drove, where her office was located, even her after-hours hangouts. He gave me one thousand dollars as a down payment and he was arrested."

"I have no further questions. The government rests." The lanky prosecutor glared down at the defense attorney wearing a hint of a smirk. The best part of any day, other than the occasional poke granted by his lawyer/girlfriend, was sticking it to the defense bar.

Agent Martini looked to the magistrate for dismissal. The wizened arthritic judge winked over the top of his wire cheaters at the agent he had known for years and had even tipped a few. "You may be excused, Doc."

Saturday, October 6th

The Alhambra
Andalusia, Spain

OMAR WAS NOT IMPRESSED WITH Ali's replacement. al Fulani was a frail man with ferret-like features. More than once he was detained by airport officials believing he was Yasser Arafat. He smelled of stale cigarette smoke and a lack of deodorant. The two sat on hard chairs in a sparsely furnished private meeting room that smelled of ancient plaster accented by mouse droppings.

al Fulani, a Kuwaiti, favored pure white robes. On the campus in Georgetown, he stood out in his attire but was even more remarkable in his academic success. He graduated with a Master's Degree in International Political Studies, magna cum laude. He was well-educated although somewhat ill-mannered was the consensus of those who met him. Even Omar fell prey to the piercing black eyes that never blinked. They reminded Omar of the sand lizards who waited patiently for their prey to pass then striking from behind. Beneath those blinding white robes, Omar sensed, beat a reptilian heart.

"I look forward to representing my country on the Council. I'm most honored and flattered."

Omar ignored the ingratiating remark. "Your half- brother, Ali Shah Masood, sat on the Council for many years. He was the informal leader and my mentor. He groomed me to assume his role if something like this happened. I have large shoes to fill, as do you."

"I understand," al Fulani said as he leaned forward to light a dark cigarette. He remained slightly forward blowing twin jets of blue smoke from his nostrils.

"Perhaps, although I doubt you truly understand. After the first Bush attacked Iraq and established permanent presence in our nations, our leaders worried that we would always be under the heels of America and its surrogate, Israel. We could foresee that the corrupt Western culture would soon change our Islamic customs forever and for the worse.

Islam itself was mortally threatened. It is our duty to Allah to prevent this from happening."

"How were you able to bring all of our brother nations to the table?" al Fulani asked.

"We had a common enemy and a common threat. So Arabs and Persians, Shiites and Sunnis, oil rich and desert poor have put aside their differences and joined to declare our independence from the West. This will be our 4th of July. My enemies' enemy is my friend."

"Why haven't we heard about this publicly?"

"Because we do not wish it to be public as you mean the word. Look at Hamas or al Qaeda, what happens to them when they lay claim to some attack on the West. Either the Americans or the Israelis track them down and kill them."

"What role do I play in this?"

"Your brother, Ali, represented your country. Each nation brings its own unique resources to the table. Some have money, some zealots, and some traditions of underground operatives. Together we have strength."

"You have said that there is this plan, what is it? When will it take place?" al Fulani asked.

"You ask too much too soon." He licked his lips becoming impatient with al Fulani. "Unfortunately, Ali's capture will force us to push ahead when we are not entirely prepared. We can't take the chance that he will talk under torture. I know you have many more questions but not now. Just listen and you will learn. If not, you will perish. Now, let us join our brethren."

Omar led al Fulani out of the room and down the stone floor hallways, their heels clicking rhythmically as they walked. As they were about to enter the conference room where the others were waiting, Farooq Al-Nahyan, the Iraqi, gently grabbed Omar's arm and led him aside. He leaned into Omar's ear and whispered, "Ali is at the American air base in Bagran. He was seen by two of our men who clean for the Americans."

Saturday, October 6th

Bagran Air Base
Afghanistan

FBI SPECIAL AGENT ANDREW JOHNSON pounded his fist on the general's heavy oak conference table. "The FBI will take custody of this prisoner." His high-pitched voice broke with anger. "These are the orders." He slammed the decoded message down in front of General Dubois.

The general, a big Texan with no discernable hair and a square jaw, squinted. "Agent, sit down and shut up. You scream or hit my table again, I'll have you shipped back to Washington in the back of a cargo plane."

Johnson remained standing, defiant.

CIA officer Casimir 'Rocky' Kowalewicz covered his mouth with his large tanned hand to hide his enjoyment of the dressing-down. He paused to recover his composure before he spoke. "General, Ali is a big catch."

The general pushed back in his chair and allowed a slight grin. "Hell, Rocky, I know he's a trophy and ya'll want a stab at him, but MI Corp has him now and the Joint Chiefs have ordered all prisoners brought to GITMO where ya'll can fight over him. We're fixin' to fly him to GITMO as soon as we get orders from Washington. It's the weekend so don't expect anything to happen until Monday or Tuesday." The general wiped dribbles of sweat from his brow. The air conditioning unit was out of service, again. The stifling heat fueled the general's already simmering temper.

"Agent Johnson, I'd suggest you fly to GITMO now so you can greet Ali when he gets there," the general said.

Johnson opened his mouth.

"Gentlemen, this meeting is over. Captain Ryan will show ya'll the way out," the general said. As the door was meekly closed, the general twirled his chair to face Colonel O'Neil, who stood behind him. "Are your men getting anything from Ali?"

"No, sir, although it's too soon to expect much," O'Neil replied.

"I understand, however, you know Ali's going to GITMO, like I said, so there's little time."

"Yes, sir, is there a reason that flight might be delayed, sir?"

The general was slow to answer. He turned his high back chair around and looked through the large steel mesh covered window to the landing strip and the control tower. After a few minutes of thoughtful silence, he moved his squeaking chair to face the officer. "Colonel, ya'll have a Machiavellian mind. I'd guess there'd be a good many reasons that flight might get delayed."

Saturday, October 6th

al Kahwa Coffeehouse
Charikar, Afghanistan

DRESSED IN THE KHAKI 511 vests and pants favored by the soldier of fortune crowd, Alex, Jake, Rooster and Lee huddled in the corner of al Kahwa Coffeehouse with their backs to a wall. They sipped strong black Arabic coffee laced with Paddy's Old Irish Whiskey poured from Rooster's silver flask, smoked counterfeit Marlboro cigarettes and waited. Except Jake, he neither drank alcohol nor smoked and deep down believed the world would be a better place without drink or tobacco. Lee held his drink in one hand and fingered the worn rosary with his left hand at the same time keeping a grip on his rifle, his index finger caressing the trigger guard.

The al Kahwa had unadorned mud brick walls, dirt floors, handmade furniture, and a single prized ceiling fan that ran when they had electricity. It didn't turn today and the only light was what came through the open doorway. At least the stone structure stayed cool and provided some rare relief from the sun and the wind. The men chose this place because it had only one door which they faced and could easily defend. Although Rooster once argued a couple of grenades rolling through the front door would give them little to defend against.

The stooped, tattered owner tended a wood fire in the opposite corner nearest the door. He tucked his long gray beard into his tunic to save it from catching fire. He was missing his left leg as a result of stepping on a mine back when he was fighting for the Northern Alliance. Two ancient copper pots, bearing the dents of ten thousand meals, were held over the fire by three foot metal rods which protruded from the floor. The rods were recovered parts from a Soviet helicopter, part of the rotor system. The aroma of stewing goat drifted across the coffeehouse. The men kept an eye on the owner. While he remained, there was little likelihood of an ambush – whenever he left their view, fingers moved to the triggers.

Jake kicked at one of the red and black roosters pecking crumbs or insects from the dusty floor. The rooster deftly dodged the kick, dropped a white and black crap for Jake to step on and resumed pecking. Typical Afghani reaction – sort of summed up the relationship between the

Americans and Afghanis. He closed one eye and sighted in the chicken, as if looking through a rifle scope. "That son-of-a-bitch walks just like you, Rooster. I believe he's imitating you."

"I believe the snitch knows a lot more but is waiting to see if he gets paid, ya know what I mean?" Rooster asserted ignoring Jake. "He's talking about al Qaeda releasing some poison frogs in Washington."

"Poison frogs? Rooster, could there have been something lost in the translations?"

"No, that's what he said, frogs that spit poison."

"Bullshit, Blackstone isn't paying us to be spooks," Alex countered as he flicked his cigarette butt on the floor. The rooster sensing a meal ran to the butt and inhaled it, burning amber and all.

"Pay him and give him to Rocky," Lee offered. Lee was the only Blackstone mercenary who had been neither a soldier nor a cop. Lee was the 34 year old son-in-law of the Party Chairman. His father was a black man who grew up on the east side of Los Angeles. Pure grit is what his father claimed delivered him from the ghetto. Lee's mother was a stunningly beautiful Latino girl, who met Lee's father in church. Lee's great-uncle was the first Black bishop in America, or so Lee was fond of saying. Lee was heir to a large privately-held company making millions from sandpaper grit. However, he was bored to tears working for dad. His father-in-law arranged with an influential Blackstone executive for Lee to live his dream. Some of the social elite wondered if the father-in-law hoped Lee's dream would turn into his worst nightmare.

Rooster shook his head. "He's danced before with the CIA, ya know what I mean, back when he was fighting the Russians and the CIA was giving 'em weapons and money. He knows they'll turn on him again. There's no man in this country that trusts the CIA or any foreigner for that matter." He paused as the beat of helicopter blades came over the little shop. The chickens, too, ceased pecking and looked skyward until it passed then resumed their eating.

"Hell, they don't trust anyone outside of their tribe. I just hate to see this opportunity go to waste if Ali doesn't talk and the snitch has more information. Besides, there may be more reward money for us if he knows where these other outlaws are hiding."

Saturday, October 6th

Bagran Air Base
Afghanistan

FBI AGENT JOHNSON AND CIA Officer Kowalewicz walked together across the austere base grounds away from the general's headquarters. The roar of jet engines coming, going, and hovering made it difficult to converse. Agent Johnson spoke loudly into his heavy satellite phone as they ambled across the rocky path.

"Carol, I want you to get into the old files and get whatever you can on General Fucking Francis Dubois, that's Dubois as in Du-bo-is. I need it NOW! Anything!"

Carol Wilkins, back at FBI headquarters in Washington, D.C., asked sweetly, "Is Francis his middle name?"

"Carol, NOW! You have no more important business, Carol, NOW," and he pressed 'END.'

"You have good people skills, Johnson," Kowalewicz offered.

"Screw you, Casimir. I'm preparing to attack from the rear and stick this up the general's ass so far the stars blow off his hat," Johnson huffed.

Johnson hadn't always been so unpleasant. He began his career with the F.B.I. after graduating from Law School at the University of Chicago, bright-eyed and eager. The Bureau snatched him up for a couple of reasons, he graduated in the lower middle of his class so he probably wouldn't be recruited away from the government service, he looked like an agent, tall, slim, handsome with no blemishes or disfigurements, and he was a devout Mormon so he had no nasty habits like drinking, smoking or womanizing. When Johnson was hired, those were all considered attributes which may outweigh whether the candidate could investigate his way out of a paper bag. Most importantly, he wasn't likely to embarrass the Bureau and he would look good speaking to the local Lions Club. That was back in the day when the last of the

J. Edgar Hoover men were still in control. Despite whatever peccadilloes Director Hoover may have enjoyed, he and *his men* expected better of the agents.

Saturday, October 6th

al Kahwa Coffeehouse
Charikar, Afghanistan

DUST NOTES FLOATED ON THE sunbeams streaming through the open doorway until Casimir 'Rocky' Kowalewicz strolled slowly into the coffeehouse trying to let his eyes adjust to the dusky interior. Someone in his position didn't want to rush into any room until he'd assessed the potential dangers. A former Oklahoma State football lineman, he filled the doorway of the smoky café. Even the chickens who were accustomed to human traffic scattered from the long shadow as though some large hawk was about to descend upon them.

"'bout time, where the hell you been?" Alex asked when Rocky joined them. Rocky sat backwards in the worn wooden chair resting his hand and chin on the chair back. He brushed the dirt from his short sandy hair.

"...playing in the sandbox with the FBI and General Francis Dubois. What you gentlemen drinking?" Rocky spoke with a voice burdened with a ½ ton of gravel heaped on his larynx.

Lee poured him a cup of coffee in a gray metal cup and spiked it with a long draught from a flask. Of course the proprietor didn't approve of the illegal act, but what was a crippled man to say to four men carrying machine guns and surly attitudes.

"Your cash is in the Pelican Case," Rocky offered after a long pull on his cup. His size 14 boot pushed the gray metal case under the table towards Alex. "I need you to sign this receipt," which he dragged across the rough wooden table to Alex.

Alex read under his breath but lips moving, "I, Alexander Stone, on this date acknowledge the receipt of $300,000 in U.S. currency from Casimir Kowalewicz. This cash is payment for services rendered to the United States Government. I understand this is taxable income to be reported to the Internal Revenue Service." Using Kowalewicz's pen, he licked the tip then scribbled "bin Laden" on the signature line, dated it, folded it and flicked it back to Rocky.

"Your government wishes to thank you for outstanding service to America," Rocky said with the sincerity of a has-been New Orleans hooker moaning 'I love you.'

"Any chance I could meet your informant to see if he has anything more to offer."

No one replied.

"There's 30 pieces of silver for anything he's got," Rocky added. A fly the size of a fat sparrow crawled to the end of his crooked nose. He swatted the pest, splattering the guts and blood onto his cheeks. He mumbled a curse and wiped the mess away with the back of his hand.

Again his offer was met with silence.

Rocky tipped his cup back draining it dry. "How are you able to communicate with the informant? I assume he speaks English."

Jake stared at Rocky with one eye squinting. He pointed to Rooster. "He speaks the native tongue."

The four agreed that without Rooster's ability to speak the native language this mission would have been impossible. Rooster never tired of pointing that out to the others. Rooster was a Pakistani born American citizen and possessed a savant like ability for foreign languages.

Rocky stood and tipped his sweat stained Yankees cap. "Call if you change your mind."

The men finished their drinks then strolled towards the door, Alex tightly clutching his new metal case in his left hand and the machine gun in his right. "Let's celebrate, boys. Goat steaks, turnips and onions on the grill, and warm beers await us! Except Jake, he can finish off the goat's milk that's been curdling in the sun all day."

Saturday, October 6th

Oval Office, White House
Washington, D.C.

THE PRESIDENT LIMPED TOWARD THE carved oak door, his 6'5" lean frame bent down several inches since the accident. Even the Secret Service agents couldn't prevent the fall he'd taken into the Grand Canyon. That little accident produced many bad jokes about being shoved by the vice president, who truly was standing by his side. President Franklin was accustomed to being the brunt of unkind humor. Coming from the trailer park in rural Alabama provided a year's supply of monologs for the late night comedians. And it didn't help that brother, Bobby Joe, was the village idiot – when he was sober enough to be stupid. The intellectual elite scoffed at the president's visit to the backwoods Baptist church, where snake handlers were the norm. The barrage of jabs and barbs had filled his face with wrinkles, turned his black hair to gray, and killed the sparkle in his baby-blue eyes.

CIA Director John Rankin continued his briefing. "Our agents have a confirmed capture of Ali Shah Masood. Mr. President, you recall that Ali is a top echelon advisor to al Qaeda. My agents are arranging his transportation from Bagran Air Base to GITMO where they will begin interrogation. Mr. President, we believe this is one captive who warrants those interrogation methods we have reserved only as extraordinary measures."

Lyov Marashov, the sharp-nosed Director of the FBI, pushed up from his chair and interrupted. "Mr. President, I object for two reasons. First, we have an agreement that FBI agents will conduct the interrogation of all terrorists suspected of conducting activities inside the United States. Secondly, my agents will not participate in any torture of suspects. We will not! Additionally, my agent in Afghanistan believes the military Intel boys have already started the interrogations."

General Leonard Highcamp, who looked simply heroic in his uniform weighted down with more medals than a Russian Commissar, sat stiffly in his high back leather chair. His bushy white eyebrows rose, trying his best to be incredulous. "I don't believe that's happening, Director Marashov. I just spoke with General Dubois this morning and he assures me that all is well and that the prisoner will be moved to GITMO as soon as an aircraft is available."

President Franklin shook his head and banged his cane on the hardwood floor. "Just once, just one solitary time, I wish you all could play in the same sandbox without the fighting, just once. Work it out gentlemen, work it out and do it by tomorrow.

"General, we have only a minute left before the reception for His Highness, the Emir of Kuwait. Are there any new developments you can share with the directors?"

"Mr. President, I want to remind the directors that as we move closer to resolving this Iranian problem with a military solution, their respective agencies must immediately pass to us all intelligence they have from whatever source. Our Command Staff must know what to expect if and when we attack."

The chief of staff stuck his head through the doorway. "Mr. President, the reception. Sheikh Jaber Al-Ahmad is waiting."

Sunday, October 7th

Grand Avenue
St. Paul, Minnesota

THE SMALL APARTMENT FACED SOUTH overlooking an avenue called Grand for reasons not readily apparent. Perhaps at one time it was. The three-story brick building held a couple dozen apartments. In the twenties it catered to single ladies, although now held no such standards, accepting all comers which made for a real melting pot. At supper time the odors of meals being prepared went from Mexican to Indian to Thai. Doc's apartment had four rooms or more accurately two… a kitchen, dining room, and living room all rolled into one and a bedroom connected to a bathroom barely large enough to sit and think. Everything had been painted white by the old caretaker and Doc saw no reason to improve on his decorating tastes. A large recliner and a few mismatched chairs around an oval wooden table completed his Goodwill furnishings. He also had a noisy brass bed, although it wasn't worth mentioning and caused many a sore and stiff back and it hadn't been making much noise lately. Beside his bed, on the night stand, rested a dog-eared copy of *The Field – The Quest for the Secret Force of the Universe.* He never grew tired of trying to make sense of the world. The apartment wasn't much, and would never be featured in *Better Homes and Gardens*, however, Doc called it home and after three failed marriages his interest in making a nest had diminished – no disappeared.

Doc didn't work on Sundays, at least he tried not to. He relished the solitude of a quiet Sunday morning and after reading a few newspapers and finishing a pot of coffee, he tended to his bonsai trees, all 29 of them. While he never thought of it as such, the bonsai gave him beauty and control in his life. Like an artist, he could actually produce beauty in a world he often found ugly.

He gave them each a drink fortified with his own mix of nutrients which included coffee grounds and crushed egg shells. He adjusted the window shades to add sunshine. It was a glorious sunny day. A French jazz artist played softly over the CD player. Looking at his watch, he rushed to finish as he intended to visit his aged mother in 'the home.' Slipping into a worn pair of jeans, some light hiking boots and a Minnesota Gopher Hockey sweatshirt, he took his dog to the lonely grandmother a floor below. He hurried back taking two steps at a time. He rinsed off the plate from which he had eaten his eggs benedict and packed the bran muffins he had baked to take to his mother. He added a thermos of freshly brewed coffee to his pack and dashed out the door.

The sunlight felt good on his face this chilly fall morning. He jumped into his Durango and pointed it north towards Duluth where his mother resided. As he drove out of the Twin Cities he noted the leaves were arrayed in a vivid autumn tapestry. He inserted a *Vivaldi Seasons* CD into the player and let his mind relax, enjoying the sounds and sights.

At Hinckley, he steered the Durango off the freeway and meandered on unfamiliar back roads just keeping a northeast heading. He crept along over gravel roads watching for ruffed grouse sunning themselves perched on stumps. Occasionally, he would stop and take his aged Beretta shotgun out of the case to chase after a bird. He had three in the bag before he moved back onto the paved highway and finished his journey. He saw no harm in mixing a little pleasure with, well, what was more of an obligation.

He could feel his shoulders tense as he arrived in Duluth. He always felt this way in anticipation of visiting his mother. The sky had turned gray and a mixture of sleet and snowflakes smacked into the windshield. He pulled into the parking lot and lit a Camel. He knew he was stalling so he flicked the half-smoked butt out the window, grabbed the muffins and dawdled into the two story cinder-block building that was a warehouse for the seniors each waiting their turn to die. Off in the distance, an incoming freighter sounded its horn signaling for the lift bridge to open for passage.

The home was well-kept, although it still smelled of old folks and depressed him to be there as a visitor. Each visit made him deal with his own mortality. He walked down the hallway smiling at those who bothered to look up. Some spoke, but he walked by having learned during prior visits, the conversations offered went nowhere except maybe in circles. He knocked and entered his mother's room trying to cast off the weight of the gloom, "Hi Mom."

The silver-haired woman looked up briefly from her cushioned chair. She put the dog-eared *People* magazine on her lap. "Who are you?"

"I'm your son, Ma. I brought you some muffins."

"My son put me in this prison. I don't think I have a son anymore. What son would keep his mother in this godforsaken place? If your father was alive he wouldn't let this happen to me."

"I know, Ma, we've gone over this before. You maybe want to come live with me?"

"Heaven forbid…you don't want me in your home anymore than…."

"Up to you, Ma…how are you doing?"

"I'm constipated and I wet myself so they have me in diapers. How do you think I feel?"

"I know it's tough getting old, Ma."

"How would you know? Do you wear diapers?"

"No, ma, I don't and I wish you didn't have to either. I made you these bran muffins, maybe they'll help." Doc extended the bag for a third time, but the old woman looked straight through him…maybe the bad eyes, maybe didn't want to see him.

"How is your wife – what's her name?"

"Sara, ma, and you know we were divorced a couple years ago. Anyway she is fine. She's dancing in Las Vegas and living with a new boyfriend."

"No, I meant that other wife, the one I liked," she said as though locked in an argument that would never end.

"You mean Kelly? She is fine, too. We had dinner together the other night and she sends her love. Can I get you anything?"

"You should have stayed with her instead of running off with that young girl. I liked her."

"I know, Ma, she deserved someone better than me."

"Least you didn't have children. That's a blessing."

"I'm happy for that."

"You were supposed to be a priest. I even told Father Louie that I'd give you to the church. Remember when you had uremia and were on your death bed? Mrs. Angelo brought Holy Water from the Vatican and Father Louie performed the Last Rites."

"How old was I then?"

"Three, no, four…."

"No, I don't remember that."

"You've made me a liar."

"Sorry, Ma…." Doc moved to the small window. Heavy raindrops smashed against the pane.

"Have you spent all of my money? Do I have anything left in the bank?"

"Yeah, ma, I squandered your fortune at the Catholic Bingo Hall and now you're going to have to live in a cardboard box under the bridge…" Doc bit off the last word as if it would help him regain control of the temper he was losing.

"It would if I could have one, just one, decent bowel movement before they kick me out. But I suppose that's too much to ask!" As the old woman made an effort to get up out of the chair she let out a sharp gasp and fell backward. Anyone else might have been reaching for the cardiac paddles, but it was a scene he'd been witnessing for years and he didn't even ask whether there was actually a problem.

She recovered as she always did. "At least you have that dog, what's his name?"

"Gumpy, Ma, his name is Gump."

"Gumby, why'd you name him after a green cartoon…"

"It's Gump, Ma, not Gumby. He's named after Gump Worsely, a hockey goalie, the last to play without a mask."

"You should have gone to play professional. But no, your father, God rest his soul, convinced you to join the Navy. You could have been rich."

"I had a draft lottery number seven. I was going to be drafted and not in the NHL. I was going to be a foot soldier in Vietnam."

"You ended up there anyway."

"Gotta go. The roads are freezing over. I'll leave the muffins in the kitchen…call if you…"

"Oh, sure, call! As if you'd come!"

"Call, ma –bye – keep your diaper pinned tight. I'll be back next weekend to take you to the reunion."

He gave her a hug and raced down the hall and out to the Dodge. The sleet fell harder as he lit a Camel with cupped hands and then turned to face the stinging northeast wind. Maybe it would wash away his feelings, his frustrations, and his disappointments.

He took the freeway back to St. Paul. The wind blew the heavy snowflakes sideways across the road. It was dark and so were his thoughts. He felt like a bad little boy and tried to dismiss the vision of his father looking down on him with great disappointment for putting his mother in 'the home.' Doc picked up his cell phone to call Kelly just to have someone to talk to. No answer. A heavy feeling as though the dark and cold of the night settled into his heart.

Sunday, October 7th

Refugio, Texas

ROGER WILCOX GLANCED OUT THE white F 350 pickup window, past his wife, Rachael, at the John Deere tractor plowing across his cotton stubble field. From inside the tractor, Enrique waved heartily as he saw his boss drive past. Roger waved back and then reached down to turn on the air conditioner. It was already growing hot as the sun burned one day closer to extinction.

The Wilcox family was on their way to the Assembly of God Church in Beeville. They held the service in an old concrete flat-roofed building that had served variously as a bar and a mechanic's shop. The congregation purchased it for a token one dollar and men, handy with a hammer, remodeled it into a respectable place of worship – although at times the odor of auto solvents still lingered. After church, they would return home to watch the Denver game. Roger preferred to watch the Texas Longhorns play. He had been the center for the team from 1978 thru 1981. So enthused about the Longhorns, he would often pilot his own plane to Saturday games.

"You kids keep your hands to yourselves back there," Roger intended them to see his scowling face in the rear-view mirror, although if they did, it wasn't the deterrent he had hoped for.

"How are those new men working out?" Rachael asked.

"They aren't like Enrique and the others. I don't even think they are Mexicans. Enrique said they may be from Bolivia or Columbia. They work hard, but I may not keep them on after harvest. They aren't like the rest of my boys. I just don't trust them. I think tomorrow I'll have them go after those rattlesnakes that have been hanging around the cattle sheds. Two steers got bit last week. I think the snakes are starting to move towards their dens and you know your father built the shed right on top of one of the ancient dens."

"I've heard this before Roger. Dad didn't know that those darn snakes keep coming back to the same den for centuries."

"Just like some men I can think of. Anyway, I'm going to turn those new guys loose on the snakes."

"Don't kill them, you know those snake handlers over in the Bayou country use them in worship services. They'll pay good money for them."

"Rachael, we gross over three million dollars from cows and crops, why should I fart around with selling some darn ol' snakes for a few hundred. They'll be killing them."

"Can we watch?" one of the children squealed from the rear seat.

"That's enough snake talk. Ya'll get your minds on going to church." Rachael ended the conversation angry with her husband.

Rachael's father built their farming business into a multi-million dollar operation before he died of heart failure. He had brought Roger into the operation after their marriage which was rushed when Roger, the football star, got Rachael, the Longhorn cheerleader, pregnant after a stunning performance on the field which was followed by an even more stunning performance off the field. Roger was penniless when he moved to the farm and now enjoyed the lifestyle of the wealthy agribusinessman. What griped Rachael was that her husband would daily point to where her father had made some bad judgment like building the cattle shed over a snake pit. He'll get nothing from me this week she thought as they drove off to the Assembly of God Church.

Sunday, October 7th

Mohamed's Turkish Bath House
Charikar, Afghanistan

THE TWO AGENTS LAY NAKED and still on the hot marble slabs. Had the steam not clouded the scene, they might have appeared to have been two cadavers laid out in the morgue. Rocky, who despised Johnson, had decided that the old adage of keeping your friends close and your enemies closer, may be worth following for a few days. At least in the steam room, Johnson couldn't find his breath enough to bitch or brag, a welcome relief.

An Afghani boy, wearing only a white loin cloth, opened the large wooden door and motioned the men to follow. Steam poured out the door past the slender brown boy. They wrapped oversized towels around their pink torsos and followed the youngster to two waiting teenagers. The larger of the teens motioned for them to loosen their towels and lay on the warm marble tables. The agents crawled up on the separate slabs and the teenagers poured cold water over their hot naked bodies. The frigid water robbed them of their breath. The boys took enormous horse brushes and rough lye soap and scrubbed the veneer of dust and sand from every inch of their bodies. Rocky waved his scrubber off when the cleansing came close to being personal. Johnson suffered no such modesty. The wash and scrub was followed by an amateurishly delivered massage that Rocky imagined was more like pygmies dancing wildly on his backside. A half-hour later, the agents were hosed off like cars in the Luther League fundraiser at the church parking lot.

Both agents rested wrapped in thick cotton towels, reclined on cushioned benches and sipped strong sweet tea. Johnson's satellite telephone rang as he was finishing a laborious tale about a heroic arrest of an ALF terrorist he had made before going overseas. Rocky Kowalewicz was jolted awake by the cell phone ring. Was the story over, he wondered and thought about excusing himself.

"Hello Carol," Johnson answered and then listened to the caller, nodding his head occasionally, uttering a series of A-Has, and scribbling a few notes which Rocky, with a practiced eye, could read upside down.

"Do we have photos?" Johnson interrupted raising his voice so it echoed around the stone walls.

He listened again for several minutes, scratching notes. As best Rocky could read, they had records documenting a sexual liaison between the general and a certain major who was a stunning beauty and yes, they did have photographs.

"Excellent. Carol, I'll repay you when I get back to Washington. You think about the reward. Goodbye," Johnson said. He snapped his phone closed.

Rocky watched Johnson flash a crooked grin, stand, dress himself, and without a word leave the bath house.

Rocky stood, and then lost his balance, light-headed from the spa and the massage. He caught himself on the door jam and waited to regain his equilibrium on his thick bare legs, scarred from battles he could barely recall. He wasn't as quick on his feet as the younger Rocky, although he remained powerful and could still dish it out in a fight. The blue-blooded Yale graduates at the CIA thought Rocky an oaf. They found him unsuitable for a diplomatic cover assignment, sipping tea or cocktails at black-tie affairs. Yet, where the Ivy League crowd dare not tread, it was most useful to send the likes of the brutish Rocky. He was more than aware of his status. In fact, he enjoyed the reputation, although he secretly feared getting old and losing his edge. He did harbor a desire to just once have the Agency deliver one of the frail preppies into the field where danger abound. It brought a smile to his face at the thought.

Rocky quietly slipped into his khaki pants and denim shirt, pulled the tan desert boots on, strapped two pistols to his side and made tracks to the airbase.

Sunday, October, 7th

Bagran Air Base
Afghanistan

THE AIR CONDITIONER WAS WORKING again and the general cranked it full-bore to ward off the suffocating heat he knew would close in as it had the day before.

Agent Kowalewicz sipped what passed as coffee the orderly had served a few minutes earlier. "My Intel is that Johnson thrived working between the lines of the F.B.I. policy and procedure handbooks just as he had 'walked the line' in the church. He learned from the older agents the ways passed down by Hoover and his team of micro-managers. Blackmail, illegal wire-taps, planting evidence or false stories were all in the tool bag of the older agents, all in the name of a greater good, however nebulous that may be."

"So blackmail won't be out of the question?" the general asked from behind the big desk.

"General, I think he's desperate. Johnson pleased his SAICs, Special Agents in Charge, and rose through the ranks. He progressed until a survivalist shot a federal agent at Ruby Ridge and Johnson was for a short time the onsite agent in charge. As that incident deteriorated into a media nightmare, Johnson's star became dimmer and dimmer as the Bureau pushed him further into oblivion."

"How long has he been in this country?"

"He was only three years from retirement when he was sent to the Middle East. He's been in Afghanistan for a year. His dreams of spending his last years as a SAIC in Salt Lake City went up in smoke. As if that weren't bad enough, his wife left him for his ex-partner who did become the SAIC in Utah. Johnson became a bitter man whose hopes and dreams were crushed. I believe he views breaking Ali as his ticket back to restore his honor."

"How certain are you of his plan?"

"You can take it to the bank. I won't embarrass you with the details, but be sure he's got some dirt he intends to drop on you to get his way."

"Thank you for the warning. I'm certain someday I will find a way to return the favor." The general summoned his aide, "Captain, show Agent Kowalewicz out and ya'll use the back entrance."

"Thank you," Rocky offered and then followed the captain out of the office.

General Dubois stood and walked across his red-hued Persian rug to the framed color photographs resting on the gray metal counter. He picked up his wife's photo, held it for a moment then looked to the photo of his children. He placed both pictures face down on the counter. As he did, his class picture of the U.S. Army War College caught his eye. A very attractive blonde major held his attention bringing back old memories and yearnings until the captain returned. "The FBI agent is waiting to see you."

"Bring him in and stay with us captain," the general walked back to his desk, sat and reached under his desk throwing a toggle switch to start the concealed tape recorder.

The captain led the visitor into the office. The general offered his hand. "Welcome, Agent Johnson." The agent's face confirmed what Rocky had alleged – the agent looked like a 16 year-old boy at a Nogales whorehouse.

"General, thank you for seeing me on such short notice. It seems I have some very important information from Washington which may bear very heavily on Ali's travel plans which seem to have stalled. Information, general, I think best shared without the captain present."

"I trust that we had no misunderstanding about Ali. We are preparing to fly him to GITMO early tomorrow. You will have full custody and in fact are welcome to join him on the flight. We are keeping him at the base because until we can make all flight arrangements, this is the most secure place in Afghanistan for him. Agent, you have our full cooperation.

"Captain, take Agent Johnson to the interrogation room and bring Ali to him. Furnish him with an interpreter, also. I'm sorry to rush off, but I must catch a flight to Kabul. The captain has my orders to give you all the cooperation we can."

"Good," replied the stunned agent. The captain ushered him towards the heavy metal door leading to the anteroom.

The general reached under his desk and toggled off the recorder.

"Agent, one more thing before you leave, please come back."

Johnson, with the captain behind him, returned to the general's desk. The officer stood, flushed with anger, leaned over his desk inches from the agent's face. "You rotten maggot, did you really believe you could blackmail a U.S. Army General? You arrogant little piss ant." Spittle flew into the agent's mouth which had dropped nearly to his chest. He tried to speak but couldn't.

Two sergeants slipped into the room unnoticed and took position flanking Johnson. Looking the astounded man squarely in the eye, the general snarled, "Let me share with you what your next 24 hours are going to look like. Have you ever been on a magic carpet ride? No? Not many have. However, I've arranged one for you."

"You camel's asshole are leaving my office rolled in that fine Persian rug. Captain, put him in a body bag first. When he shits himself, I don't want my carpet soiled." Johnson turned to leave but was grabbed by the enlisted men and spun around to face the general, no longer free to go.

Johnson turned to leave but was grabbed by the enlisted men and spun around to face the general, no longer free to go.

"These very loyal men will tie the carpet with you rolled in it to the *skids* of my personal helicopter. The Captain here will be your pilot and can assure you of an unforgettable and magical ride. Tomorrow, when the Afghan police find your very naked body, they will be furious to see your drunken ass in bed with one of their women. We have a special al Qaeda widow who we hope you will find very welcoming, if only briefly. The newspapers will report that she will undoubtedly be killed for screwing your skinny ass. You will likely be sent back to Washington and explain your drunkenness and her death to a very angry administration."

The enlisted men threw the agent to the ground. The general walked past him, pointing skyward. "Bon voyage, Pencilneck."

Sunday, October 7th

The Alhambra
Andalusia, Spain

BILLOWING DARK CLOUDS FORMED OVER the fortress threatening rain that would never come. Omar looked skyward and wished he'd brought an umbrella as he strolled along the jagged path through the woods with al Fulani. They chatted, mostly of things they missed back home – foods, family, friends. Omar missed those afternoons with his brothers, uncles, and cousins. They spent hours over tea, puffing on Hookah water pipes and discussing world politics. Mostly, he missed his father who'd imparted decades of wisdom to his son. He yearned to speak one more time to his father, to tell him of his plans and to seek his approval. Nothing had been the same since his father was assassinated by the Jews.

Finally, they arrived at the quaint stone chapel built by Christians some hundred years ago. Omar led al Fulani through the rough hewn wood doorway and to a bench in the rear of the sanctuary such as it was. A solitary gold-plated empty cross adorned the front of the dark place of worship.

"The crisis should soon be over. We have spies who have told us exactly where your brother is being held. He would never willingly betray us, however, the CIA has their ways. As a precaution we will need to take Ali out of the picture. We also have put our plans in motion to bring America to its knees and destroy the Jews. Israel will cease to exist. Next year we will be in Jerusalem."

al Fulani allowed himself a slight smile showing his nicotine stained teeth. "What is next to come?" He stood and leaned closer staring hypnotically into Omar's eyes demanding an answer.

Omar was slow to respond. His tongue wiped his upper lip as he formed his answer. He didn't like to give out information. The CIA and their brothers have too many informants. "In time, in time, you will learn."

The clouds had blown to the east by the time the two men left the solitude of the stone building. The rays from the sun shone through the forest's canopy and danced on the damp stones lining the rough path. Omar began to warm to this new partner. He seemed to be catching on quickly. Still, he reserved doubts.

Sunday, October 7th

Pend Oreille Lake, Idaho

MELISSA AND PAT KELLY LIVED IN a cedar log home along the splendid shores of Lake Pend Oreille. On this balmy Sunday morning, the quaking Aspens were at their most colorful. As they drove back home from church, Melissa wished the fall season would last forever. Pat drew up to the drive-through window at McDonald's for Happy Meals some of which ended up on the back seat floor. It was always the first place their dog checked out when he got into the SUV. He kept it first class clean.

Pat, a helicopter pilot with IRAQ #1 experience worked for the Walcott Timber Company. He spent his days flying aerial surveys occasionally interrupted by busy executives demanding shuttle flights to Denver or Seattle. The company Bell 206B Jet Ranger was only 15 minutes from home, in Dover, a fact he relished after 20 years of commuting while flying for the Los Angeles County Sheriff's Department. He was ready to draw his pension and begin a new job away from the crime ridden streets of Los Angeles. He had seen too many of his friends killed or seriously injured and wanted out before he was next. Ironically, he and Melissa were married when her first husband, also a deputy sheriff, was gunned down working off-duty at a wedding party. Pat had been assigned to care for her during the funeral and the days after. The trauma drew them close and the kids looked to Pat to replace their father. Within a year they were married and at Melissa's urging he looked for a job far away from the dangers of L.A.

An hour after returning home, Melissa was on the road again. "Pat, I'm taking the girls to Tae Kwon Do practice, be back in a couple of hours," Melissa said as she grabbed her keys and herded the girls out the door.

Pat didn't hear as his attention was focused on the Denver Bronco/Kansas City Chiefs game. He had just installed a wall-mounted television with surround sound and for all intents and purposes was live at the game in Mile High Stadium.

Melissa loaded Brenda and Amanda and all their gear into the back seat. As she backed out of her gravel driveway, she noticed a utility van parked very near the drive. She thought nothing of it and the three along with their Golden Retriever, Cody, drove to Master Park's dojo.

From a discrete distance the white van in need of a wash, followed.

Sunday, October 7th

Bagran Air Base
Afghanistan

GENERAL DUBOIS ENTERTAINED THE THIRD U. S. Senator this week. Today's guest was Senator Jason A. Ryan from Tennessee. The diminutive politician struggled to keep up with the long-legged general as they damn-near jogged across the base to the Officer's Dining Hall. Sweat dripped from his long jowls. He dabbed his face with a white handkerchief. The general enjoyed having the self-important V.I.P.s tag along like puppies that still squatted to piss. Least that's what he told the captain.

The commanding officer had his presentation memorized. "Bagran Air Base is a militarized airport and housing complex located next to the ancient city of Bagran in Parwan province. The base is home to the 82nd Airborne Division of the United States Army and the 455th Air Expeditionary Wing of the Air Force. When the last invading army, the Russians, occupied Afghanistan, the base played a key role in the Russian strategy."

There is little beauty in the clay colored rocky landscape. The poverty in the surrounding villages is a stark contrast to the billion dollars of high tech aircraft on the base. The airmen spend thousands of hours helping the locals with projects of every sort. However, as one frustrated officer said, "Where do you start and will the Taliban blow it up when we leave?"

The general pointed to the south towards a row of concrete buildings surrounded by razor wire and guard towers. "Bagran is the primary detention center for persons held by U.S. Forces in Afghanistan. The center is off limits for all except the security staff and military intelligence personnel. It's been a temporary home for many important al Qaeda and Taliban fighters. It's built like a fort within a fort with separate checkpoints and some serious looking elevated guardhouses added after four prisoners managed an escape."

They arrived at the Officer's Hall with the senator panting and five paces behind. The general waited at the top of the steps as the senator limped to the top. He held the steel door open and the cold air rushed past the men. The pint-sized politician stopped to catch his breath at the threshold.

This was a busy day at the main checkpoint. Many locals work on the base and each was required to check in and be assigned an escort. The security escort force was shorthanded because today was Women's Equality Day and the security force fielded a large team of runners in the 5K event. They would be shorthanded for a few hours.

At the appointed time, a creaking Russian army surplus truck with an empty water tank pulled through the camp gates. The guards waved the familiar driver past without a glance. The same truck came and went several times each day. Local workers used the truck to pump the septic tanks for the latrines. The contents were later sold to the local farmers to fertilize the crops which were sold back to Americans – a near perfect recycling system. A few cynics even claimed that the same truck that picked up the sewage also brought drinking water to the NCO Club.

There seemed little need to inspect the contents. Besides, the entire damn truck smelled of urine and excrement. A single security airman driving a camo Polaris four-wheeler followed the old truck keeping a respectable distance from the stench and slop.

The truck lumbered to a second checkpoint and was waived through with his military escort to the building where the driver had been told by his Taliban connection he should park and walk away. This he did and as soon as he was clear an Afghani who cleaned the American barracks removed a cell phone from his coat pocket and began punching numbers. The security escort was distracted by the gals running in the 5K race past the inner security fence and didn't notice the absent driver. .The long-legged blonde runner was the last thing on earth seen by the security airman.

The concussion of the bomb knocked General Francis Dubois off the leather-topped swivel chair. The senator rolled from his chair and landed on the general.

The waste truck vaporized as did the high security cell block which held Ali.

Sirens wailed as fire-trucks, MPs, and ambulances all responded to the horrific scene. It put an early end to the Equality Day race. Two of the competitors crossed the finish line in the air.

The general pushed the senator away, pulled himself up, and shouted for his aide. "Captain!"

Sunday, October 7th

Wilkin County, Texas
US/Mexican Border

THE TWO WHITE AND GREEN pickups parked next to each other on a treeless hilltop in the semi-arid plains. The four border patrol agents each pressed binoculars to their faces as they listened to the Denver/Kansas City football game. The score was 21 to 14, Denver with 3 minutes to go in the 4th Quarter.

Agent Bob Stanley was the first to spot the Mexicans crouched low at a trot across the arroyo. "I see at least a dozen about 2 o'clock out about 1600 yards." He pointed towards the border intruders then wiped the sweat from his bushy mustache. The heat from the desert sands was making it difficult to get a clear picture. The people looked like they were weaving between towering cacti in a wavy fogged up mirage.

Tim Bush swung his binoculars to the described area and saw a ragged line of men and women each carrying plastic milk jugs half-full of water and packs, mostly black garbage bags, over their shoulders. "Damn!" Bush muttered.

Stanley looked over to Bush. "What's wrong?"

"I don't appreciate these wetbacks interrupting this game, that's what's wrong."

"They're going to follow the arroyo to that rise. We can take them there. Relax, we'll finish the game unless it goes into overtime."

They followed the figures with their binoculars and listened to the game which ended with Denver winning 24 to 21. A touchdown, on-side kick, and field goal in the time it took the Mexicans to get to the designated capture point.

The two pickups with detention toppers were driven to opposite sides of the arroyo right up to the ragged line all of whom were too low in the dry washes to see the trucks. Then the rough men were upon them. Each of the green uniformed officers exploded from the truck armed with unslung M-16s.

"*Alto.*"

"*Policia.* Drop your bags on the ground and raise your hands. Get on the ground – NOW!" The agents trained their rifles on the group.

All nineteen Mexicans complied. The black bags and water jugs fell to the rocky desert floor. They dropped to the sand, some falling on low cactus and small sharp rocks and uttered muffled screams of pain.

There was nothing remarkable about this group, poorly dressed men and women, no children, two Sinaloa coyotes in front and one in the rear of the line. Towards the back of the line, two men carrying military style duffel bags probably with marijuana eased away from those bags and dropped spread-eagle.

The four agents slid down the brown sand into the dry creek bed to begin the process of detention.

"We have detained 19 at GPS coordinates Lat 26.098 Long 98.254. We will need transport," Stanley spoke into his microphone to the dispatcher.

"We are backed up, it may be a few hours," the dispatcher replied.

"Roger," Stanley answered.

"Let's get them cuffed and up the..." Bush's words were cut off as a burst of automatic gun fire sprayed through the back of his throat and out his front, sending blood all over Stanley's face.

Bush was dead as he dropped.

Stanley and the other two agents turned and raised their M-16s and fired in the direction of the gunfire, towards a stand of mesquite trees.

They misjudged the location of the incoming gunfire and Stanley's head burst like an exploding pumpkin, the other agents likewise crumbled mortally wounded in a hail of automatic gunfire.

Alberto Hernandez rose up from his one-kneed stance. He let the AK-47 drop, slung to his side. Off to his left and further back, Carlos Mendosa, Chuy, Memo, and Flaco appeared from the mesquite and sage, weapons at low ready. They walked over to the downed agents firing into the heads of each to be certain of their deaths. Likewise looking at their massive wounds would have assured them of the same. The calm air reeked of spent gunpowder and the unforgettable metallic odor of fresh flesh ripped from the body and blood.

The agents had no way of knowing that this group of 19 was actually a group of 24, five of whom had stopped for 30 minutes to attend to their gear after crossing the Rio Grande.

"Take their weapons and radios," Alberto barked.

He pointed to the two coyotes and ordered them to lead on quickly. "*Rapidamente.*"

They trotted for 45 minutes, a couple of women falling behind and abandoned in the darkness, the moon blackened by thick clouds. Lightning flashed across the sky to occasionally light the path and cast ominous shadows from the tall cactus. At a distant rugged hilltop, they were met by a dust covered and dented black Ford F 350 pickup pulling a rusty cattle trailer that could be heard miles away. Thirteen piled into the cattle trailer and laid in the cow shit and straw which covered the floor. Eight others, three men and five women, were left behind. The coyotes always get paid in advance. Their screams and pleas echoed in the hills as the truck made its way down the washed out road. The trailer clanged and banged heavy metallic noises at each hole and rock on the path.

The Ford traveled about 20 miles of back country dirt and sand roads finally stopping at a badly kept ranch, owned by a local sheriff's deputy and his wife. Several junked pickups on blocks and stock trailers were parked next to the mesquite pole corral which held six mangy Longhorns and a forlorn looking donkey. Angry cow dogs ran and barked loudly at the intruders. Here they could make a safe transfer. The men piled out, happy to leave the trailer alive. Buckets of cool water awaited them. They eagerly washed the desert from their faces and necks with old rags from the buckets. Large black flies from the Longhorns' corral flew to greet the visitors.

With blood covered hands, Alberto gave each man a packet of identification documents and American cash. He had one left over and cursed at his oversight of leaving Juan Valenzuela behind. Alberto gathered the men around the mesquite campfire. He gave the other two team leaders written instructions on where to proceed as well as names and addresses of their contacts. He told them that when they arrived at their destinations, they would meet with others already in place and receive the details of their mission.

Four newer Suburbans waited for the men who brushed the manure from their clothes before sitting on the Chevy's fine leather chairs. Cold beers and cigarettes were passed around as the Suburbans were driven off to Minnesota, Idaho, North Dakota, and Texas. Likewise, the day before and for several days later, other teams crossed the border to join those already in place across the nation.

The Border Patrol transport unit dispatched to move the captured illegals discovered the bodies of the officers. Within a few hours the scene was crowded with police agents, many who showed only to grieve and pay their respects. All offered to help track down the killers. K-9 tracking teams were brought in and took their handlers to where the killers were loaded in the cattle trailers. At that point the bloodhounds began working confused circles indicating the scent trail was lost. A hundred feet from the trailer track, the dogs picked up new scent and went yelping off across the sage and scrub after the killers. It would be hours before the dogs found the women who'd scattered and wandered lost in the brush. They said they knew nothing of what happened.

Texas Ranger Cullen Kingsley had been only ten miles from the shootout on another assignment when he heard the call for help on the mutual police channel. He was on the scene within minutes and helped secure the site. Then he was just a go-fer helping with whatever the Border Patrol and the FBI requested. Kingsley made the mistake of looking into Agent Bush's face as he helped roll him into the body bag. "Oh shit." He choked and turned away as he emptied his stomach.

As the crime scene team wrapped up their work, Border Patrol agent Jesus Gonzales walked off to be alone. He was Stanley's best friend. This was the worst day of his career. Suddenly, from under a sage bush, Gonzales heard a moan. He drew his pistol and shined his Streamlight towards the sound. He could barely make out a human form.

He yelled for backup.

Sunday, October, 7

Elizabeth River
Portsmouth, Virginia

HELIDORO HENRIQUES, THE PROUD PORTUGUESE skipper of the Maximiano, a 91.3 foot Raised Foc'sle Trawler, was a sturdy fellow who fished along the Atlantic seaboard. He'd done so for four decades. He required a crew of three to run the large boat and like many commercial fishermen found it difficult to find men willing to labor. The few who did show up for work often left at the first port to drink up their meager wages. His last crew, three brothers, left for the fishing grounds of Alaska to make their fortune. Two weeks ago, Henriques hired three workers from Indonesia. They seemed to know their way around the boat and fishing nets and Henriques was pleased. After two days of preparation they cast off from Portsmouth, Virginia and sailed east, in calm waters, towards a full moon.

"Martin, get up here!" Henriques shouted.

A lean little man appeared in the hatchway. "Mr. Skipper, you want me?" He wore an old slicker and a black knit cap pulled over his dark hair down to his large brown eyes. It was cool when the sun went down, even when the wind died.

"Take the wheel and keep the heading at 85 degrees. I'm going down to piss and tend to the nets," Henriques told Martin.

"Aye, Skipper. You pissed off at the nets," Martin repeated.

"85 degrees."

"Aye, Skipper," Martin nodded in agreement.

Henriques turned to go astern not convinced the order had been fully understood. He pulled up the collar of his blue wool peacoat to shield from the chilly breeze. Gentle waves rocked the boat as Henriques walked to the stern and dug inside his black Carhartt overalls to find his release over the side. He looked out over the murky water and saw he was facing the moon.

"Damn," he shouted angrily at the misdirected mate. Then he felt the course weave of a fishnet tightening over his head and upper body. He struggled, his member still hanging out and releasing a stream skyward.

"We see how you like to be caught in net like fish," one of the crew said. He unleashed a string of curses.

His screams were muted by the netting as he was lowered to the cold, black depths he had commanded only a moment earlier.

Martin continued his course to the northwest, up the Potomac River dragging the drowning Henriques behind the boat in his own net.

Hours later, Martin's seafaring partners brought bulging black duffel bags from below and unpacked compressed air tanks laying them out, valves facing the stern. When Martin turned into the wind, both men opened the twenty some valves and a rusty haze floated briefly in the air like wispy contrails then came to rest in the Potomac, about 3 miles due northwest of Washington, D.C.

Monday, October 8th

The White House
Washington, D.C.

THE CHIEF OF STAFF BROUGHT the meeting to order without the president who was late due to a photo session with the National USA Women's Softball Team. "Gentlemen, it's a daunting agenda so the president asked me to open this briefing. First, anyone who wagered against Denver with the president should make good by the afternoon. He takes his team and his bets seriously, so pay up."

"Yesterday, we had a tragic incident on the Mexican border. Secretary Wilkins, would you please brief us, the president has this information already."

Richard Wilkins, the Secretary of Homeland Security, looked like he had been too long without sleep. "Gentlemen, we lost four of our brave Border Patrol agents in a gunfight near McAllen, Texas. We are conducting the investigation. For now it looks like the four Border Patrol agents had detained 19 illegals and were awaiting transport. Our trackers, who surveyed the crime scene, tell us that five other illegals likely came upon the agents and murdered them. May God take them quickly to be by His side. For now, we have no suspects. We found a wounded Mexican under a sage brush, although we have no idea how he plays into the event. We have a working theory that the four agents came upon drug couriers who often have armed escorts on large shipments." Knowing the chief of staff's preference for brevity, he sat into the high backed leather chair.

"May we have a moment of silence in remembrance of these honorable warriors," the chief said.

The moment passed before he continued,"Two quick items on the terrorist threat – first, the media is hyping up this 'Red Plague.' The spread of red algae in the Potomac is alarming the people, particularly because it is killing the fish which stink to high heaven. If that weren't bad enough, the flies feeding on the dead fish are becoming overwhelming along the river. I don't need to tell you the problems the owners of the million dollar condos along the river could cause if we don't clean up the fish and spray for the flies.

"Very preliminary assessments are that this is some sort of exotic algae. Some believe that maybe a chemical spill has caused this unusual growth of algae. It doesn't appear to be harmful to humans. We have no reason to suspect it is a terrorist threat, however, it is early in the assessment and the scientists are all over this. Until we know, I wouldn't recommend skinny dipping in the Potomac." A slight smile crossed his face.

"The second item concerns the capture of Ali Shah Masood. John can give us the latest."

Before speaking, the round faced CIA Director, John Rankin, paused and looked at FBI Director – something the normally suspicious chief of staff noticed and wrote a reminder to dig into.

"Yesterday, a truck bomb exploded at the Bagran Air Base destroying the detention center where Ali had been held." Director Rankin stopped and wiped his brow with a CIA emblazoned silk handkerchief. "We have every reason to believe Ali was the target. He had valuable information concerning future attacks. Enough said."

"How do you know that?" Director Wilkins asked.

Director Rankin's jaw dropped and he cocked his head. "I'm sorry…"

"How do you know that this Ali had information concerning future attacks and why haven't my people been warned?"

"I'm not able to divulge our source, let's just say we have a high level asset inside the…"

Abruptly the private door opened and President Franklin limped into the room. Tall and handsome with thick silver hair and very photogenic, the best since John Kennedy the media wags agreed. According to family lore, the president was an ancestor of Jefferson Davis or Robert E. Lee – by way of a late night visit by a slave girl. The staff rose to honor him as he walked to the head of the long conference table. He set his silver cane on the table with a thud.

"Be seated, Gentlemen, we have important business this morning. First, the Secret Service agent outside the door will collect from those who owe me for the Bronco's great victory yesterday. He will arrest any welchers, on my orders," the president smiled.

"Second, could we have a moment of silence for those four courageous agents who died fighting the war on drugs to save our children?"

Pausing half as long this time, the president continued, "Most important, we need to discuss the border incident with Iran which occurred two days ago. Our soldiers were fired on from near the IRAQ/IRAN border. General Highcamp will give a complete rundown and we will spend the rest of this meeting discussing our options. I want to hear your counsel, gentlemen, although you must understand I do not choose to let this act of war go 'unanswered.' General..."

The general spent the next 15 minutes detailing how soldiers from an Army unit of Stryker light armored vehicles were fired upon. There were no injuries, damage, or enemy casualties, just a lot of incoming from the Iran side of the border.

The Iranians claimed it was American Special Forces that had violated the border and fired upon their own Stryker Group – missing by a mile. The Iranian Media Minister speculated that it was done to give President Franklin provocation for yet another invasion. He added, "Our troops wouldn't have missed."

"I have ordered the general to begin making plans to answer this attack. We have a number of attack options and I will spend the remainder of this time hearing your opinions," the president said.

Ten minutes later the meeting adjourned and seven very important persons were humbled by digging into their wallets and paying a grinning Secret Service agent.

Monday, October 8th

Refugio, Texas

THE HABIBS, UFUK AND HIS fourth wife, Katife, migrated from Turkey to live near Refugio. Having been given nearly $1,500,000.00 by their employer, Gemstar, LTD, they purchased a rundown southern Texas farm from the sons of the deceased owner. Years ago the farmer had died at age ninety-two. The farmstead suffered from years of neglect. The boys moved to San Antonio and had cash rented the land for years. Neither they nor their wives had any interest in the hardships and isolation of farming. The farm was at least 2 hours from the nearest so-so shopping mall in Corpus Christi. They decided that this century farm held more value sold for cash which could be used for more immediate desires.

They had waited for dad to die before listing the property. It sold in a day even though they were asking a premium price. In fact, the realtor was more than a little surprised when another agent walked in the office and on behalf of his clients offered full cash price with a quick closing.

It was only a few months later that the neighbors learned people from Turkey had purchased the farm. When the Habibs moved in, the neighbors were skeptical as only farmers can be of outsiders moving into the area.

The skepticism grew as they learned the Habibs were neither farming nor ranching as the locals knew it but raising goats and lambs for slaughter. The Habibs began construction on a commercial slaughter house with crews brought in from San Antonio. When asked, the Habibs explained their meat products were to be sent to markets on the East Coast to supply the demand among immigrants from the Middle East and Africa. They prospered over the last three years. And they were good neighbors.

Chuy and three of his men arrived in their Suburban after a short drive from the border. The three had too much to drink while en route and argued about who had actually killed the Border Patrol agents. Ufuk Habib showed them to their own dormitory away from the 20 other employees. Chuy and his men intended to keep to themselves. They had another mission which did not include shoveling goat offal from the slaughter floor.

At his employer's direction, Habib had spent months searching for targets. Habib had not only found targets but had located the local resources to destroy them. That would be left to Chuy and afterwards there would be no trace that Chuy and his men had ever been in the United States. The evening of their arrival and for several nights thereafter, Ufuk and Chuy met.

Ufuk and Chuy huddled at the small wooden kitchen table. "Here are the satellite photographs of your targets. I drove by the sites and took photos from my truck, although they may not be of much use to you," Ufuk said. He leaned back in his chair while Chuy studied the material.

"What about the plane? Where is that?" Chuy asked. His beery breath offended Ufuk who moved a few feet away. How can they be using such men, Catholics no less, Ufuk thought to himself.

Ufuk took a manila folder from his backpack. "These are photos of the plane and a map showing its location."

Chuy looked at the picture and shook his head. He tossed the photos back on the table.

"What's wrong? Can't you fly that plane? I was told..."

"I can fly anything. This one even has a parachute built into the plane. It's such a waste of a fine aircraft."

"I have more stuff for you."

"What is stuff?"

"Stuff is everything. It's what the Americans call everything. Never mind. Here is the name of the foreman at the farm. He will give you and your men a job. Don't let him demand more money from you, I have already paid him. The directions to the farm are on the back."

“Can you write this in Spanish?”

“No, but my wife can. She’s learned some Spanish.”

“What other ‘stuff’ do you have for me?”

“This was delivered to me only days ago, when I learned you were coming. It’s sealed and you’re supposed to open it, read it and follow the directions. That’s all I know. You’re on your own from here.”

Monday, October 8th

Arlington National Cemetery
Washington, D.C.

THE THREE SILVER SEMI-TRACTOR TRAILERS pulled up to the heavy metal service gate at the Arlington National Cemetery. The pot-bellied driver of the lead tractor crawled down to the wet payment. Rain pounded on his back as he rushed to the concrete block guardhouse. "We've supplies for the landscaping department, my instructions say you should contact a John Smith, the boss man, I guess."

The uniformed guard looked at his list of expected deliveries and found none. "I'll give John a call and get him down here to clear you through." He picked up the phone and dialed Smith's number. He explained the situation and hung up. "They should be able to send someone to get you in a few minutes."

Twenty minutes later, Oscar, a yard maintenance worker appeared at the guardhouse. Oscar was a small, less than 5'2" Puerto Rican man dressed in a blue cotton work uniform. His face was pock-marked to the point of deformity from the smallpox he'd suffered as a boy. He looked at the floor as he addressed the guard. "John sent me down to show these guys where to unload."

"You have any paper work on this deal? I can't just let them in without something in writing."

"Boss didn't give me anything. He said that I should show them where to park the trailers until we can get to unload them. They are just supposed to drop their trailers and get out of here."

"Hey, man, we're on overtime as it is, how about you just let us drop the trailers and we'll be on our way. Traffic is going to be at a standstill with these thundershowers," begged the driver of the lead semi.

The guard looked at the two and shook his head in apparent disgust with the lack of concern for procedure. "Okay, dump 'em quick and get the hell out of here. And I want the paperwork tomorrow on this." He wagged his finger at Oscar. "You tell Smith that as soon as he gets in tomorrow I want that on my desk, you hear that man?"

"Yes sir, I tell him," Oscar replied not looking at the guard. He knew that Smith would never get the paperwork because Smith was dead, his throat slashed, and stuffed behind 600 pounds of fertilizer bags.

Within forty-five minutes, the trailers were dropped next to the shed containing the landscaping supplies and the tractors had exited from the hallowed grounds. As is always the case, the groundskeepers were headquartered in the furthest most obscure part of the cemetery. After supervising the parking of the trailers, Oscar returned to Smith's small cluttered office. He answered the phone to make sure the boss's absence raised no concerns until the scheduled time came for Smith to leave work. He didn't have much to be concerned about because most everyone had left early due to the torrential rain.

As darkness settled in on the cemetery, Oscar fired up the white Bobcat skid steer. He labored for hours unloading the sealed wooden crates stored in the three trailers. It was close to midnight when Oscar finished and had the crates neatly stacked in the parking lot. Only once did a security officer swing into the lot to check on Oscar. The rain still beat down hard and the officer had no heart to even leave his squad car. He just cracked his window and asked why Oscar was working so late. He was prepared with a big lie which he aptly delivered as he stared deferentially at the ground.

Oscar had worked at Arlington for a year and a half. He got the job in landscaping with the intervention of a congressional staff from Tennessee – people he never even knew existed. When he was hired, the man in a suit told him that one day he would be called upon to perform tasks beyond his normal duties. A few days ago he was contacted by the same man and told his work at Arlington would soon be over. The well-dressed man said the time to perform the extra work had arrived. He assured Oscar he would be handsomely rewarded. He was given specific instructions and told that his cash reward would be in the crates. When he had completed the task he was to return to his remote village in Puerto Rico and his parents would be freed to join him. He even provided a photograph of Oscar's parents squatting on a dirt floor in a corner of a thatched hut.

Laboring under his damp raingear, Oscar pried open the first heavily insulated wooden crate. Tens of thousands of Leopard frogs on dozens of blue plastic shelves within the crate began to croak and leap onto the wet payment. Oscar had to wait until most of the green spotted frogs had cleared out before he reached into the crates to swish the others out. He pulled each shelf out and threw it onto the ground searching for the pouch containing his promised cash.

He pried four more containers and dumped thousands more frogs from each. In the fourth crate, he found a plastic bag containing a portion of his cash and a note stating that the rest of his money would be spread over several crates. He continued to open the crates. He was surprised to find that some contained hordes of biting flies and gnats. He flayed and swatted in order to continue his search for the cash. The humming insects formed a dense cloud twisting upward into the night sky. Some landed in the bushes, grass, and trees. The frogs feasted on those that landed within their reach.

Oscar finished before sunrise and he packed the bags of cash into the rear seat of his rusty red Kia. He pushed the blue duffel of clothes taken from his locker into the passenger seat and drove slowly through the parking lot. The road was so crowded with frogs that the car slipped off the road onto the grass making nasty ruts on the pristine lawn. He regained control and continued towards the exit. Oscar gave a hardy wave as he passed the guardhouse. When he had made good his escape, he allowed himself to ponder the purpose of his mission. It never occurred to him that he had just delivered the second and third plagues upon the nation's capital. Finding no answer, he began to dream of how he would be reunited with his father and mother and, of course, how he would spend his cash reward.

At daybreak, the incoming cemetery staff was stunned by the nocturnal invasion of swarming insects and normally pristine lawns that seemed to be spewing forth undulating waves of blue and yellow frogs. Workers tried sweeping the roads with brooms and hoses. The frogs just moved to the grass and then back onto the pavement. The changing of the guards at the Tomb of the Unknown Soldier still took place during the first shift. A guard slipped and fell onto the monument, striking his head and knocked unconscious. Future shifts were cancelled because of the disgusting sight of guards squishing the frogs. Dozens of frogs neared the eternal flame at the Kennedy grave only to be roasted.

As the staff struggled to clear the amphibians, they were menaced by tens of thousands of biting gnats and flies.

CNN camera crews were first on the scene followed rapidly by FOX, ABC, and the rest. Live coverage of the frog and insect invasion was aired across the world. There was no denying anymore that the plagues had arrived.

Tuesday, October 9th

Gran Canaria Airport
Canary Islands

WARRANT OFFICER TROY ZIMMER ASKED his co-pilot to check on the passengers. The co-pilot was happy to comply and stretch his legs. It had already been a long flight and the movement would be welcomed. Alone, Zimmer reached over and killed the number two engine on the C-31A Friendship. He calmly radioed the controller at the Gran Canaria airport.

"U. S. Army Aircraft 51505 we have an engine failure – request permission for emergency landing and fire equipment."

The Gran Canaria controller promptly granted the request. Zimmer began a steep descent through the thick gray clouds as his co-pilot returned looking concerned.

"What's going on?"

"We lost the #2 engine. I'm landing at Gran Canaria Airport. They have emergency waiting. Get back in your seat and let's start the checklist, stat!"

The shiny C31-A landed without incident and taxied to a hangar some distance from the main terminal. Three men were waiting next to an unmarked gray C-26 parked in the shadows of the hangar. Zimmer, leading four heavily armed guards walked down the gangway. A sixth man, hooded, shackled and clad in an orange jumpsuit shuffled between them.

CIA Officer Casimir 'Rocky' Kowalewicz approached Zimmer.

"The general sends his regards," Zimmer said and then motioned to the guard to bring Ali Shah Masood.

"My best to the general." Casimir grasped Ali's arm and shoved him towards the waiting C-26 aircraft. Ali stumbled and cursed at his unseen tormentor. Within minutes, they lifted off the runway and headed northeast towards Europe. Casimir Kowalewicz would never know who made the decision to divert Ali from GITMO. For years, he gave himself credit. How wrong he was.

Tuesday, October 9th

Peace Bridge Border Checkpoint
Fort Erie, Ontario

THE VEHICLES WERE SIX ABREAST and stretched a half-mile at the U.S. Canadian border crossing at Peace Bridge. Immigration, Customs Enforcement (ICE) officers worked extra hours on each shift to accommodate the rush of Canadians eager to spend their Loonies on the abundance of American consumer goods shipped from Mexico and China. The favorable exchange rate had created a bonanza for American retailers and hoteliers. Aided by an inversion, the air was a grayish blue haze of exhaust fumes.

Carlos Esteban and Flaviano Zulueta were in the queue although not interested in shopping. The Chinese products they were seeking were AK-47s and QW-2 shoulder launched missiles. When it came their turn to be interviewed by the ICE officers, they produced Canadian passports although they were citizens of the Philippines. The men were well-groomed and attired in freshly pressed white shirts and dark business suits. The officers found nothing suspicious about their passports. Not surprising as the documents were skillfully forged by experts paid by their employer. Had they bothered to search, the officers would have found bona fide documents attesting to the business travel claimed by the pair. The customs officers chose not to pull them over for a secondary inspection, however, they did remember to ask if they had any Cuban cigars.

It didn't seem to pique their interest that Esteban and Zulueta spoke halting English. Canada's open, even loose, immigration policy meant the complexion of the nation was changing and was even more diverse than the United States.

Both men were well-briefed on crossing the border. They had been told what the ICE officers looked for and most importantly to appear relaxed. Each had rehearsed their stories and easily passed their interviews. They were waved into the United States of America.

The Dodge Caravan moved at a steady 65 miles per hour along Interstate 90. They exited at Syracuse and drove to the Mail Box Store.

Esteban confidently walked into the store and opened Box 358. He removed a package they had mailed from Toronto five days earlier. Esteban returned to the van. He circled the block several times, making a couple of u-turns, stopping in a quiet neighborhood and even turning off the van. With windows down, they sat for twenty minutes, listening for surveillance aircraft. Hearing none, Zulueta got out and walked down the quiet street. He looked for young white males sitting in shiny clean cars and vans with antennas and periscope vents. Seeing none he returned to the car and they drove to the K-Mart parking lot.

Esteban ripped open the package. Inside were two passports bearing new names and showing entry via the entry port of Detroit, Michigan. Next he removed track cell phones and an innocuous gray metal box. Zulueta moved the power toggle sideways and placed the box inside an empty Kleenex box on the dash. Esteban tried his cell phone. No coverage. They tried the AM/FM radio. Static but had no reception. The gray box generated an electronic screen around the car. Any tracking devises on the car would be defeated by the overwhelming electronic haze surrounding the Dodge van.

They continued their journey and five hours later arrived near a warehouse at the Port of New York. The imported products in the warehouse had cleared ICE inspections and were awaiting delivery. The roof of the 225,000 square foot warehouse bore twenty foot letters Windsor Ltd., an international shipping company with headquarters in Bermuda. Until purchased by investors from the United Arab Emirates, the company had a 200 year history of fostering trade across the Atlantic. The Arabs kept the name and corporate structure, but they inserted loyal men in certain key positions. When the Arabs needed essentials brought into the U.S., they found their ownership to produce flawless results.

Five minutes away from Windsor warehouse, Esteban parked in a Wal-Mart lot and Zulueta stepped inside the store to call ahead to their confederates.

When they arrived, the three sealed wooden crates were waiting on loading dock #24. They merely nodded to the two disinterested workers and pushed the wooden crates into the rear of the van.

Inside the crates were RPG-7 shoulder fired rockets, QW-2 shoulder launched missiles, AK-47s, and explosives which would be delivered to their team waiting in a duplex in New Jersey. Esteban drove off having spent less than 2 minutes at the dock. He circled back on himself a few more times looking for surveillance and finding none continued to New Jersey to meet his team.

Tuesday, October 9th

The Alhambra
Andalusia, Spain

OMAR WAITED FOR THE TALL Iranian by the dry creek bed that meandered down from the Fortress. He didn't mind the wait. The air was fresh and his mind wandered to the days he spent hunting birds with the family falcons. The bed was filled with broken tree limbs and moss covered boulders the size of Mini Coopers. The ancient trees swayed in the breeze and song birds entertained Omar as he rested on a handsomely carved wooden bench. Abolhasen Mumtaz smiled as his long lean legs carried him to Omar. They embraced, kissed, and walked closely down the rocky path neither speaking for a few moments.

"I hope you enjoyed the tour of Alhambra. Our forefathers built this magnificent castle during a time of Islamic dominance to which we intend to return," Omar said.

"Very much so, I missed the tour when it was given a few days ago. Yes, it would be suitable to run our European operation from here. Do you have any news concerning Masood? I know he was like a brother to you."

"Ali Shah Masood is dead if he was in the cell block at Bagran Air Base. If that is true, the pressure to proceed without being ready is relieved. However, a brother at the base tells of a hooded prisoner leaving only hours before the explosion. Our lawyers at the American Guantanamo prison say no new prisoners have arrived in weeks.

"I have more news. Our friends in Kandahar report that Afghanistan police have found the filthy informant. She was caught fornicating with an American FBI agent. This pig is unfortunately the third sister of Ali Shah Masood. The police promise to send her quickly to hell."

"Is it necessary to proceed so rapidly if Ali is dead?" Mumtaz asked.

"We are going to proceed with our plans even though we aren't fully prepared.

Our Chinese friends are anxious to see us start this battle. They have already delivered their part of the agreement. In return, we have supplied China with names and locations of the al Qaeda and the East Turkestan Islamic soldiers in the Xinjiang province. It is in our best interest to rid the Islamic world of these renegade extremists. They are causing the Chinese no end of problems and getting in the way of our relationship with our Chinese friends. We agreed to help them in return for arms to be provided to Hamas."

"What about al Qaeda, are they ready to proceed?"

"al Qaeda has been fed information with which they may continue their warnings. bin Laden's replacement al Zawahri will make an excellent unwitting – anxious to take the offensive, and we're pleased to put them in the crosshairs. al Qaeda is fighting a medieval war and they'll die doing so. That's why we had to take bin Laden out."

"You did that?"

"We did, a representative was sent to bin Laden. He was offered center stage and declined. He was going to be a problem –an impediment – so we passed on the location of bin Laden to the CIA and they took care of our problem."

Omar stopped by the wooden corral which held the white Arabian horses – six mares and a stallion that had only this week been delivered from his home in Libya. The Arabian breed of horse also would be returned to the prominence they once enjoyed in the equine world.

"And your project, Abolhasen, how goes it?"

"We're ready to begin real time tests of our remote control program."

Abolhasen Mumtaz was a handsome man with noble Arab features. He wore a Jasper Littman tailored suit befitting of his engineering degrees from the University of Bath and Queen Mary University of London. Although he was fluent in English, Russian and French, today, he spoke Arabic.

"Since 1995, we've purchased controlling shares in leading corporations producing electronic products. Using our majority influence, we've acquired and created smaller corporations and with our Chinese partners, placed our own personnel in these small and low profile companies. These engineers and computer scientists have been dedicated to designing equipment to remotely control vehicles including those used by the military."

Omar smiled broadly. "Ali never shared the details of your project with me. I am so very impressed – but can you really do this? I mean can you really take command of a tank, for example?"

"The American Army has several programs to remotely control their weapons systems and armored vehicles. Their Crows-Lightning Program remotely controls heavy machine guns and is already in place in Iraq. The American Army Depot in Tooele, Utah has developed unmanned vehicles which are directed by onboard computers. It is those computers which make them vulnerable and at which we have aimed our attack. The Army Vehicle Intelligence Program, or AVIP…"

"They call it what?"

"AVIP."

"Those Americans, always with the acronyms…"

"AVIP is a joint operation with eight research universities. We have two students deeply involved, in particular with the Autonomous Driving Program. Our Chinese partners have also been able to design hidden programs embedded in computers which may be used for our own purposes at a later date."

"I am so impressed. Let me share with you that with Ali gone, I will assume the informal leadership. I will need someone close to me as I was close to Ali. I would like for you to be that man."

Mumtaz watched the mares lope pass the stallion in the adjacent corral. Oddly, the big horse seemed to ignore their teasing as if knowing with patience he would have a turn with each. Mumtaz looked Omar squarely in the eye and allowed himself a slight grin. "I would be honored." He knew it would soon be his turn to have his way.

They turned from the corral and strolled up the steep, rocky path towards the fortress. The sun glimmered on the pathway as it made its way through the forest's canopy. The men walked in silence for awhile, each considering the future and the ramifications of their new agreement.

Omar spoke first and softly. "As you are aware, the American elections are near and we've joined in the process, first to defeat the incumbent party and second to gain access to the other party. 'Money talks' as the Americans are so fond of saying and we will use our money to buy the politicians in the same fashion as their countrymen do."

"The Jews have been doing that for decades..."

The men reached the summit and entered the fortress with a renewed hope. They were both certain that change, real change, was within their reach.

Tuesday, October 9th

Interstate 35
St. Paul, Minnesota

DOC LOOKED FORWARD TO ENDING his workday. It had been a frustrating and disappointing day following leads sent to the Anti-Terrorist Unit. He had driven north of the Twin Cities to Forest Lake for an interview with a citizen who had called the FBI with concerns about al Qaeda terrorists poisoning the lake. He spent an hour interviewing the elderly couple who were convinced that the Hmong fishermen were scouting the lake with a mind to poisoning it on behalf of the al Qaeda terrorists. 'Why else would they spend hours out on the lake catching carp and bullheads?' Doc would have finished in less than an hour, however, it took forty-five minutes to convince the old fellow that Hmongs weren't Arabs. They weren't Muslims and that they were in our country because they'd fought on our side in the Vietnam War.

It was a waste of time and now he was locked in rush hour traffic delaying his return home to his Grand Avenue apartment. His cell phone rang as he came to a stop. It was the assistant superintendent, an ominous sign as he never called with good news. They exchanged banalities then Doc had to ask, "What's the problem, boss?"

"This is off the record. I'm calling to warn you that Sharon Risling has filed a human rights complaint against you. I just learned about it this afternoon. The guys downtown want me to suspend your ass."

"What's this chicken shit complaint all about?" Doc shouted.

"The human rights investigators won't tell me officially because of privacy act considerations, however, it sounds like you said something to her that she is claiming is harassment because she is a female. She said she has witnesses and is gunning for your head. You know how she is."

"What is she claiming I did?"

"They won't tell me because they are going to conduct an investigation. They are pushing to suspend you until after the investigation so you don't influence any of the potential witnesses."

"I'll tell you what I did. I asked her to look up some intelligence data on a terrorist we have been investigating. It's her job and I needed the data right away. She was playing Solitaire on her computer and she told me I would have to wait because she was winning. I pushed her delete key and told her to get off her lazy fat ass and get me my damn information. That's what this is all about. She should have been fired years ago. She is robbing the people of Minnesota every day she gets paid. I think I should arrest her miserable ass for theft of public funds. Someday America is going to explode because some Sharon Risling is playing Solitaire."

"Calm down. I need you to just stay out of sight until this blows over...."

"I gotta go." Doc ended the cell call and pulled over to the shoulder. He rolled to a stop some distance behind the older Cadillac and walked towards the car along the brown grass – towards a man who had his right hand around the neck of a tiny blonde woman. Her see-through red blouse had been torn away from her shoulder. Fear dominated her face. She looked like a crack addict whose mind was in a galaxy faraway. "Stubs, you asshole, I didn't..." A backhand across her bleeding face stopped whatever denial she was about to utter.

"Hey dude, you need any help with that bitch?" Doc asked.

"Hey asshole, do I look like I need your help?"

"Yeah, you look like a pussy to me. I'm thinking the little crack whore could probably kick your ass. I thought you might need some help."

The man, whose arms were filled with tattoos, shoved the woman to the grass and turned to face Doc. He rubbed his black goatee as if thinking about how to handle this interloper. The mental process produced a pained look on his face. "I'm thinking you better get back in your car before I get my hands on you." He pulled his filthy jeans up under his hanging bare stomach and started towards Doc. The woman crawled back to her feet and dove into the rusty black Cadillac.

"I don't think a fat pussy like you could even catch me and if you did, I think you would regret it," Doc said. He backed towards his SUV drawing the man away from the escaping woman.

The man closed the distance lumbering to near striking range when Doc drew his pistol in his right hand and flashed his badge in his left hand. The fat man stopped and looked puzzled at this unexpected turn of events. At the sound of squealing tires he twisted his torso to see the woman drive away in the Cadillac. He turned back to Doc. "Watch your back, you son-of-a-bitch. You're a walking dead man." His breath reeking of whiskey preceded his foul words.

"Ah, you've met my mother. Now you get into the ditch and on all fours while I think about what to do with you."

I suppose I could arrest his ass, but I know she'll be back in his arms before I clear the jail. Oh, what the hell….

The man grudgingly moved onto the grass amongst the broken beer bottles and white fast food bags. As his knees touched the ground, he cast a menacing stare towards the agent. Before he could mount an attack, Doc drove off, his tires spinning gravel and dirt back into the ditch. Doc lit a smoke and laughed at the dark world he inhabited. Perhaps he could introduce his new friend, Stubs, to Sharon Risling and given their black hearts, they'd kill each other. Problems Solved.

Tuesday, October 9th

Lakeville, Minnesota

AS DOC NEARED HOME, ALBERTO Hernandez was still working. His crew had gone off to visit some prostitutes while he waited not so patiently at the McDonald's in Lakeville. Hector was late and Alberto was getting nervous. What if they were on to them? Maybe that cigarette store owner had been caught and turned them in. Their Minnesota connection, the cigarette man, had fled ahead of an arrest warrant. The group had struggled to mend the holes the cigarette man had left. Alberto couldn't wait for the next few days to pass so he could get out of this cold city. No one had told them to bring warm clothes so they had shopped at the Goodwill store as soon as they arrived. His heavy nylon parka smelled of stale smoke and fresh mothballs.

An hour late, Hector pulled the red Mercury Cougar into the parking lot. He drove through the lot twice before Alberto reached him on a cell phone and directed him to his location. Hector jumped into the passenger seat of Alberto's Buick. "Where have you been you dumb ass?"

"I waited for you at the wrong McDonald's. Then they got robbed and there were cops everywhere so I took off. I called Memo and he told me the right spot to meet you."

"You smell like cow shit, man. Look at your boots, you've dragged that crap on my floor," Alberto complained and rolled his window down. A cold mist blew through the car mixing an odorous cocktail of cow manure, cigarette smoke, and mothballs.

"This is what I have for you," Alberto said. He carefully handed Hector a McDonald's bag. "You know what to do with this?"

"I've been told and it will be no problem to do this. I was told that you would give me money and instructions."

"In the bag is also five thousand dollars. After you finish you're to return to Mexico to rejoin your wife and son. You know that you won't get them back if you take this money and don't follow your orders. Nothing personal man, but these dudes mean business."

"Believe me, I know this well and it'll be easy for me to finish."

"Be careful when you do this. You know of the dangers?" Alberto lit his second cigarette and finished his tepid coffee.

"I do. I must get back to Rochester now. I have to get back to work." Hector was out the door before Alberto could finish telling him again to be careful.

Alberto walked into the McDonald's restroom to get rid of all the coffee he had guzzled while he was waiting. He ordered two more cheeseburgers with fries. The wind blew him off balance as he walked back to his Buick. He pulled his parka hood up and cursed the cold wind. Only a few more days and he could leave.

Tuesday, October, 9th

Finnegan's Bar
St. Paul, Minnesota

DOC PERCHED ON A HIGH metal stool at the long mahogany bar and nursed a glass of Glenlivet scotch whiskey, yearned for a smoke, and watched the Channel 7 News at ten o'clock. "We have yet another video release tonight from al Qaeda." Ayman al Zawahri's craggy face appeared on the screen. He wore his usual white head wrap and glasses that made him look every bit the physician he was. al Zawahri's promotion to the most wanted al Qaeda terrorist came with the death of bin Laden. A hero or terrorist depending on one's political bent. England's King George fancied George Washington as the greatest terrorist of his time.

A dark-haired reporter spoke over al Zawahri and offered his interpretative summary. "al Zawahri has issued what he calls a final ultimatum to the United States. The U.S., he demands, must leave Iraq and Afghanistan and abandon all support of Israel or face plagues not seen since the time of Moses and the pharaoh. Now we've been told that this tape is days old. We have been covering this story all day and it would seem as though the plagues have been unleashed. For days now, the Potomac River has experienced outrageously high numbers of a mutant form of red algae. It truly does look as though it has been turned to blood. Fish are dying and that has attracted flying insects and the stench, well, it's just overwhelming."

An airborne camera panned across the Potomac and it did indeed look as though the river had turned to blood, just as Moses had done to the Nile River to force the Egyptian Pharaoh to free the Jews from slavery.

The picture returned to the national media reporter dressed in blue rain gear and standing on a paved roadway at the Arlington National Cemetery. Rain poured down around him, dotting the camera lens. "As you can see here, I am surrounded by thousands of hopping frogs and more insects, flies and gnats than a Georgia swamp. The cemetery has been closed to the public today as workers try to herd the frogs into a large corral which you can see behind me. So far, an unnamed source told me the frog herding has failed, although they're at a loss as to how to resolve the matter without killing the frogs with poison. Animal rights protesters are outside the gates demanding a humane end to this mess. They don't want the frogs killed.

"Authorities are searching for two missing employees and are interested in interviewing them. Right now they are not suspects, although authorities have launched a nationwide search."

Photographs from their employee identification badges appeared on the screen next to the reporter who identified them as Oscar de la Vega and John Smith.

"The appearance of these frogs on our nation's most honored memorial is being blamed on al Qaeda. al Zawahri has warned of the attacks citing the biblical plagues put upon the land of Egypt. In that account, frogs, flies and gnats were the second and third of ten plagues..."

The reporter continued speaking. Doc turned away and finished his drink. "Another," he announced to the bartender. He punched his FBI partner, Pat Campbell, on the shoulder and asked, "What color alert you figure this puts us in, crimson, hot pink, blaze orange?"

Pat didn't bother to answer. He seldom bit on the wry comments that fell occasionally from Doc's mouth. The agents often came together at the end of the workday to enjoy a brew or a bump and a brew, let some steam off, tell some stories, tell some lies and enjoy the company of other officers and agents.

Doc's name, though seldom used, is Franklin Delano Martini. His father was a first generation Italian who worked in the iron mines of Minnesota's Mesabi Iron Range. Doc was named after the president who the old miner considered to be the working man's greatest friend.

Five years ago, Doc became a special agent with the Minnesota Bureau of Criminal Apprehension and was assigned to the FBI Joint Anti-Terrorist Task Force. Doc was a hard looking cop. Since being out of his Minneapolis Police uniform, he shaved only occasionally, somehow maintaining a permanent three day growth on his face.

Doc suspected Pat had orders to keep an eye on him. Doc's 30 year career had many successes, although he often took the road less traveled and that proved to be a very bumpy ride, indeed. His style didn't fit well within the narrow fog lines laid out by the FBI's policy and procedure handbook.

Pat was one of the athletes hired by the FBI, not that it was part of the official qualifications. Tall with blond hair and boyish good looks, he cut an impressive image in his FBI blue windbreaker. More than once, his SAIC had detailed him to escort a high profile prisoner past photographers. Pat had no law enforcement experience when they hired him. He was a tennis pro with an accounting degree from Syracuse. Yet he was bright and knew enough to learn all that Doc had to offer. For Doc, Pat was the son he never had. It was a good and productive relationship.

Wednesday, October 10th

Bansko, Bulgaria

CIA OFFICERS HAD LEARNED THAT with the right amount of cash, preferably dollars, in the proper hands they were welcomed worldwide. It helped to have needy and greedy secret police executives and government controlled media. Bulgaria was just such a place and that is how Ali Shah Masood came to be in a mountaintop castle near the village of Bansko. The medieval stone castle was the former retreat of a ranking member of the communist party, hence its audacious interior decorating, primarily in red. Most recently the former secret police executives used it as a party house for their mistresses. The liquor cabinet was well-stocked with local wines, Kralska Vodka and Kehlibar Brandy. The sheets were seldom changed and dust bunnies and cobwebs hung like artwork in every corner.

Tucked away in the lower level of the fortress were CIA Officers Ed Mitchell and Joseph Young. These young men were uniquely trained in Interrogation Arts. Oddly, they even thought of themselves as artists. They took their tasks seriously and were in no way sadistic in their endeavors. They'd long ago convinced themselves they were doing this nasty job to defend their country. They knew that doing this correctly would take time and had settled in with that notion in mind until yesterday when they received a message from CIA Headquarters in Langley.

Casimir had called Mitchell from the tiny bare room where he had been speaking with Ali Shah Masood, who spoke excellent English.

"How's it going?" Casimir asked.

"He was telling me of a diabolical plan to destroy America. You interrupted us and that might be the last word out of him..." Mitchell answered.

"Nothing huh, better send the A team in while you warm the bench, Junior."

"Rocky, what do you need?" Mitchell asked impatiently.

"We just got an urgent message from Langley authorizing us to turn up the steam."

"Any limits?"

"Yeah, keep him breathing and regular bowel movements."

For the next 24 hours, they turned up the heat. Mitchell had given Ali an opportunity to avoid the change in tactics going so far as explaining how much pain he could expect. Ali's reply was to spit towards Mitchell and kick at Young. Mitchell kicked the wooden chair from under Ali who landed on his back. It sounded like a ripe watermelon crashing on the ground when Ali's head hit the cold stone floor. That wasted an hour while the men waited for him to regain consciousness and for his vitals to settle to where he could bear the strain they intended to inflict. Mitchell regretted his loss of self-control.

Young blindfolded the bound Ali and roughly pushed him across the room through a doorway into an adjacent room and onto a rough pine board. The board was inclined and Ali's feet were shackled to the top of the board while his head lay somewhat below his legs and feet. It was cool if not cold in the room and Ali's naked body was shaking.

Mitchell took a roll of cellophane and wrapped it tightly over Ali's face and back behind the two inch board. Young sprinkled cold water on the bare skin, causing an even more rapid decline in body temperature. Ali struggled to free himself from the heavy leather straps across his chest.

Young slowly poured a measured amount of water unto the cellophane which covered Ali's head. His gag reflex led him to an unavoidable feeling of drowning. Again and again the process was repeated broken only by fresh requests for his cooperation. Always it was asking for the cooperation and punishing the negative response. Finally, Ali passed out from his excessive struggles and his perceived inability to breathe.

Then another message arrived from Headquarters, "POTUS, President of the United States, wants no extraordinary means used during your interrogations."

"Probably doesn't matter as he either really knows little or we will kill him getting it," was Mitchell's only comment.

They decided to take a break for the rest of the day. Ali was in no shape to have civil discourse for awhile. They left the prisoner on the filthy stone floor of his makeshift cell. The cell had no light and was cold and damp. Ali's teeth chattered and he shivered uncontrollably. Tiny Tim's *Tiptoe Through the Tulips* played through the unseen speakers over and over and over again. Ali wondered how much they paid this madman to 'sing' such a song.

Young and Mitchell both wore blue coveralls over their jeans and white shirts. They walked on the two-inch unfinished boards that served as steps and out of the dim hallway into the blinding sunlight. They squinted as their eyes adjusted. They lit French cigarettes, Gauloises, sharing a pack and a lighter as they strolled along the mountain paths near the castle. Tall conifers shaded the cobblestone pathway. Young rubbed his neck trying to free muscles from the grip of stress. Remnants of manicured flower gardens and rose bushes provided a border to the path and a hint of the beauty of the estate before the Nazi and Russian invaders pushed the wealthy Jews from their home. They discussed other possible techniques as though they were two medical researchers searching for a cure of some fatal disease. By the time they'd reached the rushing waters of the stream below the estate, they'd concluded that the most likely outcome was no information and a dead Ali.

Wednesday, October 10th

Grand Avenue
St. Paul, Minnesota

DOC WOKE WITH HAPPY THOUGHTS as he felt the warm tongue on his ear. His dog, Gumpy, stood on the pillow licking where Doc's ear used to be before the Viet Cong tossed a grenade which trimmed off the bottom half. That wasn't the only scar the grenade had left on his face, just the most noticeable. The pug licked as though he could heal it if only he tried hard enough. Doc playfully pushed him away. The heavy hard cover book, he'd fallen asleep reading, fell to the floor with a bang.

It was going to be a good day he thought as the night's last moonlight shone through his half-opened shade. It was cool in the room as he'd slept with the window partly opened. He had pretty much worked past the visit to his mother, although on Sunday night his dead father visited his sleep with a red hot poker and chased him much of the night scolding him for putting his wife in 'the home.'

Doc and the pug finished off the bran muffins and Doc drank black coffee, strong Kona brew, freshly roasted and ground. As he read the newspaper, he looked forward to beginning his day until he remembered that he had to attend a mandatory staff meeting for the FBI's Anti-Terrorist Unit. His attitude took a turn for the worse. He hated meetings and didn't like to start his work day until about mid-morning. Most criminals he knew slept in. He was frustrated with the inability to penetrate the terrorist organizations that everyone in the Intelligence community knew existed. Never in his career had he met with such failure.

Doc dressed in his usual uniform, a starched white shirt, today with thin blue stripes, pressed lean blue jeans, and brown loafers. About the only item that varied from day-to-day was his belt. Sometimes he wore a black belt and switched to black loafers. About every fourth day he shaved or at least trimmed his graying whiskers. Doc dressed Gump in his ranch coat and took him out for his morning constitution – a process that had to be hurried today if Doc was going to make the 7:30 meeting.

Traffic came to a standstill as he tried getting onto the bridge over the Mississippi River. Doc was about to try a different route when his cell phone rang. It was his mother and she was crying. "You need to get me out of here," she bawled.

"Calm down Ma, what happened?"

"I hate this place. I want you to come and get me out of here."

"Ma, I can't do that. Where would you go?"

"Take me back to my house in Ely."

"We sold your house last year."

"You never told me that. Why did you sell my house?"

"Ma, you signed the papers. I don't know where you could go."

"You shouldn't have sold my house. Now where am I going to go?"

"Ma, you're going to have to stay at the home."

As the traffic cleared on the bridge, Doc accelerated the Durango into the right lane. He took the cell phone from his ear momentarily. When he brought it back to his ear his mother had hung up. A twenty-something man driving a low riding green Toyota, cut in front of him and to add insult flipped him off as he sped away weaving in traffic.

At 7:15, Doc pulled the SUV into the parking lot in the Minneapolis warehouse district where the old brick factories and warehouses had been remodeled into chic office space along the Mississippi River. His mood had turned downright surly by the time he reached the Anti-Terrorist Unit office. He'd been listening to the media reports concerning terrorist threats and felt guilty that while he was on the task force, the best he could do today was attend a meeting.

When Doc strolled into the office, he was greeted by the Assistant Special Agent in Charge (ASAIC) who proudly displayed a selection of sprinkled covered donuts purchased at a nearby convenience store. It irked Doc that the ASAIC felt the need to put out donuts like bait for hungry rodents. He nodded at the ASAIC as he hurried past the pastries and took a seat as far to the rear as he could get and still say he attended the meeting.

At exactly 7:30 the ASAIC welcomed the dozen agents and officers, reminded them to eat the donuts which he paid for out of his own pocket, and introduced his guest presenters. First would be the district's legal officer, an attorney who needed to remind the unit members to observe all the rights afforded to America's criminals. Especially, they were to be sure to notify the arrested foreign citizens that they could contact their consulate. He reminded the agents of court rulings and international treaties that provided a bundle of protections and rights to the uninvited guests.

Next, the diversity officer reminded them during over an hour presentation to be civil in a non-sexual manner to all they encounter. A nervous young clerk was next, stumbling through new report writing procedures. The ASAIC told all of his guests to take some donuts during the break. Doc sat in the back with his feet on the chair ahead of him, working behind a leather portfolio on a series of Sudoku puzzles. The ASAIC smiled at Doc's apparent enthusiasm for the topics, actually taking notes.

By 11:00, Doc put down his puzzle as the agenda seemed to be changing to real police matters, catching terrorists. After ten minutes, he was back at his puzzles. The terrorist discussion centered on an investigation of an animal rights organization intending to free research animals at the University. Doc figured they could take care of this security matter without him.

They afforded the last ten minutes to the plague. It was too early to up the threat level. All agents were put on standby in case the Homeland Security Advisory System color-coded terrorism threat advisory scale was elevated to RED and an emergency command post was initiated. If that national crisis was declared, all leave would be cancelled and every agent was to report for assignment. The ASAIC's final words, "So far it's just algae, bugs, and frogs and just in Washington. Keep your ears to the ground, boys."

They mercifully ended exactly at noon with a reminder to respect the sanctity of the holy places and passed a signup sheet for volunteer speakers to attend meetings at local mosques. Doc finished his puzzle, got the signup sheet, printed his partner's name, and quickly made his way out into the sunshine.

Wednesday, October 10th

Chattanooga, Tennessee

THE VENERABLE SENATOR JASON A. Ryan had worked relentlessly to get military contracts to his home state of Tennessee. As a powerful member of the U.S. Senate Committee on Armed Services, he had pushed through the contract bidding process, his staff actually writing many of the specifications for the military advanced drone program. Senator Ryan knew how to bring home the bacon. He was so proud of the reputation, that he prominently displayed a gold-plated statue of a hog at the forefront of his desk.

Not far from the senator's office in Chattanooga, Frampton Navigation Systems, FNS, had a small nondescript office located in a nearly abandoned strip mall in Chattanooga until they were awarded a contract for the Army's AVIP program. Internationally, FNS was a leader in this technology and had it already working in farm tractors. Their facilities were largely in the Midwest. That changed when they received the contract and before long they had leased over 310,000 square feet of commercial space and relocated dozens of researchers, technicians and the ambitious management teams to Chattanooga. The price in political contributions they paid the senator was paltry compared to the millions, no billions, of revenues generated. He cost little more than a couple of pretty but overpaid executive secretaries.

FNS stock was largely owned by Advanced Dynamics, a U.S. corporation traded openly on the U.S. stock market. It also had subsidiaries in Panama, Grand Caymans, Switzerland, and Dubai. Through a variety of accounting schemes and damn good lawyers they were able to shift millions of profits to these tax haven nations even though the U.S. Government contracts were a large share of their revenues. The government regulators' lack of zeal made it far easier to put cash in the politicians' pockets and profits untaxed and offshore.

A substantial share of Advanced Dynamics, about 62%, was owned by investors outside America. Not that anyone would have known as the 62% was split up into 6 different separate and distinct foreign investment trusts which in turn were owned 100% by other foreign trusts, the trustees of which were all Swiss lawyers and bankers and paid handsomely through lawyers from Oslo and Copenhagen.

None of this mattered to Howard Chung who had emigrated from China to Hong Kong and later to Canada. FNS eventually transferred him to the United States. With the help of the senator's staff he was able to gain U.S. citizenship – citing his unique skills in the field of GPS Navigational Systems. He had led the project to develop the operating system that allowed computers to control the movements of farm machinery.

This day, Chung just transferred back to Vancouver, Canada, on special assignment. He was happy to go where he could eat his native foods and speak his native tongue. He looked forward to returning to Canada's relaxed attitude towards marijuana. A daily user, he didn't like looking over his shoulder for the Chattanooga Police.

Although Chung didn't know what organization was behind his research, he'd been sent to do their bidding by his Chinese handlers. He knew better than to ask or raise some philosophical or moral questions. As the various bits and pieces of this special program flowed through FNS, the final product, the dark side of the project, came to Chung. He would be the puppet master when the time came to bring the project to completion. He would be the operator who would grab control of the American military hardware. It would be his honor to change the balance of world power. With America out of the way, his homeland would have a clear playing field. That's what motivated Chung to work 18 hour days, seven days a week – and, of course, the bonus, enough to last a lifetime.

Wednesday, October 10th

Refugio, Texas

ROGER WILCOX PULLED BACK ON the controls and the wheels of the gleaming white Cirrus SR22 Turbo and lifted off the grass runway into the bright blue sky. At about 500 feet he banked slightly to the left and looked over his 18,600 acres. It brought great joy to survey his farm from the air. A smile crossed his face as he continued the slow banking ascent.

Below, Wilcox saw that the John Deere 9030 tractor was plowing a cotton stubble field. At 1000 feet he leveled off and had completed a full circle.

"What the hell," he muttered as he watched the John Deere veer off its assumed straight course and first traveled severely to the left then to the right and then make a full circle and then another.

"Either that damn GPS guidance system is acting up or someone is getting a severe ass kicking when I get back." He set his course for Austin. He had a meeting at the University of Texas with the Longhorn Club and the Athletic Director. They were meeting about that damn football coach. Not about his win loss record, that was beyond question. No, Wilcox was beside himself because the coach had benched Wilcox's young cousin, the aspiring quarterback. It was time for a new coach and maybe even the AD needed to go, too. After spending the last days sleeping on the couch, Wilcox was in an exceptionally foul mood.

Below in the green tractor, one of the new men, Gordo, held a coffee cup in his left hand and a Nextel cell phone in his right. As the tractor turned and circled without his touching the steering wheel, he reported on the Nextel. On the other end of the Nextel direct connect conversation was Howard Chung, who was making the tractor do his bidding using a simple joystick connected to his computer using a not so simple program and a satellite uplink. At times, because Chung spoke English with a heavy Chinese accent and Gordo with a Spanish twist the two shouted at each other trying to be understood. In fact, the inability to understand each other was the only shortcoming of an otherwise highly successful experiment.

Chung sat in a small FNS lab in a nondescript concrete block building along Vancouver's pine-lined coast. He was pleased with the success and his supervisor would be also. Like a child with a new toy, Chung spun Gordo and the tractor round and round, pushing the machine and his control to the limits.

When he was done with his test, the chubby pale Chung turned his system off, excitedly rubbed his hands together and hit the favorites list on his Internet Explorer. He rewarded himself with an hour in his favorite porn sites. He fired up a joint of fine British Columbian hydroponic cannabis. He deserved the break. He kicked back and dreamed of his next conquest of the American military fighting vehicles.

Wednesday, October 10th

The Empire Club
Washington, D.C.

THE CLUB WAS FILLED WITH senators, representatives, their staffers, and lobbyists all plying their trade. Power, influence being bought and sold, all wrapped in civil discourse and a thin pretense of honor and integrity. One could feel the intensity of the game as though strolling into a cheap Bangkok whorehouse, looking for bargains.

Filled with leather and fine old wood, the smell of exquisite dishes prepared by highly-paid and well-regarded chefs drifted through the air. Grants, buildings, bridges, jobs, trips and contracts were all for sale for the price of a political contribution.

Darrin Watkins excelled at this trade. A Harvard educated blue blood attorney, he was born and raised to be in this world. Picture what such a man would look like playing that role in the movies and you have Darrin Watkins to a tee. Beneath his refined manners, he was a savvy street hustler who never let ethics or morals distract him. Those academic concepts, along with his Armani overcoat were to be checked at the door.

Mr. Watkins sat at 'his' table, linen covered and decorated with silver, china and crystal. His round table, in the William Howard Taft Dining Room, was next to a rear wall and his chair always faced the door. Above his chair was an original oil painting of George Washington with his troops in a snow covered camp. Senator Ryan from Tennessee stopped by to exchange pleasantries and information. He expressed his gratitude again for the large contribution Watkins had arranged on behalf of Frampton Navigations Systems (FNS).

Darrin stood as Tommy Jenkins approached his table. Tommy, as everyone called him, was a handsome, well-groomed man who wore his satin black hair in a ponytail. Tasteful rings and a diamond stud in his ear. He dressed in a tailored black suit but no tie. Ties were too common. Tommy was an up and comer in the party with a knack for attracting big money. He was wealthy by way of an inheritance of a fortune in the cosmetics industry made by his grandfather. Power not riches was what mattered. Once there was a dream of running for office, however, his promiscuous lifestyle kept that off the table. Didn't matter, he had the power now in his real talent, hustling political contributions. When political wags spoke of 'Tommy,' everyone knew it was Tommy Jenkins.

"Tommy, my friend, so good to see you again," the lawyer offered his hand and at the same time motioned for his friend to be seated.

"Darrin, how's the family? Well, I hope. What did you bring me? I hope you brought some real money this time – the candidates are spending like lottery winners. What do you have for me?"

"Tommy, I know your people will be pleased. I've some clients who have deep pockets and more importantly some wealthy friends. Here is a list of six locations, Palm Springs, Vail, Hollywood, Miami, New York City, and San Francisco, where we will host fundraisers for your party. I think I can guarantee you $50 million without exaggerating."

The hustler responded with a soft whistle, "What are you expecting for this?"

"I want nothing more than a candidate who will stop the crazy wars in Iraq and Afghanistan and maybe a couple of other little favors, nothing big."

They ordered another round of martinis, a Commedia Dellarte and a Foxy Squirrel.

Tommy actually felt sexually aroused at the thought of bringing in $50 million or maybe it was that and Darrin was damn good looking for a straight guy.

Over lunch they discussed the details of the fundraisers which would take place in a week. As they concluded, Tommy rose and shook Darrin's hand holding it too long and making too much eye contact.

As the attorney walked away from The Empire Club he dialed his office to speak with the executive manager. He excitedly told of the meeting. The manager was pleased and told Darrin what a fine job he had done. Darrin was employed by the law firm of Rosencrantz and Feldman in Washington, D.C. They represented clients from all over the world. The client offering to sponsor these six major fundraisers was Gemstar Technology from Boston. The majority owner of Gemstar was Holdingford LTD., a Bermuda corporation. The officers of Holdingford were headquartered in Zurich.

That evening, Darrin was back at his table, this time meeting with the other party's 'Tommy,' Pat Baldwin. If Tommy was the flashy man about town, Baldwin hardly warranted a second look, stocky and bald with a gray pinstripe suit and black oxfords. Baldwin drank decaffeinated coffee and wiped his sweaty brow often with the linen napkin.

Darrin made the same offer to Baldwin except for the locations of San Antonio, Coeur d'Alene and Minneapolis. Also, the amount was reduced by $20 million and the demand for war's end disappeared.

Darrin did add one request. "The Harvey family who lives on Lake Minnetonka, Minnesota, has close friends in the grain and food industry. They are very loyal and can be counted on for a large contribution. One of the agribusiness contributors is awarding FFA scholarships. They would be very pleased if the president's son could present the awards at an event right before the fundraiser. There will be a number of big players in agribusiness there for the awards. It is a great combination event if you can put it together. These are good people to have on our side. Agribusiness is in a boom period and there's a lot of cash looking to advance the farm bill. Apparently the Harvey daughters have a crush on the president's son and they have lobbied the parents to have him visit."

Wednesday, October 10th

The Rising Road Farm
Rochester, Minnesota

THE SUN WAS SETTING INTO black thunder clouds forming on the horizon as Hector walked into the gray metal milking barn. He wore torn and tattered blue coveralls bearing the name tag 'Hector' and walked in twelve-inch rubber boots that were three sizes too large. He carried the same McDonald's sack he had received from Alberto the day before. The other workers would assume that Hector was bringing his dinner to work. Hector was a hired hand at Swanson's Rising Road Farm where they milked hundreds of purebred Holsteins around the clock in an automated plant. Human hands never even touched the cows' teats. Hector had worked for Swanson's about six months.

Back in April, an American with a pocket full of pesos had recruited him from a similar farm in Sinaloa, Mexico. The recruiter told him that if he would travel to Minnesota and take a job with a milk plant, he would be handsomely rewarded. He knew that the job would be temporary and that he would be asked to do other things. That was apparent from the recruiter's offer. He assumed it would have to do with smuggling drugs. He didn't wrestle with the moral issues. Since NAFTA, his small family farm had been destroyed when the American Grain Industry flooded his nation with cheap corn. He stopped being concerned with laws and thought only about feeding his family. It was worth a dash across the desert past the rattlesnakes, scorpions, jumping chollo cactus and armed border agents.

A week ago, the American, a crude man with a foul mouth and whiskey breath, approached him in a local bar. He told Hector that the time had come for him to carry out his promise. Hector was given a cell phone and told to expect a call with further instructions. The American also produced a photo of Hector's wife and son. They looked distressed to the point of tears. He said that they were safe but being held to insure that Hector followed his orders. The American left the bar while Hector sat staring at the photo through tear-filled eyes. It wasn't but a few days when he received a call from Alberto to meet him at the McDonald's.

Hector moved swiftly through the barn and into the granary. Ordinarily his job was to mix the sophisticated grains and chemical additives for the cows. He worked twelve hours on and twelve off to keep the food flowing down the automated feeder shafts. Tonight he donned a mask and gloves and slowly removed the vials from the McDonald's bag. He carefully poured a small portion of the contents of each vial into the mixture of feed. As the conveyor belt carried the feed to the cattle, he spread out the contents over the next hour to insure the entire herd would ingest the Anthrax spores.

Cows are ruminators. The cows would eat the contaminated feed and then regurgitate the rumen to enjoy again. It would then pass through the digestive track, be absorbed into the blood stream and finally passed into the mammary system. By Sunday evening, the cows will be giving Anthrax contaminated milk. By Monday, the milk will be at the dairy and within a day on the grocery store shelves.

Within 7 days, the consumer's first symptoms will appear. Boils come first to indicate that the victim was ill. Shortly after, ulcers will form at the base of the tongue; vomiting and fever would precede abdominal pain and bloody vomit and diarrhea. Within 2 to 4 days, death would be the likely outcome.

The cows would also show similar symptoms as the disease spreads throughout the herd. Before the outbreak could be detected, workers along with movement of cows, calves, rats, mice, and birds would contaminate the surrounding area. Even the renowned Mayo Clinic only a few dozen miles away would not be able to mitigate the pain and suffering of its victims.

Hector had no idea what he had just added to the feed. He couldn't let himself care. Hector thought only of his family. Well that and the money which would afford him the small ranchero near his hometown. He followed his instructions and stripped off his clothes. He quickly dressed in the second set he had brought into the barn...put the McDonald's bag and his contaminated clothes into a large black plastic bag and left it in the dumpster as he departed. He stopped by the hygienic station and scrubbed one last time. Hector wasted no time getting to his Mercury Cougar and heading west on I-90. In his rearview mirror, the moon was rising as he sped into rain showers driving towards Mexico. He had just unleashed the fifth and sixth plagues. Within days livestock would begin to die and boils would appear on the skin of those who consumed the Anthrax-laced milk.

Wednesday, October 10th

Parkland Hospital
Dallas, Texas

JUAN VALENZUELA LAID IN THE hospital bed connected to tubes and monitors. His bed was surrounded by modern technology that was unknown to much of his homeland of Peru. He gazed alternately between the ceiling painted in soft beige and the various flashing, humming, and beeping instruments. A single barred window was overwhelmed with sunlight. The rays hit the instruments reflecting dancing light on the ceiling and walls. A single uniformed guard sat in a steel chair beside the windowless blue door. He was reading *Sports Illustrated*.

Spanish was Juan's native tongue, although he had survival English skills. He understood little of what the doctors, interns, nurses, aides and guards had to say about his medical condition. Even when they explained it in Spanish, he didn't understand the medical terms they used. What the hell was a 'nosocominal infection?'

While in the Peruvian military he had been trained by America's Special Forces units. He even had a seven week course at the U.S. Army School of Americas at Fort Benning, Georgia courtesy of the United States of America. Later, Valenzuela had been among the troopers who led a coup against President Perez. He was jailed briefly, although soon forgiven along with the other conspirators. That was all before he decided to become a mercenary and was sent to Iraq. They had recruited him from an elite unit of paratroopers. They paid him less than 20% of what they paid the American mercenaries, but still, it was a fortune for a Peruvian soldier.

Valenzuela and the others had been in Iraq for over 3 years when he was told they were to be deployed in a special mission. They would be paid an additional $20,000.00 each, although now employed by a new company Shantel, Ltd. an Irish corporation. Valenzuela didn't know it, nor would he care that Shantel, Ltd. was owned by Gemstar, through two other corporate entities that also inhabited and prospered in the shadows. The soldiers were moved from the Middle East operations to Libya where they were issued weapons and gear and flown via charter to Simon Belivar Airport, Maiquetia, Venezuela. At the airport, they were met by 3 military trucks, 6 x 6s, and quartered for a week at Base Aerea Generalissimo Francisco de Miranda, near Ala Carlota. During their stay they were given a mission briefing. Juan, one of the squad leaders, along with Alberto Hernandez and Carlos Rodriquez, was briefed in detail about the next phase of their mission. A week before crossing the U.S. Border, they all boarded a modern fishing vessel and motored through the Gulf waters to Tampico, Mexico.

They were met by three Ford F 250 crew cabs escorted by hard men whose day job was protecting narcotics shipments across Mexico. They moved to the U.S. border south of Roma, Texas, where the coyotes met them and they waited along with the others, mostly Mexican citizens, young men and women. They were split into two groups each lead by a pair of coyotes, Mexican guides, and each entering the United States over a couple of hundred mile stretch of the border.

All had gone well with his group's crossing. They had crossed the shallow Rio Grande River just before daybreak. Wading in waist deep muddy water, they held duffels high overhead looking like a line of African porters on safari in bygone days. The heavier loads were floated in waterproof bags. They gathered on the sandy American shore to account for each member then quickly disappeared into the maze of cactus, sage, and mesquite bramble. After hiking about 40 minutes, Alberto Hernandez called the march to a halt. Several of the waterproof bags had taken on water as they were floated across the river. The river water was now slowly draining down the backs of the soldiers. Alberto Hernandez feared the water would damage the equipment.

Hernandez ordered four of the larger men to stay with him to dry off the gear and repack it in dryer bags. He told the coyotes to continue as the women were slowing the group down anyway and he and his crew could easily catch up by following their tracks.

Juan continued with the coyotes just to keep them honest. His weapon remained stuffed in a military style duffel bag. When confronted by the Border Patrol, he simply dropped the bag to the ground. He was face down on the desert floor near a cactus when the firefight erupted. He rolled behind a mesquite tree impaling himself with a mess of cactus. The soldier jumped up to escape the thorns and ran away from the fight and about 75 yards into the brush he was hit in the lower abdomen by one of the last wildly fired rounds. He fell back in pain, hitting his head on a rock. Unconscious and bloody, he lay in a heap on the thorny and rocky desert sand until discovered by the border agents.

As Juan rested in bed thinking about how he had got there, he was angry at having been deserted by his partners. He was bitter about being shot and was in a lot of pain as his body fought the nosocominal infection which resulted from having been gut shot.

He wondered, if he lived, what they would do with him. He desperately wished to return to Peru, to his wife and children. He could see her at the clay oven behind their home cooking tortillas while the children played soccer in the yard. He could even smell the food and the wood fire burning and wondered if he could bargain with the U.S. authorities. Maybe they would make him a deal if he told them the plans.

Thursday, October 11th

Emirates Office Building
Dubai

MAURICE SMITH SAT IN HIS spacious office on the 50th floor, checking his figures for the third time. The high walls were paneled in mahogany. The office was intended to be occupied by an executive. Maurice was hardly that, more of an accounting toady. There was room for a couple of couches, a bar, and a conference table. Smith had none of that, just a little metal desk and a fake leather chair.

He was getting more frustrated as he went over the same accounting documents. Maurice worked for Blackstone as an accountant. A single man and a loner, he was well-suited for his assignment in Dubai. He actually enjoyed laboring over the numbers and the lack of interaction with other humans.

Maurice was a diminutive, even frail man. As a youth, he was often the victim of bullies' attacks. He stopped going to the playground and found comfort staying in his basement room pouring over math books and working number puzzles. He graduated from Montana State University, Bozeman with a 3.95 GPA. Maurice never fit in with the other students at Bozeman. Most of the Bozeman students had difficulty showing up for class when the snow was good on the mountains or the fish were biting in the trout streams. He told his mother that he wanted to attend a school in Connecticut. His mother reminded him that they couldn't afford out of state tuition. He couldn't wait to leave Montana where he was reminded daily of his physical frailties. He traveled east and landed an accounting job with Blackstone again surrounded by tough active men. Within a year he found himself in Dubai.

Maurice would not let himself make an error so he studied his figures a fifth time before he decided to notify his superior in the corporate headquarters in Washington, D.C.

E-mail was his preferred means of communicating. Maurice typed:

Mr. Olness:

I have found a discrepancy in our payroll numbers of men in the Iraq missions. There are 373 employees who are being paid but are not in Iraq. In fact, these 373 men are nowhere to be found on any of Blackstone's active missions. I fear that this may be a fraud on the part of the payroll clerks. Please advice. Details attached.

Regards,
Maurice Smith

Thursday, October 11th

al Kahwa Coffeehouse
Charikar, Afghanistan

HAVING JUST FLOWN INTO AFGHANISTAN from Bulgaria, Rocky was uncharacteristically early and had coffee waiting. Alex Stone settled into his usual chair with his back to the corner wall, M-16 resting across his knee. Alex added a kicker from a leather-covered flask and took a long pull before he said a word. A dust storm blew a thick brown haze into the dimly lit room. The fan wasn't turning as the electricity had been off for hours. A couple of kerosene lamps provided the only light. Alex noted that the brown and red chickens were not present. He took this as an ominous sign and moved his right hand to the pistol grip, his finger resting near the trigger. The proprietor may have gathered his chickens in anticipation of an attack. No sense losing one's chickens over some fight that didn't concern him. Alex remained nervous and vigilant as he knew CIA agents were even more of a prized target than civilian contractors.

Two local men huddled in the corner table opposite the Americans. They leaned towards one another as though they didn't want to be heard. It didn't matter, neither American spoke the local language much beyond 'get the fuck away.' Alex stared at them with the intent of making them nervous. He stroked the M-16's trigger and let the barrel slide towards their table. The two local men scurried out the open doorway into the bright sunshine.

Without looking at Rocky, Alex asked, "What's your story anyway? Everyone has a story."

Rocky didn't answer immediately. When he did, he simply asked, "Which one?"

Alex didn't know if that meant Rocky had a long background or just so many lies and cover stories that it didn't matter which one he told. He dropped the subject.

"The informant says that Ali's friends have put a hit out on him ..."

"On the informant?"

"No, on Ali."

"Little obvious from the bomb."

"Anyway, Ali is a main player in an attack that will make 911 look like noth'n. He says the plan is already in play because they are worried Ali will puke up on them. He can find out more, but he wanted money and protection first," Alex said.

"Does he have specifics on the plan?" Rocky asked.

"If he does, he isn't giving it away. I don't know much about him and I think he may be getting this all second or third hand from a relative who is high up and on the inside of the operation. Oh, yeah, he also wants you to make him a U.S. citizen."

"We need another citizen like him like I need another asshole."

"I'm just telling you what he wants – I'm not looking to sponsor him."

"Can I meet with him?"

"Look, I already told you he thinks that the CIA will mess with him and doesn't want to meet anyone until he has the money and passport in hand. Tell you what Rocky, I've got no interest in playing this spy game, ain't my thing especially if there's no money in it for me. How about I just show you this guy and you boys just grab the son-a-bitch and do what you will with him."

Rocky nodded in agreement.

"Man, pick him up, but do it far from the prayer service or you'll have a riot. Bring a couple of vans so you can grab him and I don't want to be involved. It's your deal."

"I got another problem. You know that little explosion they had over at the base?"

"What about it?"

"There weren't but a handful of us that knew Ali was being held there."

"Stop beat'n around the bush."

"Rooster, I've been able to vet everyone but your man, Rooster. What's up with him?"

Stone threw down another shot. He didn't like the feeling of having to defend his men. "Rooster's father was a minor State Department official assigned to Pakistan long enough to fall in love with and impregnate a local girl who cleaned the Embassy. After a payment of a small fortune they were married and lived for a decade in Islamabad. When Rooster graduated from the University of Paris, he landed a job with the State Department's Executive Protection Service. By the end of his career, he spoke 6 foreign languages. He and I have...."

"Yeah, but do you trust him?"

"Every day, with my life ..."

Alex stood, his M-16 in hand and walked away. "Back here tomorrow before prayer service." He noted that the chickens had returned and relaxed a little as he walked into the blinding sunlight.

Rocky's was a very dirty business. No one could be trusted and that cynicism took its toll. He pulled himself up and wandered off thinking about the wording of the telex he would send concerning Ali. He assumed that the snitch was referring to the plague bullshit, although a few frogs and some algae wasn't going to beat the attacks of 911. He needed to pass on the information, however, the wording had to be such that if it was true about a plan of destruction, he would have given proper notice. On the other hand, he did not want to raise the alarm on bad fourth hand information, something he would be blamed for later at his annual review. He would word his communication very carefully. A man needs to protect himself from those second guessing assholes in Washington. He'd feel better when he had the informant in hand.

The wind raged as he lit a cigarette after three attempts while he trudged back to his white Range Rover. He pulled his sweat-stained black baseball cap down to prevent it from blowing away and inspected the Rover for a bomb which might have been planted in his absence. He looked for footprints in the sand and where someone maybe had slid under the Rover. He never trusted the youngsters he hired to watch his truck. As soon as he handed them a coin they rushed off as though they knew enough to escape the blast. Sometimes, he tossed the coins under the Rover to see if the little shits would venture under as he started the engine. His was a dirty business in a dirty country.

Thursday, October 11th

Phoenix, Arizona

BOBBY LEE HAD GROWN LETTUCE for two decades but had never had the experience of driving to his field and seeing the produce black with locusts. He thought briefly to get out of the Ford F 350 and chase them away. Then he realized the futility of a man shooing millions of the black and green insects from his fields. He powered his window down ever so slightly and the noise created by the multitude was shocking. He could hear them plainly chewing away at his livelihood and felt as if they were gnawing at his very being. Hundreds flew through the pickup window and landed on his face. He couldn't swat them away fast enough to be free of the menace.

It hadn't taken the mercenaries but a few minutes to stop the semitrailer along the field and literally kick hundreds of crates out the back. Three men on the ground rapidly pried open the covers releasing the swarms and delivering the eighth plague. That scene repeated itself dozens of times throughout the night all across Arizona.

Soon Bobby Lee's white pickup was black with crawling insects, their buzzing overwhelming the music on his radio. Stunned he sat for maybe ten minutes then he snapped. Just snapped and drove the ¾ ton truck into the field, shouting, screaming at the glimmering hoards that rose into the air and blocked the rising sun, turning Bobby Lee's world dark.

In a day, a local newscaster would report the odd incident that resulted in Bobby Lee's untimely demise – seems that as he gunned the big Ford over his produce, the locusts covered his windshield blinding him. Now a rational man would have stopped. He was anything but and pushed the accelerator to the floorboard until he ran headlong into the irrigation center pivot.

Thursday, October 11th

St. Paul, Minnesota

FBI AGENT CAMPBELL CALLED Doc at about 3:30 p.m., "I need you to help us on surveillance tonight, are you available?"

"Sure, nothing waiting for me at home unless you count the dog and I can get my neighbor to let that little turd out to pee. Or, I could bring him with. What you got going? Some leads on the terrorists bringing on the plagues, I hope."

"I'll explain to you in person. Meet me tonight at the University Golf Course. Seven o'clock in the parking lot."

Doc's pulse quickened. His mind raced. Finally, he hoped there'd be a break, finally, he'd be chasing the terrorists that had eluded law enforcement officers.

At 6:30, Doc and Gump were parked in the shadows next to the clubhouse. The old building was deserted. The wind blew his cigarette smoke back into his car window. He sipped bitter tepid coffee from his Thermos cup as he watched Pat drive his white Ford van into the lot and wait for Doc. The little pug curled on his lap, snorted and snored. After five minutes, Doc got on the radio, "I'm over by the clubhouse."

Pat pulled next to Doc, "Try to listen without giving me a bunch of crap. The domestic terrorist unit has information, likely from a wiretap, that some Animal Liberation Front, you know, ALF activists are going to hit the livestock genetic engineering lab. They believe based on the intercepted conversations that a couple of scouts have arrived from Boston and will be entering the lab tonight, probably testing security in advance of the main sabotage event. They want our unit to give them a hand and see if anyone shows."

Rain began to blow into his window. Doc took a long drag on his cigarette, exhaling the smoke towards Pat's open window. "Why would you think I might have some bullshit comments to make about this deal? Just because the country is awash with Islamic terrorists bent upon our destruction?"

"Look, all we have to do is watch the lab for a few hours, starting at ten and then we can get about capturing the al Zawahri family, just give me a hand here. I have three more agents, who have already given me a ration of crap, late but on their way. Here is a run sheet with the details and a map of the area with your surveillance post marked on the map. I'll be watching the lab with my guys. We'll be on channel three on the radio. I'd like you to watch the barn where the cows live. There's a part of the lab in the barn so I guess they could go there. If we see anyone looking like they may be scouting the place, just stay with them and we will get a uniformed U cop to stop and I.D. them. Any questions?"

"Yeah, what do they look like, little 'Elfs,' you got any photos or a description?"

"No idea. I'm sure I can rely on an old fart like you to know an 'elf' when he sees one. Just play with me, this isn't my idea, but the boys out East want it done."

"Then done it shall be, my son. And you should be more observant when you pull into a parking lot. I watched you for five minutes – in an ambush, you were mine. I'll be on the air."

Doc drove the black Durango into the darkness and found the surveillance post marked on the map. He parked, got out, and walked the area with the dog on a leash for a half-hour sizing up the likely routes of approach a scout might take. The large white barn rested in a narrow hollow surrounded by dry brown grass. The sides of the building were lined with windows each lit dimly from the few lamps left on for the night. Doc counted eight doors – all were unlocked. A handful of black and white cows lounged in paddocks next to the barns. A few pigeons drifted lazily above the barns but not a student was to be seen. After emptying bladders, they strolled back to and crawled into the SUV for a long watch. He took his Sudoku puzzle book out of his backpack and played with one eye and watched the area assigned with his other eye.

About 2:30 a.m., the little pug stopped snoring and growled. Doc dropped the puzzle and looked towards the barns. Two figures dressed in dark clothes walked near the lab. They ducked suddenly into the sliding door at the end of the barn. He picked up his mike then set it back on the seat and lit a smoke. When he finished, he picked up the mike and announced that he would be off the air for a bathroom break. He slipped out of his car and walked to the barn entering the same door he had seen the dark clad persons go through a few minutes earlier. The smell of fresh manure and urine filled his nostrils. He un-holstered his Glock pistol and waited in the shadows.

A few minutes passed and as his eyes adjusted he could see the two persons, both wearing night vision goggles, coming towards him. As the first passed from the shadows, he powerfully kicked the second in the left knee. The first figure turned and he received a size ten in the groin. Doc stood over them as they lay on the ground writhing in pain. "Now, you little assholes, we need to talk."

"What the hell…" was all the first man got out when Doc gave him a boot to the side of the head. He gave the second a boot also just to be fair and make his point. "You little punks shut up." He cuffed them and took their night vision and backpacks containing radios. He removed their wallets and took their driver's licenses.

"Listen you little pukes, I do not like wasting my time chasing you sorry little bastards when there are real criminals to catch. Have you turds heard we have real terrorists trying to blow our fat asses to hell and if the FBI has to spend time following you maggots we aren't going to catch them?

"I see you two are from Boston. I am going to tell you both how this is going to work. I am only going to tell you once. If you don't understand, speak up and I will kick the crap out of your other ear. Am I clear? Good, no response means you understand and I don't need to clean the shit out of your ears.

"Look at my face. I want you to remember me. You are both going back to Boston and take this message to your fellow 'elves.' There is a cop in Minnesota that will pull your brains out of your noses if any of you ever set foot in my state again. After you deliver that message, you will personally give up 'elfing.' Am I clear?

"Now despite your current predicament, you are saying to yourselves, 'This asshole will never know if I follow his directions.' Ah, but I will. The Bureau obviously knows about your plans just as they obviously have plants inside your 'elf' kingdom. I will find out if you two are still little 'elves' and if you are then I have an evil plan to deliver to you.

Do you want to know my plan?" He kicked them each in the ass, squarely. "Aren't you listening?"

Collective groans issued from each to avoid another boot.

"I have what I would hesitate to call friends in the Hell's Angels although I can count on them to return some favors. The Angels have a soft spot in their corroded hearts for cuddly animals, but they despise long hairs such as you. If I find that you ever are back in Minnesota, I will get them to do what I cannot legally do. The same is true if either of you ever complains about this meeting. The same is true if you remain 'elves.' I changed my mind. I think I want you both to remain 'elves' but as informants for the FBI. In fact, I think when you get back to Boston, I will give you each a day to ice your balls down then you will be able to walk to the Boston FBI and become informant 'elves.' If I learn that you have not followed my orders, I will call my heathen motorcycle friends. They have a chapter in Boston. They are well represented throughout the world.

"Worst case scenario, you little dickheads go about your business and the FBI puts you in jail. Believe me, I will keep a watchful eye and if you land in jail, you ladies will have wonderful new dating opportunities with some real Angels. Any questions my little 'elves?' Good, hearing none, I will release you and wish you well in carrying out your new marching orders."

Doc threw their wallets on the ground, keeping the licenses and took the cuffs off. Neither said a word and both remained on the ground as Doc slipped away from the barn.

He returned to the car. The pug growled at his approach. Without getting in, he picked up the radio mike, "I'm back from the piss break. No change here."

Friday, October 12th

Near White Plains, New York

AS THE SUN WAS SHOWING its face on the horizon, Flaviano Zulueta and his three companions drove the red four-wheel-drive pickup down the dusty back road towards the Brunswick Wildlife Preserve. They followed the barbed wire fence to the left. Posted signs noted the area was open to public hunting. The four men weren't hunting although they wore the blaze orange vests and had shotguns in cases on the floor of the pickup box. They'd even purchased nonresident hunting licenses in case they were stopped by a game warden.

Zulueta had been a busy man since crossing the Canadian border with Carlos Estaban. After picking up the weapons and explosives at the warehouse, they had gone to a safe house where others waited. Zulueta took some of the cash and purchased the old rusty red pickup and two ATVs with a trailer that they'd found for sale on the internet. They believed that using cash and the internet was preferable to retail purchases. All of the retail stores had cameras. As long as they paid the full price, the seller had little reason to question them – or even remember them for that matter.

He pulled the pickup and trailer into the area reserved for hunter parking. The two Filipino men jumped from the back seats and quickly unloaded the Polaris four-wheelers unto the brown grass. As they warmed the engines, Zulueta and his partner loaded green canvas bags from the pickup box onto the ATVs. They carefully strapped the bags to the front of the machines and set off in opposite directions.

Enormous steel power lines carrying electricity to New York City and points south ran through the hilly country and along the game preserve. The men ran for several miles to the north and south using the road ditch and then cut over to the power line right-of-way. The sites to place the explosive charges had been carefully selected from satellite photographs. They wanted the sites which could not be easily observed and that would be difficult to access to repair. Once they'd selected the locations, they noted GPS positions and set out on the pre-programmed course.

All four men had been trained by the U. S. military in the use of explosives. They'd been hired because of that specialty and paid well for it, at least by Filipino standards. They kept in contact by inexpensive hand-held radios. Zulueta and his partner arrived at their first structure. He was surprised to see that the tall steel tower was protected by only a chain link fence and three strands of barbed wire. They promptly cut through the fence and dragged one of the bags through the opening.

They spent the last two days preparing the charges so that when the time came to set them on the structures, there would be minimal effort and time. The blasting caps and timers were packed separately and once the explosives were placed on three of the tower's legs, the caps and timers were added and the men zoomed off to the next selected tower. Four towers each over a span of about sixteen miles would be sufficient to bring the ninth plague, darkness, to hundreds of square miles of the east coast.

It took less than three hours for the men to complete their mission and meet back at the pickup. Zulueta instructed the men to load the ATVs on the trailer. As they did that, he could hear loud pops to the north and the south. Off to the west he saw the thick electrical wires strain, break, and whip wildly in the air, sparks flying. He was filled with satisfaction as he drove out of the parking lot. He knew nothing about the big picture of the scheme, but he grinned with the knowledge that he'd carried out his mission and within a few days he'd be back in his homeland with his pockets stuffed with pesos.

Friday, October 12th

Oval Office, White House
Washington D.C.

CIA DIRECTOR JOHN RANKIN WRAPPED up his intelligence briefing. "We've received a communiqué from an officer in Afghanistan. His message was short on details but states the informant who gave us Ali Shah Masood is now saying that Masood is a party to a plot to bring massive destruction to America. This new plan, which has already been set in motion, will make 911 pale by comparison. Our agents intend to snatch this informant and put some flesh on the allegations. Mr. President, I believe we need to authorize the interrogators of Ali Shah Masood and this new informant to use all means available to protect our soil from attack. This is the very issue the polls say citizens overwhelmingly support."

"No, No, No! We're Americans and we don't torture people." President Franklin pointed and shook his cane at the Director. "I'm not ruling by polls. That issue is off the table, Mr. Rankin. Please continue."

"Yes, Mr. President," Rankin continued, noticeably flushed at his leader's reprimand. "We've had no telephone or internet intercepts that support any imminent plot or threat aside from the algae and frogs – not to be dismissive of those – however neither has resulted in any permanent destruction or fatalities."

"The calm before the storm," F.B.I. Director Marashov piped in. "Mr. President, through back water channels we've received a personal communiqué, authenticated as coming from no other than bin Laden's replacement, al Zawahri. He addresses this to you personally. It states that within one week you must announce the defeat of U.S. military by the Islamic fighters in Iraq and Afghanistan and begin your retreat. al Zawahri states that after one week the nation of the United States of America is in peril as are you personally…."

"Mr. President," Director Rankin interrupted.

The president held his hand up to stop Rankin's protest. "No torture and I do not want the topic brought up again.

"As for Mr. al Zawahri, I don't fear this cave dweller and furthermore we'll answer his ultimatum with some military advances of our own. His threats of bringing biblical plagues to our country are absurd. That little stunt with the frogs and bugs shows how little they can do. It just shows how he must think of himself as God's equal. We will crush him. For too long, we have waited for Iran to comply with the nuclear weapons protocol and it is time we get their attention the way we got the Iraqis' attention. We'll be working on this with the Joint Chiefs.

"I must emphasize that Iran is a nuclear threat and each of you must take every opportunity to advance this cause with the American people, every opportunity. Mahmoud Ahmadinejad, that little bastard, excuse my language, is behind all of this and I'm going to destroy him the way we destroyed that punk, Saddam.

"Now, we'll reconvene this meeting after lunch which I understand is a Texas BBQ. Let's meet back here in 2 hours. Nate, you stay," the president said to his chief political advisor.

After the room cleared, the president spoke, "Nate, what do the contributions look like?"

Nate shook his head, "Mr. President, there's no doubt we are behind the opposing party. The war is unpopular and a lot of the big contributors are throwing their money at the opposition because they believe that they are the frontrunners. We have major fundraisers next week in Coeur d'Alene, San Antonio, and Minneapolis. The first lady and your son will represent you in all three. These will be some of the largest contributors we get this season. That money will allow us to outspend opponents ten to one during the last week blitz."

"Unless we have some major victories in the Middle East, our people predict fundraising will be slow," President Franklin said.

"Mr. President, I've been twisting President al-Yawer's arm and a few other body parts to get him to get his people under control. He tells me that unless we are willing to support him as the new Saddam Hussein, there'll be continued fighting. It was only Saddam's savage repression that kept the order. al-Yawer does not believe democracy can work in Iraq.

"And Hamid Karzai, he's not likely to be Afghanistan's George Washington. In fact, I believe the situation is….."

"Nate, I think what we need is another front, another enemy to rally the citizens and Iran is a solid choice for that enemy. I'm convinced of this. A new enemy always adds up to support for the incumbent. A week before the election, we'll put this entire mess at Ahmadinejad's feet. We need a photo of bin Laden or al Zawahri hugging that little toad – can Rankin get that done? "

Nate looked sadly at the president but said nothing.

"Nate, let's join the others for Texas steak and Mexican beans," the president put his arm around Nate as they strode out to join the others. His limp seemed more pronounced today. The doctors had been disappointed that his leg wasn't healing. They said that perhaps the diabetes was contributing to the slowness of the process. The president yearned to get back on his bicycle.

Sometimes, Nate thought the president just wanted to ride away from it all – just get on the bike and go like Forrest Gump.

Friday, October 12th

44 Wall Street
New York City

BERNIE SILVERSTEIN GREW UP WATCHING the New York Stock Exchange with his father. While other boys his age played ball and followed the Yankees, he sat by his father's side and they talked about financial matters or more specifically how to make money with other's cash. When Bernie graduated from Columbia University, his father used his influence to land his son a job with Brace & Hartford, a top Wall Street investment firm. That was 33 years ago and at 55, Bernie had seen the ups and downs, the cycles, both predicted and unexpected. He had seen fortunes made, lives ruined, fortunes lost and more lives ruined.

He had come to some firm conclusions over the years. He no longer saw the price of stocks as a function of value determined by a corporation's earnings, net worth or innovative products – he had learned that a typhoon in Asia could send a stock tumbling. He watched American money leave the NYSE and pour into China where native investors use the stock exchange like a casino, betting on lucky numbers. He had seen plenty of inside traders make hundreds of millions for trusted friends and relatives. And then there were the mistresses who lived in Fifth Avenue condos kept by the money they made buying and selling stocks with inside information more precious than the diamonds and furs. Bernie had seen over the last two decades that the stock exchanges around the world were inter-related. When big money leaves the London Stock Exchange, it has to go somewhere and it may mean large buying sprees on the NYSE.

Bernie had seen much, earned an encyclopedic knowledge of markets – from gold to hedge funds, and had come to expect surprises. By the end of this day, he would have seen some new tricks, some that would cause him to dig out the bottle of brandy. He rarely drank.

Bernie was a tall, pale man with thinning hair. He combed the six-inch long hair on his left side to his right side and when he bent to pour a tumbler of brandy, the long hair fell onto his narrow face. He flattened it back. The battle continued everyday to keep his hair in place.

Despite pleas from his wife to cut his hair, he refused to surrender to baldness. He settled his lanky frame back into his swivel leather chair and put his Armani Italian leather loafers on top of the small safe he kept in the knee well. It was where the .32 pistol rested, just in case. He wore a serious look of concern and pondered his next move while he awaited directions from his overseas clients. They seemed to be in a selling mood.

Acting in concert with investors from Russia and China, trusts and corporations controlled by the men unknown to Bernie, began an unprecedented selling spree, unloading carefully selected stocks on the NYSE. Calls were made to reporters who were told that fear of al Qaeda's threats was causing a panic. Having planned this for months, the investors had hedged their losses by selling short. They had no intention of losing money or destroying the United States economy. They had every intention of getting the attention of the United States Administration and Congress to withdraw their forces from the Middle East, and later, at the urging of Russia and China, from Europe and the Pacific.

Friday, October 12th

Pend Oreille Lake, Idaho

LIKE THE HABIBS IN TEXAS, the Shaloubs brought substantial cash with them to win the prized EB-5 visas. They too arrived 2 ½ years ago from Lebanon and settled near Sandpoint, Idaho, where they purchased a dilapidated timber mill from the bankruptcy trustee. Their operations recovered logs harvested a century ago and then unintentionally lost in rivers and lakes used as timber highways. Timbers recovered from the cold waters produced fine and expensive woods for furniture, floors, and walls. In the booming economy with all of its excess, business was excellent.

Like the Habibs and many others, the Shaloubs had been sent to provide a base for future operations. They all operated legitimate businesses and to the public eye led stellar lives – not so much as a speeding ticket. They received occasional orders and requests from their employer. These communications came from overseas via encrypted flash drives, hand carried by unwitting foreign students and sent to mail drops monitored by the Shaloubs, the Habibs, and the others.

They were never asked to do anything illegal. Most of the assignments were to find certain types of businesses or persons. Sometimes they were asked to watch a person, learn their routines. Occasionally, they facilitated the movement of the people or money. Never were they knowledgeable of the actual intent or plans. Most soon assimilated into the community, oblivious to the role they were playing in the defeat of America. However, if one strayed too far they would receive a visitor who spoke of family and relatives in the old country and brought them back into line.

A year ago, Djoko Sutarto and his crew joined the Shaloubs as skilled divers and settled unnoticed on the mill property. The six of them had been recruited from *Kopaska*, Indonesian's Navy Underwater Combat Team. They immediately set to work making dives but time underwater was so severely restricted for safety sake it allowed them plenty of time for their real mission.

Last week, with directions provided by Shaloubs, they had found the Kelly residence and followed Pat and Melissa Kelly to the grocery store. She noticed nothing even when they joined her shopping for their own groceries. Playing a covert little game, like a cat toying with a mouse, they even engaged her in conversations about the freshness of the lettuce.

Endriartono and Feisal watched from across the grocery store parking lot as Pat waited in the SUV listening to the local football game. It was Pat's day off from flying for Clearwater Timber Company. The Bruins were winning over the Oregon State Beavers with 3 minutes to go. Between quarters, the local station KSPT announcer, Bob Bernard, gave the same forecast he had for weeks. Warm and dry. The forests were dangerously dry and getting worse by the day.

After their short surveillance, they returned to the timber mill. There they met with Carlos Mendosa and his crew, having just arrived in their Suburban from the Mexican border. They had little time to prepare.

Friday, October 12th

Lake Street and Mississippi Avenue
Minneapolis, Minnesota

"THE COPS ARE STOPPING US," Alberto Hernandez shouted.

Juan, Memo and Lalo tensed and pressed their hands against the polished steel in their waistbands. They were still on edge from their unexpected shootout with the Border Patrol in Texas. He coasted the sedan to the right curb.

From out of their squad, two Minneapolis Police officers approached on opposite sides of the 1992 Buick Century. The officers noted the brakes lights stayed on – never a good sign if the transmission is still in drive, there'd be a chase.

"You know why I stopped you?" Officer John Erickson asked the driver through the open window. His partner often pestered Erickson, "Why do you ask them why you pulled them over? Are they supposed to read your fricken' mind?" Not today, he was more concerned about the driver keeping the car in gear.

Alberto, who understood perfectly the officer's question, simply looked bewildered, held his hands up and shook his head.

"*Hable* English?" Officer Erickson asked the driver.

"*No, hablo español, verdad*?" Alberto replied.

From across the Century, Officer Garcia who had learned a little Spanish from his grandmother, offered, "John, he wants you to speak Spanish."

"Driver's license and proof of insurance."

Again, the driver feigned ignorance and held his arms out palms up to show a lack of understanding.

Officer Erickson pulled his Spanish Q-Card from his blue uniform pocket and asked again for the license and insurance in something that resembled Spanish.

Alberto smiled, nodded approval, and produced a Texas driver's license in a false name of Pablo Martinez and a State Farm insurance card for the vehicle in the name of Armando Gomez. The license he had been given after he'd crossed the border in Wilkin County, Texas.

The officers returned to the squad car. Officer Erickson wrote a tag for faulty equipment and they ran the registration on the vehicle and it came back to Armando Gomez.

"I know Armando, he's a cocaine dealer from Lake and Hennepin but he's not in the car, I know him because I busted him about a year ago on cocaine charges. He went to Drug Court and was back selling within a week," Garcia commented.

"These guys look like they are newly arrived to this country," was Erickson's only reply.

"Give them their fix-it tag and kick them on their way. John, you know the mayor has made this a sanctuary city and wants us to embrace our very illegal cousins. Do you still have some keys to the city we could provide or perhaps some voter registration cards?"

Erickson waited impatiently for the warrant check to come back on the squad's computer.

Neither officer noticed that a black Grand Prix, which had been traveling in front of the Century, had crossed the Mississippi, made a u-turn and returned to park about a 1/4 block to their rear. Beto and Chole both removed Glock .40 pistols from the Burger King bags which lay on the seat between them. Should things go poorly with the police, Beto and Chole were prepared to intervene. The time was too close to their mission to lose any team members to the Minneapolis Police.

"Clear of warrants. Come on partner, put a big smile on your face and let's welcome our newly arrived friends. Don't forget the welfare and unemployment applications and let's not forget to remind them about the free college programs."

Officer Garcia smiled and joined his partner in sending the men on their way. The wind whistling across the Mississippi lifted his blue hat from his head and onto the road. Cursing, he chased it across the road where it came to rest under the Grand Prix. Beto tensed as he saw the officer running at them although he hadn't seen the hat blowing his way. His finger moved to the trigger. Officer Garcia reached under the rear tire, retrieved his hat and returned to the squad never knowing how close he had come to lacking any head for a hat.

The Glocks returned to the bags and both the Century and Grand Prix crossed the Mississippi.

The mission as planned for Alberto and his men had not gone well. Alberto had been told to meet the cigarette man, Abbas Ali Jaafar, when Alberto arrived in Minnesota. Alberto's instructions were that they would be provided shelter and vehicles by the Jaafar family who owned 14 smoke shops in the Twin Cities. That plan failed when Jaafar fled the area ahead of IRS special agents who had a warrant for his arrest for tax evasion. It was only two days ago that Alberto had finally made contact with Jaafar's brother who was able to get them on the right track.

Within a day of arriving, Alberto and his men met Armando Gomez in a Lake Street bar and Gomez invited the men to live in a two bedroom duplex he owned on Pillsbury and Lake Street. He offered them 'jobs' selling heroin and cocaine. They agreed to the relationship, although they had no need for money. The men took the cocaine on a front. Occasionally they brought money to keep him satisfied. They used the unsold dope to party with hookers. The local girls were happy to take the cocaine in trade – saved them having to take cash and go out and buy the stuff. It eliminated one step in their daily quest for the drug.

Armando even let them use his business cars as they went about his drug dealing. In Armando's case, business cars were old beaters bought at the police auction. He had learned long ago that driving a new Cadillac or BMW was an invitation for police attention. A couple of times they did make large deliveries to his other dealers, a low risk deal in Alberto's mind. It got them through the first few days until they could hook up with their contact.

After crossing the Mississippi River, they drove to Cretin and north to the freeway. Lalo and Memo huddled in the back seat over a small metal case with an eighteen inch antenna. They played with a small joy stick and watched a variety of dials and digital displays. The instructions and control labels were especially written for them in Spanish. Both men had operated sophisticated radio equipment in the military so they found this quite simple if not childlike.

They exited Highway 5 turned left and after a few blocks pulled the two cars across from the Minnesota Department of Transportation (MNDOT) Regional Headquarters. From their vantage point they saw rows of orange MNDOT snowplow trucks. Although still October, a few of the massive rigs stood ready for duty outfitted with snowplows. Memo pressed the red power button and then a green button labeled *EMPEZAR*.

Memo very slightly pushed the lever labeled *ESTRANGULAR* with his left hand and held the joy stick with his right hand. The six men could see that the last in line of the orange trucks blew diesel exhaust and inched forward about 10 feet. Then it reversed and returned to its parking spot. The driverless vehicle repeated this maneuver four times and parked. The men exchanged the South American equivalent of a high-five.

Friday, October 12th

Pend Oreille Lake, Idaho

PAT KELLY RELAXED IN HIS favorite recliner watching ESPN when he heard the front door open. Melissa had just departed to take the girls to their soccer game. He assumed that they had forgotten some equipment and his attention turned back to the game.

He felt a presence before an arm reached across his back and around his neck. Half standing on his own, half pulled to his feet, he struggled and threw his head back into his assailant's nose. He was free and turned to face his attacker who lay moaning on the recovered timber floor the family purchased from the Shaloubs. He saw three more men each armed with pistols all aimed at his head.

"We've your wife and daughters. They'll not be harmed if you cooperate," the dark-complexioned man with the scarred face barked in something resembling English.

"Let's put your hands on your head and turn around."

"Where's my wife? I want to see my daughters. What do you want from us?" Kelly shouted.

"You are going to give the three of us a ride in your helicopter and then you can have your family back."

"No, I want them here now or I do nothing."

Carlos Mendosa pulled himself up – blood streamed out of his nostrils. He slipped from behind the brown Lazy Boy chair and kicked Kelly squarely on the side of his knees. Kelly dropped to the carpet and Carlos put a shoe to his head with the skill of an accomplished soccer player.

Djoka Sutarto and his crew followed Melissa Kelly from a discreet distance. His cell phone rang. It was Carlos and he sounded excited and angry. "We have Kelly at his home. He refuses to go further unless he talks to his wife."

They hadn't anticipated Melissa's sudden departure. It complicated the operation, although these soldiers were used to reacting to changes in battle plans.

"They are almost to the soccer field. We can grab them in the parking lot."

"No, there would be too many witnesses. Do it now, we can't be standing around here."

Sutarto waited until the paved road narrowed and curved in a wooded stretch. Pushing the accelerator deep into the mud caked carpet, he pulled his vehicle along side of her left rear quarter panel of the SUV. He gently touched his right front bumper on the fender, turned the wheel hard right, accelerated and watched her spin uncontrollably in front of his Buick Riviera. After two full spins she came to rest into a patch of small aspens. Within seconds, the men had Melissa and the two girls in their Riviera. Sutarto grabbed the screaming Melissa by the throat and shouted for them to be quiet. They drove another mile and turned on a deserted gravel road.

Sutarto dialed Carlos. "We have them. I'll put you on speaker phone. You do the same."

"Melissa, are you and the girls alright? What have they done with you? What do they want?" Kelly shouted as he sat on the carpet still groggy from the blow to his head.

"Pat, they ran us off the road. Who are they? Why are they doing this? Where are you?"

"Everything will be alright. I just have to fly them somewhere and then they promise we'll all be okay," Kelly replied.

The cell phone went dead.

Sutarto shot the Golden Retriever whose big brown eyes looked trustingly and never blinked. The girls screamed until he put a bullet in each of their foreheads. Melissa watched and then fainted, mercifully. Sutarto nodded to his partner and two 9mm rounds were dispatched to the back of Melissa's head. Then it was silent in the woods except for the wind through the pines carrying their spirits skyward.

....

"You see, your family is just fine. Now my friend, you and I will get the chopper ready, go for a little ride, and shortly you will all be back together."

Forty minutes later, Kelly along with Carlos, Javier and Pedro jogged to the shiny white and blue Bell Ranger. They loaded the flight deck with six wooden crates while Kelly prepared the bird for flight. Kelly lifted the noisy machine off the tarmac without communication with air traffic controllers. His flights typically were all over timber country and required little FFA contact. Kelly tried a last ditch effort to convince his abductors that the 35 mph wind was too dangerous to fly in over the mountains. It fell on deaf ears. The strong wind is what they'd hoped for – in fact, last night they'd even prayed to the blessed Virgin for winds just short of a typhoon.

Kelly brought the helicopter to an altitude of 1,500 feet. Carlos sitting on the port side told Kelly he would take the controls. He flew due south for few minutes then turned over his right shoulder and nodded. Pedro who sat behind Kelly touched the muzzle of his Sig Sauer .40 pistol against the left side of Kelly's head and fired once. Carlos reached across Kelly's body and opened the door – slit his safety harness, tilted the chopper to the starboard, and pushed him out into the sky to join his family.

Carlos lowered the Bell Ranger to tree-top level and flew by knap of the earth, a technique he had perfected during his three months tour of duty with the U.S. Army before returning to duty in Peru. As he cruised over the mountain terrain, Javier and Pedro threw traffic flares out and into the timber about every twenty miles.

With about 20 minutes of fuel remaining, Carlos landed the Bell Ranger almost hitting the waiting tanker truck which held the jet fuel. Men quickly refueled and loaded more flares into the Bell Ranger. Within minutes, they set off again and continued tossing flares into the dangerously dry forests.

Within several hours and a couple of more refueling stops, they arrived over the San Bernardino Mountains. Buckled by Santa Ana winds, Carlos brought the Bell Ranger to maximum altitude to dump the remaining flares. Javier and Pedro reached into the crates removing a flare at a time. They twisted the igniter cap and quickly tossed the flares into the downdraft of the helicopter. As he flew, Carlos looked for areas where the trees had died from insect infestation. Those dry brown trees stood out among the healthy green pines. Carlos avoided populated areas, believing they would be easily apprehended if a witness saw their activity. Even using those precautions, he knew their chances of escaping without being shot down were poor.

With no flares remaining, and about 30 minutes of fuel, Carlos headed south towards a remote desert along the Mexican border, dropping to less than 200 feet the last ten miles. Carlos strained to spot the banditos who would pick them up and take them to safety. They left behind an inferno and the only evidence would be a burned up Jet Ranger on the Mexican desert floor. As the flames consumed hundreds of thousands of acres, the skies across the West darkened. Street lights in the cities nestled in the mountains remained on both day and night as they became indistinguishable. As the heat from the fires drove moisture laden air even higher, hail storms appeared in the foothills and plains. The seventh and eighth plagues, thunderstorms, hail, and darkness had been delivered.

Friday, October 12th

Castle Creek Chalet
Aspen, Colorado

THE CHALET OVERLOOKED THE ASPEN ski slopes. It was owned by a Saudi sheik who bought it from one of Hollywood's leading actors who decided Aspen was passé and moved to a ranch in Montana's Gallatin River Valley. The sheik didn't know Aspen was yesterday's news and paid $5.8 million for the big home. That's what the public records show, however there was additional funds paid to the seller in the form of a yacht resting in a port in Bermuda. The chalet could have been easily mistaken for a resort lodge. Its 23,000 square foot of living space had every amenity including an indoor pool, commercial grade kitchens, riding stables, and cabins for staff. A cedar deck surrounded the log home and provided million dollar views of the ski slopes which had been blessed with the earliest opening day on record. Two massive stone fireplaces warmed the decks during the winter months.

The twelve Council members had no trouble entering the United States as all but two carried diplomatic passports issued by their respective governments. They had decided some time earlier that they would implement their plan from the United States. It was a bold move. Ali and Omar had convinced the members that the Americans would never be looking for them in their own backyard, their own playground. Besides, he argued, they would be able to better assess the effectiveness of the plan with front row seats. "Maybe if the U. S. President was living in Afghanistan or Iraq, he too would have a better perspective and improved sense of reality."

They met in the great room all facing the forty-foot stone fireplace. Not a skier amongst them, they none-the-less had shed their Arabic garb and were outfitted in freshly purchased après ski wear from Aspen's finest shop, Gorsuch, Ltd. – a one day sales spike that pushed the store manager to pop the corks on a case of champagne when the store closed.

Omar stood facing the Council, his back warmed to the fire and for the first time in recent days, a hint of a smile on his face.

"Allow me to update you on a few matters. Our gracious host has prepared a feast which will be served tonight. We'll meet for the next two days to work on details. Tonight we feast."

He spoke for over an hour before winding down.

"Gentle reminders, my brothers, no telephone calls regarding our affairs and be mindful of email messaging. Let's speak English to avoid unwanted attention.

"And lastly, our lawyers tell us that Ali is still not in Guantanamo and that may be evidence that he was killed in the explosion at Bagran ..."

Mumtaz excitedly interrupted, "The first tests of our ability to remotely control equipment hundreds or thousands of miles away have been a success. We used American farm equipment to avoid too much attention. There has been no media report on these events as they seldom pay attention to events away from their Coasts. Most of you know this from your school days in America and England. They call the rest of America the 'Fly over Country.' We may use some of our contacts in the media to plant stories or at least push for more coverage."

"With that I will end and we will talk no more of these matters for tonight we celebrate our successes. Praise Allah."

As the men paraded down the hall decorated with antique skis, Omar grabbed Mumtaz's elbow and guided him aside. He leaned into the younger man's ear, "al Zawahri has made contact and is ready to consummate a deal with us."

Saturday, October 13th

White House Lawn
Washington D.C.

Facing a stiff easterly wind, Marine One, the president's VH-3D helicopter, lifted off the White House heliport at full power and immediately banked to the portside. At a few hundred feet it began evasive maneuvers designed to give maximum protection from shoulder-fired missiles. Marine One was quickly joined by four identical VH-3D helicopters and they created a formation that constantly shifted the president's position to confuse would-be attackers. As soon as Marine One reached a safe altitude it began a zigzag course to 'Cactus' as Camp David was known to the Secret Service.

From the overstuffed, reclining chair on the starboard side, President Franklin leaned over and stared at the Potomac River. His chin rested on his cane. The river appeared a brackish red in the bays and slow backwaters. He could see where the water could be mistaken for blood.

He waved for an aide to join him, "Are we making any progress on this 'red plague' as the media have taken to calling it?"

"Mr. President, CDC scientists know it's an algae and it is harmless to humans. They have not been able to say how it started and why the fish are being killed."

"What do our polls say about what the people are thinking? Are they concerned about this?"

"Our pollsters say most people are largely unconcerned about the algae. I don't think most Americans get past the sports page or gossip column to read much about some pollution in the Potomac."

"Good, let's keep a lid on this. We don't want the people to panic over what is of no consequence."

"Yes, sir."

"What about the frogs? What are you doing with that mess?"

"Fortunately, it was a one day event. It's cleaned up and we are back in business burying the dead at a record pace."

"That's good news. We can down play that as nothing more than a childish prank."

"The blackout is creating the greatest problem. The bombs took out a crucial area of the power grid. They've been able to reroute some of the service although there are still massive areas in the dark. The governors are complaining that the National Guard troops they'd normally use to keep order are deployed to the Middle East. They demand federal troops to patrol the cities after dark."

"Well, we just don't have any extra troops. They are already committed to other engagements."

Nate Holstein, the Chief Political Advisor, slid into the empty seat across from the president, "Mr. President, may we go over the last minute changes to the fundraisers?"

"Understand we expect to raise $30 million for the war chest?"

"We've hired Randolph Watson Detective Agency to check out the donors and make sure there is nothing for the media. The first lady and Cody will have paid photo ops and the Watson Detectives have approved the list. There should be nothing embarrassing. The Secret Service also found nothing."

Ever since First Lady Rosalynn Carter was photographed with serial killer John Gacy, the political parties made extra efforts to review and conduct background checks on those persons coming in close contact with the president and his family. While the Secret Service routinely conducts checks, some still slip through. Hillary Clinton's photo with fugitive Norman Hsu made headlines. Some speculate that if enough money is contributed, such trivial matters as arrest warrants may be overlooked.

They spent the remainder of the trip reviewing the itinerary and finished just as Marine One approached the landing site using fewer evasive maneuvers in the secure Camp David setting. Coming in fast, the helicopter cleared the canopy of trees and settled into the tarmac. The ground crew promptly pushed the steps to the helicopter and a tall Marine opened the bird's door. The president hurried down the steps offering a weary salute to the two Marines on the ground. At the landing, Randal Chang, National Security Advisor, waited for the president. A slight man of Chinese descent, he wore a serious expression, one which the president dreaded because it meant more trouble.

"Mr. President, NSA and CIA have been watching al Jazeera and they report al Zawahri is on TV, they think on a live up-link and . . ."

"Good morning, Randal. A bright sunny day my friend. al Zawahri, does he have his own talk show now?"

"Mr. President, al Zawahri is speaking to you personally and warns you have 12 hours to announce a pullout from Iraq and Afghanistan and abandon military support of Israel or the jihadists will rain holy terror upon you. He is threatening to visit even more plagues on America. He is claiming that the blood in the Potomac waters, the frogs and insects, and the darkness are only the beginning."

"Can we get a location on him?"

"We are obviously putting every effort towards locating him however al Jazeera isn't going to help."

They walked to the lobby and sat in the lounge while Secret Service agents pulled a limo up to the door for the impending departure of the first lady and their son.

"Randal, get together with Press Secretary Mahoney and get going on our reaction to this, something like this is why we continue to take the fight to Iraq and Afghanistan and spin Iran in there somehow. Maybe they are sheltering the al Qaeda leadership. Get the Center for Disease Control to issue a statement that the algae are harmless – the frogs a childish prank and the rest we don't even know if they are acts of terror. Find something!"

The heavy wooden door opened and the first lady and Cody entered the room. The president hugged them both.

"Please, I'd like a few minutes alone."

The staff hurriedly departed as Julie Franklin, the first lady, settled into a plush cloth covered chair. She was a lovely woman who emanated grace and a peaceful countenance. In many ways she was stronger than the president who doted on her.

"Dad, what do you think about this al Zawahri threat? All the TV stations are in a panic and speculating about all sorts of disasters and plagues."

"Son, I've no idea what will happen. In many ways our Intelligence community has been a disappointment. We're constantly being misled by internet and telephone intercepts. We are running in all directions following false leads. Our FBI and CIA agents are terrified that they will be crucified by Congress and the media if they get information and don't follow-up on it. In the meantime, we've few spies on the inside of the terrorist organization. The military, the CIA and FBI along with a host of others are still fighting over who has jurisdiction. They don't share information or they ignore what they have like they did with Zaccarias Moussoui. The FBI spent hundreds of millions of dollars on a computer system designed to do that and it doesn't work, they scrapped it. I'm sorry. I don't mean to rant about this, but I feel so helpless – and they say I'm the most powerful man in the world."

"Dad, where do you think they'll strike?"

"Son, pick any one of a thousand locations that are vulnerable. We have given billions to states to harden security, although by the time every village, town, county, city and state got their share, I fear we're still very vulnerable.

"I'm afraid my generation has had many failures and we've been greedy and power-hungry, not about the people's business but about the party's business."

Cody looked down, not sure what to say as he prepared to leave on more party business of collecting money. Another 'money run' as he jokingly called them. At twenty-two he had hopes of following the family tradition of politics. He was having his doubts. A handsome, articulate young man often cited as America's Prince William, he would have no trouble following in his family's footsteps if that was his wish.

"I guess I'm a hypocrite, ranting about the failures of our political leaders and then sending you two off to raise more money. Son, I hope your generation can turn this around. I really do. When I was your age I'd no idea how much our government runs on the power of money. We've been reduced to buying votes for political favors and stabbing each other in the back to make the other guy look bad.

"Julie, Cody, I'm sorry to go off like this. I can't say these things to anyone else. There is really no one close to me that I trust. There are way too many Brutus' in this office."

"We understand and we'll always be here for you. We must get going to be on time, can we say a prayer together before we leave?" Julie replied.

"Certainly," the president came to his feet as did his wife and son. They held hands and bowed their heads.

"Father, we ask your guidance as we go about these days of difficult times. We acknowledge that you are in control of our lives and events and ask for wisdom and your blessings.

"We feel the presence of the evil one in our world and ask that you protect us. Father, I ask for protection from our enemies and your special blessings on Julie and Cody as they travel today."

Cody knew it was wrong and he'd probably go to hell for it – while Dad prayed, he couldn't help but wonder if the Islamic terrorists praying for the death of all heathens would have more juice with God. Is God going to take sides?

"Amen," they said and hugged a last time.

As the Boeing 747 jet climbed rapidly over the Potomac, the first lady leaned over to see the river, now in the sunlight, looking blood red. She opened her well worn Bible to Exodus and read, "Thus therefore saith the Lord: In this thou shalt know that I am the Lord: behold I will strike with the rod that is in my hand the water of the river and it shall be turned into blood. And the fishes that are in the river shall die and the waters shall be corrupted and the Egyptians shall be afflicted when they drink the water of the river." She continued reading, "...and all the firstborn in the land of Egypt shall die, from the firstborn of the pharaoh that sitteth upon his throne, even unto the firstborn of the maidservant that is behind the mill; and all the firstborn of beasts." She closed her Bible and closed her eyes.

The Boeing reached cruising altitude of 35,000 feet and set a course to Minneapolis and then on to Coeur d'Alene. The plane rocked with turbulence from the storms below. From about two thousand meters behind, three F-15 fighter jets shadowed the 747 on orders of the president.

Saturday, October 13th

Minneapolis International Airport

IT WAS THE KIND OF fall day that Minnesota travel brochures always promise although seldom deliver – blue skies, no wind, and the cool night air slowly being warmed by the sun. Secret Service special agents, who had been in Minneapolis for days preparing for this visit, patrolled the perimeters of the airport in anticipation of wheels down for the first lady or 'Rainbow' as they called her by her code name.

Secret Service Agent Donna Lyons and her local partner were an Intel Team assigned to patrol the airport and motorcade route looking for anything suspicious. Since 911, the taxi waiting area at the Super America drew special attention. The airport taxi drivers were generally Muslim African immigrants and their waiting area ran parallel to Runway 4/22, an easy missile shot.

Agent Lyons heard via her radio that Rainbow was "5 out" and they parked between the waiting taxis and Runway 4/22. She had to admit to herself – she would have been helpless had a shoulder-fired missile launcher protruded from the back door of one of the taxi vans. In exactly five minutes she saw the Air Force Boeing coming in fast and when the tires squealed on the tarmac, she heard "wheels down," through her earpiece. She enjoyed being a part of the precision of the most professional law enforcement agency on earth. Despite the personal sacrifices, including her ex-husband and a few other failed relationships, she would want no other career, a fact noted by her superiors. Despite being only a five and one-half year veteran, she had risen rapidly within the ranks. It didn't hurt either to be drop-dead gorgeous. Stationed in Washington, D.C., she was assigned to the first lady's protection detail – usually on the outer perimeter. Political hacks didn't want Donna's beauty distracting from Rainbow.

"Head down to the Air Jet Way Terminal," she said referring to the private terminal often used by those who enjoyed executive protection.

Tony Brothers, a state agent who drove because he knew the local roads better than Agent Lyons, nodded in agreement and turned his unmarked Impala around towards the terminal.

"Park short of the gate until we hear that Rainbow is in the limo," Agent Lyons directed.

Tony flipped on his grill mounted emergency lights to avert suspicion from the nearby marked patrol units and pulled onto the grass next to the fence.

"She's in the limo. Let's run the route a few minutes ahead of the motorcade," Lyons ordered.

Tony, who had worked many times with the Secret Service, still marveled at the sensation of driving through a major city at mid-day without any traffic interruptions. Every intersection was closed and there would be no traffic on the route. It was a powerful feeling to be cruising down the freeway, no speed limits, free of all other traffic. He eased down the curb onto the road ahead of the motorcade, looking for any threats which could be dealt with or detour the motorcade.

They rode, mostly in silence, the entire route without incident. When Agent Lyons heard via the radio that Rainbow and Lightening were inside the Wayzata mansion, she said, "Let's get some lunch. We've got about 90 minutes. Where can we grab something other than more bad news on a bun?"

Tony looked at her and smiled. "This isn't actually my neighborhood, but there are probably some fancy restaurants in downtown Wayzata."

"I'm buying. I haven't eaten since noon yesterday. Let's go!" Agent Lyons said enthusiastically.

They drove past Lake Minnetonka mansions, the priciest property in the state. The wealthy bought older lakeside mansions only to tear them down and build bigger mansions. It was no coincidence that Rainbow's 'money run' brought her and politicians from both parties to be courted by people who were regulars on the Fortune's list of the wealthiest Americans.

Tony arrived at the Lakeside Café and parked in a no parking zone. He put his police placard on the dash.

"I hope you brought a credit card because I'm very, very hungry," he smiled at her and winked.

Saturday, October 13th

Mandan, North Dakota

MANDAN IS ONLY FIVE HUNDRED miles West of Wayzata, although Ted Schaffer had more in common with African Masai herders than Wayzata bankers and brokers.

Ted put the front sights of his Ruger .22 rifle between the serpent's eyes and pulled the trigger. The 3 foot diamondback rattlesnake sprang from its coil towards Ted but died mid-strike. Reno, Ted's Blue Tick Heeler, grabbed the snake and shook it viciously as though Reno had something to do with its death.

"Reno, you dumb sum-a-bitch let that thang alone before you shake its fangs into your own ass!"

Rodolfo came at a trot from the bunkhouse, "What you shoot at boss?"

Ted reached down and took the snake from Reno, "Supper," and tossed it near Rodolfo who recoiled at the dead viper.

Ted had been on this small ranch all of his life. His great-grandfather had been in General Custer's 7th Calvary stationed at Fort Lincoln, ten miles to the north. Great-grandpa had been in sick bay with dysentery when the general marched his Grand 7th off to the Little Big Horn. He was angry to see his buddies ride off without him although a few weeks later he was relieved when he learned it wasn't his time to join them in death. A year later, he was honorably discharged and he rode his newly purchased pinto to stake out a ranch. A plump and jolly laundress followed him out of the fort on a buckskin mare. Ted's father was born there as was Ted.

Ted's sons and daughters saw no future in ranching. They all settled in Seattle with careers in computer technology. Except the youngest son, he went to the dark side and paid the price when he overdosed on heroin beneath a freeway bridge in downtown Minneapolis. When his wife died, Ted and Reno took to the bottle. The ranch fell into disrepair and the neighbors complained when his barbed wire fences no longer kept his bulls or cattle on his land. Ted never again spoke with his neighbors, but in a sober moment, two months ago, he did place an ad in the *Mandan Pioneer Press* for a ranch hand. Neighbors gossiped that since losing his driver's license, Ted needed a hand not to mend fences but to run to town for liquor

Rodolfo showed up in response to the ad and brought his brother. Ted told Rodolfo he only wanted one wrangler and that was all he would pay for, however, the brother could stay in the bunkhouse for a few weeks. Rodolfo didn't mind. He only needed a place to remain unnoticed until the others came to join him. Until then, Ted's place would do nicely as a place to scout out their intended targets.

Last Wednesday, Rodolfo's cousin, Eduardo, showed up in his Chevy Suburban with two others. Rodolfo bribed his boss with several bottles of Wild Turkey Whiskey to permit his cousins to stay a few days while they looked for work.

"Boss, here is the skinned snake," Ted heard Rodolfo say an hour after the shooting. Ted and Reno sat in the kitchen in front of the wood cooking stove. "Anything you want in town, Boss?"

Reno growled as Ted turned to answer, "More Whiskey." He was met by a .357 revolver to his forehead. That was the last thing he saw and he never had a chance to ask for more Old Turkey.

Eduardo ordered the men to the Chevy but not before Rodolfo had poured kerosene on the wood stove. They could hear old Reno cry from behind the closed door as the little wooden frame ranch house burned. They had been ordered to leave no witnesses.

The SUV drove off well ahead of the arrival of the volunteer firefighters. It proceeded north along the Missouri River bottoms stopping at the Burlington Northern Railroad Bridge spanning the Missouri.

Before coming to the United States, Eduardo had been in the Columbian National Police. He was an EOD specialist, a bomb man. He had plenty of experience responding to FARC bombs laid for the police, judges and elected officials. Later, he was trained by the DEA and U.S. Special Forces to blow up cocaine labs. He was even tapped occasionally to blow up FARC officials hiding in the Ecuadorian border country.

Last Friday, Eduardo and his partners had driven to the two railway bridges and he surveyed the spans to be blown. He had been furnished photos of the bridges with markings as to the precise location where the metal burning incendiaries were to be placed.

Every day dozens of freight trains carried tons of coal from the fields to the west to electric power plants in Wisconsin and Minnesota. The loss of those bridges and two others in South Dakota would effectively close the power plants. As winter closed in on the Upper Great Plains, millions would be without heat or electricity. Within days, as the stockpiles of coal dwindled at the power plants, millions of Americans in the Midwest would be in darkness and as the winter winds blew across the prairies, they would be without heat. They had just delivered the ninth plague, darkness to the Upper Midwest.

It was late evening by the time the last man crawled down from the next bridge to the north. By then the first bridge had crumbled into the river as would this structure before the men drove off. Eduardo set the SUV's GPS system to the location he had been given to make the border crossing into Canada's vast farmland.

Saturday, October 13th

Refugio, Texas

GORDO HAD MADE MANY TAKEOFFS and landings on clandestine airfields flying for Columbian narcotics traffickers. He had no trouble taking off from Roger Wilcox's field. Well, his increasingly big stomach actually got in the way of pulling the yoke back on takeoff. He had to pull a couple of inches into the fat to get off the ground. He wiped his thick black mustache and enjoyed the thought of how angry the arrogant Wilcox would be at the loss of his Cirrus. Gordo was still stinging over the ass-chewing he received for the ride Chung gave him in the tractor. The smile grew even broader at the thought of the C-4 packages they had left on Wilcox's diesel fuel tanks and on the propane tank next to the residence. Come to think of it, Wilcox may be too dead to be pissed.

In perfect weather, he and little Chuy flew a low altitude course to the southwest, towards Corpus Christi. In the rear of the plane lay explosives which would be dropped on their targets. Weeks ago, Gordo and Chuy had practiced their technique in the deserts of Mexico flying in a plane provided by the Mexican Army courtesy of the narcotics traffickers. For two days in the desert, Gordo flew over big oval targets drawn in Mexico's big sandbox. As they passed over each oval, Chuy threw pineapples out the door onto the makeshift targets. By the end of the second day they had reached near perfection with their accuracy.

Acting as navigator, Chuy directed Gordo towards their first target. Chuy had downloaded satellite photos from Google Earth along with the GPS coordinates. As they approached Corpus Christi, he saw the first refinery and elbowed Gordo, pointing to the large storage tanks several miles away. The obese pilot dropped the Cirrus to below 500 feet and gunned the engine. They expected no antiaircraft protection and they weren't disappointed. As they were only meters away from the first tank, Gordo dropped his airspeed and banked to his starboard to allow his passenger the best target opportunity. He hurled his first incendiary directly onto the tank. Gordo repeated his maneuver on a tank a hundred meters beyond and the second incendiary landed dead center.

One more pass and two more throws and they flew off to the next refinery and then a third. Chuy kept his accuracy at 100% which they celebrated by popping two Coronas. Flying at about 50 feet off the gulf water, they headed for Mexico where they would be picked up after landing on a desert airstrip. As they crossed the Mexican border unmolested, Gordo swung the plane to the north and gained a few thousand feet of altitude so they could admire their work. Plumes of black smoke could be seen in the horizon as they rose thousands of feet into the clear blue sky. As the clouds covered the area, day turned into night. The ninth plague, darkness, had just been delivered to southern Texas. Although Gordo couldn't see it, the workers on the refinery grounds were engulfed in flames and smoke. Only hell could produce a worse inferno. Fortunately, for most, death came mercifully quick.

Saturday, October 13th

Lakeside Café
Wayzata, Minnesota

WITH 15 MINUTES TO SPARE before the motorcade departure, Agents Lyons and Brothers finished lunch and were on their way out of the Lakeside Café. Her cell phone rang as she slid into the passenger seat. Tony started the car and waited.

"That was the command post. Evidently some genius just remembered his Sunday School lesson and realized the last of the plagues sent on Egypt was the death of the first born males including the pharaoh's son. We're going to triple the detail when we get back to the airport and the president wants the first lady and his son back in Washington.

"Let's head back to the mansion and when 'Rainbow' and 'Lightening' are in the limo, we'll run the route ahead of the motorcade again."

"Yes, Ma'am," Tony offered a sloppy salute.

Tony dialed the radio to KSPP and he heard news reports first of the cleanup of the insect and frog infestation at Arlington and then breaking news of refinery fires raging out of control in Texas. The national news ended with an interview of a U.S. Forest Service public relations representative who cited unprecedented forest fires in the Rockies and speculated that severe lightening from thunderstorms on Saturday may have been the cause. Local news began with the visit of the first lady and Cody and ended with a prediction of increasing thunderstorms.

"Have your people hardened security at the White House since the plagues?"

"On POTUS and the V.P., we've increased tremendously. Of course, that leaves us stretched thin on the other protectees. Then it doesn't help that half the foreign dignitaries in the world are in New York City or Washington. They all come with their hands out and we have to provide liaison agents for each."

"So, you're a little short-handed?"

"That would be an understatement. And with elections coming up, it's one money run after another."

They waited in a church parking lot near the mansion for only six minutes when an agent reported over the radio that 'Rainbow' and 'Lightening' were in the first lady's limo.

"Let's Go!" Agent Lyons said a little too loud.

Again, without exchanging words, they drove along the route, taking Highway 12 to eastbound 494. Tony watched the freeway ramps which were guarded by patrol cars, fill up with waiting motorists, most of who were impatient and had no idea why their lives were being interrupted. Neither agent saw any potential threats on the route – no stalled vehicles or people on foot.

Saturday, October 13th

Bloomington, Minnesota

LACKING THE PRECISION OF THE Secret Service, however, still on time, Alberto Hernandez, Juan Robles, Beto and Pepe rode in two freshly washed black Suburbans. Both bristled with antennas and had concealed police emergency lights in the grills and the rear windows. They looked no different than the Suburbans in the motorcade. The men monitored the local police radio frequencies which had been designated for the first lady's trip and heard the State Patrol, Hennepin County and local officers report the progress of the motorcade. They listened without speaking and waited. Pepe, whose English was superb thanks to an American college student he lived with for two years, followed the motorcade's progress on a large colored map laid out on his lap. His finger followed the route so Alberto could time his movement.

They were tired as they had been awake going on 20 hours. Only Beto who had furtively snorted some meth an hour earlier didn't feel the fatigue. At 1:00 a.m. they had returned to the MNDOT parking lot and remotely started the two orange MNDOT trucks. Memo and Lalo 'drove' them away from the unguarded parking lot. They parked two blocks away where Memo and Lalo got into the driver's seat with their controllers and took them out on the freeway. They practiced until they were satisfied they felt they could accomplish their mission and only then driving the two trucks to a rented warehouse in Bloomington.

Alberto held a last briefing which concluded with each man reciting his exact responsibilities. They loaded 20 round magazines into their AR-15s, tested their Motorola Sabre portable radios as well as the lights and sirens on the Suburbans and waited.

Hernandez listened intently to the police radio traffic describing the movement of the first lady and her son to the fundraiser. Pepe held his right index finger on the ambush site. His left finger moved across the map with the motorcade. The fingers came closer together as each second ticked by.

Earlier, allowing themselves a cushion of time, they slipped out of the rented warehouse at intervals each following exactly the route laid out on their briefing papers. They conducted radio checks as they drove to their posts to wait.

Lalo and Memo drove the two MNDOT trucks to the freeway entrance ramp located at France Avenue and I-494. They were followed by an orange MNDOT van which had been purchased months earlier at a state surplus auction.

Memo and Lalo each stepped down from the truck which they had parked next to a Hennepin County Sheriff Patrol squad. The deputy was assigned to the intersection to close access to the freeway entrance before the motorcade even got close. The deputy powered his window down. A ball game was playing loudly on his radio. He reached over and turned down the volume.

"Shut down the I-494 ramps," the dispatcher ordered over the police radio.

Memo, who spoke the best English, addressed the officer, "Officer, my boss say we park here to block the freeway ramp. Where you want us?"

Deputy Quam looked at the Hispanic man wearing a blue cotton work shirt. Reading his name tag, he addressed the worker, "Ernesto, I don't know nothing about no MNDOT trucks, who sent you?"

"The boss man sent a bunch of the trucks, man. Said we were to block traffic. I got lost so I'm late, but boss say go anyway."

"No one told me about MNDOT trucks but not telling me is pretty much the norm. Let me check with Dispatch and see what they know."

As Deputy Quam reached for his microphone, Memo stepped back from the brown and white squad and removed his Twins baseball cap. Seeing Memo's cap off, Chole flipped the toggle switch on the control panel of the Audio Jammer.

Deputy Quam's radio and MDC went berserk with static. He dropped the microphone and tried sending a message on his mobile computer, nothing. He picked up his cell phone and dialed, nothing. It was as though he had been delivered to electronic purgatory.

"Ernesto, you two just wait next to your truck. I have to stop traffic here. Just sit next to your truck," Quam ordered not knowing what else to do.

"I just wait here like boss say," Ernesto replied agreeably.

Forgetting about Ernesto and pissed off about his radios and even more pissed about missing the Gopher football game on his AM radio, Deputy Quam lit up his squad's emergency lights and blocked the east bound entrance ramp to prevent traffic from entering as the motorcade passed.

Memo and Lalo slipped away and joined Chole in the van. Memo and Lalo each opened a Pelican case exposing a computer screen and a control panel. The controls they manned were rudimentary but functional.

There were nine vehicles in the motorcade. A State Patrol squad led the procession followed by a Secret Service full sized SUV. Four glimmering black limos containing the protectees and staff were sandwiched in between two more Secret Service SUVs. Trailing behind the motorcade was a State SWAT truck positioned to protect the rear. The motorcade continued towards the France Avenue exchange about five minutes away.

As the motorcade passed the highway 169 ramp, the two black Suburbans with lights flashing approached the deputy blocking the bridge. Driving the lead Suburban, Alberto gave a short burst of his siren and waved for the deputy to move aside. Without hesitation or question of authority he did and both Suburbans blew by him racing down the ramp, lights flashing, sirens blaring.

The last vehicle in the motorcade was the armored SWAT truck operated by the Highway Patrol. It carried the State Police SWAT team running tail gunner duties. As the two Suburbans closed on the State Patrol rig, the team leader spoke excitedly on Statewide Radio.

"Trooper 6, we have two black SUVs closing on us fast with police lights flashing, are they your guys?"

The detail leader quickly responded, “No, Trooper 6, stop and identify or engage them. You’ve permission to leave the motorcade.”

To the lead vehicle driver, Trooper Lt. Moss, the detail leader ordered, “Pick up the pace now and fast until we sort this out.”

Lt. Moss and the rest of the motorcade pushed to over 100 mph as Trooper 6 dropped behind to confront the SUVs.

Lt. Moss reached 105 mph and then grabbed his microphone, “We’ve two MNDOT trucks approaching in our lanes coming from the France off ramp.”

At speeds over 100 mph and little reaction time to sort out this newest transmission, the detail leader shouted over the microphone to bootleg turn, however, those few delayed seconds of reaction allowed the MNDOT trucks to pass both sides of the Lt.’s Crown Vic and the first motorcade limo. The first lady saw the trucks, covered her eyes and screamed. Cody had been playing a video game and never saw the events unfold. As the trucks cleared the first limo by feet and were meeting the second limo both exploded causing the entire motorcade to careen, roll or simply disappear.

Trooper 6, a mile back, had stopped, the SWAT Team jumped out, M-16s trained on the Suburbans which had slowed but still sped by Trooper 6, weaved through and passed the crumbled motorcade.

Deputy Quam ran to the orange MNDOT van when he saw the large trucks enter the exit ramp. He drew his pistol and screamed as he approached the van. Chole leveled a machine gun and through the rear window unleashed two bursts into the deputy.

In the chaos, the two Suburbans drove past the destruction without interference and exited France Avenue to join their MNDOT partners to drive to the warehouse.

Saturday, October 13th

Camp David, Maryland

PRESIDENT FRANKLIN WAS MEETING WITH staff when he noticed the net of Secret Service around him double and then triple. Artis Dumont, the lead Secret Service agent, had a worried if not panicked look on his face as he uncharacteristically interrupted the president in mid-sentence.

"Mr. President, I have terrible news, your son has been gravely injured during an accident in Minneapolis. The first lady is in critical condition." He continued talking, although the president heard nothing he said. Falling back into an executive chair, he covered his face and began to sob. His chief of staff rushed to his side and embraced him. The press secretary broke into tears. The president's medical staff had been led in and escorted the president to a lounge off the conference room. They gave him tranquillizers to calm him. It was as if his very soul had left his body.

Dr. Conner took Agent Dumont aside along with the chief of staff, "You better get the vice president over here now. I don't think he is capable of performing his duties."

Saturday, October 13th

White House Press Room
Washington, D.C.

IN FRONT OF THE THRONG of reporters and cameras, Peter 'Petey' Mahoney, the Presidential Press Secretary did his best, "We all share our sorrow with the president and his family for these unspeakable acts. I want to assure you that despite this cowardly terrorist attack on the president's family, the president is in control and the American people need to know that we will find those responsible. I ask all Americans to support President Franklin and pray for him and his family."

Saturday, October 13

Brainerd, Minnesota

DOC HAD RETRIEVED HIS OLD hunting dog, Snip, from his ex-wife, Kelly. He promised to have the English setter returned in one piece before dark. They were up before sunrise and headed to the Lake country to hunt grouse. By 9:00 they were already at the fast food drive thru in Little Falls where he ordered McMuffins and coffee. Snip devoured his McMuffin and then vultured Doc until his was spilt and shared.

Just north of Brainerd, the home of Paul Bunyan and Babe the blue ox, Doc hit the old logging trails he had hunted for weeks when he returned from Vietnam and needed to clear his mind. He parked the Durango and they set afoot alone in the miles of rough paths. It was a clear and windy day. The last of the leaves from the white birch were being blown to the ground after stubbornly clinging to the treetops. Nose to the ground, Snip set a brisk pace for Doc who was a few thousand cigarettes past prime condition. Two miles down the trail, he stopped for a smoke as Snip chased two ravens feeding on a deer carcass. The screaming black birds retreated to a nearby Norway pine and hurled insults. They had put several miles over the next four hours when Doc called the dog to a downed tree where they rested in the sunshine, Doc scratching the dog behind the ears and enjoying each other until the cell phone vibrated in his pocket. He cursed, reached into his pocket removed his phone and read the text message, 'Presidents son killed in motorcade ambush. Call in to dispatch ASAP.'

He quickly dialed his dispatcher in St. Paul only to find he had no service. He swore again and slowly jogged back to the Dodge, ignoring the grouse flushed by Snip. His mind raced. What could have happened? Then, as always, guilt darken his mind – I shouldn't have taken a day off – repeated itself like broken tape player. Doc would feel remorse at missing the Titanic slipping into the deep blue sea. He felt guilt when the Space Shuttle Challenger blew to smithereens before his very eyes. If he'd been there carrying out his duties, he could have prevented these disasters. He would carry those neurotic burdens to his grave.

Saturday, October 13th

Executive Airport Terminal
St. Paul, Minnesota

AFTER THE VICIOUS ATTACK, ALBERTO Hernandez and his men returned to the Bloomington warehouse. They changed clothes and cars and left the deserted metal building in Armando Gomez' Buick Century and Gran Prix driving to the Executive Jet Terminal in St. Paul. Dressed in expensive looking suits they'd purchased at the Goodwill and carrying briefcases, they walked past the State Patrol Air Wing headquarters. To the Trooper pilots rushing past the men, the assassins appeared to be busy business executives.

They wasted little time boarding the Gulfstream V executive jet. The pilot filed a flight plan showing a trip to Vancouver, Canada. As the jet rocketed skyward, they left little trace behind of their brief visit to Minnesota, except for the carnage on the bloody freeway.

Sunday, October 14th

Camp David, Maryland

VICE PRESIDENT GRINLING GIBBONS CALLED an emergency Cabinet meeting. He didn't comprehend the totality of the circumstances which seemed to change by the minute. It was no great secret that he and the President were not close, in fact the vice president was added to the ballot as an unpopular party compromise. Truth be known, he despised the president and he was as much surprised that the President would relinquish control as he was to learn of Cody's death.

The vice president ordered his staff to set the wheels in motion to formally pass the presidential authority.

He entered the Hickory conference room where all available cabinet members and executive staff crowded the room – others appeared on T.V. monitors. Many clutched Kleenex in hands and wet bloodshot eyes dominated the faces.

"Gentlemen, Ladies, I would never wish to take this seat under these circumstances, however, fate has cast me for this position. I want to assure you that I am in charge and the government will continue to function to protect our borders. We will break for 55 minutes to allow each of you to meet with your designated groups to initiate the protocols for my assumption of the presidential duties. When we reconvene you will provide me with your recommendations on what immediate actions are required.

"General Highcamp, I will meet with you and the Defense Secretary now."

The general and Secretary Herrington moved off in a corner. CIA Director John Rankin joined them and spoke first, "Mr. Vice President, forgive my interruption – I believe this is crucial to our immediate actions."

The vice president, who oddly had never had a personal conversation with Director Rankin, nodded for the man to continue.

"We have intercepted cell phone calls between al Qaeda members. We have been listening for about a week. They normally aren't so careless, but there's been a lot of chatter about the al Qaeda threats. Shortly after the attack on the first lady, we intercepted a call which seemed to be a congratulatory call to Rashid Rauf, an al Qaeda lieutenant. Our analysts think that Rauf must have been a player if not the mastermind in this attack. It's unusual but Rauf has been residing in one place for the last week."

"Where is he?" asked the vice president.

"He is in a tiny village south of Ahva, Iran, on the Iran/Iraq border. We have two of our operatives watching the compound. Iranian soldiers have the place well-guarded. They aren't able to move in for a confirmation of the target."

General Highcamp spoke up, "We have two Stryker groups in that area."

Defense Secretary Nelson Herrington quickly noted, "General, that would be an invasion of Iran."

They all looked to the vice president, "I want Rashid Rauf captured or killed, tough shit if Iran chose to hide this assassin. General, set that in motion, immediately!"

CIA Director Rankin, sensing an opening for a change of policy, took a chance, "Mr. Vice President, one more thing. Our officer in Charikar, Afghanistan picked up an informant who gave us a terrorist named Ali Shah Masood. By applying some extraordinary persuasion, the informant admitted that Ali has much information about al Qaeda plans. The informant has no specifics about the attacks, however, he knows Ali Shah Masood does have the knowledge. Sir, if we could take off the gloves perhaps. . ."

"Do it, use whatever means that will produce fast results. I'll take care of your people if the media gets a hold of this. We will never have a better opportunity."

Monday, October 15th

Bansko, Bulgaria

FOR THREE DAYS THE THUNDERSHOWERS had pounded the mountain. The temperatures set new lows as the clouds blocked the sun for the fifth day in a row. The Bulgarian version of flash flood warnings were issued over the television and radio. There would be no travel near the deep ravines and canyons until the waters had receded.

"Ali Shah Masood is an unusually strong man. I don't have high hopes that we'll get much, if anything, using these extraordinary measures. You know when they're this committed to a cause, it's like thinking St. Peter would climb down off the cross," Ed Mitchell said.

"We need to get with Director Lang and explain this to him before we kill Ali and are left here empty-handed," Joseph Young suggested. He rubbed the back of his neck to relieve the fatigue. Torture is hard work.

Twenty minutes later Mitchell, Young, and Rocky were enjoying cognac and fat cigars with Michael Lang, the CIA Deputy Director of European and Russian Operations. The Director had set up a temporary office in the third floor. Lang was a handsome man in his mid-fifties, silver hair parted in the middle. He looked like a Boston blue blood patrician. His background, however, was far from that. He was born to humble circumstances on the South Dakota prairies where his parents eked out an existence from a rocky farmstead better suited for buffalo than growing crops or grazing cattle. His maternal grandparents, both German immigrants from the Ukraine, lived with the family. With six brothers and two sisters there were a lot of mouths to feed at the Lang homestead.

Oddly enough, this familial arrangement gave Lang his purpose in life. He learned to speak and write both German and Russian from his grandparents during the long winter evenings. His mother was a teacher before marrying his father and home schooled young Michael. He received an academic scholarship to Georgetown and was recruited by the CIA after his first year of graduate school. Lang had no desire to return to the farm although he missed his family and visited frequently.

His language skills and quick mind earned him rapid promotions in the CIA and he was an unrecognized hero of the Cold War.

"Director Lang that's our dilemma, we can push the issue although it's likely we'll kill him without getting the desired results," Mitchell offered after he had described in detail their efforts to extract information from Ali.

"Gentlemen, I appreciate your candor. Let me add something you don't know. Apparently friends or perhaps enemies of Ali are at our doorstep. Our counter-surveillance group has been watching at least seven men who have this castle under surveillance. Given what happened to Bagran Air Base, I believe we need to move Ali. That being the case, I've another idea how we may use Ali Shah Masood."

Lang strolled to a large cathedral style window and to view the sun breaking through the thick dark clouds. He continued, "What I'm telling you if we go through with this plan, and it fails, we alone will know. To all others, our superiors, Congress, the vice president, will know only that Ali died as we transported him away from danger. Is that clear?" Lang asked.

"Yes Sir!" they replied somewhat relieved that their boss had a plan that would remove some of the pressure to perform in what would be a crap shoot at best. Their spirits buoyed as they departed the great room.

When they were gone, Director Lang made a hurried phone call back to America – on a cell phone that didn't exist.

Monday, October 15th

44 Wall Street
New York City

RAIN WAS BEATING ON THE large office window pane as Bernie Silverstein pulled out a bottle of Armagnac Brandy from the freshly polished mahogany cabinet and called his secretary, "Cindy, come in here, I'm not going to drink alone." Bernie shuffled to the conference table and poured two glasses. He plopped into the red leather chair and put his feet on the table, something he'd never done before. This day was different – he sensed there had never before been a day like this.

"This isn't good, is it?" Cindy asked Bernie after she'd joined him. She sensed a look of concern if not panic on his face.

"Not if you own stocks, or bonds, for that matter."

Bernie pushed the buttons on his remote until CNN News appeared on his television. Cindy and he watched the reports of the attack on the first lady and the death of her son. By now the reporters were re-playing al Zawahri's threat to bring plagues to the Americans. First they showed the refinery fires. Then they played al Zawahri. They played footage of the frogs and insects at Arlington Cemetery and then al Zawahri and his predecessor, bin Laden. Tired looking reporters provided live coverage at the collapsed railroad bridges, the downed power lines and the out-of-control fires in the Rockies. Retired military generals provided expert commentary connecting of all of these disasters to al Qaeda. Bernie turned the sound to mute upon hearing that these events had caused panic in the market until the Board closed trading to halt the fall.

"Tomorrow is going to be worse than today, I fear." Silverstein shuffled over to the window and peered through the closed blinds to see if the investors were jumping from the windows. "It's not raining brokers yet."

"What's going on?" asked Cindy.

"The first lady thing is to be expected, everyone thinks it's an Islamic terrorist attack, probably is, however, the selling began before that news. Then you've these retired generals saying that all of the other events are terrorist attacks. There is more going on here, it's hard to put my finger on it – last Thursday and Friday, it was mostly foreign investors who put sell orders in unheard of numbers. This is going to be worse than 911 if we open tomorrow and the foreign money continues to pull out."

He poured her another glass of brandy, "My father gave me this brandy thirty years ago. Save it for a time when things don't look so good. It will make it better. That's what he told me. To a better tomorrow!" He found comfort in the fact that years ago he had sold much of his stock and bond portfolio and bought diamonds and gold.

Monday, October 15th

Castle Creek Chalet
Aspen, Colorado

ABOLHASEN MUMTAZ, DRESSED IN A neon green warm up suit and matching sneakers, joined Omar on the deck in front of the massive stone fireplace. Fragrant pine logs burned brightly on the grates. Omar sported a new après ski outfit and with his feet on the deck's railing, he looked very American. Snow was again blessing the skiers who were enjoying the earliest opening on record.

"Allah is with us, our successes have been many," began Omar happily. "We've much to discuss as couriers bring news.

"A friend in Europe has found Ali Shah Masood. I've sent men to Bulgaria to watch the castle where he is confined. Allah has protected him from these men, we know he hasn't talked or quite frankly many of us would be dead.

"Our source in the White House press corps says that rumor is the president has been ruined and the vice president is now acting as the president. He is anxious to find the attackers and we are going to help him." Omar leaned forward and took a drink of strong tea served in a white porcelain cup.

"Do you believe it is time to give al Qaeda to the Americans?" Mumtaz asked almost in a whisper.

"Last week, we arranged for a loyal brother to travel to Iran near the Iraq/Iran border and stage cell phone conversations which will lead the Americans to believe al Qaeda is responsible for the death of the president's son. We've watched the Americans staging near the border. We welcome their attack as it will give us an opportunity to show the Americans that they are vulnerable."

Not wanting to push Omar on the timetable, Mumtaz changed the subject. "I was just looking at the headlines on AOL before I joined you. I was surprised to read that Venezuela's president publicly applauded the attacks on American soil. He even praised the attack on the first family."

"Our agents arranged with Venezuela's president to accommodate travel for our operatives to America. The president has been assisting narco-traffickers with transportation and refuge for several years so this sort of thing is nothing new to him. He supports these narcotics dealers as they contribute to the internal destruction of the United States. We have a common goal in that regard.

"I might add that we've provided our aid to the cocaine traffickers from Columbia. They can triple their money by selling cocaine in Europe instead of America. We transport the product to a safe haven in Libya where it is moved to the southern coastal area of Europe. We also profit substantially for our efforts."

Mumtaz smiled at the irony of assisting the drug dealers when in his homeland they would be put to death for selling the narcotics – whatever it takes to destroy the enemy.

"I was reading the *Wall Street Journal* website and the American economy is in turmoil."

Omar was slow to comment as if assessing how much he should disclose to his new protégé – his tongue slightly protruding feeling the air. "This plan is working as we had expected. As you know the stock market has crashed. Markets in India, China, and Europe closed to avoid a panicked run to sell. As important, our actions conducted through our trusts and international corporations have remained anonymous. As we knew when the crash was coming and know when it will be relieved, we will not only avoid losses but profit handsomely. We'll keep this pressure on until America is out of our homelands and Israel is no more."

Mumtaz continued with his assessment of the news coverage. "The American media have cancelled all other programs and are covering the plagues 24/7. I believe the president will listen when we present our demands."

"Events will unfold rapidly." Omar had decided that he'd gone far enough for the moment. "Have you ever skied?" Omar asked as he gestured towards the ski runs of Aspen. A few skiers were shushing down the newly opened runs as snow seemed to kiss the slopes nearly every night.

Mumtaz looked curiously at Omar and sensed he'd pushed enough for now. It would be foolish to push for more.

Monday, October 15th

Camp David, Maryland

PRESIDENT FRANKLIN LAY ON THE plaid upholstered couch, barefoot and wearing exercise pants and a sweatshirt bearing the Presidential Seal, staring at the ceiling.

"Mr. President, I appreciate you seeing me in private," offered Vice President Gibbons. "I know you are suffering and I'll keep it brief.

"We have a major crisis on our hands. The refinery fires will be an economic disaster. They will take years to rebuild and we were already years behind on increasing refining capacity. I have ordered all National Guard Units not serving in the Middle East to the Rockies to fight the fires. The railroad bridges will stop the flow of coal to major Midwest Cities and they will soon be without power and heat. New York is a mess with the downed power lines. Looters have taken to the streets and we have little resources to send to restore order. I've directed private security forces to harden the defenses of the nuclear power plants.

"The CIA believes that the Iranians are harboring al Qaeda terrorists who are responsible for these horrendous attacks. I have ordered our Army to enter Iran and seize or destroy these terrorists.

"Mr. President, you and I haven't always got along, however, I want you to know, I will get revenge for your loss. If the soldiers entering Iran find al Qaeda terrorists responsible for this, I will reduce that country to rubble, even if it means using nuclear weapons."

The president looked up and feebly nodded. "I just need a bit more time to get back on my feet. Just a bit more time…." He waved the vice president away.

Monday, October 15th

FBI Anti-Terrorist Unit
Minneapolis, Minnesota

THE F.B.I. ASAIC CALLED A 4:00 a.m. emergency meeting for all hands in the squad. No donuts and coffee for this meeting. The ASAIC had not slept since the attack on the motorcade. He looked frazzled and frankly panicked. The investigation had put him in the national spotlight and he clearly was uncomfortable with the attention.

"We're dropping every other investigation until we have these murderers in custody. I want 110% from each of you. All vacations are cancelled. We are going to live here until we have these guys behind bars."

Doc interrupted the ASAIC's failing attempt to motivate the troops, "Do we have any suspects, any leads?"

"Of course, the phones are ringing off the hook. We've had dozens of citizens visiting our office offering leads. We'll follow up on each of these leads. I've a dozen analysts grading each one as we speak. A priority number, one through ten, will be assigned to each lead. We'll start with the tens and work our way down to the poorest leads."

"Are there any ten leads yet?" Doc asked.

"No, although I am told there are a couple of fives."

Doc continued, "Do you have a working theory of who may have done this?"

The ASAIC was clearly agitated by Doc's questions. "Of course the Islamic terrorists are behind this. al Qaeda's al Zawahri has been threatening to bring plagues on the Americans and you might recall the biblical account of the plagues included killing the pharaoh's first born son. He as much as warned us this would happen."

Doc ignored the ASAIC's impatience, "I agree, but do we have some local suspects in mind? Anyone we could go put some pressure on?"

"For the moment, we will follow what's been called in and send agents to solicit more leads from the local Islamic leaders. Let's move on. I want to make some assignments here and get moving on this..."

It took a few hours to make the assignments and then the ASAIC retreated to his office. Doc followed him. "Sorry to put you on the spot, boss. I just have the feeling that there aren't any good leads on suspects and that we'll waste a lot of time and talent."

"There'll be no wasted time here. We have a plan and we'll be adhering to it. The major crimes unit from national headquarters will be up and running in Minneapolis today. They'll take over the leadership and we'll support them."

"Do any of the agents have solid informants into the radical Islamic community? I mean I have a whole herd of informants in the criminal world but zilch in the Islamic world. I may be out of place, but it's not the average Joe practicing the Muslim religion we're looking for."

"You know we've few assets in that community. Many are still upset after we combed through their families after 911. The informants we do have aren't al Qaeda, many are just seeking favors concerning immigration matters. Unfortunately, we found many times they make allegations against their enemies just to cause them trouble."

"And they waste our time pointing fingers at their own enemies..."

"Doc, between us, I don't think we have a single good lead, however, we have to give it our best effort. The HQ guys are beside themselves again."

"I'm here to support you, although I gotta tell you that I'm not in favor of just running roughshod over the Muslims. That makes enemies of half the world and right now what we need are friends!"

"You got any better ideas?"

"Boss, I gotta tell you, I got zero ideas. I'm embarrassed to say it. I just don't know where to start. I mean the crime scene is taken care of. We just need some leads on the perps."

"That makes me feel better that a hot shot like you isn't out in front of this."

"I can follow up with the MN Department of Transportation. I will check the cameras on the ground where the trucks were taken and see if there was an insider. It beats following leads offered by the kooks who come out of the woodwork when something like this happens."

"Have at it – be sure to take one our agents with you and bring the film back to the guys from the national office," the ASAIC said.

"Sure."

Doc drove faster than prudent to the MNDOT building on the east side of St. Paul. He parked in front of the large brick building. The gates to the rear which were usually open were locked shut and a maroon Patrol squad was parked behind the gate. Nothing like shutting the barn door after the horses have gotten out. He walked into the reception area where an older woman at the switchboard was overwhelmed and on the verge of tears. Doc waited for her to acknowledge him, "I'm a special agent with the FBI Anti-Terrorist Task Force and would like to speak with the site manager."

"All inquires are being handled downtown at the Commissioner's Office."

"I understand the media is being referred to the Commissioner's Office, however, I need to talk to the manager here."

"He is in a meeting."

"I'll wait."

An hour later a pink-faced chubby man dressed in an ill-fitting pinstripe suit and matching striped tie waddled up to Doc, "I understand you're with the FBI and want to see me."

Doc stood and offered his credentials to the manager.

The manager held his small smooth hands up as though to fend off an attack. "No, no. I can't answer any questions. The Commissioner's

Office is handling this. You will have to go downtown to talk to them. I can't say anything."

"I just wanted to get some basic information that I'm sure the Commissioner's Office would only have to ask you anyway."

"No, no, no, I have been told to answer no questions."

"I was hoping to get the TV surveillance tapes covering the time period when the trucks were stolen."

"No, no, the tapes have already been sent to the Commissioner's Office. You must go down there to deal with them." Heavy beads of perspiration formed on his flushed forehead.

"You know you are really starting to piss me off. I'm starting to wonder if you have something to hide. I'm thinking maybe I should arrest your sorry bureaucratic ass and then see if you would be more cooperative."

"No, no, no. I have nothing to hide. I'm just taking orders. Those are my orders. I have to go back to my office now." He turned quickly and clumsily jogged back to the refuge of his office.

Doc was so utterly disappointed he didn't know what to do other than make the drive downtown. He lit a smoke as he walked back to his car and promised himself that he would not make a scene at the Commissioner's Office. He knew he would not keep that promise.

Tuesday, October 16th

Desert Country
North of Basrah
Iran/Iraq Border

LT. JOHN MATTHEWS HAD JOCKEYED tanks for almost 17 years. He was in Bush's first war and fought again for Bush's son, rolling into Baghdad 15 years later. He wanted little in life other than to drive tanks for the United States Army. Matthews had risen well before dawn, grabbed a quick cup of watery coffee, and hurried to the tank corral at the edge of the tent camp. Two of the enlisted men were already warming the engine when he arrived. They spent the next hour before daybreak preparing the behemoth for battle. As the sun broke the horizon above the sand, a dozen tanks rolled noisily towards Iran. Lt. Matthews knew he should be fearful or at least apprehensive at attacking however, after watching the Iraqi armies fold before the American forces, he expected an even more dismal showing by the Iranians. He stood tall in the turret and felt proud to be a part of the invasion force rolling across the border, kicking up dust that rose a hundred feet into the air.

His driver set GPS coordinates in the FNS system of the on-board computer. Not unlike an aircraft auto-pilot, the tank required little guidance once its course was laid out. Earlier, Lt. Matthews had joined the other officers at a lengthy briefing which the colonel began, "Gentlemen, we are invading Iran this morning!" The colonel, in a style General Patton would have envied, went on to describe a mission to invade Iran to capture the al Qaeda terrorists responsible for the attack on the First Family.

Lt. Matthews' tank group rolled across the border without incident and cruised towards Ahvaz, Iran. Lt. Matthews stood in the Abrams M1A1 tank turret with binoculars in hand. "Slow down to 10," he ordered as he strained in his gyro binocular. "We have three trucks shadowing us about 2 klicks to the south," he reported to the tank squadron commander.

"Any threats?" was the reply from the commander.

"Just trucks, can't see any weapons." The wind and the tanks were stirring up a large cloud of dust driving visibility down to nothing.

"Keep an eye on them. I'll send Apache helicopters above and behind them."

"Roger that," replied Lt. Matthews.

The tank group was about four klicks into Iran when Lt. Matthews' tank jerked violently to the right, increased speed, turned sharply right again and headed back towards the border.

"What the hell are you doing? You idiot!"

Sgt. Collins defended himself. "Sir, I didn't do this. I can't get control of this bastard. It's gone berserk."

"Take this tank back on track, Sergeant!" the lieutenant shouted.

"LT, I can't."

Lt. Matthews dropped down to the controls and elbowed Sgt. Collins aside.

Col. Harris in the rear of the squadron couldn't believe his eyes as four more tanks moved out of formation almost colliding with nearby tanks and headed back towards Iraq.

It took two hours for the crews to regain their composure and regroup at the border. The mission aborted, Colonel Harris met with General Arnold who, with staff and technical specialists, had flown to the border. The general's first order was for the colonel to get the imbedded news reporters under wraps. His second order was to determine, "What the hell is wrong with the computers!" Junior grade officers rushed to obey both orders.

"Under no circumstances are they to make any satellite uplinks, do you understand, Colonel?" the general barked referring to the reporters.

"Yes Sir, we will take their phones."

"Do what you have to do."

....

Back in Vancouver, Howard Chung was pleased with the results. The Iranian trucks trailing the tank column reported a smashing success. That deserved a commensurate reward. He picked up his cell phone and called Elite Escort Service ordering not one but two escorts for the evening. His next call was to his marijuana source. He ordered enough for himself and the two girls to last the night. That being done, he methodically shut down his computer up links and did his best to destroy and delete any trace of his activities.

Tuesday, October 16th

Cotoctin Mountain Park, Maryland

CARLOS ESTEBAN AND PEDRO FRANCISCO wearing full-body dry suits crept along the bottom of Hunting Crook Lake tethered by a loosely attached black nylon ski rope. Using GPS positions, they knew they were close to crossing the Camp David boundaries. Both skilled underwater divers, they were comfortable using the rebreathers and navigating with GPS.

Swimming behind them, Amir and Datu dragged Chinese made QW-2 shoulder launched missiles. They had rigged four neutral buoyancy harnesses to keep them below surface although off the floor of the lake. The rigging required frequent adjustments and slowed their progress. They harbored no hopes of surviving if they were discovered as they had no intentions of surrendering.

The brackish water allowed about three feet of visibility, however, they dared not surface to get oriented. When Esteban reached what they believed was the border they slowed to a standstill searching for sensors. With the poor visibility, Esteban wasn't confident he would see any sensors anyway. He plodded along more feeling his way than seeing. The others followed, each taking turns pushing the gear ahead of them. They worked deliberately and breathed shallowly knowing they were stretching the limits to get to their desired launch site. Each man carried a Russian APS underwater 5.56 rifle, MREs for a week, and water purification tablets.

When Esteban reached their intended hidie-hole which they had selected from satellite photos, he switched to a snorkel and allowed his diving mask to just break the water's surface. He studied the shoreline of the wooded marsh for 20 minutes and then went back down, signaling for the others to go to snorkels. They did and each surfaced again showing nothing more than black tubes and a tiny part of the masks. For an hour they watched and waited before Esteban broke away and crawled to shore.

As he waited for his partners, he thought about his friend, Flaviano Zulueta. They had split up shortly after crossing the Canadian Border and securing the weapons they'd picked up from the shipyards. Zulueta had traveled to a second safe house to wait for orders to carry out his assignment. Esteban wished he could trade places with Zulueta knowing that Zulueta wouldn't be laying in the weeds for days. His thoughts turned back to the woods in front of him. He watched and waited another 30 minutes before he was joined by the others.

Ashore, without speaking, they slowly created a hideout from available brush and cover suitable to begin their vigilance.

Tuesday, October 16th

St. Paul, Minnesota

DOC WAS UP EARLY AND finishing his first cup of coffee and second Camel when his cell phone rang. He set down *A Connecticut Yankee in King Arthur's Court* and answered the phone with a mumble. It was Austin, the Assistant Superintendent. They dispensed with the niceties as both knew an early morning phone call would be contentious at best. Austin got right to the point, "Her Highness, The Highway Commissioner herself, called me yesterday. She tracked me down in Duluth and she was not happy."

"Boss, you don't have to call me at 6:30 to give me the Commissioner's Happiness Report. I know we both have better things to do."

"She said that you threatened to arrest her manager and then barged into the headquarters office making demands and that you were rude at best."

"That's partially true. I did tell her fat-assed manager that I was thinking of arresting him because I was truly harboring that very thought. He was a pussy and he pissed me off."

"She said that you were rude when you came to her office and you upset her receptionist."

"The president's son and over a dozen agents were killed when two of their orange trucks blew up next to the limo. I went to pick up the video footage of the parking lot where the trucks were stolen from. You know the video just might give us a photo of the suspects. When I get to their office, I find that they have sent the video downtown which I would have preferred they had just let me remove it for chain of custody purposes. So I get downtown and I'm nice. I explain that I am investigating the attack and the whole thing. You know what they tell me?"

"What?"

"They send some media rep out to see me and she tells me that I will have to wait at least a day to get the tape. Why, I asked. Because she and a crisis team were reviewing the tape to prepare their official response. You know what they were doing? They were delaying this investigation so they could review the tape to see if they had even more bad exposure to this event. So I told that little media wag that she had ten minutes to get me that tape or I would be back with a search warrant in two hours. And then I added that she was obstructing a federal investigation, a felony for which I could arrest her."

"Doc, I agree with how you handled this. That being said, you already have a complaint against you and I'm hearing the Commissioner's Internal Affairs dickheads are making a project out of you. You can be sure they'll add this to their files."

"'As fire when thrown into water is cooled down and put out, so also accusations when brought against a man of the purest and holiest character, boils over and is at once dissipated, and vanishes and threats of heaven and sea, himself standing unmoved.'"

"Plato?"

"Nope, Marcus Tullius Cicero."

"Look maybe you can get Mr. Cicero to defend your ass. In the meantime, you know you can do the right thing and still run afoul of the outrageous policies and rules. You know that these employees can mess with you just by making the complaints and they are totally protected. You know that, Doc."

"Sorry, boss. You're right, but they generally really piss me off."

"Listen, I'll get back to the Commissioner and make the appropriate apology for what had to be a misunderstanding. You, on the other hand, keep up the good work and watch your back. Was there anything on the tape, by the way?"

"You're not going to believe this – those trucks drove off by themselves. Turns out the MNDOT had a few experimental trucks that could drive themselves or more accurately be operated remotely. MNDOT and a company, FNS, from Tennessee were testing the trucks to be used in big snowstorms to be able to run four abreast cleaning the entire freeway system at night. Hell of a deal."

Doc put his cell phone on the kitchen table, "Gump, remember, it's always better to act and beg forgiveness later than to never act at all. No, I don't think that would include you pooping in the house. Come on, I'll take you out. Get your coat on you little turd."

Wednesday, October, 17th

Basra, Iraq

COLONEL HARRIS HAD BEEN THE army's media man in Iraq for two years. He was used to the dog and pony shows trying to sell the U.S. news media a storyline. The media had their own agenda and had little interest in what the colonel had to offer. They would show up, just in case the colonel messed up, however the good news stories the colonel had to offer seldom got air time. The media was having plenty of stories about dead and crippled civilians and soldiers. They delighted in playing video clips of children without limbs and screaming parents.

A.P. Reporter Scott Worth thought this field trip may prove different. He listened as Colonel Harris pointed to the dead bodies and how some wore partial uniforms of Iran's conscripts. Worth made notes of weapon types and Iran military vehicles. He thought he could see something big coming from this story. The other newsmen eagerly shot pictures with cameras shielded from the blowing sand.

"Our soldiers intercepted and destroyed this unit at 1030 hours. We returned fire after being fired upon. Let me make it clear, we are over 30 miles inside the Iraq border. I would say this constitutes an invasion of the sovereign border of Iraq, an escalation of hostiles, and an act of war upon the nation of Iraq."

Worth looked around, "Colonel, excuse me, I don't see any Iraqis around here complaining of an attack on their border." He knew he was not likely to be invited on the next field trip, like he cared. "What can you tell us about the Army losing control of its tanks during a counter attack into Iranian soil?"

"Worth, I don't know where you get such pure bullshit information. Do any of you reporters who have not been smoking hashish have questions?"

Wednesday, October 17th

9 Smolenskin Street
Prime Minister's Residence, Jerusalem

A VETERAN OF 1967 AND 1973 wars, Israeli Prime Minister Har-El was battle-hardened and scarred. His tanned face wore many fine imprints where the shrapnel from the mortar had entered. Every morning when he shaved he was reminded of the hatred that permeated his nation.

Har-el did not care much for politicians and knew that American Ambassador Hamilton was nothing but. Hamilton wasn't even Jewish. He was getting his reward for the substantial political support he wielded in upstate New York. The ambassador was a tall handsome man with thick dark hair and broad shoulders. Thankfully, he looked so fine because he lacked any intellectual or moral substance.

"Mr. Prime Minister, I assure you that the support of the United States has never been stronger. We stand..."

Har-el cut him off, "That's strange Ambassador because I am hearing different. Can you tell me about the ultimatum the president is faced with to abandon Israel or face destruction?"

"There has been no such ultimatum. That crap that al Qaeda gets on al Jazeera is just that, crap. We put no stock in that."

"I am not in America to make my own assessments, however, I have men who are and . . ."

"We are well aware of your intelligence forces in our country, although I'll not bother to make any formal objections even though their actions certainly border on spying."

"My sources tell me that America is under attack on a variety of fronts, the president's own family, a river full of blood, pipeline eruptions, school bus attacks, oil refineries, fires, stock market crash, bridge collapses, I could go on and on . . . ."

"Mr. Prime Minister, the FBI assures us that there is no evidence, I repeat, no evidence, none, that all of these events are connected. Yes, we have been attacked, the attack on the president's family and the bridges and electrical transmission lines, although that doesn't mean that every tragedy that happens in our country is terrorist sponsored or necessarily all related to al Qaeda's threats. Hell, he could take credit for a Kansas twister if he wanted, but he can't make one."

"Mr. Ambassador, can you look me in the eye and assure me that the president is under no new pressure to abandon support of Israel?"

Ambassador Hamilton mustered up his best steely-eyed glare, "You have my word."

Wednesday, October 17th

Castle Creek Chalet
Aspen, Colorado

HAVING JUST COMPLETED PRAYERS, THE twelve men filed back into the Great Hall where they found a scrumptious buffet of Syrian cuisine and tea waiting. They ate, drank and talked like a conference of plumbing hardware salesmen, minus the alcohol and lingerie models. Omar was a man who believed Allah would acknowledge and reward punctuality so at the appointed time he asked for their attention.

"Praise Allah my brothers, we must be about our business."

"Abolhasen tell us the news of the Americans' reaction to the plagues. I know your people have been monitoring the media."

"They have taken our bait and are convinced that al Qaeda is responsible for the attack on the president's family and that Iran is helping them. They have attacked the Iran border town of Susangerd, or at least they tried to attack until we took control of three tanks and turned them around. As expected, they still sent missiles directed at the cell phone conversations they were intercepting. All they destroyed was a shed with a cell phone which we were using on a three-way conversation."

The others smiled and nodded. Abolhasen did not and continued, "We know we can successfully control a few of their tanks. When the tanks had new computers installed, Frampton Navigational Systems buried programs which allow us to remotely capture control. The tanks with the old systems, we have no control over."

Omar stepped forward as Abolhasen finished, "Unfortunately, the president has shown no intention of withdrawing their invading forces. No, instead I think he will expand into Iran. On the other hand, the governors are clamoring for troops to be sent to their states to restore order. We shall see if he relents in the next day. We can certainly add to their misery to apply more pressure.

"As we had planned, al Qaeda will claim responsibility for all of these events. The Americans are more than willing to believe this and are directing all their reprisals at al Qaeda, although they can hardly ever find members of that group who are not handed over to them from some other nation and mostly just so those nations can get rid of their own garbage.

"Tomorrow, al Qaeda will announce that an unnamed Pakistani general has defected to al Qaeda with a nuclear weapon. They will threaten to use it to destroy Israel. To support that false threat, we have arranged for a Pakistani general to willingly go missing. We need to keep the pressure on the Americans, we know we can't defeat them in a face-to-face battle, however, we can force our will upon them."

Wednesday, October 17th

Finnegan's Irish Pub
St. Paul, Minnesota

DOC WAS IN A DARK mood. He and Pat had closed over a dozen leads in the last two days. The analysts had stretched their imaginations to grade any of them a five. Chatting with the other agents, Doc found they were chasing equally unproductive leads.

He stood smoking a cigarette under the awning protecting the bar's front door. He slowly blew the smoke towards the stars and wondered if it would freeze and crash to the ground. It was so cold that he thought it would snow soon.

As he approached the bar's entrance, Campbell could tell from the scowl on Doc's face that he would not be civil. He wondered how much he had to drink.

"You and I are supposed to be interviewing Arabs over at the Middle East Deli. The bosses are wild over this assassination."

"Told you before, I'm done doing cold Arab interviews. All you end up doing is pissing 'em off and writing meaningless 302s. I'm done with that!"

"Doc, the ASAIC is pounding the desk. He wants results on this, he's got the mosques under surveillance and we are interviewing the Imams."

"Bet you ain't getting crap are you?"

"Let's go in, it's getting chilly out here."

"Chilly?"

Doc led the way to his usual table where a Glenlivet waited. At Finnegan's a patron could always count on ales and lagers from the old world and Irish music blaring over the aging and poorly tuned stereo system. Twice a year, in the old days, fundraisers were held for the IRA, although some said it was for bringing the wee ones from Ireland to spend the summer months away from the gunfire and bombs.

"What'll you have?" Doc said.

"Listen, I'm serious, I got interviews piled up and the Muslims aren't much on alcohol."

"Hey, take Dewey – he thinks he is actually catching terrorists every time he interviews a Muslim."

"I'll take him but you gotta pitch in here somehow."

"Have I ever failed you, buddy? Tell the boss, I got pulled off to follow some bullshit leads by my own agency and I've promised to let you guys know if B.C.A. has anything hot, he'll go for that. I need to think. I can't think properly if I'm running from Arab to Persian and writing reports about what they don't know. I need to think, alone."

"You owe me . . ." Campbell said and then left taking long strides towards the door.

"Don't worry, I'll take care of you," he said halfheartedly and then turned his attention to anchor woman Rhonda Cooper. She reminded him of a cheerleader in high school he had pursued. Being a cheerleader, she spurned his clumsy attempts.

He could hardly hear Cooper over the din of the bar noise and background music by the Chieftains playing Bob Marley's Redemption Song. He was forced to read the closed captions as CBS showed the funeral highlights. The camera scanned the VIPs from China, Russia, the Arab countries, nary a nation was missing, except Iran. The president still looked in shock or excessively tranquilized. Catholic priests, Protestant ministers and Muslim imams shared the clerical duties.

After the commercial, Rhonda appeared again with forest fires raging on the monitor behind her. Closed caption described fires burning from Idaho to Southern California. A U.S. map appeared on the screen with animated flames across the mountains with the largest being in the San Bernardino Mountains. Without a break, Rhonda went to an out-of-control oil refinery fire in Texas. A bearded seminary professor from

Texas told an interviewer that the plagues visited upon Egypt were done so by God. He quickly added that the Muslim terrorists had no such claim and that God had nothing to do with these so called plagues.

Another commercial break gave Doc an opportunity to order a second Glenlivet scotch and relieve himself before Rhonda returned with the stock market crash – huge arrows showed massive downturns of the Dow Jones Industrial Average and NASDAQ. The experts offered their paid for opinions of the downturns, agreeing that a 32% drop was probably more than a market 'correction.' He assured them that now was the time to buy because prices were low.

After another commercial break, a balding Edward Jones analyst assured the viewers that the market would adjust and he hauled out the statistics kept since 1920s to show that the market does this downturn and then pulls right back up again.

Doc took a huge swallow as he imagined his pension fund and deferred compensation stock investments plummeting. He may not retire as soon as he had hoped. He took another gulp and nearly got it down when he felt a powerful slap on his back.

"Hey, Asshole, wha 'sup?"

Doc twisted in his chair. Michael Hornsby stood over him wearing an endearing grin that reminded Doc of Donkey, Shrek's best friend and sidekick.

"Wha 'sup my ass? Sit down, son, and tell me what's goin' down. What you drinking?" Doc asked as he reached for cash to buy a round.

"Nothing man, still trying to lose some pounds and beer isn't on my diet menu, unless they make lettuce beer, they do that, man?"

Hornsby was a muscular man with a pleasant disposition. He had been a cop for most of his young life. He sat with the chair back facing him.

"Doc, what do you think of the al Qaeda threats with the plagues from the Bible? You remember what plagues there were?"

"Not really, seems God was always sending floods and fire down on his enemies or on the sinners who disappointed Him. I always half-ass expect to have a bolt of lightning come flashing my way."

"Man, you work this terrorist gig, so I thought I'd pass this on to you. I've told a few of the Feds. They're too busy running all over trying to shake up the Arabs. Anyway, I was in the SWAT truck, tail gunning on the motorcade when it blew up. Just before we got hit, there were two police vehicles, Suburbans, coming up fast on the backside of the motorcade. The lead Secret Service agent ordered us to stop them. They weren't supposed to be there. The first lady's limo sped up to give us a chance to drop back and check them out. We stopped and jumped out to address the two SUVs. Both had emergency lights and sirens going.

"Anyway, we bailed out and were hailing for them to stop. Then the MNDOT trucks blew and the Suburbans just drove by us and we lost sight of them in the smoke and confusion."

"Who were they? I mean who was in the Suburbans?"

"That's the thing Doc, we had M-16s leveled on those guys, safeties off and ready to lay into them, but they were all in digital BDUs and looked like SWAT. None of us were going to fire on cops who got their assignment screwed up. Thing is, I know most of the SWAT operators from the State SWAT Association. These guys were all Hispanics and I didn't recognize them. I thought at the time maybe they were Feds. Later, the Feds denied that and everyone is sure they were a part of the terror attack, however, they sure weren't Arabs and they for sure had a military cut to them."

"Have a drink, Michael. They got some great diet whiskey," Doc offered, his interest and adrenaline in overdrive for the first time since the attack.

As they discussed the different possibilities, Doc and Michael promised each other that this would be the last one. It may have been except they were joined by BCA Special Agent Vasco da Gama, 'Topo,' and Guiermo Munoz, 'Gato,' a St. Paul cop. The two men had formed an informal partnership based on their mutual love of the hunting of drug traffickers. Doc and Michael settled back and ordered some wings and a pizza knowing their evening was going to be longer.

"Topo, you guys hear anything on the street about Mexican soldier types being around? Maybe look like hired guns or something?"

"Nope," Topo said and looked to his partner to add his recollection.

Gato added, "You know, every once in a while we get one and we find they were in the Mexican Army or Special Forces. Zetas they call them 'cause they are all tatted up with military designs and Zs. Dealers, well-connected dealers, use them for protection. The tats keep changing and the original Zetas are likely dead. The younger guys are using tats of Santa Muerte, the death saint."

Doc felt his shoulders being massaged, tossed his head back into a pair of 38 Cs belonging to Susan Rivard. "You say you need protection, Big Guy?" Rivard asked. He nuzzled his head back into her breasts and she slapped him roughly alongside his head. Sue was a pretty woman of medium height, blonde hair pulled tight into a ponytail, and large breasts, at least that's how Doc always remembered her.

"Hey, Sue, how you been, pull up a chair. What are you drinking?" Doc asked.

Sue was a veteran officer who found great satisfaction working prostitution and specifically catching pimps and slave traffickers.

"What are you buying me you big stud?" She pulled a metal chair from a nearby table and sat next to Doc.

Topo motioned the waitress over and ordered another round. Sue added Crown Royal and Seven.

"What are you Sherlocks talking about?" she asked.

Doc repeated the entire story and added a few new thoughts which had been brought on by another dose of whiskey. He felt good for the first time in days, finally his mind was engaged. Finally, he had a bone to chew on. He was happy.

"I can ask around. You know, Blondie, a working girl near Lake Street, was telling me about some new dudes, Mexicans, all tatted up with a shitload of money for her and her friends."

The drinks came and Sue took a long pull, ordered another, and then slid her cell phone from her jeans pocket. "I'll call her. Anything you want me to ask her? Any specifics you want me to ask her?"

They each offered several, all at the same time until she held her hand up to shush them. "Blondie, hey you remember them Mexicans who're thrown the big bucks at you and the girls? Yeah?" Sue couldn't hear the response over the advice being offered, so she moved towards the woman's restroom to talk.

Ten minutes later, she returned smiling. "She couldn't talk long, she was entertaining, however, she did describe eight Mexicans who could have been soldiers – had a bunch of tattoos like skeletons floating on parachutes. A few of them packing heat. They were brought over by Armando Gomez. He's her cocaine source. He was just bringing them over to intro them. You know like vouch for them.

"We're having lunch at Me Gusto's tomorrow and I'll get more details. That enough to buy a girl a drink?" She smiled broadly at her success. Years of working prostitution details and rubbing shoulders with the girls had left Sue with a rough edge that her mother wouldn't be bragging about at church circle.

Another round.

Rhonda Cooper's blushed face played on the bar's television screen. It had quieted enough to hear Rhonda trying to connect the dots. Rolling out the ever available retired FBI agents as experts, she pressed them to connect the attack on the president's family, the oil refinery fires, Arlington Cemetery, the West Coast fires, the red Potomac, the pipeline spill in Illinois, the collapse of a railroad bridge across the Missouri river, a high school band bus leaving the highway and toppling over a mountain cliff, and a couple of other human tragedies that happened to fall on the same day. The gray haired agents, who had probably never even seen a live terrorist, offered thoughtful insights concluding that it may all be terrorist related or it may not be related at all.

Thursday, October 18th

Lake Prespa
Near Ritola, Macedonia

WHEN ALI REGAINED CONSCIOUSNESS, HE was on his back looking at blue skies dotted with fluffy white clouds and knew he was in heaven. 'How pleasant,' he thought until he realized how much he hurt and heaven was suppose to be pain free. He reached his left hand to brush blood running down his face and watched his right hand follow, caught by the handcuffs which encircled both wrists. Blue smoke, smelling of aviation fuel, surrounded him. Tiny flames burned near his feet and he pulled away from the heat. As he gained his senses he realized he was surrounded by the wreckage of a small aircraft. His feet were still attached by shackles to the aircraft seat legs.

Two men lay near him – one young man dangled upside down hanging from his seat belt harness. A pistol secured in a shoulder holster hung near his head. Two more men, both without heads, were in the area of what once was the cockpit.

Ali's memory was coming alive, he could recall being driven from the castle grounds and boarding an aircraft. He could not recall being in a crash. It didn't matter because as the CIA officers knew, Ali's mind would fill in the blanks. He would survey the wreck and his mind would create its own version of what had happened, all without any recollection.

Through his binoculars, CIA Officer Ed Mitchell watched Ali stir and roll over. It took about a half-hour before he saw Ali crawling to one of the corpses. Mitchell felt a little guilty about taking the four corpses from the Sofia morgue – all had died in an auto accident and were properly mangled although it seemed disrespectful. He couldn't recall having ever purchased corpses during his long and strange career – with the CIA, anything was possible. He was surprised at how little it cost him, less than a thousand dollars for all four bodies. Ali finally stood, he must have found the handcuff keys and released himself from his bondage to the chair because he slowly moved away from the smoldering wreckage limping down the brown hillside towards the lake.

"Get the donkey cart moving, Ali is moving down towards the trail next to the lake."

"Roger that," Joseph Young answered.

"How're we reading the tracker?" Mitchell asked.

"Reading at 93% – we won't lose him as long as he stays on earth." Young reported.

A local farmer, hired by Young, traveled in the two ruts which passed for a road. The man urged a forlorn looking donkey to pull the worn wooden cart up the steep hill. He whistled, shouted, and swung a short whip at the donkey that was almost as old as the ancient farmer. Finally the creaking cart reached the crest. Ali bloodied and sore, struggled to wave the old man down to claim a ride. The farmer slowed the donkey to a snail's pace and waved Ali aboard the cart's box which was full of straw and produce. Ali limped on what surely must be a broken leg and slowly pulled himself onto the cart.

It was evident to Mitchell that neither spoke a common language as there was much gesturing and pointing. Good, that would prevent the farmer from betraying the agents. Ali crawled in the back of the cart with the squash and pumpkins. The farmer resumed his coaxing and pointed the little beast down the rocky path towards the village.

Thursday, October, 18th

Prime Minister's Residence
Jerusalem, Israel

Alon ha-Koheim, the Director of Mossad and Prime Minister Joby Har-el had been meeting for two hours, much of it filled with reminiscence of old battles, shared brawls, and chasing young female soldiers. They rested in old but comfortable black leather chairs, their feet on the coffee table relishing the camaraderie that they'd enjoyed around many a campfire during their military service. The conversation was punctuated by hard laughter. Har-el enjoyed a fine Cuban cigar as he sipped his ice water. As the sun's rays moved across the open window to warm Har-el like an old friend, he stood and moved to the square teak conference table.

"I wish we could be young and relive those days – back to business," Har-el ordered.

"Joby, I'll give you the bottom-line as we in the Mossad see it."

"Please do," Har-el answered.

"We believe that the Americans are about to abandon all of the Middle East including support of Israel. They're pre-occupied with the terrible chaos in America. We shouldn't be fooled by this tough talk of invading Iran. In fact, they've already tried that and had to turn back for reasons I've yet to determine.

"They'll pull out for two reasons. First, they're incapable of defending themselves internally when all of their forces are occupying our neighbors. We believe they'll also be forced to reduce European and Asian occupation forces. That will suit the Russians and Chinese. We're right back to where we were two decades ago when Russia armed Syria and Egypt to destroy us. Second, they will pull out because the attacks on their soil have been tied to their Middle East occupations and bottom-line, if they pull out the attacks will end, at least that's what our people inside the White House are hearing.

"We have sources, double agents, working for the Russians under duress because of relatives back in Russia. They are being pressured to provide real time moments of military deployments and troop strength. We'd be fools to ignore this. It's typical of the Russians before they attack – or their surrogates attack."

"How soon should we expect this to happen?"

"Imminent, I would estimate. As for us, good friend, we will be left to fight for our lives. There are forces to our north in Syria building near the border. The Saudis to our east have been flying forays into Jordan and lighting up our radar. Egypt, to our Southwest has been moving tanks near the Gulf of Suez. It would seem we may soon be surrounded with the noose tightening and we'll have to call upon God to do some more parting of the Sea."

"*Fercockt*," uttered the prime minister.

Thursday, October 18th

Lake Street, Minneapolis

AGENT SUSAN RIVARD SLOWED THE Ford Explorer as she passed the blonde woman sitting at the bus stop bench, mini-skirted and legs immodestly spread, without underwear. 'Good grief,' thought Rivard. 'Is she always trolling?' They made eye contact and Rivard turned right at the next intersection, pulled over and waited. Within seconds Blondie was at the door and jumped into the SUV. A working girl couldn't afford to be slow, too much competition on the street.

"Hey, Honey, how ya doing?"

"Doing good girl, you hungry?"

"You buying?"

"Yeah, what about *Me Gusto* around the corner?"

"You cheap ass, what 'bout the Calhoun Beach Club?"

Rivard looked at Blondie's colored hair, pink tank top with no bra, white mini-skirt, and ankle high boots and considered the request, 'what the hell nobody knows me there.' "You got it baby," and she cruised to the Beach Club talking about tricks, dope, and baking bread.

They were seated in the rear corner of the swank club. That suited Rivard. They ordered turkey wraps and Cosmopolitan martinis from the skinny waiter who seemed to know Blondie at some level.

"So tell me about the Mexicans."

Blondie was a great witness. All Rivard had to do was ask a single opened-ended question and then sit back and sip her martini – like putting a coin in the jukebox and listening to the music.

"Well, Armando brought them over. He's my coke guy you know. He said they were roofers, but they weren't no roofers. I seen plenty of them and these guys weren't no roofers, they loved to party, tequila and

Coronas, good tequila, they had a lot of money and weren't afraid to spend it, not like roofers who expect to pay Tijuana prices. No, they gave good tips, well they should. And roofers, they got rough hands like sandpaper on my boobs. Me, Nikkei, and Fancy showed them boys a fine time. Armando never came back with them after the first time, but they would come around almost every night to party at my place. Normally, I don't take nobody to my place, but they's too many of them and we'd party all night so we made good money so I let them come to my place," Blondie paused just long enough to take a drink.

"They speak English?" Rivard asked. She set her drink down and picked at her wrap.

"Yeah, they talked English just fine. Pretended they didn't but they did. Fancy speaks some Spanish so she would mostly talk to them anyway, but one day I told Nikkei that the guy I called Jose II, I called them all Jose, I told Nikkei, in front of all of them that Jose II had a unit the size of a hamster. Jose IV asked Fancy what was a hamster and when she told him in Spanish what it was they all laughed except Jose II who was really pissed off, so I know they spoke English 'cause they knew everything I said except they didn't know hamster. So I was more careful after that."

"You remember what they drove?" Sue asked.

"They usually drove Armando's wrecks, a Gran Prix and maybe a Buick or something like that. Only one time they had a couple of real nice Suburbans."

Blondie took a bite of her wrap so Rivard saw an opportunity to ask a question, "Tell me about their tattoos, you said they were unusual?"

Blondie set the wrap down and continued to talk with her mouth full, "They were all tatted, which ain't unusual, but they was eight José's, one through eight, and each one had the same tattoo on their right shoulder, they was like a skeleton in a parachute and some Spanish writing around the tatt, like they all was from some gang or something, they all wore their hair like Marines, ya know, real short…"

They continued their lunch over the course of two hours and three martinis, each. When they finished, the waiter just waved them off as

Sue tried to pay the bill – said something about taking it out in trade some other day.

Rivard dropped Blondie at her house and dialed up Doc on her cell, "Doc, listen, my snitch has some pretty good descriptions of these guys, says they all wore the same paratrooper tattoos, spoke English, were young studs with a lot of money and while they use to come every day, she ain't seen them since the day before the first lady was killed. I got a bunch more, however, I think I'll make you pay for it.

"Tonight at Finnegan's would be fine, see you at 7:00 p.m. and remind me to tell you about the Tequila bottles I picked up from Blondie . . . maybe got some fingerprints, Bye Sweetie."

Thursday, October 18th

Minneapolis International Airport

ALEX STONE STEPPED ASIDE FROM his fellow Delta passengers, knelt on all fours and kissed the U.S. soil. He was full of joy to be back in the United States and off the long hours of flight from Amsterdam. He loitered in the concourse and waited for Jake and Rooster to join him.

All three had been jerked from their Afghanistan duty by Blackstone and sent to Minnesota. Their new assignment was to augment security at the nearby Koch Refinery and Prairie Island Nuclear Power Plant. Newly released homeland security funds in response to the 'plagues' had provided lucrative contracts for Blackstone to provide high octane security.

"Com'on, let's get our bags," Alex motioned for the others to pick up the pace, "my sister will pick us up at the baggage level." He looked at his watch and gave it a twist around the wrist.

"I gotta piss," Rooster said as he grabbed his crotch like a grade school boy as if to emphasize the point. He turned and strutted away. Rooster wore his black hair long. He naturally had a dark complexion and the days in the sun and wind made him look years older. His salt and pepper beard hung down to his chest. He acquired his nickname at the State Department's basic agent training where one of his instructors, a retired SAS sergeant, thought he strutted like a Rooster. The name stuck and some of his recent acquaintances didn't even know his real name.

"Me too," Jake added and grabbed at his privates to mock Rooster.

"I'll meet you at claims."

They were reunited at the baggage claim and soon were out the automatic doors. Dressed in jeans and tee shirts, they quickly pulled jackets from their bags and put them on. Their blood had thinned from the months in the desert. Alex, cell phone in hand, shouted to be heard over the traffic, "Where you at? What you driving? Hit your high beams. OK, I got you, stop at door 7."

The blue Trailblazer pulled over and the driver got out.

"Blondie, baby, I missed you." Alex said. He picked his baby sister up and swung her in two circles.

"Boys, meet my kid sister, Blondie," Alex said as he set her down in front of the two as if she were a display model. Stone had always been proud of his sister. In her younger days, she'd been a real beauty. They'd grown up in Western Wisconsin, on a dairy farm ruled by their drunken father and depressed mother. In their younger days, they spent hours hiding in the barn hay loft to escape the attention of their increasingly abusive father. Alex took the brunt of his father's beatings, but it was Blondie who attracted his sexual attention. Alex felt helpless until he reached his sixteenth year. That was the year he'd had enough and beat his father so severely the old man spent two weeks in the hospital. Alex and his sister, who was only a couple years younger, took the two week hiatus to make their break to the Twin Cities. For two years they hustled on the streets until Alex got crossways with the law and the judge suggested he enlist in the military to avoid the jail sentence he intended to hand down. That turned out to be a good move for Alex, although it left Blondie without a male protector until she was swallowed up by Sly, her first pimp.

Friday, October 19th

Camp David, Maryland

"MR. PRESIDENT, THE VICE PRESIDENT is here."

"Send him in."

Gibbons strutted into the private office looking very presidential.

"I'm pleased to see you are up and feeling better. I've got everything under control."

"The hell you say. I don't think I ever had the feeling, even on one single day, that I had everything under control. You're either a great man or a damn fool."

The vice president looked like he had been backhanded, however, he remained quiet.

"Look, I appreciate that you gave me the time to grieve. I appreciate all you have done, however, I intend to resume my duties as president."

"Mr. President. . ."

"That is who I am – and you, sir, are the vice president. I'd suggest you return to the Executive Office Building today."

The vice president saw no point in arguing, he had no cards to play, he simply left.

The president called to the Secret Service agent, "The vice president will be returning to the Executive Office, he may use my helicopter."

"Yes, sir."

Friday, October 19th

Castle Creek Chalet
Aspen, Colorado

OMAR LOOKED TIRED WHEN HE left the Council meeting. Mumtaz followed him out and suggested they walk to the path along the creek. Omar declined, however, at Mumtaz's insistence, he relented. They donned their bright colored ski jackets and strolled into the cool air. The sun warmed their backs as they walked north towards the village. The sweet smell of burning pine drifted across the valley.

Omar enjoyed looking at the ski slopes, the pure white snow brought memories of his family's visits to the mountains. He shook the thought as he realized Mumtaz was speaking.

"...I don't think that will be necessary. I have to believe that President Franklin is a practical man and will do what he must know is his only choice."

"We lay ready to finally deal with Israel. For several years, the Russians, Chinese, and Americans have been sending weapons, tanks and fighters to Saudi, Syria, and Egypt. These forces stand ready to push the Israelis into the Sea," Omar said.

Mumtaz continued, "We've used the tunnels to arm the Palestinians to fight on the backs of the Jews. Our tests with the American tanks proved successful. We should be able to do likewise with selected Israeli tanks, at least enough to disrupt and demoralize the Israelis."

Omar allowed himself a crooked smile, "All seems to be going so well. And to think a few days ago we were worried about Ali and that our plans would be compromised."

Neither man spoke as they passed two middle-aged women, tanned and dressed in clothing that cost enough to feed a hundred – no more like a thousand–Somalis for a month.

Omar held his head in his hands, "Our surveillance team at the Bulgarian castle believes the Americans have left with Ali or perhaps he has been tortured to death. I believe we can safely assume that he has not talked and will not disclose our plans. I am confident that matter has been put to rest."

"What remains to be done? Will we wait to see if President Franklin yields to al Zawahri's demands?" Mumtaz asked.

"No, we will promptly send an emissary to the president to press our demands. So far the requirements have been set forth only by that old fool, al Zawahri. We will turn up the heat as the Americans say and I believe he is a broken man who will take the opportunity to save what remains of his country."

Mumtaz looked at his watch and stopped. "My brother, please, to prayers. We have much to ask of Allah."

Both men turned back and quickened their pace to get back to the chalet and join the others for prayer, their common bond.

Friday, October 19th

South Minneapolis, Minnesota

AGENT SUSAN RIVARD MET BLONDIE at the same bus stop, this time with new intentions.

"OK, you've done this before for us so you know the drill," Rivard said after Blondie settled into the Explorer.

"Is Gato, that cute cop, going to search me again?"

"I think I'll do the honors this time."

"Damn."

Rivard pulled the SUV into the Burger King parking lot. "Let's go into the restroom."

The agent picked up her radio mike, "1233 would you make sure no one bothers us in the bathroom?"

"Copy," came the reply from 1233. The two women hurried into the Burger King to the restroom. It smelled of stale urine and unflushed toilets. "Take your top off and put this bra on, there's a bug built in the bra."

"Honey, that's not good. Armando ain't likely to shake my hand, but he might give my boobies a squeeze, do you have anything else?" She pushed her ample bare bosoms skyward as if to emphasis the point.

"Give me your cell phone and take this one," Rivard said impatiently as she handed a Motorola phone to the near naked woman.

"OK, put your arms up and spread 'em," Rivard directed as she patted Blondie's body looking for money or drugs. Blondie had put a month's worth of cheap perfume all over her body. The smell mixed with the odor of excrement and urine was gagging. Finding no contraband, she handed Blondie $350.00 cash. "OK, this money and that phone is all that's going in with you. We will be outside watching and listening to you. Don't sell or trade anything with him. No sex. I can't have you giving blow jobs while we are taping the deal. Not like last time. Are we clear on that?"

Blondie smiled slyly and nodded that she understood. She recalled how she'd ignored that rule and how Rivard had screamed at her. She slipped her tight spandex shirt over her skinny torso, nipples protruding in the cold bathroom.

"Make some sort of comment about the quality of the dope so we know you have the coke and then leave. Don't stop anywhere on the way there or on the way back. Clear?"

"Yes, officer, what am I getting again for doing this?"

"You know damn well you're getting $200.00 for doing this. If we find more, and I expect you to ask him if you can buy more later, you will be paid accordingly."

"Accordingly to what?"

"Look Honey, we get a pound and I'll give you another $500.00 – you get a kilo, I'll give you $1,200.00. Now let's go. I got a crew waiting on us. Oh yeah, while you're walking to the house I'd like you to comment on Gato's lack of manhood, can you work that in?"

"Yeah, for another $50.00."

"Done. Now spit that gum out, I don't want to listen to a half-hour hour of gum smacking."

They walked quickly back to the Explorer. The polluted air of Minneapolis never smelled so good. Rivard keyed the mike, "I'm turning the bug on . . . 1440 can you copy?"

"10-04."

"OK. I'll drive you nearby his house, drop you off and wait in the same spot." She sped through the narrow streets of south Minneapolis taking alleys and shortcuts at times.

As they drove, Blondie began one of her long stories. "Hey, I was talking to my brother about those tattooed Mexicans and he said. . ."

"What the hell are you talking to your brother about that crap for? This kinda stuff is between us only. You know. . ."

"Chill out sister, my brother just flew into town. He's a Special Forces soldier, he knows about this crap, so chill out, Babe."

"Sorry, what's he say anyway?"

"With your pissy attitude, I'm not so sure I'd even tell you."

"I said I'm sorry."

"Alright, he said that skeleton tattoo is for Peruvian Special Forces guys. He said they are a tough bunch of soldiers who were trained by the Americans. He worked with some of them in Iraq and Afghanistan."

"What the hell are Peruvian soldiers doing in Iraq and Afghanistan?"

"My brother isn't in the Special Forces any more, he works for Blackstone in Afghanistan. They hire cops and soldiers for protecting people. That's where he met those dudes. In fact, he's here in town guarding the refinery and nuclear power plant."

The police radio interrupted, it was Doc's voice, "1442, we are all hearing this on the bug, let's cut the chatter and you, me and the CI finish the conversation later."

Embarrassed at her lapse in security, Rivard answered, "Copy that," and turned to Blondie, "So what do you think about Gato?"

"I liked when he searched me last time, but he got a little too close and let me tell you….."

The Explorer pulled to the curb and Blondie jumped out and beat a straight path to Armando's house. It was a modest story and half stucco painted brown. The front picture window was covered with plywood and bars. She pushed through the broken white picket fence gate and up to the barred door. Barely two knocks and the agents could hear

Armando greeting Blondie and inviting her into his house. Within five minutes the agents could hear Blondie tell Armando, "it looks like good shit, but it ain't a whole ball, baby."

"You got a scale?" Armando asked.

"No."

"Then it's a whole ball, baby."

"Screw you, here's $300.00. I ain't paying you for what ain't there. Don't mess with me honey, I'm just gonna sell half to another dude, and he said if it's any good, he'll take 4 OZs. Can you do 4 OZs if I come back?"

"Not a problem, baby. Not a problem."

The agents could hear the door slam and the clicking of Blondie's high heels as she headed back to the Explorer. When she arrived she handed Rivard a small clear plastic bag. Rivard immediately took a pinch of the white powder between her fingers and dropped it in an Ident test kit. It turned a light blue, turned very fast. She keyed the microphone, "Okay, I got it and it tests positive for cocaine. Go get the search warrant."

Saturday, October 20th

Rome, Italy

USING THE U.S. CASH HE had pilfered from the dead bodies, Ali had made his way to Skopje where he purchased a flight to Rome and checked into the Dei Mellini Hotel.

CIA Officer Ed Mitchell and his crew had no problem keeping track of Ali. The tracker worked perfectly and Ali had no apparent skill at counter-surveillance or he was in such a panic he didn't care. It helped that his leg was severely injured. It considerably slowed Ali and Ed was still boasting at his brilliance of disabling their target to make him easier to follow.

Ali had settled in at a sidewalk café at the Ambasciatori Palace Hotel. The café was only half-full. The other customers were mostly Middle Eastern men. Ali could be seen talking to several, in fact carrying on lengthy conversations. It was a lovely fall day, sunshine abounded and a hint of a breeze to whisk away the heat. The smell of baking sweet pastries and brewing Arabic coffee filled the air. Towering waiters wearing long white aprons moved gracefully among the tables serving cups of brutally strong coffee. By the time Ali had left the café, the shadows had moved across the striped umbrellas sheltering the metal tables. He limped down the busy sidewalks to his hotel and disappeared into the lobby.

Saturday, October, 20th

Armando Gomez Residence
Southside Minneapolis, Minnesota

DOC HAD BEEN INSIDE ARMANDO'S house for about an hour. As with virtually every drug dealer's home, it was a mess. The kitchen was littered with decaying food scraps. Used pizza boxes and fast food bags rested on the counter. Roaches scurried from box to bag as Doc searched the kitchen. The smell was overwhelming and disgusting. He retreated to the rear of the little house and into the bedroom – clothes, old and new, clean and dirty, piled on the floor. The bed had sheets which years ago might have been white, now they came closer to brown from who knows what. He turned on the light switch. Nothing happened. It never did. Working lights weren't a priority for the likes of Armando. Probably had a light when he moved in – when it burned out, that was it. Wearing latex gloves Doc poked around through the clothes and then was called into the basement.

Doc walked down the dimly lit steps shining his flashlight on the creaking wooden planks. The basement smelled of dog excrement and mold. He carefully stepped between the piles to the rusty white washing machine. Two agents had found 34 ounces of cocaine in the two sealed boxes of Cheer laundry soap and another two ounces in the opened box. The discovery gave the agents a laugh – anyone would know that a drug dealer like Armando doesn't use three boxes of Cheer in a year. In fact, the washer obviously didn't work, it had no door. He needed to improve on his hiding spots.

Doc stepped carefully picking his way through the dog crap. Not careful enough, he walked in a large greasy pile and slipped forward catching himself on the steps. Cursing, he ignored the mess on his brown loafer and climbed up the steps leaving tracks, brown smelly footprints. He moved across the living room carpet, his shoe prints nicely matching the existing color. Doc was looking for evidence other than drugs. He ordered Armando from the sofa to the recliner and removed the sofa cushions. Cautiously, he pushed his gloved hand in the area where everyone keeps their change. Feeling something solid he pulled out a set of car keys with an alarm fob. Holding them up in the air, Doc pushed towards the smirking drug dealer and asked, "Hey, Armando, are these Suburban keys yours?"

"I never owned no Suburban, man, I got no money for that, I'm just a roofer."

"Listen, Armando, I've little patience for your bullshit. If these aren't yours, who do they belong to?"

"I want my lawyer."

In a blur, the smaller Doc lifted the tubby Armando by the front of his shirt and held him suspended two inches from his face, "Tell me whose keys these are or you and I are going in the basement to see if there might be a good lawyer down there!"

"Let me down you . . ."

Doc kneed him and pulled him closer, "Whose keys?"

Armando tried to speak through the pain, nothing came out.

He pushed Armando back to the chair and waited. "If the next words out of your mouth are not to tell me whose keys these are, you. . ." he pointed a finger in Armando's face, "and I. . ." he pointed a thumb at his own chest, "are in the basement."

"Man, I don't have a Suburban," Armando whispered hoarsely.

"You are one dumb shit. I asked you who lives here or who visits you that owns a Suburban?"

"Alberto and some of his friends, they were roofing with us, but I ain't seen them for weeks, man."

"That's a small beginning . . . maybe only a white lie. I think we can work on this. Let's hear more about Alberto and his friends."

Saturday, October 20th

Finnegan's Irish Pub
St. Paul, Minnesota

"DOC, THIS IS BLONDIE'S BIG brother, Alex," Sue Rivard said when she brought Stone to Doc's table. She leaned into Doc's ear and whispered, "Don't say anything bad about Blondie. He loves her dearly, flaws and all."

Doc offered a sloppy salute and pointed to a chair. "Have a seat sailor. What are you drinking?"

"Whatever you're buying, mate."

Special Agent Susan Rivard delivered the order to the bar.

"Blondie tells me you know about the Mexicans wearing the parachute tattoos. Why are you interested?" Stone asked and he settled into his chair.

"What do you know?"

The drinks arrived and that stopped the cat and mouse game.

"Okay," Alex began, "I work for Blackstone and spent time work'n in Iraq and Afghanistan. Blackstone hires soldiers and police officers from many different nations, including Mexico, Bolivia, Peru, and the Philippines. We served in Iraq with a group of Peruvian paratroopers. They're a tough bunch. Many were trained by Special Forces at the School of the Americas at Fort Benning in Georgia. They are skilled operators. Some went to work for Blackstone, others, I'm told, work for the Tijuana drug cartel. My sister described the tattoos and I'm sure she is talk'n about Peruvians. Now, why you want to know?"

"Between friends here, I think they were the assassins of the president's family."

"Seriously?"

"Yes, very seriously."

"You know there was a guy who worked for Blackstone who said a bunch of foreign soldiers disappeared from the Middle East but were still on the payroll. He got transferred to Bosnia for what he knew."

Doc made mental notes to follow-up on what Alex had laid on the table.

Alex reached across the table towards the half-full pitcher of beer. Doc noticed a tattoo on the man's biceps, an anchor with a chain wrapped around it and a naked woman.

"You were in the Navy?"

"I was... retired a few years ago."

"I've a matching tat on my ass – Miguel's Tats, Tijuana, Mexico, 1969."

"Miguel's, 1968. I was stationed for a time in San Diego."

"Vietnam?"

"Two years – how about you?"

"Navy Corpsman detailed to the Marines."

"Navy Corpsman sewed me up once in Rung Sat Special Zone…"

"On your right buttock, you're the Navy Seal they called The Stone."

Saturday, October 20th

Camp David, Maryland

WARREN HARRINGTON, A SLENDER MAN with perfectly trimmed silver hair and matching mustache, waited outside the President's Office. Other than the receptionist and the two Secret Service agents, he waited alone on a surprisingly hard and uncomfortable wooden chair. Harrington was an old school lawyer with the law firm of Powers, Harrington, and Adams. At 82, he had served many presidents, senators and congressmen in their private affairs. He was apolitical, as much as one could be in Washington, and known for his integrity and discretion.

"Mr. Harrington, the president will see you now. You have 18 minutes. Please hold to that even if the president doesn't," directed the chief of staff who'd suddenly appeared in the doorway guarded by stone faced agents.

Harrington, dressed in a dark well-tailored suit, brought his 6'5" torso up slowly from the chair and walked with the assistance of a black cane into the office. "Mr. President, a pleasure to see you again. My deepest sympathy for your tragic loss."

The president nodded and warmly shook Harrington's sturdy hand with both hands.

"Mr. Harrington, always a pleasure. What is this urgent matter my chief says requires my immediate attention?"

Harrington removed a folded paper from his coat pocket and sat in the leather high back chair the president had offered.

"Mr. President, I have served many presidents and congressmen on discreet matters for five decades and I've seen some unusual situations. However, this matter is the most unusual and disturbing I've ever been charged to handle.

"I received this letter delivered to my office via courier. I don't know its origins. I do not attest to its veracity, although given the manner in which it was delivered to me, I believe it warrants your time and consideration. It directs me to bring it to your attention, personally.

"I will obviously give you this letter which directs me to read it to you, and I quote:

President of the United States of America,

You personally and your nation have experienced extraordinary tragedy in recent weeks. Beware. There are even more horrific events of monumental proportions about to befall your country unless the demands detailed in this letter are met. Within 6 hours, you will order the immediate withdrawal of all American troops waging war against the Islamic nations. You will announce to the world that all soldiers will be withdrawn from Iraq, Afghanistan, Saudi Arabia, Egypt, Qatar, Bahrain, Turkey, Kuwait, Oman, and the United Arab Emirates. The American naval fleet will be directed to withdraw from waters contiguous to those nations.

You will inform the Israeli ambassador that the United States will no longer provide for Israel's defense, even if they are attacked.

To support your announcement of withdrawals, Sunni, Shiite and tribal leaders in Iraq and Afghanistan will announce a cessation of the hostilities and establish a rule of government under Shariah Law.

Following your announcement, your CIA will be furnished with the precise location of al Zawahri and the leadership of the al Qaeda organization. You may seek the deaths of those responsible for the murder of your son.

The nations of Islam will no longer tolerate American interference with our religious, political, or economic institutions. We will rule ourselves according to our ways. We are not interested in your imported democracy or capitalism.

Be assured, if you fail to act within six hours, commencing at midnight there will be renewed attacks on America and the American economy. This will be followed by the oil producing Islam nations denying oil to your country. You have seen already the plagues that have been visited upon your nation. You must believe that more devastating events will befall your country.

We have spent a decade preparing for this jihad. We do not want the destruction of America, but wish not to be under its Imperialist military rule and occupation or economic domination.

You were correct to be concerned about the Pakistan nuclear security. We have received two such missiles from a sympathetic Pakistani general.

You will also find attached to this letter, copies of schedules of political contributions to you and your party which will be made public should you fail to heed this warning. These schedules show over $8 million in illegal contributions over the last 9 months.

By now you know that we have the ability to disrupt and even control military vehicles and aircraft. Those small demonstrations should serve to convince you that further military action will be met with failure and high losses of American lives.

You have until Sunday at noon.
s/s The Islamic Council

Sunday, October 21

Camp David, Maryland

PRESIDENT FRANKLIN HAD A FITFUL night's sleep. Just like his deceased nemesis, bin Laden, he also woke at night in a cold sweat. Twice he rolled over to touch his wife and awoke to find her absent. He pushed the switch for his bedside lamp and reread the letter delivered by Warren Harrington. Finally, at 4:00 am he crawled out of bed and called his chief of staff to meet him immediately in his office. He pulled a linen robe bearing the presidential crest, over his linen pajamas, found his cane nearly under the bed and shuffled down the hallway to the elevator and his office. It was dimly lit when he entered and he kept it that way.

The chief of staff ambled into the office looking every bit as though he had just rolled out of his own bed. His normally coffered hair sticking straight up in the air on one side and smashed and flattened on the other side. They both sipped coffee that the steward delivered and tried to wake up. After suffering heavy silence, the president leaned toward the chief and handed him the Council's letter. "Read this very slowly and carefully."

Minutes passed and the chief finished reading and looked at the president. "Where did this come from and when did you get it?"

"Last night, it was brought to me by Warren Harrington. He does not know its origin. Other than me, you are the only person in the administration to know about this."

"You want my reaction?"

"Yes, of course."

"I don't know that I can fairly give you a shoot from the hip opinion that would amount to a damn."

"I had the party treasurer check last night to verify the contributions made to our campaign funds. That information is accurate at least as to the amounts. We must assume that they are accurate in terms of their illegal nature."

"Is there a way to verify any of the other information? Do we have a foundation of facts that would lead us to believe they can carry out the threats?"

"Good Grief, man, they killed my son and my wife lies in critical condition. What more proof do we need?"

"I'm sorry."

"Are you familiar with the biblical plagues in the Book of Exodus?"

"Mr. President, I'm sorry I don't recall them. I remember watching the movie with Charlton Heston, although I can't recall each event. I know the Nile was turned to blood."

"Last night, I looked them up. Let me refresh your memory..."

The chief squirmed restlessly while the president launched into a rendition that was befitting his rural Baptist roots.

When he finished with the plagues, the president stood and stretched his long arms back trying to shake the stiffness from his bones. "I checked with General Highcamp about the claim that they can control some of the military vehicles."

"What does he say about that?"

"I was not pleased to have learned about the problem in this manner. The general said that there was an incident in Iraq where an attacking squadron lost control of their tanks. He said it was an isolated incident, probably caused by some computer programming errors. They are trying to identify the problem."

"What about the Pakistani missiles – have you confirmed that?"

"I made some vague inquiries without specifically asking. No one has any information that would verify that threat."

The president added, "I also checked with the FBI about the refinery fires, the Rocky Mountain fires, the loss of the railroad bridges, and the electrical towers tumbling on the East Coast. The director said that his agents believe that they are all the acts of terrorists. They are not making that opinion public because the news media is pointing to every tragic event and calling it a terror attack. Yesterday, a ferry in Port Aransas sank in the Gulf of Mexico and the media calls it an attack."

The chief held his arms up in mock surrender, "I'm ready to give you my reaction. I think we have a real problem."

"I was expecting some brilliance beyond that."

"I would give you my real reaction, however, I know your dislike for profanity. As you say, al Zawahri has been publicly claiming responsibility for attacking America and you personally with plagues."

"And we have dismissed that as his usual blather."

"I don't think he is capable of putting this together."

"Well, he certainly surprised us on 911."

"This letter is signed by the Islamic Council, have we ever heard of them?"

"I asked the CIA and they have nothing on such an organization." The president began to pace around the mahogany desk.

"They have delivered the so called plagues, they maybe have some capability to control some of our military hardware, and they can publicly embarrass you with illegal contributions."

"That's about it. They are claiming that a Pakistani general has given the terrorists two nuclear weapons. It would be the ultimate understatement to say that they seem to have us by the short hairs."

"What if we ignore their threats?" the chief asked.

"Perhaps it is a bluff and the worst is over. Or they could deliver the nuclear bombs and thousands would be killed."

"Not to mention your credibility may be destroyed by the disclosure of the contributions."

"What if we agree with the demands?" The president stopped his pace for a moment as if stopped by a roadblock.

"If they can be trusted, and that's a big if, they will bring an end to the attacks and give us those responsible or at least the al Qaeda network that had claimed responsibility."

"If they have the power to bring these plagues, if they are the responsible parties, why would they deliver their own?"

"Unless they have used al Qaeda as their foot soldiers, their toadies and they are willing to give them up."

There was a long silence as they both paused to ponder what they had just discussed. The president poured more coffee and continued, "The Jews what about the Jews?"

"Ah, yes, what about the Jews? The letter implies that they intend to attack the Jews. Would we allow that?"

"No, we will stand behind the Israelis. They have been a surrogate for our own military presence in the Middle East for decades. If we abandon them, and pull out our troops from the rest of the area, we have no military presence."

"And that means our oil supplies are left to the whim of the Arabs."

"On the other hand, if this Islamic Council really has their hands on the controls of the oil wells, they can indeed squeeze us." He resumed his walk around the desk, drinking coffee as he paced. He yearned for a cigarette which he'd given up to become president.

"We could force the flow of oil with our military."

"We could although right now that isn't working so well. Besides, if they have control over some of our weapons, that could be a disaster. The American public would never put up with that kind of mess," the president said. He finished his coffee and set the china cup on the walnut table.

"Oh, I don't know, they don't seem to pay a lot of attention to these matters. They are more interested in the NFL season than they are in spending time thinking about a military operation in the Middle East."

"I don't share that opinion. Back to our options–I think we could comply with their demands," President Franklin said.

"Mr. President, we don't negotiate with terrorists."

"We are not going to negotiate. We seemingly have nothing to negotiate. Look. I can make this announcement that we will pull out and declare a success. The governors are crying for their National Guard troops to be returned to restore some order and provide security for some vulnerable targets. We wait and see if this Islamic Council delivers on their promises and the feuding factions announce reconciliation. We will then wait to see if they produce the assassins. All this will give our FBI and CIA time to identify this Council and then we will have our way with them."

"And we can make some effort to undo the embarrassing campaign contributions."

"Yes, that too."

"What about the Jews?" the chief asked.

"They will have to take care of themselves for awhile. I will contact our allies including the Egyptians and the Saudis and ask for their support for heading off any attack on the Israelis. Until then, we'll buy ourselves some time."

"What will we release to the media?" the chief asked.

"I will think about that and you should, too. My first reaction is to simply announce our intent to withdraw and declare a victory and bring our troops home to protect the citizens of this country. I think it would sell."

"This is going to raise many problems with the State Department and the Pentagon. How do we explain it to them?"

"We will tell them that there have been secret discussions which have brought us to this point and that the details will become clear as events unfold."

"I think they may accept that, although not for long."

"This is going to stay between you and me. We'll have to react as this mess unfolds. Just between you and me, is that clear?"

"Yes, Mr. President."

"I'll be flying back to the White House to make the formal announcement."

Sunday, October 21st

Catoctin Mountain Park
Maryland

CARLOS ESTEBAN HAD GROWN IMPATIENT and uncomfortable lying up in the bush for days. He was tired of the insects and bugs crawling across his body and biting him. They had neglected to bring sufficient heavy garments and the nights were unbearably cold. They lay huddled together – shivering and teeth chattering. They'd have given their first born for a fire.

Over the days, he and others watched the Marine helicopters make several flights into Camp David. Each time, Esteban, using a rangefinder, noted that they would be in range of their missiles. It was shortly after noon when he received a text message to attack if an opportunity presented itself. Esteban directed Pedro to a nearby hilltop inside the park. Pedro would be able to see the presidential helicopter before it joined the four decoys. He would keep Datu and Amir apprised as to which craft was the president's among the five helicopters. It would be tricky because the helicopters would constantly change formation position. At least that's what the scouts who watched the White House for the last year reported.

Pedro peered through his spotting scope to see a Marine helicopter lift through the forest canopy to be quickly joined by four identical helicopters. Pedro keyed his microphone and told Esteban what he was watching.

Esteban pointed for the men to ready their Chinese weapons. Amir and Datu shouldered the QW-2 missiles and waited.

Pedro strained to keep his tri-pod mounted spotting scope trained on the president's chopper. His scope in one hand and radio with the other hand, he broadcast continuously the target chopper's location in the sortie.

A ways back from Pedro, Estaban was the first to spot the five helicopters gaining altitude and heading a little to the left – generally towards their position. He pointed skywards for Amir and Datu to see.

Estaban fixed his range finder on the five choppers and when they were within range, radioed to Pedro, "Which one? Which one?"

"It's the one to your far right. Now it's moving to the farthest to the rear."

Estaban turned to Datu and Amir, "Listen to Pedro, they are in range, fire as soon as you have the chopper Pedro is describing."

"Now, it is the one in the center."

Datu fired first followed quickly by Amir. The missiles flew at supersonic speed towards the center helicopter.

Datu's missile hit the center chopper's rear rotor causing it to spin and crash into the chopper to its starboard.

Amir's missile missed the center chopper but landed in the cockpit of the chopper directly behind.

The three crippled choppers plummeted to the earth crashing and exploding upon impact.

The two remaining choppers veered off immediately and retreated in a zigzag fashion back to Camp David.

Sunday, October 21

Grand Avenue
St. Paul, Minnesota

DOC WOKE EARLY, DRESSED QUICKLY, and strolled with Gumpy to the nearby Caribou Coffee. It was his first day off since the assassination. The sunshine felt wonderful on his face and he breathed the fresh air in deeply. It only took five minutes to get to the little shop. He tied Gump loosely to one of the curb side tables and went inside. A fresh faced young girl, her long blonde hair pulled back into a ponytail, took his order. He ordered scones for each of them and coffee for himself. Outside on this warm humid morning, Doc broke up Pug's scone and made him stand on his hind legs and bark for his breakfast.

That entertainment finished, he read the Minneapolis Tribune, eliminating the ads, sports, and fashion. It didn't take him that long because he only read the by-line and the first paragraph of each story. The AP reported the latest on what they were now calling the 'plagues.' Massive aerial spraying of insecticides and a messy cleanup ridded Arlington Cemetery of the bugs and frogs. Similarly, algaecide halted the spread of the 'bloody water.' The refinery fires destroyed three entire processing plants although the flames were at least under control and would be allowed to burn out. The price of gas already increased over a dollar at the pump.

Three St. Paul Police squads went racing past, lights flashing and sirens blaring. Good grief, Doc thought, more attacks?

Electricity was being slowly restored to the eastern seaboard. The Rocky Mountain fires were still out of control. Trains were being rerouted to bring coal to the Midwest. Politicians were exchanging allegations of blame. Reports of a possible Anthrax attack in southern Minnesota. A coalition of state governors was demanding that their National Guard troops be returned from the Middle East and Bosnia. The first lady was out of intensive care and expected to recover. The violent deaths of the families in Texas and Idaho didn't even make the back pages with all the major events unfolding in the United States.

He slurped the last of his coffee and they walked back to his apartment stopping at every fire hydrant along the way. He dressed in his black testifying suit and the two of them left again headed towards Summit Avenue.

Doc and the one-eyed pug enjoyed strolling down Summit Avenue along the century-old mansions. The stately elms lined the street and he could envision the horse drawn carriages carrying the empire builders from their mansion to their downtown offices. From those offices, all building of the nation north west of the Mississippi took place. Lumber barons, railroad tycoons, and bankers plied their trade to the taming of the West by the immigrants drawn in from Europe.

He took his time admiring the architecture of the buildings and imagining who lived in each when the Avenue was the place to live – before the word suburb even existed and the big mall's parking lot actually produced crops. They arrived at a renovated brownstone owned by his ex-wife, Kelly. He knocked at the back door and was met by the barking setter. Kelly shouted for them to enter adding that she was getting dressed. Her housekeeping hadn't improved since their married days. That was one of the many differences that led to going their separate ways – that and being habitually late while Doc was compulsively early. Leaving the two dogs to play, Doc and Kelly continued on to the St. Paul Cathedral to attend Mass.

They seldom missed the Sunday worship service even during their fighting days. Doc felt that the refuge from the craziness of his work kept him with a semblance of sanity. Father O'Reilly met them after the service. "Good Morning, Doc and Kelly. How are you folks on this fine, sunny day?"

"Great now that we have been refreshed by your inspirational message. It was a message of hope at a time when there is little of it. Are you still joining us for dinner at Kelly's place this evening?" Doc asked.

The small man with big freckles nodded vigorously, "I wouldn't miss it. What delights will you be cooking might I ask?"

"I thought I would grill some of the bison steaks and of course the sides which you favor," Kelly replied.

"I'll see you at six."

"Come early and we'll get into the wine cellar."

"So it will be."

Doc had first met the good natured priest when Doc was working in a uniform in Minneapolis. The good father had gone to the annual Emerald Society fundraiser at the Fort Snelling Officers' Club. The priest had given the blessing of the dinner and then stayed to visit with all of the cops. The officers bought round after round for the priest and by the time he stumbled out of the club, he should have taken a cab. He didn't and Doc found him off the road, having driven his compact car into Minnehaha Creek.

It didn't take Doc but a moment to notice the white collar worn by Father O'Reilly. Doc called Twin City Towing and arranged for the car to be put back on the road. He paid the driver with cash and got his partner to drive the slightly damaged car back to the Cathedral. He drove to the St. Paul border as the smashed priest sang Irish ballads from the rear seat. At the city limits, Doc handed him off to a couple of sympathetic St. Paul officers who took him home. The priest later sought out Doc with a bottle of Jameson and they struck up a lasting friendship. During tough personal times Doc would lean on the man he had helped years earlier.

Doc's cell phone rang as they were nearing Kelly's brownstone. It was his FBI partner, Pat.

"What do you need?"

"Sorry to call you at this time, but I need you to help me. The on-call agent just spoke with a guy who is the next door neighbor to the fundraiser host out in Wayzata. He says he knows who attacked the first lady and her son. The on-call agent phoned the ASAIC who wants this guy interviewed right now. He thinks that because this is a sophisticated and wealthy guy, there may be something to it. The caller said we should phone ahead so he can open the driveway gates and we shouldn't let the neighbors see us arrive. Can you join me for this interview?"

"Sure, can we get it done now, I have dinner plans?"

"I'll meet you at the Wayzata Police Department parking lot in an hour."

Doc prevailed upon Kelly to watch Gump and entertain Father O'Reilly if Doc was delayed. She rolled her eyes but agreed. That, reminded Doc when he got certain urges towards Kelly, was another one of the reasons they were best unmarried.

At precisely 1:30, they were at the entrance of the McGovern estate. The gates opened as the FBI car pulled to the entrance. No one could be seen along the pine-lined boulevard, however, Doc felt certain they were being watched, closely. The caller, Dustin McGovern, had instructed them to drive to the carriage house where he would meet them. As they drove, Doc could see the neighbor's estate where the presidential fundraiser had been held. Pat had asked the duty agent to provide some background on the caller. Just before they entered the estate the duty agent had called back and reported that the McGovern family was among the twenty wealthiest families in Minnesota. They had made their money in the agricultural commodities business which dominated the Minneapolis business community in the early decades. They were a highly regarded family and the ASAIC had reminded them to be most respectful. An audible gasp could be heard when Pat told the ASAIC that Doc was going to be doing the interview with him. "We don't want any problems out there. I want you to call me as soon as you leave that interview. Do you understand?"

Pat pulled up to the massive brick carriage house door. It, too, was opened by an invisible operator. He drove onto a painted gray floor and to an open stall sandwiched between a Bentley and a Mercedes. Doc got out, marveling at the immense garage. It was cleaner than his own immaculately kept apartment. This was a place where he could live and be content. He wondered if they needed a security boss.

A silver-haired man appeared from behind a black Citron. He approached the two law enforcement officers with great confidence and swagger holding out his hand in greeting. "I'm Dustin McGovern. And you are?"

The agents introduced themselves and he invited them to sit on the tall stools in front of the bare maple workbench. Above the bench, platinum and chrome-plated tools lay, organized like fine silverware. He gave the striped tie a tug and pulled on his sport coat sleeve before he began. "I have invited you here today because I know who attacked the first lady and who killed her son."

Doc and Pat looked at each other and then back to McGovern, waiting for him to continue. For the moment it seemed he had no intention of going beyond his bold pronouncement. He stood in front of them as they sat on stools like pupils in grade school. He was obviously pleased with this arrangement. When he didn't continue, Doc, without raising his hand finally asked, "Who?"

McGovern paused and cocked his head for effect, and then waved his hands in the air, as if it were plain to see, "Why Grinling Gibbons, of course. Surely the FBI must have suspected him from the beginning. He has an obvious motive and I have been told by others in the Administration that the vice president is running things. I have also learned that Grinling Gibbons despises President Franklin. Why it was only a month ago that the vice president was at my next door neighbor's for a fundraiser. And then, the next thing you know, the first lady and her son are next door and then they are attacked as they leave. I can assure you I wasn't at the fundraiser. I believe that the vice president made the arrangements for the attack during his first visit. My neighbors are Bilderbergers, you know. I'm really quite shocked that the FBI hasn't already investigated this matter. That would have already been done if I ran the FBI. I applied to be a FBI agent once, however, I was turned down due to my poor eyesight. I likely would have been running the place by now."

Pat and Doc traded looks and Pat finally asked, "How do you know this, Mr. McGovern?"

"Would you two care for some refreshments? I keep some rather rare brandies in the tool boxes."

Pat remembering his ASAIC's admonishments, "No thank you, Mr. McGovern."

"Sure, if you join us, sir," Doc said not meaning to overrule Pat.

"Of course." He walked to the shiny black and silver tool chest pulling open the doors to reveal a full bar bereft of tools. He poured three drinks without consulting them and served them with great seriousness and formality. “Gentlemen, I propose a toast to our most important investigation.” He poured down half of the drink and raised his glass again, “May that scoundrel, the vice president, be brought to justice and become the devil’s concubine in hell.”

“Off to hell with him and his evil mates.” Doc was getting into this performance.

“Gentlemen, now that I have provided the suspect, the motive, and the opportunity, I shall leave you both to carry on. It shan’t take you long to bring this matter to a close. I shall charge you both to arrest the vice president when you have sufficient evidence.”

He turned to leave disappearing behind ‘48 Cadillac convertible as the garage door slowly rose. “I shall also expect frequent reports updating me on your investigation.”

“Yes sir,” they both replied as they got into the FBI car.

They drove in silence along the pine bordered boulevard, not certain whether to laugh or cry for the odd fellow. Finally, Pat reached for his cell phone and called his ASCIC, “Sir, I don’t think Mr. McGovern has any great insights into the matter at hand. In fact, I think he has a bit of a gentleman’s drinking problem. No, sir, Doc was most well-behaved. Yes, sir, I will thank him for you, Good bye.”

“The boss thanks you for your uncharacteristic restraint.”

“I’m flattered.”

“I almost forgot to tell you. I got a call from one of the agents from back east working on the ALF wiretap. He said that the two ALF members who were suppose to do the scouting in Minnesota came into the FBI Office and wanted to be snitches. The agents were highly surprised as they have never had anyone inside the organization turn before.”

“That right? Good for them – upstanding citizens doing their duty for God, country, and the coin of the realm.”

"The Boston agent said that both men had some crazy story about having been to the U of M on a scouting mission and being caught by a FBI agent who beat them and threatened them into becoming snitches. He wanted to know if I knew anything about this happening during our surveillance."

"Do you?"

"Nope."

....

By 5:00, Doc, Kelly, the two dogs, and the priest were enjoying a fine Cabernet Sauvignon as the bison steaks and ruffed grouse kabobs sizzled on the grill. Kelly left the two alone in her cluttered den where she turned out romance novels the way Henry Ford turned out black model A's. Another rift between them – Doc couldn't compare with her male characters, in or out of bed. He always wondered where she acquired her vast knowledge of sexual encounters.

"Father, what do you think of the al Qaeda threats of bringing biblical plagues upon America?"

"That's a hard question to answer." The priest ran his hand through his thin carrot colored hair.

"Why?"

"The biblical account of the plagues teaches us that God brought the plagues on the ancient lands of Egypt to force the pharaoh – probably Ramses – to release the Jews whom he held in servitude. God's man Moses went before the pharaoh and warned him that the God of the Jews was demanding he free them. The pharaoh, of course, wasn't going to do that because the Jews were busy building the pyramids and tending to the crops – all of the things that the Egyptians didn't want to do because it was back breaking labor."

"Kinda like America bringing all the labor from Mexico and Central America to work in the slaughter houses and as roofers."

"I think you could make that analogy. Anyway, the pharaoh basically told Moses and God to get screwed – however a pharaoh would say something like that. Moses told the pharaoh that God would visit these terrible plagues upon the land of Egypt."

"What were the plagues?"

"Well, God began the program by turning the Nile River red with blood. Then he brought in frogs in great numbers. Moses would go back to the pharaoh after each plague and basically say 'Ok, have you had enough?' and the pharaoh being a stubborn SOB held firm. Could I have another glass of the wine? All this talk about Egypt is leaving me a bit parched."

"Easily remedied," Doc replied and reached for the bottle to pour a healthy glassful. The father took a large draught and continued.

"So on it went, God continued to bring on the plagues of gnats, flies, frogs, disease on livestock, boils, hail and fire, locusts, darkness, and then topped it all off with the death of all first born of every Egyptians' family including the pharaoh's son. It was very similar to what we have seen the last few weeks."

"That was kinda a show stopper," Doc offered.

"Indeed it was because the pharaoh finally agreed to free the Jews and allow them to migrate to the land of milk and honey which today they call Israel."

"So, back to my original question, how do you think that relates to al Qaeda's threats to bring the plagues to America?"

"Well, as I say, it's similar, although they have it all wrong."

"Why?"

"Because, according to the Bible, God brought the plagues to Egypt and I certainly don't believe that al Qaeda has garnered Allah's support in bringing the plagues to America."

"I see your point, but the pharaoh likewise didn't think Moses had God's support until his son was killed."

"*Touché*. I'll give you that. There are more liberal theologians that say that the plagues were actually naturally occurring events that the Bible authors later sculpted to its present form."

"How so?"

"Some say, for example, that the blood in the Nile was really naturally occurring red algae that made the river look blood red. Algae sometimes contain neurotoxins that could have killed the fish and driven the frogs from the water. The dead fish would have attracted an unbelievable number of flies and other insects to eat on the fish. The frogs came to feed on the flies. Those flies could have brought disease to nearby livestock and so the cycle goes. All of this, of course, is modern scientists trying to explain an ancient story and cutting God out of the picture."

"What do you believe, Father?"

"I believe that God can bring such events into play. It may be that He warmed the river and increased the red algae knowing that all of these events would fall into place. I believe that al Qaeda is replicating the events, using current technologies, to force the president to leave the Middle East and abandon the Jews."

"Seems ironic that now we have Arabs playing god by using the same plagues to force the Jewish people back out of the Promised Land...."

Monday, October 22nd

White House
Washington, D.C.

The cosmetologist made final additions to the president's make-up – fading away some wrinkles and erasing the dark bags below his eyes. His nose looked like a ski slope on television so she took care of that. She trimmed a few misbehaving hairs and stepped back to admire her work. He frowned and waved her away, like a royal dismissing a servant and resumed studying his script.

"Mr. President, one minute to air."

President Franklin took a deep breath, put his game-face on and stared into the camera lens above the teleprompter screen.

"I am proud to announce that our American military forces have achieved victory in the Middle East.

"Our presence in this war torn area has led to the unity of national leadership in both Iraq and Afghanistan. Shortly, those nations will declare a unified ruling coalition and a cessation of the fighting.

"As I speak, our forces are attacking the remaining al Qaeda and Taliban forces. They will no longer be a threat to America.

"Agents from the FBI are near to arresting the al Qaeda forces in America. These unprecedented arrests will bring an end to their terrorist activities in our nation.

"My fellow Americans, while it has been an arduous war – today I can confidently claim victory.

"I have ordered what we all have been waiting for, the immediate return of all military forces deployed in the Middle East.

"They will be reunited with their loved ones.

"Join me in welcoming these heroes home.

"I will end with an expression of appreciation to all who supported our armed forces and my administration during these trying years.

"Lastly, I wish to express our grief and condolences to the families of the pilots and crew members of the three Marine helicopters who perished as a result of a mid-air collision last night near Camp David. These men were true heroes and deserve our prayers and our nation's appreciation."

It all seemed so simple – a few words, carefully crafted together, a snap of the fingers, and no more war, no more killing, no more disabled vets.

Tuesday, October 23th

Finnegan's Irish Pub
St. Paul, Minnesota

ANCHOR WOMAN RHONDA COOPER LOOKED quite pleased with herself as she reported that "American forces have begun a withdrawal of massive proportions reminiscent of the American military helicopters leaving the American Embassy in Saigon. General Highcamp is quoted as saying, 'Our mission has been accomplished, and our troops leave victorious.' The general says within 30 days all remaining forces should be home."

"Victorious, my ass, just like Nixon in Vietnam," Doc muttered. He still woke at night dreaming about the Marines who'd died in his arms. That inglorious withdrawal from Southeast Asia still stuck in his craw.

Sue Rivard brought Doc back from his dark thoughts of Southeast Asia, "I got the lab results back today from the whiskey bottles I picked up from Blondie. They lifted six distinct prints from the bottle. I ran the prints nationally and found three men who were printed during some sort of military training operation. I'll check more. They were all Peruvian soldiers," Sue Rivard told Doc.

Doc looked across the room to see Pat Campbell strutting towards their table. "What's he so damn happy about?" Doc asked.

"Well, partner," Campbell began as he slapped Doc on the back and held his hand there, "I ain't going to have to work with your dumb ass no more."

"Say no more and leave," Doc begged.

"Nope, I suspect I'll be in my own SAIC office in New York or LA, maybe Washington."

"Whose fat ass did you kiss to make you arrive at that conclusion?"

"I caught the attackers of the first lady and her son. We hit a Muslim house at midnight last night and arrested three al Qaeda trained assassins. They were all from Saudi Arabia, just like the 911 hijackers."

"How'd you know they did it?"

"Because, my ex-partner, and this is very hush, hush until the Director announces it tomorrow morning, we got uniforms, guns, police radios, remote controls for the MNDOT trucks and notes in Arabic about the plan. Plus, we got keys to a building in Bloomington. We searched that building and found two Suburbans and an orange MNDOT van. They also had a bunch of al Qaeda training material and photos of themselves in Afghanistan with bin Laden."

"Thanks for inviting me to go with."

"This was a very secret FBI only operation, you understand."

"I sure do, my boy, I surely do. Anyway, congratulations, young man, sit down and let me buy you a drink," Doc offered and pointed towards an empty chair. He hoped Pat wasn't serious about a transfer.

"Can't, ex-partner, I got a racquetball game to get to. Later pal," and he turned and left still bouncing with a lightness Doc could only vaguely recall in his own life…maybe a Christmas 30 years ago.

"Hey, Pat," Doc shouted, "where'd they impound the Suburbans?"

Campbell turned, looking puzzled, "Minneapolis Police Indoor Impound, why?"

"Have a good game and call me when you get to New York!"

Doc gently elbowed Special Agent Brothers. "Let's go for a ride."

"Where to?" Brothers asked.

"Minneapolis Police Impound, my son, mount your horse."

…………………

When they arrived, two bored Minneapolis Police Officers guarded the door. Doc threw a handful of breath mints in his mouth as he approached the officers. "Evening, officers, I'm an agent with the FBI Anti-Terrorist Unit, this is Agent Brothers. I'm going in just for a minute to verify the VIN for a search warrant."

"You got ID?" the smaller of the two asked.

"I do." He flashed his credentials as he continued past them through the doorway.

Brothers and Doc stepped inside the impound room where the two black Suburbans were stored. "Watch this," Doc said. He removed the Suburban key fob he had taken from Armando, the Southside drug dealer. Doc pressed the door unlock button and heard an audible CLICK from the Suburban. He pressed the lock button twice and the horn sounded.

"It would seem we have some unfinished investigative work to do."

Wednesday, October 24th

FBI Office, Joint Terrorist Task Force
Minneapolis, Minnesota

DOC PUNCHED THE KEYS OF his cell phone and waited for Special Agent Lora L'Engle to answer. "Lora, are you still friends with that Texas Ranger you met during the Schilling homicide?" Doc asked.

"Well, Tex and I aren't as close as we once were if you get my drift, although we are still friends, why?"

"Because as I remember he was some sort of expert on Latino gangs, wasn't he?"

"He was an expert in a couple of areas, my friend, gangs being just one. I'm thinking you need a favor?"

"Would you call him and ask what he knows about Peruvian Special Forces wearing a tattoo of a skeleton hanging from a parachute? I think they may have been a paratrooper unit from which some sold out to Mexican drug traffickers as hired guns."

"Might this involve the need for me to travel to Texas?"

"If you would like that, I think I can arrange it. Would mind taking a military flight?"

"You cheapskate, I'll call him, good bye."

Lora pulled her Impala into the Cub Food parking lot and dialed up the Texas Ranger Headquarters in Austin.

"Lora, what a surprise to hear from you again. It's been too long. Where are you?" Cullen Kingsley said in a voice that expressed caution and curiosity.

"I'm in Minnesota. We've got an investigation and I was wondering...."

Forty-five minutes later, Kingsley had pretty much summarized his knowledge of Peruvian gang members who are ex-military and work for the drug cartels.

“That help you?”

“Sure does – do you guys run into these gangs often?”

“Last one I saw was part of a shootout at the border. Four Border Patrol Agents were killed and we found a Peruvian wounded in the bush. He’s at the Lakeland Hospital in Dallas. He might have been part of a bigger group that got into a gunfight with the Border Patrol.”

“When’d that happen?”

“Happened on Sunday, October 7th.”

“I’ll get back to you.”

Wednesday, October 24th

Castle Creek Chalet
Aspen, Colorado

THE TWELVE FINISHED THEIR PRAYERS a half-hour later than expected. They prayed longer than usual as they had much to praise Allah for and much to ask of Him. They paraded back to their rooms in silence to prepare for the evening meeting.

When Omar began the session an hour later, he announced, "The President of the United States of America has conceded our triumph albeit in his own declaration of victory. I don't believe we are concerned if he saves face in his defeat. In fact, we will give him a few real victories to assure our goal to wipe Israel from the earth."

"Hakeem Al-Busaid, share with us the plan of attack upon Israel."

Al-Busaid was a Persian, who was born and raised in occupied Palestine. The list of family members killed battling the Jewish oppressor was long and growing. He was proud and anxious to be permitted to orchestrate Israel's defeat. He stood smiling, "We will do nothing to Israel as long as the United States has a military presence in the area. We'll bide our time as they retreat and use that time wisely to prepare.

"Already, we are deploying mercenaries to the borders. They are well supplied and will be the vanguard of the attack from every inch of the border. This time the Jews will not be facing boys with rocks, they will have to fight real soldiers.

"We have made two very limited tests on Israeli tanks. We know we can disrupt them by controlling their on-board computers. The tests are limited because we do not want to call attention to our ability. We are uncertain if the Americans have brought this issue to the Israelis. I believe they likely are keeping the problem quiet.

"The military forces of Egypt, Saudi Arabia, Syria, Iran, and Pakistan are ready to support our efforts. Americans have bolstered some of these nations' military forces for a decade. Russia and China have secretly armed Iran with missiles and fighter jets.

"For the first time, we are getting intelligence from spies in Israel. Jewish immigrants from Russia have penetrated the Israeli Defense Forces Command. The Russians hold family members hostage to motivate these spies to betray their country and people. Consequently, we will have valuable real time battle plans or at least as much as one can trust that type of spy.

"The question is, will Israel use their nuclear weapons and against what target? And if they do what will be our response? Pakistan has committed its nuclear missiles and that is an option, although it makes Pakistan a logical first strike by the Israelis. It would be our desire to refrain from nuclear weapons as our own people are too close and would be killed. Not to mention the land we conquer will be uninhabitable.

"In the broadest terms, our plan of attack will be to immediately slow the supply of fuel to Israel. We can use our own corporate influence to accomplish this. Additionally, we will send divers to the Ports of Haifa and Ashdod to scuttle three vessels which will be strategically placed so as to shut down the ports.

"When we have squeezed their oil supply and the Americans are out of sight, our mercenary forces will provoke the Jews to attack Lebanon. Hamas has been re-supplied with arms from the Russians and Chinese and will take the brunt of the attack – sustaining we believe large losses. We all agreed Hamas and Hezbollah need to disappear. They have served their purpose, but will threaten our new Islamic Order if they survive. Those that the Jews don't destroy will be later dealt with by the mercenaries.

"When the Jews are close to victory over Hamas – Syria, Egypt, Saudi Arabia, Iran and Pakistan will jointly attack Israel.

"It is then we will do as much damage using our ability to penetrate their computers and disrupt their communications. Frankly, we do not know how successful this will be as we have such limited tests.

"We have only one opportunity to finally destroy Israel and restore the Palestinian homeland. More importantly, we need to chase the American military surrogate from our lands. As long as they have Israel to do their fighting and dominate the battlefield, we'll be unable to determine our own destiny.

"Once the Jews have surrendered, we'll give them safe passage across the Red Sea to Sudan. I believe they'll ultimately be delivered to America according to the ultimatum the president has tacitly agreed to.

"In their place, we have leaders ready to be installed to join the new Islamic Order. I believe we will be in Jerusalem by the Jew's Passover next year – Second Passover for certain. It will be the last year the Jews defile our city with their filthy presence."

"Your plan will be blessed by Allah," Omar spoke after letting Al-Busaid's speech settle in their minds. "I have more good news."

"Ali shah Masood is alive and free. He has made contact with us and is asking for direction. Obviously he wishes to return to us.

"Right now he is in Rome. We have sent him money and identification documents. We have our own counter surveillance looking for the CIA and to date, they say Ali is free of anyone following him. I'll put that discussion aside for you to think about.

"Let me tell you about the plans for al Qaeda and the Taliban." Omar kept it brief. He was growing weary of the endless meetings and yearned to be free of the others who demanded his attention for even the most mundane of matters.

"We will time the demise of al Qaeda and the Taliban with the American military retreat...

"...Finally, let me say a brief word about our partnership with the President of Venezuela and FARC.

"During our talks to these parties, we learned we had mutual interests and problems. The president sees himself as the heir to Castro in that part of our new world order. He despises America and is anxious to assume Castro's role as a major thorn in the Americans' side. What distinguishes him from Castro is oil money available to facilitate the drug trade. FARC and several drug cartels allied with the president to use Venezuela as a shipping point for cocaine. We have access to endless amounts of heroin from Afghanistan and transportation companies to move the narcotics. We will transport our heroin to Venezuela where it, along with the South America's cocaine, will be readied for shipping.

Venezuela's President has a government owned factory that will seal these drugs in a variety of products which our boats will bring to America and Europe. The profits will be substantial.

"Ah, and speaking of profits, our investment moves in anticipation of the crash of the American stock market have turned a handsome profit. The American people are financing our revolution and establishment of Islamic order.

"My brothers, we are awash in cash."

Wednesday October 24th

J. Edgar Hoover Building
F.B.I. Headquarters
Washington, D.C.

F.B.I. DIRECTOR LYOV MARASHOV WEARING his favorite gray suit stood before the microphones in the Media Relations Room on the first floor of the J. Edgar Hoover building. Surrounded by flags and eager looking staff who were brought in as props, Director Marashov began, "I am pleased to announce that yesterday special agents from the F.B.I. Office in Minneapolis arrested three al Qaeda members for the attack on the first lady and the assassination of the president's son, Cody. Acting upon fresh information found during our investigation of the assassination, agents executed a search warrant at a residence in Minneapolis. Agents were met with gunfire upon entering the residence. They returned fire which resulted in the death of five assassins and the wounding of three others, who are in custody.

"I am told that agents found overwhelming evidence that the eight al Qaeda operatives are indeed the assassins.

"As this is a continuing investigation and there are three suspects in custody, I will not answer any questions or go into further detail.

"I do want to express my personal thanks to the dedicated special agents of the F.B.I., who painstakingly brought these criminals to justice."

Amid shouted questions from the media, Director Marashov performed a perfect pirouette and left the stage.

Wednesday, October 24th

B.C.A. Headquarters
St. Paul, Minnesota

DOC'S VISITS TO HEADQUARTERS WERE rare. He felt uncomfortable among the brass. He nearly always misspoke saying something, however well-intended, he later regretted. Mostly, entering headquarters brought him to the reality that he did have a boss and did have rules and regulations, policy and protocols – something he mostly elected to ignore.

He made appearances when he needed something and today was no exception. He needed 'favors' from his boss, Brian Millard, the Agent in Charge of Special Investigations. Millard was an affable fellow who'd once been a superior investigator, perhaps Doc's equal. Acting upon poor judgment and bad advice, he took the supervisory job only to find that his new job consisted of attending meetings…sometimes meetings about meetings. Like a prisoner in his cell, he began to X off the days until retirement and a termination of meetings, endless and pointless meetings. He yearned for the freedom enjoyed by Doc.

Doc entered Millard's spacious corner office and exchanged greetings. When Doc was in Millard's office, he remained standing near the door, as though he might make a faster exit. Today he sat. Millard smiled knowing that Doc must have a long list, not that he would ever write a list of needs.

"Shall we exchange meaningless pleasantries or do you want to get on with just telling me what favors I may bestow upon you?" Millard asked.

"Just as soon get right to the favors if that's okay with you, boss?"

"Shoot," replied Millard as he took a pen to scribble the list he knew was coming.

"First, let me tell you I think the FBI is wrong about Cody Franklin's assassins. There's more to this . . ."

Millard held his hand up, "Doc, I went to the FBI briefing this morning. They shared what evidence they got on these guys, believe me they are nailed – signed, sealed, and delivered."

"Boss, listen to me. There were at least eight Mexican or Peruvian paratroopers in town before the son was killed. We got prints from a couple who were trained by U.S. Special Forces. They disappeared after the assassination; nowhere to be found. I spoke with a witness in Minneapolis where they stayed and found a Suburban key fob that belonged to them. I tested the key fob on one of the Suburbans the FBI took from those al Qaeda guys. It worked. One of our own agents who was in the motorcade saw those guys in the black Suburban as it was closing on the motorcade. He swears they weren't Arabs but Latinos. I think there is more to the story, that's all boss."

"I will regret asking you, have you shared this with your FBI partner?"

Doc shook his head, "Hell, no, boss, you know they are fine with wrapping this up and they do not want other evidence messing up their theories."

"So, what part do you want me to play in your diabolical plan to prove the FBI wrong?"

"Just a few small favors – first, we could use some cash to conduct this little investigation. We already have some informants and will need some travel money."

"What else?"

"I'd like you to assign Sue Rivard, Topo, Tony Brothers and Lora L'Engle to work this for 2 weeks. They are available, I already checked with them."

"What else?"

"I'd like you to keep this between the six of us until we know what if anything we have here."

"What else?"

"That's it, boss."

Millard waved his pen in front of Doc, "All your wishes are granted . . . good luck and call me once in a while."

"I owe you boss," and he was out the door wasting little time getting out of headquarters.

Doc's cell phone was pressed to his ear as he moved towards his car, "Lora, I am just leaving Millard's office, we are good to go. Can you get down to Dallas today? Good. I've got a flight for you, call Amy at HQ she'll give you the details. Good luck."

Doc hit 'END' and immediately dialed Agent Tony Brothers.

"Tony, we're on. What did you find out about your Uncle's place?"

"I spoke to him yesterday. He is in Tucson, Arizona and won't be back until spring. He said we can use his place."

"Later Buddy . . . see you out there and thanks."

Seconds later, "Sue, this is Doc. Millard gave his blessing. Can you get Blondie and start out to Taylors Falls? Call Brothers for directions and ask Blondie if her brother can join us. I'll see you out there… later beautiful."

Doc was right back on the phone, "Topo, Doc here. Millard gave us a green light for two weeks. We are going to work out of Brothers' uncle's estate near Taylors Falls. Can you get food for two weeks and meet us out there tonight? Yeah, some meat for the grill – call Brothers for directions."

Doc headed back to his Grand Avenue apartment to pick up clothes and the one-eyed pug.

Wednesday, October 24th

Rome, Italy

A LOVELY FALL DAY – SUNSHINE abounded and a hint of a breeze to whisk away the heat. The smell of baking sweet pastries and coffee filled the air. Tall waiters wearing long white aprons moved gracefully among the tables serving cups of brutally strong coffee. By the time Ali had left the café, the shadows had moved across the striped umbrellas sheltering the metal tables. He limped down the busy sidewalks to his hotel and disappeared into the lobby.

While Rocky watched Ali enter the hotel he felt his cell phone vibrate in his coat pocket.

"Rocky, it's Alex Stone, I need a favor."

Rocky hated when anyone started out a conversation mentioning favors, "What's that, Stone?"

"When I was working in Iraq for Blackstone there was an accounting type who worked in Kuwait or Saudi, he went back and forth, his name is Maurice Smith. Anyway, he was suddenly promoted and sent to be in charge of things over in that hellhole in Bosnia. Rumors among my drinking buddies are that he had uncovered a bunch of missing mercs who were on the payroll. The rumor is that Blackstone shipped him out to keep him quiet. I was wondering if you could locate him in Bosnia?" Alex asked.

"And do what, why should I be interested in finding him?"

"Because, I think those miss'n mercs are working for al Qaeda and are in the United States, that's why."

"Are you crazy? Blackstone is one of the largest contractors over here and a huge supporter of the president."

"Be that as it may, I have good reason to believe it's true, can you help?"

“Listen, I’m up to my ass in alligators and really don’t have time.”

“What if I told you that these guys may have killed the president’s son?”

“I’m not working that, take it to the FBI.”

“What if I told you I’m record’n this?”

“You prick,” Rocky shouted into the phone.

For a half a minute there was silence, “Okay, I’ll get one of our guys to locate him and call you when we find him. We’ll take it from there if you have some solid evidence.”

“You are a true patriot.”

Wednesday, October 24th

Castle Creek Chalet
Aspen, Colorado, USA

OMAR SOAKED UP THE SUNSHINE which had been hard to come by while he sat on the massive deck and read the Koran. "When ye encounter the infidels, strike off their heads till ye have made a great slaughter amoung them, and the rest make fast the fetters." Omar wondered how his people could ever fix the fetters, the shackles, to the Americans. They were such a rebellious, unruly lot.

When he appeared at his side, al Fulani, the Kuwaiti, interrupted Omar's study, "Omar, may I speak bluntly?"

"Of course, Qadir, what's troubling you?"

"You know Ali shah Masood is my half-brother and my father's favorite. My father is deeply troubled as he's heard nothing from Ali. Omar, I'd like to bring him in."

"I also would like to bring him back but we just don't know if this is a trap."

al Fulani sat next to Omar and leaned in closer. "However, leaving him out there is dangerous, also. What if the CIA finds him again or if they are watching him? They could grab him anytime or, and I pray this is not the case – it's possible that Ali has been tortured into cooperating. If that were the case, we shouldn't let this opportunity slip through our hands. For all those reasons, I believe we must bring him in."

Omar let those thoughts sink in, his pointed tongue playing on his open lips. "What do you want from me?"

"I want you to let me handle this. He is my family."

"If he is being watched how would you grab him without being compromised?"

"I have the men who can handle the matter."

"Qadir, let me pray on this and give you my answer tomorrow."

"Can I ask you a question…a matter that has troubled me for days?"

Omar shifted in his chair, "Yes, of course," although he was concerned that al Fulani would press for too much.

"Why the plagues?"

Omar was relieved. "al Qaeda brought that to us. It was not our plan but it seemed to fit our needs."

"But it won't bring the Americans to…

Omar held his hand up, "It's symbolic. Just like the towers and the Pentagon were symbolic. The damage far exceeded the immediate harm to New York or Washington. The same with the plagues and because al Qaeda had been working on the project for years, we simply accommodated their plagues."

An aide brought a cellular telephone to Omar. He leaned down to the seated man and whispered in his ear.

"Excuse me, sir, it's my mother, she says it's important." Omar accepted the phone and walked away speaking softly.

Thursday, October 25th

Sheppard Air Force Base
Wichita Falls, Texas

IT'S A LONG BUMPY RIDE in the jump seats of the C-130 cargo area. Agent Lora L'Engle cursed Doc every minute for arranging this free ride from Minneapolis to Dallas on the National Guard plane. The agent rocked in the webbed seat while she spent the last forty minutes applying her make-up. The mirror bounced so much, she couldn't be certain that she wouldn't look like a clown when they got to Texas.

She gave a silent word of thanks when the massive wheels fell onto the tarmac. When she disembarked, she was blinded by the Texas sun. There hadn't been sunlight that intense in Minnesota since the Fourth of July. She pulled her sunglasses from her purse and looked for her ride.

"Lora, over here," called Texas Ranger Cullen Kingsley.

It took a moment for her eyes to adjust then she saw the lanky ranger with the trademark white Stetson hat.

"Cullen, it's great to see you again." She hugged him so tight she knocked his hat off. "Sorry."

"Not to worry, darlin', a ranger should take his hat off to a lady anyhow." He bowed slightly. "Let's go and I'll fill ya'll in on the way to Lakeland Hospital."

They caught up on personal news until they hit the freeway. "I'd better tell you how I see this before we get there. Ya'll know some of this already so bear with me – I don't want to miss anything.

"Two weeks ago, Sunday, October 7th, four Border Patrol agents were on patrol along the Mexican -Texas border in Wilkin County. They radioed Dispatch that they had stopped 19 illegals and were waiting for transport when they were ambushed and killed. The illegals disappeared after the shootout except Juan Valenzuela who was wounded and unconscious in the sage brush. He remained unconscious until last week.

"The FBI has been trying to talk to him although they aren't getting anywhere. I'm not involved with this investigation in any official capacity. I am getting my information from my old partner in the Border Patrol, Jesus Gonzales.

"Jesus is the Border Patrol agent assigned to tag along with the FBI. He also does the translations because the FBI agents don't speak a lick of Spanish.

"We are meeting Jesus at the hospital and I'll let him tell ya'll what he's learned.

"OK, now, where do you want to go to dinner tonight?" Cullen asked.

"Oh, surprise me, you choose – I want real Tex-Mex food not the Taco Juan's version."

"I know just the place, the best carne seca in the state," he said. They resumed catching up on personal news until they arrived at the hospital.

Kingsley pulled the big sedan to the emergency entrance. Jesus Gonzales, a squarely built man, walked to the car and got into the back seat.

Greetings were exchanged and Gonzales got right to the point, "Ma'am, this visit ya'll are 'bout to make is off the record. I'll get you into the room and translate."

"I speak Spanish. What's your take on this guy? How does he fit in with the murders of the Border Patrol agents?" L'Engle asked.

"Honest opinion, Ma'am, the FBI's working theory is that the Border Patrol agents apprehended a group of illegals some of whom were smuggling drugs. We know from footprints some of the illegals in the group were women, so they were likely not all smugglers 'cause they don't use women in that type of operation. We know from the tracks that some of the men were carrying heavy loads – like sixty pounds – maybe marijuana.

"When the FBI interviewed Juan, they set out to prove he was one of the drug smugglers who engaged in the gunfight. They threatened him with the death penalty unless he confessed and identified the others."

"What do you think?"

Gonzales paused – conflicted with helping his old partner and crossing the line with the FBI, "I don't know if he is a drug smuggler. He denied smuggling drugs and when they demanded he confess to this and being a part of the gunfight or get the death penalty, he clammed up. He comes from a culture that distrust police – rightly so – and he seems like he believes that the agents are telling him lies."

"Do you think he was one of the smugglers?"

"Ma'am, I don't – for a couple of reasons. The smugglers used are normally the peasants of Mexico. Juan is no peasant, he has a military bearing and he isn't Mexican. Judging from his speech I think he is from Peru, Ecuador, Columbia, somewhere along the West Coast of South America."

"Have you told this to the FBI?"

"Ma'am, ya'll ever worked with the FBI?" as Gonzales rolled his eyes.

"Enough said, let's go talk to him."

"Good luck, I'll wait here for you. I'll catch up on a bunch of reports," offered Kingsley.

When they arrived at the hospital bedside, L'Engle noted Juan Valenzuela did indeed have a military bearing, even lying in bed. He looked directly into her eyes and held her stare, emotionless. She didn't know it but Valenzuela wondered if L'Engle was the angel he'd been praying to the Blessed Virgin to deliver him from this cursed place.

Thursday, October 25th

Brothers Estate
St. Croix River Valley
Taylors Falls, Minnesota

DOC SAT ON THE GLEAMING wood deck of the opulent guest-house belonging to Tony Brothers' Uncle Fred. He sipped coffee and watched two bald eagles gliding on the morning updrafts from the St. Croix River which coursed through enormous boulders. The cedar log guesthouse was nestled on the 400 foot bluffs and the eagles were only a little above that. The oak and white paper birch trees had lost nearly all of their red and yellow leaves. He felt the warmth of the wood fire inside the natural stone fireplace which rose from the sandy soil three stories along side of the house.

While one eagle flew out of sight, the other perched in an enormous dead pine. Within seconds, four gray birds, too small to identify, began to dive at the eagle, coming closer with each pass. Doc marveled that such a powerful creature could be so harassed by the weaker birds. The eagle pecked at the attackers but missed as they flew by like a squadron of F-4s. Hardly three minutes passed when the eagle had enough and dove from the dead branch towards the river. It gave Doc pause to wonder if he was an eagle or one of the little grey birds endlessly fighting to stay alive and protect his own.

Taylors Falls is a village lying between the rapids of the St. Croix River and the steep sandstone embankments. The village was larger when Scandinavian lumberjacks worked the virgin forests and sent the timber floating down the river over the falls. The lumberjacks have long since disappeared, however, the tall pines have returned and line the pristine river banks. The falls were mitigated by the dam although upstream still has plenty of fast water. Doc wore the scars on his elbows and forearms where jagged rocks tore his flesh when he tipped his kayak in one of the class three rapids.

Tony Brothers' Uncle Fred never married and his family was that of his brothers and sisters. The nieces and nephews were always welcomed at the estate and treated like princesses and princes. Tony Brothers never doubted that Uncle Fred would open his house to his partners.

The ex, Kelly, had just completed her manuscript for a new romance novel, *Heavenly Lust*. When she handed Doc the typed version, she explained it was about a priest who was rescued from the Mississippi River when he jumped from the High Bridge. He falls in love with his young rescuer a St. Paul Police Officer. She won't say male or female. In return for watching Gump when Doc went skiing at Big Sky last year, he now was obliged to read her copy and comment on the police procedures she cites in the book. Comment not criticize were her last words. He promised himself to set aside a half hour every morning to fulfill his vow to read what was decidedly was not his genre.

Doc was in poor spirits. He had planned to get started with the investigation yesterday, however, all the agents had personal matters to attend to before they could set aside two full weeks. Doc only had Gump to tend to, although he was a handful. "Shut-up, you stupid fart-hound. What the hell is the matter with you?" Doc walked towards Gump who was barking himself hoarse out in the cobblestone driveway.

"*Merda* . . . What in the hell is going on here?" he said to himself, although loud enough to be heard.

Doc flew down the steps shouting at Tony. "Who are all these people?"

Tony quickly put his arm around Doc and took him off to the side of the house. "Look, Doc, I know this looks a bit crazy, but it will make sense when I explain it to you," Tony offered.

"I doubt it, what's the story?" Doc asked.

"Listen, Topo went to get Alex Stone and Stone insisted on bringing his partners Jake and Rooster. Stone said they know as much as he does. On the ride out, they told Topo about a guy named Ali who they kidnapped in Pakistan who claims to know about a plot to destroy the United States. Anyway, you should ask those guys about it."

"That makes six with you and me. Who are the girls?"

"Well, Sue picked up Blondie like we agreed, to get her off the streets until we can assess the danger to her. So she brings Nikkei and Fancy, working girls who also partied with the Mexicans or South

Americans – whatever the hell you think they are. Blondie figures these gals are in danger just like her because the soldiers may still be in town. She says Nikkei and Fancy got some more information plus I guess Fancy can cook," Tony concluded, resting his case.

"Oh, *merda*, what have I created? Oh, *merda*. That's ten so far. Who is the good looking broad with you – your sister? Can she cook?" Doc put his head in his hands.

"That beautiful woman is Special Agent Donna Lyons from the Secret Service. She and I were working together on the motorcade when the first lady was attacked and Cody Franklin was killed. The FBI, as you know, is the lead investigative agency, however, the Secret Service detailed Donna and a few other agents to stay in Minnesota to assist in the investigation. I think you'll find she has some very interesting ideas. And yes, she can cook, although she may well kick your skinny little ass if you ask."

"That's eleven…where are we going to put everyone. What have I done? Gump, you little farthound, let's go!" Doc walked back up the stairs to the deck lighting a smoke on the way. It was only the first morning of the first day and the small covert investigation he'd envisioned was already swirling out of control like his capsized kayak in the fast water.

Thursday, October 25th

J. Edgar Hoover Building
Washington, D.C.

F.B.I. DIRECTOR LYOV MARASHOV WAS again before the camera in the headquarters press room. As before, in the background were the obligatory flags and well-dressed executive-agents who were ordered to stand behind the director and look interested and supportive. Only the most photogenic were ever asked to make a showing. One never saw fat buck-toothed balding agents smiling behind the director.

"I am proud to announce the arrests of several terrorists who were responsible for the recent attacks on American soil. Yesterday, FBI agents conducted search warrants in Cambridge, Massachusetts and Austin, Texas. Additionally, the Royal Canadian Mounted Police at our request executed search warrants in Winnipeg, Canada.

"Bearing in mind that no charges have been brought and that twelve men are in custody, I am not able to provide exact details. FBI agents arrested three Egyptian citizens who are students at MIT in the engineering program. Later today, these men will be charged with the explosive destruction of electrical power lines in New York State just days ago. Agents found substantial physical evidence including maps and documents which makes us confident as to their involvement in this destructive act.

"Yesterday evening, FBI agents arrested three Texas University students for the firebombing of refineries in Corpus Christi, Texas. These students are enrolled in chemical engineering and two are members of a flying club in Austin. Agents again found significant evidence including car rental agreements, bomb making materials, maps of the ranch from which the airplane was stolen, and false passports all in a storage rental unit leased by the students. We expect they will be charged tomorrow.

"Lastly, the RCMP arrested six University of Winnipeg students after finding evidence that these Iranian visitors blew up four railroad bridges in North and South Dakota. RCMP officials also found Composition 4 explosives, photos, maps and two stolen vehicles all of which were used to destroy these bridges. We will be working with Canadian officials to extradite all six men.

"These arrests were possible only by the dedication of highly skilled and committed FBI investigators. I thank the men and women who accomplished this task under extreme pressure to bring the terrorist attacks to an end. I might add – additional arrests are imminent.

"I will not be able to take any questions for the reasons I have already stated, thank you." The director executed a rather clumsy exit resembling a *fouetté*, bumping into two props that failed to get out of his way and would never be invited back to share the stage.

Thursday, October 25th

Castle Creek Chalet
Aspen Colorado

AL FULANI WAS ENJOYING A cup of herbal tea, figs, and red grapes on the balcony. He watched the skiers race down the slopes and wished he dared an attempt to ski. "Maybe another day," he thought.

"Qadir, I've thought about the predicament we spoke of yesterday." Omar spoke as he joined al Fulani at the large pine table.

"I agree that we should bring Ali in to talk. Do you have a plan to pick him up?"

"Omar, my family thanks you. Yes, I'm aware of a dozen or more men, who at a moment's notice could do the job. Are we to take this to the whole Council?" al Fulani asked.

"I leave that to you, Qadir. I personally believe that it best be done by you and you alone. If it goes poorly, it should be your decision to remove Ali. Either way, you have my blessing and I believe it's the right decision."

"Thank you, Omar. I'll take care of this matter immediately."

"Have you ever wanted to ski, Omar?"

"I would like that, although perhaps I'm too old. Having fun is not something I ever learned to do."

"I know what you mean. I watch these Americans and they spend so much time and money 'having fun.' My entire life has been spent working, praying, and taking care of all my family and relatives. I don't understand this 'having fun' or 'playing.' It seems to me that is for children."

Thursday, October 25th

Brothers Estate
St. Croix River Valley
Taylors Falls, Minnesota

FANCY, WEARING SHOCKINGLY TIGHT JEANS and a University of Minnesota Golden Gopher sweatshirt, stood on the deck cooking rib-eye steaks on the enormous stainless-steel grill. Fancy was a large black woman – a beauty the likes of Queen Latifah – who could sing like Whitney Houston. As she turned the steaks, she sang softly, *I will Always Love You*, to no one is particular. She used to sing at the Baptist Church in Minneapolis. That was before she met 2-kee, a dope slinging pimp who charmed her into the ugly world of crack and tricks. That was three years ago. Three years since her mama had talked to her. Three years since she'd lifted her voice in praise at the First Baptist church.

Gump lay beneath the grill enjoying the singing and hoping for something to fall within his limited reach. Large billowing clouds moved lazily pass the sun. A slight breeze blew the fresh scent of pines mixing with the sizzling steaks. Crows on tips of swaying cedars watched the humans come and go from the deck. There would likely be morsels of food after the two-leggeds leave.

'Maybe this will work out,' Doc thought while he surveyed the tranquil scene. The stage was set for success or so it seemed.

"Stop giving that dog beer, Fancy, he'll get drunk and roll off the deck," Doc said as he began the descent down the sturdy cedar steps.

Tony opened the screen door and shouted, "Doc, Lora L'Engle is on the phone in the study."

"Get Donna, Topo, and Sue and we'll put her on conference call," Doc ordered.

When they had all arrived in the wood paneled study, Doc began, "Okay Lora, we're all here. Tell us what you've found."

Lora's deep raspy voice – some would say sexy – came through loudly over the speaker phone. "I'm here with Jesus Gonzales a Border Patrol agent in the Lakeland Hospital room of Juan Valenzuela. We have been talking to Juan for three hours. I will spare you the details of how we got to what I'm about to tell you.

"Juan is a Peruvian soldier…a paratrooper trained by American Special Forces. He was recruited by former American Special Forces Commandos to work for an American security company. He and some of his buddies were sent to Iraq until several months ago. They were split from their units and sent to Libya.

"Juan said that within a couple of days of arriving in Libya a charter flew the men and equipment to Venezuela where they were met by soldiers and taken to a military base. He then described a journey by boat to Mexico and ultimately led across the border by two coyotes.

"He swears they were not smuggling drugs. He said that when the Border Patrol stopped them, others in their party who had lingered behind, caught up with the main group and shot the officers. He was wounded, crawled under the sage brush and passed out."

"Why were they sent to America, what was their mission?" Tony asked.

"I'm getting to that. He says that his group was one of several independently sent across the border. He only knew that at the final rendezvous, he was to be given a truck and specific instructions as to where to go, who to meet, and what their mission would be. When they arrived at their destination, there were collaborators already in place that would furnish them with supplies and a final briefing on the mission. He says it would be a mission using their combat skills."

"What about his tattoos?" Tony asked.

"I took photos of his face and tattoos which I sent to your cell phone."

Tony checked his cell, "OK I got the photos. Topo, ask Alex and Blondie to step in here for just a moment?"

"Lora, what's your assessment?"

"I think this is close to the truth. I believe I may get more if I get to talk to him again. I'm doing this sub rosa, and have to be careful not to cross the FBI and U.S. Attorney's Office more than I probably have already. I like Texas but would prefer to not be here behind bars. So, my inclination is to leave this alone for a few days until we can approach the U.S. Attorney with something more than a gut feeling."

"I agree," Doc offered.

"Lora, we have just been joined by Blondie, her friend Nikkei, her brother Alex and his friends Jake and Rooster. Where's Fancy?" Tony asked.

"She said she can't leave the grill because the damn dog will steal the steaks," Blondie declared.

Tony handed his cell phone to Blondie and said, "OK, I'm going to pass this cell phone around and I would like each of you to look at all the pictures."

Blondie and Nikkei looked first, "I don't know this guy, but he has the same tattoos as the Juans – right Nikkei?"

"Yeah, it's the same," Nikkei said.

Jake took the cell phone looked at the photos closing one eye and sighting in the picture. He passed it to Alex and Rooster who viewed them together. They knowingly looked at one another then Rooster said, "We served in Iraq with this guy, you know what I mean. He is a Peruvian paratrooper named Juan. . . ."

"Valenzuela," added Jake. "Hell of a soldier."

The agents exchanged glances and Doc said, "Thanks guys, please, let us finish talking to Lora."

When the room cleared, Doc spoke, "Lora, I believe we are on to something here, however, I agree, let's give it a rest. Can you stay in

Dallas a few more days until we can give a proper presentation to the U.S. Attorney if it comes to that?"

"I think I can occupy myself."

"Be very careful, this could come back to bite us!"

Friday, October 26th

Prime Minister's Residence
Jerusalem, Israel

U.S. AMBASSADOR HAMILTON WEARING HIS 'Friday suit,' a tan Dolce & Gabbana, was ushered into the waiting area of the prime minister's personal office. A somber looking steward/bodyguard offered to get him tea or coffee. Not an early riser, Hamilton eagerly accepted the coffee – hoping the caffeine would give him the boost he needed to face the prime minister – and waited. He was unhappy about being summoned on short notice and at such an early hour, before dawn, without explanation. He was increasingly annoyed at being kept waiting under any circumstances. When he was a CEO, he kept others waiting.

At the end of twenty minutes, Hamilton was on his feet pacing and pestering the young steward. Prime Minister Joby Har-el entered the room unnoticed by Hamilton until he felt a firm hand on his shoulder. "Ambassador Hamilton. Thank you for accommodating my request for this meeting on such short notice and at such an early hour. Please come into my office and we can finish our coffee."

Har-el, attired in his favorite khaki cargo pants and bush jacket, led Hamilton into his spacious corner office and offered a seat at the round table. An aide brought more coffee and opened the bullet resistant windows a bit to let the cool morning air freshen the office. Har-el said nothing, poured coffee and then as if on cue, the loudspeakers on the minarets began their call to prayer throughout the city. Har-el let them finish, "It's a shame you have to drive to Jerusalem from your embassy in Tel Aviv. You know our capital is here in Jerusalem not Tel Aviv. Most nations post their ambassadors in the nation's capitals, do they not?"

"Mr. Prime Minister, you know how contentious this issue is. The Arab and Persian states claim Jerusalem as their holy city and reject Israel's occupation of the city."

"Ah, so they do, I think their endless calls for prayer around our capital are a constant reminder of their claim. Wouldn't you agree?"

"Our position is to try to negotiate a settlement to resolve the dispute."

"Yes, indeed, negotiations have gone on for decades and my people have been bombed and shot for decades while they wait."

"Mr. Prime Minister, why did you ask me to come here on such short notice, I have meetings scheduled and have had to make many changes."

"I know that you had a meeting scheduled with the Palestinian Authority to discuss access to water and have lunch with that pretty news reporter, what is her name again, and dinner plans with friends from New York. Our business today will end this evening at the beginning of our Sabbath. I would suggest that all of these meetings may be delayed as you meet with Israel's prime minister. That, I would suggest to you, is your purpose for serving here. You may also consider in the future not scheduling your social events on our Sabbath. I will remind our Ambassador to your country to respect your Sabbath, such as it is, in the same manner."

Hamilton flushed with rage. He drank his coffee and said nothing for fear of revealing his feelings. Deep down, in his gut, he feared the battle-hardened Prime Minister. Har-el had won round one.

"It has come to my attention that I have not been such a good host since your arrival to my country. I thought we could spend the day together – how do you say it in your country – so we could 'bond.' Har-el smiled broadly showing heavily nicotine-stained teeth, a feature that matched well with his bulbous nose turned red from too much hard liquor.

Hamilton continued holding his tongue.

"I just want this opportunity to show you around and I can assure you that I will have you back to Tel Aviv for dinner. That pretty news woman will be happy to reschedule, in fact I will pick up the tab and you can tell the Palestinians that we will continue giving them adequate water as long as they keep the bombs and rockets in their own backyard and not ours."

Hamilton warmed a little as Har-el showed him around his office, explaining many of the photos which hung on his wall, especially his war photos. He described his role and offered as how many of his friends in the photos had been killed in battle. He spared no detail on their deaths until Hamilton looked as though he was becoming uncomfortable. "Come Mr. Ambassador, let's take a ride."

Under heavy security their motorcade drove to the nearby Holocaust Memorial. Hamilton explained he had already been to such a memorial in his own capital. Har-el ignored the remark and they spent 90 minutes, mostly in silence, walking through the museum. As they exited, Hamilton looked a little green around the gills. "You have never been in battle have you? I apologize if this offends you. However you need to remember always that this nation was formed after the Holocaust by survivors of those terrible events. Never forget that."

As they drove along the busy streets of Jerusalem, Har-el pointed across the valley to a small tel or mountain top. "Ambassador, if you look across the valley to the top of the tel, you will see the United Nations Headquarters for this city. Do you know the ancient name of that mountain?"

Hamilton looked puzzled as if questioning why he would know such a thing. "No, I must admit not being well read on ancient Hebrew mountain names," he said with obvious sarcasm.

Ignoring Hamilton's manners, Har-el answered his own question, "The ancients called it the mountain of evil council. I've seen U.N. maps and you know there is no Israel only Palestine. You may have heard that some believe UN forces have been bribed to actually escort shipments of weapons, under the color of their neutral blue flags, to terrorists in this city and into Jericho which the Palestinian Authority controls. Look to your right, to the horizon, that is the town of Bethlehem. I can't go there. They still fire upon us from Bethlehem. The Palestinian Authority controls that area. We have had to put bulletproof windows in the homes facing Bethlehem that are within rifle range." 'Oh little town of Bethlehem,' Har-el hummed ever so softly.

The motorcade took them to Police Headquarters where a Bell Ranger helicopter waited on the rooftop. They boarded and headed north through the Jordan River Valley. The chopper landed in an isolated military post in the Golan Heights on the east side of the Jordan River. The prime minister led the ambassador to an observation post overlooking the river valley.

"We are standing on the east side of the Jordan River on land that used to belong to Jordan. As we look across the valley, you can see all of the Kibbutz farms in Israel. This is what the Jordanian Army and the Palestinian terrorists saw before we took this land. Every day they shot down into the valley at the Kibbutz and the farmers in the fields and the children in the playground, everyday. We put a stop to that. Now we all live in peace along this valley. That is a result of war not negotiations."

As they moved slowly back to the helicopter, Hamilton, who had been mostly quiet, asked about the signs warning of landmines.

"The Russians sent soldiers, advisors they were called, and military hardware to Jordan. One of the first things they did was to mine the valley slopes to prevent Israel from attacking them. It didn't work, and now we are left with miles of useless land filled with hard to detect plastic mines. The wandering goats occasionally find them and we make a little sacrifice. No?" The humor escaped Hamilton as he crawled back into the Israeli Defense Force helicopter.

The pilot aimed the noisy machine on down the River Jordan staying in Israeli air space, also advising the Jordanians of their peaceful intent. They circled high over Mount Nebo. "Our Rabbis tell us that when the Lord brought down terrible plagues on Egypt and pharaoh freed my people, He led Moses to the Promised Land. It was a journey that took forty years. At the end of the journey, Moses stopped at the top of Mount Nebo which is in Jordan right down below us. The Rabbis say the Lord pointed Moses to the west to look across the Jordan River's west bank towards Jericho and Jerusalem. That land the Lord said was the Promised Land and he gave it to the children of Abraham, my people. That land is today, once again, in the hands of Abraham's descendants. The prophets said that this would happen. That Jews from all parts of the world would one day return to this land and it would be restored as the Promised Land."

Har-el thought for a moment he saw a sense of understanding in Hamilton, but then realized Hamilton was on the verge of being air sick. Har-el told the pilot through his headset to make a steep descent back to Jerusalem. That was enough to put Hamilton over the top to make a fast grab for the nearest bag. Har-el smiled at Hamilton's predicament. He is not much of a man, Har-el thought.

As the motorcade hurled back to his office, Har-el suggested a late lunch and named off a number of menu choices. Hamilton shook his head and the driver headed to the old city walls. They drove past companies of armed soldiers near the wall. Har-el didn't get out right away. He rolled his window down for Hamilton to see. "That is what many call the Wailing Wall. Do you know why it is so called?"

Hamilton had just about lost his spirit and simply shook his head.

"When the ancients settled in the Promised Land, they built a huge temple within the city gates. Inside the temple they put the Ark of the Covenant, containing God's Commandments. It was in the place of the Holy of Holies. Do you know what stands over this site today?"

With almost impossible timing, the loudspeakers on the minarets began to call their followers to prayer.

"The Muslims built a mosque over our temple. And so it stands today. The closest a Jew can get to the most Holy of Holy places is the Wailing Wall. Every day hundreds of Jews go to the wall just to be near to their temple which is buried under the Mosque. Every day, they pray to be reunited with their temple. We have begun to excavate the outside of the wall so that the original walls will at least be visible. Come I will show you what we are doing and then I promise to get you back to Tel Aviv. Come."

They hurried past the hundreds of black clad orthodox worshipers, men and women on separate sides, into the stone building where excavation was proceeding. Har-el led Hamilton into a small dimly lit room. When their eyes adjusted, they could see a perfect scale model of the old city as it is today. Using a laser, Har-el pointed to the Mosque of Omar, the Dome of the Rock, which lay over the old Jewish Temple and the Wailing Wall. "This area of the old wall is currently under homes dominated by the Muslims. We intend to renovate this wall. Let me show you." At the press of a button on his laser pointer, the Muslims' houses disappeared below the model and the entire ancient wall was exposed.

Hamilton looked quickly at Har-el as though he had just dropped a bomb on the Muslims.

"We have plans beyond that that you should be aware of and take back to your president." Har-el pushed the laser button again and the Golden Dome Mosque dropped from sight and a new Temple slowly rose to replace the Mosque. "At the conclusion of Yom Kippur service and the Passover Sedar, the words, 'Next Year in Jerusalem' are recited. Make no mistake, this is our holy city and our Capital and we have no intentions of leaving, none."

Friday, October 26th

Dei Millini Hotel
Rome, Italy

AS HE HAD BEEN INSTRUCTED, Ali shah Masood left the Dei Millini Hotel at 8:00 a.m. and hobbled southbound on Via Muzlo. He moved as briskly as his bum leg allowed in anticipation of being approached by his half-brother's rescue team. Only last night, while in the cramped elevator, a man had passed the message to him. Be prepared to come home.

"He's out of the hotel, walking south bound," Ed Mitchell reported over the encrypted radios.

"James and I have him. We're on foot across the street."

"Stay on him. The tracker is transmitting at 85%."

"Copy."

As Ali approached the second intersection, two men dressed in dark leather jackets came behind him stopping uncomfortably close.

"When you cross this intersection there is a white Mercedes van coming to a stop, curbside, the side door is open, do you see it?" the taller of the two men spoke English, in a hushed tone with a French accent.

"Yes," Ali replied without looking around.

"Step into the van quickly and follow their instructions."

The pedestrian light changed and Ali crossed the busy intersection. Traffic was snarled due to a minor accident. Horns and curses filled the air as drivers tried to move around the two vehicles.

James spoke into his microphone concealed inside his shirt collar, "He's across the intersection, out of our sight blocked by a van."

Moments passed, the van cleared the light and James reported excitedly, "I've lost him! Anyone have him? He must have gone into the chocolate store."

From the command center, Rocky watched the tracker. "Don't worry we got the tracker signal. Damn, we don't have him, I've lost signal. Tighten up where he was last seen."

Ed Mitchell called the Command Post, "Rocky, get that C-26 surveillance aircraft overhead now!"

Seconds passed.

"Copy, they're moving into our air space now."

When Ali came to the van, Jean Claude helped him climb aboard – actually, he pulled him as roughly as Alex had just a few long weeks ago. "Quickly, on the floor…I will cover you with these blankets in case they are tracking you," Jean Claude commanded. He tossed more protective curtains on the prone man. Ali heard others in the van speaking French which he did not understand.

The driver of the van turned left at the second intersection, somewhat too quickly. It was followed by a gray Mercedes C230 occupied by four heavily armed men.

The men were former legionnaires with the French Foreign Legion. Jean Claude was their commander both in the Legion and at Blackstone. They had been through many difficult times together and Jean Claude had always brought them through. They had been recruited and hired two years ago. Although all were Europeans, they seemingly had no strong national ties, a characteristic their new employer found most useful.

As the van continued towards the outskirts of Rome, the men in the gray Mercedes conducted counter surveillance. Over the radio, they reported to Jean Claude the clean backside.

Ed Mitchell could smell the stench of failure as he heard the confusion in the voices over the radio of his surveillance agents.

"He's not in the chocolate shop."

"He's not in the stores on either side of the chocolate shop."

"We've got the end of the block capped – he didn't continue on Crescenzio Avenue."

"Nor did he cross over."

Playing on instinct alone, Mitchell turned right several cars behind the van, "I'm following the van the target was next to when he disappeared."

"Why?" Rocky asked from the command center.

"Just a hunch, just a hunch…we are making a left on Via Plinio."

Mitchell felt more confident in his hunch when the agents on foot reported that Ali was not in any of the shops. "We are making another left on Orazio, there is a gray Mercedes occupied four times taking turns with the van…aircraft can you get with me?"

"OK, we're making another left. We've gone in a circle. The gray Mercedes is still with the van. Aircraft, we are stalled in front of Piazza Theatre. I'm in a white Audi tapping my brake lights."

"OK, we got you, is that the van about 8 in front of you?"

"Yes, and I am going curbside. Aircraft, stay with the van…we need a few more ground units to assist. Don't lose him!"

Friday, October 26th

Brothers Estate
St.Croix River Valley
Taylors Falls, Minnesota

"FANCY, YOU ARE ONE FINE cook. Are you trying to fatten up me and Gumpy?" Doc asked.

"No, sir, but I do enjoy watching you two double-team a meal! Like Jack Spratt and his wife."

"Well, thank you from both of us, although keep in mind all of my wives were better looking than Gump here...well, one of them anyway."

"Tony, can you get the others and we will meet in the study?"

A few minutes later, Tony entered his uncle's den. Doc was seated in a fine upholstered swivel chair with Gumpy on his lap. He rested his feet on the desk, and had a lit cigar, one of uncle's, in his mouth.

"Make yourself to home, Doc," Tony said.

"I don't think you really want to see that," Doc grinned broadly. "Let's get started!"

"Sue, would you be so kind as to begin?"

Sue Rivard looked at her notes. "I took statements from Blondie, Fancy, and Nikkei. They all agreed that Juan Valenzuela's tattoo is the same as all the tricks wore. They told me something new. Nikkei and Fancy were given keys to Armando Gomez's Century and Gran Prix. One of the Juans paid them $200.00 to pick-up the cars at the St. Paul Airport and told to abandon them with keys in the ignition on the North side of Minneapolis."

"Did they do it?" Doc asked.

"Yes, they sure did. They hitched a ride to the executive jet terminal. The cars were parked right next to the State Patrol squads, kinda spooked them out."

"When did they do this?"

"They remembered that it was the day of the assassination, because it was all over TV and Fancy was pissed because Judge Judy and Oprah were pre-empted."

"Where're the cars now?"

"Well, they claimed they dumped them, but I don't think those girls would let a few bucks slip through their hands, anyway, I'll press this issue later. I did interview Armando again and he confirmed that Alberto and the others went missing with his two cars the day of the assassination."

"What about . . ." Doc began but Sue was already ahead of the question.

"I already have the State Patrol Air Wing Captain checking video and jet departures. The State Patrol Air Wing is headquartered at the executive jet terminal. It is really unusual to have a bunch of guys like this flying out of that little terminal."

"You'd expect to run into executives from 3M or Target, but not foreign soldiers," Tony added.

"And something else, on October 12th, MPD made a routine traffic stop of Armando's Buick Century. The driver provided a Texas driver's license bearing the name of Pablo Martinez. Two days ago, that license was referred to the fraud unit – seems they busted a false ID ring and seized the computer used to produce the license. There are hundreds of photos on the computer. I've already got a copy of the Pablo Martinez photo – it's a photo of Alberto Hernandez. They're sending me a complete list. Maybe we can identify some more of the jerks."

"Topo, have you learned anything more from the Blackstone boys?" Doc asked.

"A few things…one of our military intelligence analysts who used to be assigned to BCA from the National Guard's Counter Drug Program had a military chum assigned to what they used to call the School of the Americas in Fort Benning. They changed the name because too many of the graduates had happy trigger fingers. His counterpart at the School was able to find student photos of the three Peruvian soldiers whose prints we lifted from Blondie's liquor bottle. Turns out there was a large squad sent to the School for training and the analyst sent all 16 photographs. Sue, you want to pick it up from there?"

"Blondie, Fancy and Nikkei, picked out six of the soldiers from the sixteen they sent," Sue said as she handed the photograph to Doc. Six soldiers were circled with yellow highlighter by the women – including the one Blondie remembered had a dick like a hamster.

"I showed the photos to Stone, Rooster and Jake. They said they could identify seven as Blackstone mercenaries. They identified the same six as the ladies, and guess who the seventh was in that training squad? Juan Valenzuela!" Tony said.

"Donna," Doc said, "before we get to you, I want to say mostly for your benefit, but for all to hear, we are not conducting this investigation in a dark manner to exclude the FBI. Well, yes, we are, allow me to explain why.

"I have a sincere respect for the agents at the Bureau. I have spent a career working with them and they have some of the world's most skilled investigators and for sure the world's finest equipment and resources.

"It's their management that I have concerns about. No, more accurately, it's the politicians in Congress I am concerned about. Those politicians have rendered the FBI ineffective on large-scale investigations – Ruby Ridge, Waco, Zacarias Moussanoui. The politicians call the FBI executives before the oversight committees after each high publicity event and if things don't go perfect the FBI gets kicked in the ass. That never happened when J. Edgar ran the outfit cause he had files on many of them and they weren't about to pick a fight with that fat prick in bloomers.

"After taking it in the butt so many times, the FBI management has written a policy and procedure for every possible situation and each of these procedures require minute management by executives in Washington who are more interested in making sure some senator won't get another shot at their behinds. They have as many senior agents auditing the working case agents for policy compliance as they do agents on the streets. The working agents might be tossed under the bus while the big boys proudly wave their policy before the congressmen and claim innocence.

"We're working on some very limited circumstantial evidence and we may be off the mark. However, if we are right, the FBI has either arrested the wrong bad guys or at least not all of them. I am suspicious at how fast and easy the FBI seemed to have solved this crime. If the FBI missed something the congressmen and senators will be kicking the collective FBI balls like a field goal kicker at the Super Bowl.

"Anyway, if we find we're on the right track, we'll give it to the FBI in a package that will require their attention. I want you to know that. Also, I don't want you to be put in a barrel – however this turns out." Doc waited for Donna's reaction.

"I'm a big girl and you needn't worry. I'll give you whatever help I can."

"Thanks, what can you add?"

"To keep me busy, the FBI sent me back to Washington to interview the man who had a hand in arranging for the first lady and her son to visit Minnesota. It was just a loose end and a low priority because the man is in no way a suspect. I wanted to do something constructive so I flew to Washington, D.C. and interviewed a guy named Darrin Watkins. He's a D.C. lawyer who's a lobbyist and a real big man in the campaign fundraising. He puts the folks with money together with the party bosses. I set up an appointment and when I arrived, he was most charming, inviting me into his office, very friendly, until I told him I was there regarding his role in setting up the first lady's visit to Minnesota. I mean he turned six shades of red, damn near stroked-out and lost the friendliness, like right now."

"Why?" Sue asked.

"I don't know, I mean he has some secret and he looked like a pole-axed ox."

"What'd he say?"

"I was so taken back by his reaction I hardly heard him – bottom line is he claimed attorney-client privilege and had his secretary show me the door. I wrote a report, however, there is much more to do with him," Donna said. "I reported this to the agent in charge. He basically told me to stand down – they have the assassin in hand."

Friday, October 26th

Via della Muratella
Outskirts of Rome, Italy

THE DRIVER OF THE MERCEDES van pulled off the road into a mature olive grove where it rolled to a stop. Inside, Jean Claude and two others removed the x-ray curtains from Ali. They stripped him of his clothes and possessions bundling them in a black garbage bag and throwing it out into the grove. The nude Ali was handed a white nuclear radiation protection suit. He donned the radiation suit, a SCBA, self-contained breathing apparatus, and radiation hood. Jean Claude quickly scanned Ali for any R.F., radio frequency, and detected none, including the test transmitter he had taped to Ali's back.

The four men in the gray Mercedes got out and scanned the skies for aircraft. Seeing none, they reported this to Jean Claude.

In French, Jean Claude directed the interpreter, "Tell him, we've been sent by his half-brother and have been instructed to ask some questions."

"Were you being followed in Rome?" the interpreter asked in broken English.

"No."

"Did you cooperate with the CIA?"

"No."

"Did you tell them of your plans?"

"No."

"I've been instructed to kill you if I do not believe you."

"I tell you only the truth."

"What are all of the wounds on your body, could they have put a tracker on you?"

"I got them in the aircraft accident. I survived, my guards did not. I don't believe there is a tracker."

"I don't believe you are telling the truth!" Jean Claude yelled in French. He pushed a pistol into Ali's right temple. The interpreter shouted in English and pointed his Beretta at Ali's left temple.

After a very long moment, "However, I suppose your half-brother would prefer I deliver you alive," Jean Claude said. "Let's move out you bull-legged toads. Let's Go! Let's Go!"

"Helmut, wait here hidden to see if anyone comes to a tracker in those clothes. We'll pick you up in less than one hour."

…………………

Rocky still monitored the tracker at the command post. "I had a signal for a brief moment. It's at Via della Muratella north of da Vinci Airport."

"Command Post. We have that van and the gray Mercedes at the location where you just got a signal." The C-26 radio operator reported from miles above.

"Stay with them."

"Roger, we are filming all of this – a moment ago they tossed a large dark object out into a grove of trees where they are parked. It's big enough to be a body."

"Roger that."

"The guys in the Mercedes are out of the car with binoculars."

"Roger. Stay with them. Ground units stay back until they leave then get in there to see what or who they threw out."

"Okay, C.P. they are back on the move."

Minutes later, the van and Mercedes pulled into a secured area of private hangars at the da Vinci Airport.

"C.P. they're going into an airport, looks like they're going towards private hangars. You better get some ground units in there. If we try to move in closer, the air controllers will be screaming at us for violating the air space. We can watch the airport entrance when they come out." The C-26 pulled back a mile or so to avoid a conflict with the tower.

"Roger. Ground units get in there, if you find him again, we need to end this ASAP!"

Friday, October 26th

44 Wall Street,
New York City

THE POLISHED LIMO NUDGED CURBSIDE in front of 44 Wall Street. Darrin Watkins directed the uniformed driver, "I'll be in here for only an hour, why don't you stand down until I call you."

"Yes, Sir." The driver closed the passenger door behind Watkins. He walked next to Watkins carrying an opened black umbrella to protect against the beating rain.

Watkins dressed in a Bermini Italian gray wool suit nodded to the doorman/security as he passed through the gleaming gold doors and moved to the elevators. Men in Bermini suits don't stop for doormen or explain their presence. He was lost in thoughts about the recent visit from Agent Lyons. There were many sleepless nights since her visit. He was certain that he had been set up to accommodate the first lady's visit to Minnesota. There was just the nagging question of what to do about it. Should he meet with Agent Lyons and disclose all? That could be very dangerous. He got off at the seventh floor – without answering his own questions – and went to the door labeled "Bernie Silverstein, Financial Consultant."

"Good Morning." Watkins smiled warmly at Cindy, who was surprised to see a client walk through the door, a rare occurrence. Cindy didn't have many duties around the Silverstein Office. Bernie conducted much of his business on the phone and his computer. Mostly, he kept Cindy around because she wasn't bright enough to be inquisitive or suspicious of Bernie's business affairs and she was pleasant to look at through the glass window of his office.

She smiled, put her nail file down and sat up, "Good Morning, how can I help you?"

"Mr. Silverstein is expecting me, I'm Mr. Watkins."

Cindy called Bernie and a moment later waved Watkins through the door.

"Good morning, Bernie. It's wonderful to actually see you again."

"Likewise, how is my favorite client? What can I do for you? Have a seat, please. Coffee? Something stronger?"

"Nothing, however, I do have some important business we need to discuss," Watkins opened his briefcase resting on his lap. He quietly activated a bug detector searching for signals from transmitters or tape recorders. He stared at the green lights indicating no electronics were present. Nonetheless, he activated an Audio Jammer and then removed a binder of accounting papers.

Watkins began, "First, you've control of over $900,000,000 that was earned by my clients as a result of the recent crash of the stock market. I've written instructions on how these profits are to be handled. I'll wait while you carry them out. When you've completed the transfers, return the instructions and a printout of the verification of the transfers, do you understand?"

"Of course, let's see what you have."

Watkins reached across the desk and handed Silverstein the paper. He leaned back in his chair and parked his Italian loafers on Silverstein's antique desk.

Bernie turned to his computer and began to type orders, with the speed of a stenographer, to transfer profits to the accounts belonging to Peris, Ltd. at the Euro-Credit Ltd. bank in Grand Cayman.

He typed further instructions to transfer $250,000,000 from the Cayman account to the Mercantil Provencial account at the Central Bank in Caracas, Venezuela.

Simple instructions thought Bernie, wondering what was behind the transfers. He never knew although he was well-paid for his service.

What he did not know was that the Mercantil Provencial account in Venezuela was controlled by Libertad S.A. which was wholly owned by FARC – the leftist guerillas who have bombed and shot their way to near dominance of the cocaine market. The money would later be sent to Colombia where FARC would use it to support its war and narcotics trafficking in South America.

The financial wizard, after a few minutes, tore a document from his printer and handed the instructions and verifications back to Watkins. He dropped his feet from the desk, letting his chair fall forward and studied the documents. Satisfied, Watkins opened his briefcase and turned off his electronics and filed his papers.

"Bernie, maybe now we should have our refreshments, a libation on the stronger side, perhaps?"

"Of course." Bernie rose and went to his bar pulling out a bottle of brandy pouring two glasses. For his role in moving the money, he had just profited over a quarter of a million dollars and all done outside the preview of the SEC and the IRS.

"To our continued success."

Friday, October 26th

Brothers Estate
St. Croix River Valley
Taylors Falls, Minnesota

"GUMP, WAKE UP. IT'S TIME for our meeting. Get your bare-butt in the study!" Doc chided the little dog. Gump cocked his tawny head and perked his black ears. He gingerly followed Doc into the study – his curled tail wagging vigorously.

The others waited inside the study, Tony behind the desk, feet on the rosewood top.

Doc glared at Tony, "Is this a mutiny?"

"No, not at all, just wanted to feel the power – it's all yours."

"Youngsters should know their place. Up, Pugs, up." The little dog leaped into Doc's lap, landing hard on his privates. Doc winced.

"Sorry for this late hour. We wanted to wait for Lora to get back to Juan. Topo, is she on the conference call?"

"I am. Thanks for waiting until I could get to Juan. I showed him the photos that you e-mailed and he picked out those who crossed the border with him. I'll send you the details in my report. He gives a lot of background on each soldier."

"Excellent!" Doc exclaimed. "Just Damn Excellent!" He gave Gumpy a celebratory hoist into the air.

"Sue, Topo, what about the State Patrol?"

"They found the videotape of eight men, all Latinos, well-dressed in business suits, carrying luggage. The men in the video appear to be the same Peruvian soldiers. A ground crewman remembered what jet they boarded, owned by a Canadian Charter service. They filed a flight plan to Vancouver, Canada."

"Topo?"

"The Blackstone guys had to go back to work at the nuclear power plant, but they threw out a couple of ideas before they left."

"Geez, now the mercenary partners of the assassins are running the show?"

"No, No, Doc they're good guys. Stone said he served in the Navy with the founder of Blackstone and he is a straight shooter. Stone said there is no way this guy would be a player. However," Topo added, "the company was bought four years ago. They kept some of the executives on at first although over the years replaced most of them."

"Who bought them?"

"Stone doesn't know for sure. He thinks it was a holding company owned by foreign investors."

"What else did the mercs suggest, although I kick myself for asking?"

"Jake said a friend of theirs, a mercenary named Lee, is back at headquarters teaching firearms to new hires. Lee has a girlfriend who is vice president of H.R. so she could pull the personnel files for the Peruvians. It's a risk, but this gal is one of the few remaining from the original Blackstone organization."

"That's good, obvious downsides, although maybe worthwhile if this Lee gives the right story. Let's think about that one for awhile. I hate to blow this deal on some guy we don't know who's doing some VP we don't know. What else?"

"Rooster has a friend in Blackstone's Middle East Headquarters in Dubai. He says the friend could find out about why the accountant was suddenly transferred to Bosnia. Remember, he believes the transfer had something to do with 'black' off the books operations, at least that's the gossip."

"Anything else?"

"I talked to Lora, she's getting very nervous about keeping this from the FBI. Juan Valenzuela could tell the FBI agents about her interview. She wants to return to Minnesota," Tony said.

"Just a couple more days, a couple more days," Doc said. "Anything else?"

"Stone told me about an Arab named Ali they captured in Pakistan. They got $300,000 from the CIA for grabbing Ali. The CIA was very pleased because Ali had knowledge of plans of attacks upon the United States. Stone says he can put us in touch with the CIA Agent, his name is Rocky."

"Donna, what's your input?"

"I'm convinced we're on to something big. I've got to spend tomorrow with the FBI but will come back in the evening. In the morning, I'll have one of our liaison agents in Canada follow-up on the executive jet. I can also call Rocky and feel him out.

"Doc, if you agree, I believe we should let Stone and Jake make their calls to Blackstone. I've met the founder, Gene Overland, several times. He's a close friend of the president's family. He's been to Camp David a few times. Stone's right, he's an honorable guy."

Friday, October 26th

Rome, Italy

"JAMES, CAN YOU GET INTO the airport quickly on your motorcycle?" Rocky asked.

"I'm already in. The van is inside a hangar, Persis Ltd, is the name on the outside of the hangar. They are helping a person in a Haz-Mat suit out of the van and over to... looks like a twin engine... Beechcraft. Stand-by." James straddled his BMW motorcycle and held a small monocular to his eye.

"We are moving in towards the olive grove to see what they moved out," one of the other agents announced on the air.

"Negative, Negative — stand down on the olive grove – there are only three in the gray Mercedes, they may have left one behind," James shouted.

"Aircraft look at your video fast and tell us how many of the four in the Mercedes got back in the car," Rocky asked.

"Roger."

"The three in the Mercedes are outside the hangar watching the area –everyone stay out of here. Okay Haz-Mat man is in the airplane. Engine started, only driver back in van...van's away...Mercedes's away occupied three times," James reported.

"Tail number on Beechcraft is November1342Zulu, taxiing to runway," James said.

"Roger, if we are certain our target is in the Beechcraft, we can pick it up on takeoff," the surveillance officer aboard the C-26 announced.

"Affirmative Aircraft, we will contact Aviano Air Base and request the base radar lock on and follow the Beechcraft," Rocky said.

"Let's stay away from the olive grove until we can sort this out."

Saturday, October 27th

Brothers Estate
St. Croix River Valley
Taylors Falls, Minnesota

DOC WAS AWAKENED BY CROWS cawing from an apple tree outside the bedroom window of the caretaker's cottage. At the foot of the bed, Gumpy was softly moaning and crying bedeviled by the nightmares of a dog's world.

The crows were migrating south and gathering in large numbers. At dawn, when they realized they were all roosting too close to one another, they cut loose with cursing calls warning each other away. Doc joined in the obscenities as he rolled out of bed. He lit a cigarette and took a sip from the thermos of coffee he had prepared the night before. "Get up you lazy son-of-a-bitch," he said to Gumpy in a voice sounding like John Wayne. He rolled the little dog on his back and rubbed the soft stomach. His blood pressure dropped and his mood mellowed. "Let's go for a walk as long as we're up this early."

Doc and the dog got dressed, Doc in an old canvas Filson hunting coat and Gumpy in his tan corduroy ranch coat. The dog hated being cold and would only go outside to do his morning duties if attired in outerwear. Doc used to feel ashamed of having a dog that wore clothes, however, he eventually decided it was better than the dog fertilizing the carpet twice a day.

Red and golden leaves carpeted the ground. Gumpy chased some that the wind blew in front of him. They strolled northbound on an old logging trail. The air scented with the wonderful aroma of wet fallen leaves. Overhead, in formation, Canadian geese honked goodbye as they flew south.

Doc's cell phone rang. It was Tony. "Where the hell are you?"

"Just out for a walk along the old logging trail to the north of the estate."

"Don't go beyond the fence. The old coot who lives there carries a shotgun and still thinks the Revenuers are sneaking on his land. He'll shoot at you although I don't recall he has ever hit anyone. Fancy is making pancakes and we have some real maple syrup from across the river. When you coming back?"

"Soon as the dog finishes with his morning constitution. That can take awhile. Put my name on some of those pancakes."

They walked up to the fence where Doc stopped and settled into a downfall of pines. He got comfortable, lit up a smoke and poured some coffee from the thermos. He watched as the billowy white clouds raced the geese southward. Maybe next year, he'd put his papers in and join the birds in Texas.

His phone rang again. It was the Assistant Superintendent. "Doc, sorry to bother you so early – I'm flying to Bermuda for a conference this morning, in fact, I'm at the airport about to board. I wanted to talk to you before I left."

"What's the problem, boss?"

"I was at the Sheriff's Roundtable yesterday and the ASAIC from the FBI cornered me. He said you have disappeared from his radar and that your FBI partner claims our agency pulled you back to conduct our own investigation. He was pissed that we would be unilaterally conducting our own investigation of the president's son's death. I assured him that wasn't true. I wasn't lying to him was I?"

"It must just be some crossed wires, boss, I'll straighten it out before you get back."

"The other matter, this human rights complaint won't go away. They're dragging their feet on conducting the investigation. They want you to be suspended until they finish the investigation. A word to the wise – stay out of the office. You know, out of sight – out of mind. I'll do all I can to run interference, I'll be gone for ten days so who knows what they will do behind my back. I gotta go."

"Have a nice trip, boss."

"Pugs, let's go back and get you started on another eat-sleep-and-poop cycle."

As they were walking along the grassy path, Gumpy half-glimpsed a cottontail rabbit hopping out onto the trail and he rushed almost sideways tail tucked between his legs in pursuit. Code 3. A great horned owl saw the same rabbit from his perch behind Doc and flew inches over the agent's head towards the rabbit. Doc, who hadn't seen the rabbit shouted a warning and sprinted towards the dog, and the owl. "*Merda*," he screamed as his feet tangled in the underbrush. He stumbled face-first just as he heard a scream as though from a child. His heart raced. He looked up to see the owl carrying off a screaming hare.

His phone rang covering the cries of the rabbit as it drifted away.

"Hello, ma, how are you?"

"I've been robbed. Someone broke into my room last night and stole my gold necklace, the one your father gave me, the only jewelry he ever gave me."

"Are you sure, ma? Did you look around your room?"

"Of course, I did. The gold cross was on my neck when I went to bed last night. I know it was because every night I hold it and pray that I'll see your father in heaven."

"I doubt that someone slipped into your room and stole it off your neck."

"Well, it's not on my neck and it's gone. I want you to investigate this. What good is it to have a son who's a cop if he can't investigate a theft from his own mother's neck?"

"Where are you now?"

"I'm sitting on my bed. I just woke up and felt for my cross to say my morning prayer and it was gone."

"Stand up and jump a few times."

"Oh lord, some help you are. I always wanted you to be a priest. You'd been better suited for that."

Doc waited as she was silent for a few seconds.

"The thief must have dropped it on the floor. It's on the floor next to my bed."

"Ma, I hope your day gets better. I have to go, bye." Doc picked himself up from the dry grass and put his phone into his pocket.

"Pugs, this is starting off to be a horseshit day – the kind you want to rewind and erase."

They strolled back to the estate in silence, except for the shuffling of crispy leaves, each lost in their own thoughts.

Saturday, October 27th

Castle Creek Chalet
Aspen, Colorado

THE PINE LOGS CRACKLED IN the fireplace at the feet of Omar and Mumtaz. They'd retreated to a private room adjacent to Omar's opulent suite. Full timbers held the cedar ceiling twenty feet above the leather couches and rough western log tables. They sipped strong tea and watched large snowflakes drift lazily past the floor to ceiling windows. Several sudoku and crossword puzzles lay unfinished on his night stand. They were becoming close during this crisis and Omar looked more and more to Mumtaz for advice and counsel.

"al Fulani left to meet with Ali shah Masood in Europe. Yesterday, mercenaries picked up Ali in Rome. There was no CIA surveillance. He'll have more to tell us after he talks to Ali. If al Fulani is assured there has been no compromise of the Council, Ali will be taken to a safe house and we can put an end to this crisis."

"Do you trust Qadir's judgment?" Mumtaz asked.

"No, I don't – at least not much of the time. In this instance, he personally has everything to lose if he is wrong and I pray that will sharpen his instincts. Regardless, Ali will be taken to a safe house that I have selected. It is indeed safe and my trusted people will kill Ali and blow the house if there is a problem. Ali will never be allowed to associate again with the Council."

Mumtaz sensed that matter was put to rest. "I just spoke to a friend back home. American forces are making haste in their retreat from our homelands."

"Does this clear the way for our attack on the Jews?"

"We are moving all of the necessary mercenaries, including the ones we used in the American attacks, to the Israeli border. I've ordered that they be shot, if not by the Jews, by our own."

"The Jews are nervous, very nervous, they are increasing their presence on the border, and they've activated all reserve forces. They smell trouble," Omar paused and looked away.

"We're slowing down those oil deliveries. Within 48 hours, we'll have two ships in the ports of Haifa and Ashdod, which the mercenaries will sink to effectively shut down access to the Jewish seaside oil terminal." Mumtaz shifted uncomfortably, "I believe the time to attack has arrived."

"As long as the Americans are pulling out, we'll wait for our attack on Israel." Omar smiled, licked his lips, and sipped tea. He said nothing. He seemed mesmerized by the crackling fire. Mumtaz respected the silence and drank his tea.

"How goes it with al Qaeda and the Taliban?" Omar asked as he broke the solitude.

"They have been emboldened by the defeat of the Americans. They are already moving rapidly back into areas as the Americans move out. I realize we'd hoped to wait until the Americans were gone from our land before offering their leadership to the Americans, however, I fear we will regret any further delays."

"What do you propose?" Omar asked.

"We should immediately set our trap and give the Americans as many as possible. If not, we will be battling these outlaws for generations."

"I will put it to the Council to vote upon this evening after prayers."

Saturday, October 27th

The Alhambra
Andalusia, Spain

"MY BROTHER, HOW GREAT IT is to see you again. I'm so pleased we were able to rescue you!"

Ali did not look well. Pale, thin, and covered with scabs and scars. al Fulani could not tell if his obvious wounds were from torture or the airplane accident.

"Qadir, you have no idea what I've been through, you have my gratitude." He hugged and kissed his half-brother.

"Our father will be so happy when he sees you again. We're concerned that the CIA may be following you, that they may have surgically implanted a tracker, you have so many wounds and scars."

"I don't know. I have no recollections other than the torture. I didn't betray you or any others."

"How can you be certain?"

"I'm certain. They never questioned me about anything beyond the same simple questions. They never asked me details which might have indicated that I told them something under torture." Ali suddenly slumped towards the table, his legs wobbling.

"Sit, you must tell me everything they did and everything they asked."

They sat on hard wooden chairs and drank tea for almost three hours. Ali related all details he could remember. When they were finished, two men came with electronic scanners. al Fulani left the room.

The dour young men gave Ali a simple purple cloth robe and straw sandals to wear while they performed their examination. The dark-haired man took a small hand-held devise with blinking lights and moving dials from a metal suitcase. He walked away from Ali, made some adjustment to the settings on the machine then slowly moved toward Ali. He watched as lights came on and dials moved. Neither of the men spoke except to direct Ali into a certain position or to lift his arms or legs.

The bald man, with a beard like a billy-goat, removed a smaller devise from the metal suitcase and went to the farthest corner of the stone room. He made adjustments – turning this dial and that switch and then approached the seated Ali. Ali's eyes grew wide and he pulled back as if expecting a shock. Lights blinked and numeric codes flashed.

The dark-haired man took metal probes from his canvas bag and probed gently at Ali's wounds. He settled in an area of the lower back and his partner ran a menacing looking devise near that area several times.

Where the tests hastily conducted in Rome took only seconds, these operators with more sophisticated equipment worked for over forty-five minutes. When they were done, a cart with a feast was wheeled in and the brothers dined. They talked for hours about good times they'd had as youngsters and al Fulani spoke of the bright future they would both enjoy when the Council triumphed. Ali asked if he would be able to resume his role and position on the Council. al Fulani assured him that would be the case.

"Now, I must leave you for awhile, please get rest and we'll make plans for your travel when you awake."

al Fulani shut the heavy metal door to the electronically sealed room…it slammed loudly and finally. With his head hung low he shuffled down the long hallway to the room where the technicians and Jean Claude were waiting.

"He has a transmitter in his lower back. It is still functioning," the bald man announced.

Saturday, October 27th

Brothers Estate
St. Croix River Valley
Taylors Falls, Minnesota

TONY AND DOC RELAXED ON the deck for the first time in days. Doc exhaled blue smoke from his nostrils. "This is moving too fast and we are losing control."

"I know, but we need to press this as far as possible before we hand it over to the Feds," Tony replied. "We need to hand them a prosecutable case. We have to locate the rouge mercenaries. We need defendants – not ghosts."

"I got a call from the Assistant Superintendent. He said the FBI thinks the BCA is conducting its own investigation of the assassination and he is pissed."

"What did you tell him?"

"The truth, there is a misunderstanding and I would straighten it out."

"How is that the truth?"

"Because I think the FBI misunderstands who killed the president's son and I do intend to straighten that out."

"I think you love courting disaster."

"Did Donna get a look at the surveillance video?"

"You mean the video of the warehouse in Bloomington?" Tony asked.

"Yes, of course. Are there any usable pictures?"

"Donna looked at three separate videos which the agents had seized from nearby businesses. She said that the Suburbans, the DOT van and the trucks are clearly caught on camera coming and going. There is a single time when a dark haired man is seen outside the building, looking up and down the street. He is on only a dozen frames. Donna says the FBI has identified the man as one of the al Qaeda terrorists they shot. She took a closer look and believes it is one of the Peruvians, a soldier named Alberto Hernandez."

Doc shook his head and moved to the railing surveying the valley below. "We need one of the killers, I mean Valenzuela is good but he wasn't in Minnesota. We need one of the soldiers identified in the photographs." He paused to massage his neck – the muscles tightening as he spoke of the challenge which at the time seemed insurmountable. "I'm still not sure how to react, when I learned Alex contacted Blackstone's founder," Doc said trying to get a sense of how Tony felt.

"Doc, we just need to roll with the punches, Alex has picked the man up at the airport and called to say they would be here in 15 minutes. How do you want to handle this?"

"It's a little late to be making a plan. I think we need to assume Stone and Lyons are right and that the guy is going to be on our side. I do worry that he could carry this entire message to the president." Doc finished a smoke and went into the den to wait.

....

"Doc, this is Gene Overland, the founder of Blackstone," Stone said and then moved aside allowing Overland to step forward.

"Pleased to meet you, thanks for coming on such short notice. Have a seat. Coffee? "

Overland was a compact sinewy man, dark graying hair and piercing dark eyes. "Nothing for me, I don't wish to intrude on your affairs, however, when Alex told me of your suspicions, I came in hopes that I might help."

"Mr. Overland, let me put it to you bluntly. I think Blackstone employees attacked the first lady and killed her son. How could this happen?"

"You understand, I sold the company..."

"Who owns the corporation now?"

"It is still a private corporation. I was bought out by two separate groups at different times, each group picked up fifty percent. Both groups are holding companies and represented by lawyers, mostly European. If you look at the actual stock certificates, they will read, Persis Ltd. and Windsor Ltd. Now who owns each of those corporations, I truly do not know. When I sold, I wanted to pursue other interests. It speaks poorly of me – they paid me such a premium for the company, I really didn't care who was behind the purchase.

"After 911, Blackstone grew twenty-fold and they hired thousands of new employees and management. It's a totally different company than when I owned it."

"So how could this happen? Where should we be looking?" Tony asked.

"Blackstone remained unchanged at first and then new management gradually replaced our executives all of whom were provided for with fantastic severance packages. The board members are all lawyers or bankers from Europe, all reputable persons.

"As we were driving here from the airport Alex told me about an accountant who got transferred because of phantom employees. I could help you nail that down, although quite frankly we all know the risks of me or anyone else asking questions."

"Could you give us a history of the company, how it works, gets contracts, everything you think might be important?" Doc asked. He leaned forward across the desktop.

Two hours later, Gene Overland finished. "So the sale, both times, was handled by a Washington law firm. One of their attorneys brought the purchase offer to me. My attorneys and accountants scrutinized the offer. I accepted and made a lot of money."

"What law firm did the buyer use?" Doc asked.

"Rosencrantz and Feldman, they are mostly known for lobbying, Darrin Watkins was the attorney who brought the offer."

Doc sat upright in the chair. "Who?"

"Darrin Watkins was their attorney."

Sunday, October 28th

The Alhambra
Andalusia, Spain

ED MITCHELL, JOE YOUNG, AND Rocky leaned against the Audi Quatro at the wayside rest. They smoked and kept their thoughts to themselves. They looked up at the Alhambra Castle waiting for some moment, something that would allow them to resolve this matter, to end the chase. Earlier, they'd even discussed an assault – that remained a possibility although that wouldn't be their decision. The temperature was dropping as a cold front moved in bringing winds and threatening storms.

Mitchell asked for the tenth time, "Rocky, are you sure you got this place locked down?"

"Ed, you're no rookie, you know there is no 100%, but yeah, we got a tight lid on it and the guys are taking photos of everyone in the courtyard. The C-26 saw the Haz-Mat man go inside. Fortunately, it's early Sunday and not much traffic at the castle. As the day goes on we have some big decisions to make if we go after Ali or how to play it."

Young interrupted, "We got some good photos of a couple of men who arrived after Ali – they drove in a green BMW. I have had photos of all the people in play over the last 2 days sent to Director Lang to see if we can get them identified."

"What's the word from back in Rome?" Mitchell asked.

"We're still following the group that picked up Ali. The Mercedes went back to the olive grove and picked up the fourth man who must have hidden in the grove. After they picked him up, our guys retrieved what had been tossed out, it wasn't Ali, but it was all of his clothes and identification which he must have purchased earlier. The pickup men look like soldiers. They're all at the Rome Airport now. We should be able to identify them soon. We're arranging for customs to give them a close inspection," Rocky said.

"I've laid this entire deal out to Director Lang with a request for direction. He said he would call back shortly, hopefully before anyone moves out of there," Young told the men.

The radio crackled from the voice of the 'Eyeball,' "Three men are moving towards the BMW, looks like the same three that arrived yesterday in that vehicle, doors shut, Beemers moving."

"Damn," said Ed Mitchell on the radio, "Stay with the BMW."

"Roger that, the aircraft has the BMW."

"Two men are wheeling a cart with a large gray duffel bag…cart is to back of a covered pickup…no, it's a van, back of a white van, two men, and one on each end of the bag is tossing it into the back of the van…van's away," the Eyeball called out. The CIA Agent had climbed a nearby cell tower where he remained suspended in a harness. He had a superb view of the courtyard and the main entrance. The wind had picked up to close to 30 kph. He struggled to cling to the tower and maintain a solid view through his binoculars.

"Stay with the van, also."

"Are there any other vehicles in the castle that can be seen?"

"Negative, unless they are parked out of sight, wait a minute, two more vehicles, looks like two Citrons are coming out," the Eyeball reported.

Mitchell swore, "Damn it to hell, we are not going to have enough resources to stay with them all."

"Could that duffel have been a body?" Mitchell asked.

"Affirmative, consistent with a body bag – affirmative," the Eyeball confirmed.

The aircraft interrupted, "BMW has arrived at a private jet port, only two out of the Beemer, walking towards a business-class jet on the tarmac. We may have to move out of the area until this thunderhead passes through."

“Damn.” Mitchell’s phone rang.

“This is Director Lang. What is your current situation?”

Mitchell quickly described his predicament and begged for some direction.

“Ed, I want you to stay with what is likely Ali’s body and let the rest go. I will take full responsibility. If that body goes towards an aircraft have the local police make a routine stop. No, on second thought have them make a routine stop a few miles from the castle and have them discover the body. You will have to direct this from a distance, can you do that?”

“Yes sir, it’ll be done. What about the private jet?

“I’ll take care of that. Good luck, you men are doing outstanding!”

“Thank you, Director Lang.”

Sunday, October 28th

Brothers Estate
St. Croix River Valley
Taylors Falls, Minnesota

THE EAGLES WERE BACK, GLIDING on the morning's updrafts from the St. Croix River Valley – this time without the pesky attackers. The few remaining leaves were rapidly falling in the wind as the sun was rising across the river valley.

Doc, Alex, and Gump enjoyed early morning coffee on the deck which overlooked the rushing river. The many rapids below created a muffled roar. Doc broke the silence, "Alex, I have a gut feeling that the Washington attorney, Watkins, is involved with this assassination, maybe only as an unwitting, however, he may provide the link between the assassins and their controllers."

"Yeah, I hear you Doc, but like Donna told you he claims attorney-client protection," Alex offered.

"Privilege, not protection – I've another idea how to get him to talk."

"What? Kidnap and torture him?" Alex asked.

"Exactly!"

They both stared out into the spreading pink sunrise and drank their coffee.

"You thought 'bout how to do this?" Alex asked.

"Matter of fact, Gumpy and I had a brainstorming session last night over some beverages on this very deck."

"And?"

"Well, we were thinking that some highly trained Special Forces soldiers could easily grab a pansy-ass Washington lawyer. Take him for a voyage into the Atlantic where he may be inspired to tell the identities of his clients who purchased Blackstone and who paid him to set up the first lady's trip to Minneapolis."

They watched one of the bald eagles dive into the shallow river seizing a surface feeding smallmouth bass. The eagle flew to the top branches of a nearby dead tree and began to devour its breakfast.

"If some former Special Forces soldiers were to do such a deed, they probably wouldn't want to have a lot of discussions with others about this, would they?" Alex asked.

"Probably not."

"If a guy did this and things turned to crap, you'd have to take care of Blondie, agreed?"

"You have my word. I have a priest friend looking into some alternative lifestyle for her. But, yes, I would watch over her."

"Cuz, she's all I have, all that's important, anyway."

They both took a moment to ponder the conversation and lit some Cuban cigars Alex had smuggled from Germany. Alex looked at his watch, twisting the band once around his wrist.

"Tell me about this Ali fellow you boys kidnapped?" Doc finally spoke.

"He's some sort of big shot in the al Qaeda organization. The CIA put a bounty on his fat head and the boys and I made a quick trip to Pakistan, got lucky, and put the grabs on him. We turned him over to the military and the CIA. I don't know what they learned from him, but I do know that he was supposed to have information about an attack on the United States."

"I assume the plagues," Doc said as he blew smoke from his nostrils like a small dragon.

"Well, in hindsight, I think we could make that assumption," Alex replied. "I think the CIA has him now."

Sunday, October 28th

Over the Azores
Atlantic Ocean

QADIR AL FULANI'S CELL PHONE was in his hand when it rang. "*Marhaba*," he answered.

"*Marhaba*, Michael Lang speaking, how are you my friend? We have not spoken for a while."

"I am in good health and yes, it has been too long."

"How is your family, your father?"

"All are well although my father ages and suffers those problems."

"Your brothers and sisters I hope are well, all forty-six of them?"

"As you may imagine, it is difficult to keep track of them all, but I think they are fine, and you my friend, how goes it?"

"I am thinking of retiring – maybe move to Dubai to live in luxury. We'd be neighbors."

"You would enjoy it in Dubai. They have more French chefs than Paris. What can I do for you?"

"I would like to meet with you, are you in Kuwait?"

"No, I am traveling, however, we should meet, I have much to tell you."

"Yes, I understand the Israelis are concerned about military buildup on their borders and the American military departure."

"I am sure they are very concerned. I will call you back when I have an opportunity to speak with you in person. Where would you like to meet?"

"You know I'm fond of Paris."

"Paris it is. I will call you. *M'asselema.*"

"*M'asselema.*"

al Fulani pushed 'END' on his cell and then #33 on his memory. "Good morning, Mr. Watkins. I have a favor to ask of you."

"What can I do for you?"

"I have a close friend who is visiting Washington and would like the White House and Congressional tours. Can you get him in?"

"I'm sure I can. When?"

"Monday afternoon."

"That's short notice. Can I get back to you?"

"No, just do it. His name is Jean Paul Duvoire, that's D U V O I R E – he will get the pass at the White House. Leave a message on my cell as to the time." He pushed 'END.'

"Jean Claude, tell the pilot we will stop and clear Customs in Washington, DC instead of New York and you should plan to get off in Washington. You are going to visit the White House and not New York."

Sunday, October 28th

Brothers Estate
St. Croix River Valley
Taylors Falls, Minnesota

STONE, ROOSTER, AND OVERLAND SAT at the card table drinks in one hand and cards in the other and cigars dangling from their lips. Jake joined them but sat near a window he'd cracked open to escape the smoke.

"Last hand boys, I have to make some calls before supper. Fancy said she has a turkey on the grill," Alex directed.

"Gene, what'll you have?"

"I'll take one card."

"Rooster?"

"Give me two."

"Jake?"

"I'm good."

"Dealer takes three," Alex said as he dealt three cards to himself.

"Lay your bets down."

"Five."

"Call, raise ya two."

"I'm in. Let's see your cards."

Overland laid down a straight flush – jack of spades high.

"Beat that you sons-a-bitches."

"You always have been more lucky than smart."

"Yeah, and you've always had a first-gear brain and a fifth-gear mouth."

"Gene, I'm going to make some calls, before I do, I'll give you one last chance to back out," Alex said looking to Overland then to his watch, turning the band once around his wrist.

"I'm in and we're on my jet immediately or we can leave after turkey, which I would prefer."

"OK, I'll make the calls to get what we need."

"Make 'em, I'll have my boat ready with no crew."

Alex called Lee who was back in Washington spending time with the wife and kids. "We're on, rent a couple of rust buckets from some place without cameras that'll take cash, you'll have to get the gear we need – which won't be much. We'll start surveillance at his Georgetown row house at 0500 hours, tomorrow. If we see an opportunity to make a safe grab we will, otherwise we'll get a pattern over a couple of days."

"Anything else?"

"Yeah, Overland is com'n along."

"Like old times, see you tomorrow."

Alex dialed again, "Rocky, it's Alex Stone. I need a couple of favors."

"Where the hell are you?"

"We got sent to Minnesota to protect a nuclear facility, but I got involved with some local cops and I need a favor."

"Yeah, Yeah, and what do you need?"

"Did you locate the Blackstone accountant for me?"

"I did, and odd, you a Blackstone employee couldn't find out on your own, and odd, I'm in Europe right now with two men who were stopped with the body of a murder victim, and one of the men has a Blackstone pay stub in his pocket."

"What's his name?" Alex asked.

"What difference does it make – it won't be his real identity anyway. The local cops say they have French Foreign Legion tattoos on their shoulders, name of the pay stub is Claude Le Berne."

"I don't know that name but I know Blackstone hired a bunch of Legionnaires after their enlistments expired. Can you send me a photo on my cell?"

"What's your other favor?"

"I was goin' to do you a favor. These local cops believe and I think they're right, that some Blackstone mercs did the hit on the first lady and her son. I think that the mercs are work'n for Blackstone and are likely the phantom employees that accountant, Maurice Smith, found on the Blackstone books, you got a home address for him?"

"Yeah, I'll text it to you so you don't mess it up. What else?"

"I remember the Ali snitch said that Ali knew about a bunch of bad crap is going to happen in America."

"The FBI said they caught the assassins and they were al Qaeda."

"Well, the FBI may not have the whole story. Did you get anything from Ali?"

"No, matter of fact, I was thinking that we should get our money back from you."

"Fat chance."

"The body the Legionnaires were hauling is Ali," Rocky told him and hung up.

"Rooster, grab me another Coors," Alex ordered.

Rooster came back with a Heineken. "Fancy says the bird is on."

"OK, give me ten minutes. I got one more call to make." He looked at his watch and twisted the band once around his wrist.

"Bobby, sorry for the late call, how are things in Bosnia?"

"That's good, fine wine, women and no one blow'n you up, hey, I'm going to text you that accountant's home address. Grab him up and squeeze him 'til he tells you the whole story about those Blackstone employees, thanks man."

"Last call, Rooster, save me a place."

Alex dialed again, "Andy, this is Alex Stone. When you get this message on Monday, Rooster, Jake, and I will be off the clock for several days. I've arranged for our shifts to be covered. Thanks, Babe."

Sunday, October 28th

Paris, France

"DIRECTOR LANG, THIS IS COLONEL Andrews, I am the CO of the AWAC squadron over the Atlantic. My duty officer tells me you made a personal emergency request for deployment."

"Yes, Colonel, I did make such a request. What can you tell me about the aircraft in question?"

"Sir, it is a business jet tail number N1322C, owned by Persis Ltd., and is currently on a reported course to Washington, D.C., ETA, 93 minutes."

"What about the telephone activity?"

"I am told that we intercepted two calls, one apparently from yourself and a second to an unidentified caller. The man you spoke to told the caller he wanted a guest pass to the White House and Congress for his friend Jean Paul."

"Is that all?"

"Yes, Sir. In about 92 minutes they will reach Washington D.C. and we will drop our coverage. The pilot called the executive airport manager asking for a U.S Customs officer to clear the passengers. He said they would need service and fuel for a continuing flight to Aspen, Colorado."

"Colonel, I would like your AWAC to stay with that jet."

"Negative. We can't conduct military surveillance or telephone intercepts in U.S. airspace...get my ass in the brig for doing that, Director Lang."

"Colonel, can you at least keep a ground radar fix on the aircraft to tell me when it flies from Washington to Aspen?"

"Roger that sir. I'll take care of it and call you with updates."

"Thank you, Colonel, and by the way, please send the original and any copies of the recording of the telephone calls to me."

The director turned to his aide, "I'll need for you to arrange an aircraft for tonight. You and I will be flying to Spain to pickup Kowalewicz, Young and Mitchell. We will need a safe-house in Washington and get an appointment scheduled early tomorrow morning with Director Rankin. Better arrange for the FBI liaison to be there also, and do we have any cognac left?"

"Affirmative on all counts, sir. Would you like the cognac first?"

"Yes, of course."

The aide left the office to fetch the liquor. Director Lang quickly dialed on his cell phone.

"*Je me suis occp`e de cette mati`ere. Il n`y a rien pour s`ingui`eter de*," Director Lang said when he received an answer.

Monday, October 29th

North Waziristan Region, Pakistan

THE EGYPTIAN, NASIM AL THANI, first met bin Laden on the soccer field. Both tall men, they stood out on their opposing teams. Neither was very talented – too tall to compete against the shorter more agile players. Those school day contests developed into a lifelong friendship. They shared long talks about world affairs and found a mutual hatred for the moral excesses of the West. After graduating, al Thani continued with his education receiving a graduate degree in Business from MIT in Cambridge. While bin Laden took up arms to battle the West, al Thani became a wealthy man from his shipping business. His cargo ships, under the flag of Greece, brought commodities throughout the world, gaining him valuable relationships in the capitalist circles. Behind the scenes, he maintained contact with bin Laden and mustered financial support from like-minded businessmen. It was bin Laden who'd introduced al Zawahri to al Thani, and shared that his old friend could be trusted with the highest confidence. When al Thani joined the Council, he was outspoken against eliminating his old friend, bin Laden but bent his will to that of the Council.

It was to that end that al Thani contacted al Zawahri through an intermediary. He arranged for a meeting on this day in a village located in the Shawal valley in North Waziristan, an al Qaeda stronghold. His private jet flew him to Chitral, Pakistan, where he was met by al Zawahri's security forces. They drove al Thani to an obscure village about 50 kilometers from the Afghanistan border.

"Get out!" the leader of the security detail ordered.

al Thani pulled his lanky body from the back of the mud caked Range Rover. "Are we here?"

"No, take all of your clothes off and give them to him," the leader directed as he pointed to his minion. "Put your hands on the Rover and spread your legs." Without touching the man he carefully examined al Thani's naked body as his minion felt every inch of clothing and sandals. The leader removed an electronic instrument from a briefcase and slowly ran the detector over the clothing and al Thani. "Put your clothes back on and get in." After he was dressed, the aide put a black hood over al Thani's head and helped him back into the Rover. Over rocky roads they drove another two hours without any words exchanged.

When they arrived at the village, al Thani was searched again by the chief of al Zawahri's bodyguards. Finding nothing, they led al Thani down a narrow mud brick stairway. Still hooded, he slipped several times on the wet stone floor, however, the bodyguards had strong grips on his arms and prevented him from falling or escaping if he'd a mind to. He reached the bottom of the stairs and was led through several doors until they paused and removed his hood to reveal a small cave-like room with mats and two doors. The room smelled musty and foul from too many souls crowded into a room with no windows. They left him alone in that room.

About an hour later, the door opened and, led by two bodyguards, al Zawahri entered, "My old friend, how wonderful to see you again." They exchanged embraces and squatted on the mats. The bodyguards stood by each of the two doors. al Thani thought al Zawahri looked like he might die any moment. He had grown very thin. His skin was yellow and greasy – his long hair mostly gray. He had lost some of his teeth and open sores were on the tops of his dusty feet. Perhaps he would not have to assassinate the man.

"What exciting news do you bring?" al Zawahri asked.

"Where do I start? We have made so much progress in defeating the Americans and the Jews."

"I have followed closely the many victories, all thanks to Allah."

An hour later, al Thani finished describing the same events al Zawahri had been viewing on the Internet and added that the Council was responsible for the catastrophes. "We could not have done this without your assistance and I am here to offer you a partnership in the future of the Islamic world."

"What is the Council's proposal?"

"We believe that you should be a party to drafting the final constitution which will form the body of the new united Islamic nations."

"Are you suggesting that I, Ayman al Zawahri, be the Thomas Jefferson of the Islamic world?"

"I hesitate to use that description, but yes, that is what we want. Do you need to take such an offer to others?"

"No, I will make that decision, although I should discuss the matter with my advisors."

"I would like to take an answer back to the Council today. Is that possible?"

"Yes, all of my advisors are here with me. How does the Council think that such a public status for me would be received by the Americans?"

"Frankly, the Americans are on their knees. They will no longer meddle in our affairs, particularly with the Jews gone from our homeland. To use your analogy, the King of England didn't bother Thomas Jefferson or George Washington after the Revolutionary War."

The old man cracked a hint of a smile through his thick gray bread at the thought.

The discussion went on for another hour, when al Zawahri suddenly stood, "I will discuss this with my advisors, wait here. Bring him tea and fruit. I shall not be long."

After al Thani enjoyed his tea and fruit, he explained, "I need to relieve myself."

The bodyguards looked at each other and then one replaced the hood and led him through a maze of cool dry doorways and hallways to a primitive commode. He removed the hood and motioned al Thani to the make-shift toilet. al Thani pulled the modesty curtain in front of the commode and sat down. After several minutes of straining he passed the cylinder which back at the airport, he'd keistered. He quickly unscrewed the cylinder and pushed the small 'ON' switch. After twisting it back together, he placed it in the excrement at the bottom of the hole and returned to the guard. "Where can I wash my hands?" The guard shrugged and replaced the hood. He gave al Thani a slight push and led him back to the room.

al Zawahri returned to the small room, "I will accept your offer. I will become Islam's George Washington. However, I would like the Council to demand my safety from the Americans to return to a public life. I need that protection in order participate."

"That would not be a problem. As you can see, the Americans are at our mercy and will agree to that demand or pay a price."

"My brother, send a courier as soon as you can regarding these matters. Use the same methods as before. We will not be at this location for long. I wish you a safe journey and will await your word."

"May Allah guide you. I will send word soon and we will meet in Tehran."

They embraced and al Zawahri left the room with his bodyguards. al Thani recalled how similar this departure was to the evening he left bin Laden – just before Seal Team Six burst into the bin Laden living quarters and filled him with lead.

Two rough looking men came into the room and shoved a hood over al Thani. He was led in reverse order out to the Range Rover.

Monday, October 29th

Georgetown, Washington, D.C,

STONE COULD SEE BEDROOM LIGHTS come on at 5:13 a.m. Rooster sat next to Stone in the Dodge ½ ton pickup with a topper over the box. "Lee crawled all over the place in the dark. He said that if Watkins is alone when he goes to the garage behind the house, he and Jake could wait inside the garage and it would be no problem. We could even stuff him in his own car. He's got an Audi A-8, lots of trunk room."

"Sometimes the simplest plan works the best. Is Jake sure he can get in the garage?" Stone asked. He looked at his watch for the fourth time since arriving and twisted the band once around his wrist.

"Yeah, door's not even locked, they have been in there already. They'll grab him when he comes through the door."

"How certain are they that he's alone?"

"Jake says the thermal image in the place only shows one person. They are fairly certain. He isn't married and lives alone by all accounts."

"OK, tell 'em to get to it now while it's still dark."

Jake and Lee left the Olds 88 and made their way along the paved alley. There were no city street lights, although as they passed by the garages they triggered many motion detector lights. Jake took care of most of them with a quick shot from a pellet gun. Fortunately, Watkins didn't have any lights on his garage. The men dressed in black and wearing hoods, slipped easily through the personnel door and into the garage. Jake slipped behind the personnel door. Lee waited crouched behind the Audi. After ten minutes of being in this position he wished he'd taken the door.

Watkins scurried out the back door of the colonial and went straight to the garage door, coffee cup in one hand and a briefcase in the other. He held both in his left hand just long enough to turn the door handle and push the garage door open with his foot. He took the cup back in his right hand walked through the door and elbowed it shut.

Jake said nothing when the door shut exposing him. He simply unleashed a brutal blow with his forearm to the right side of Watkins's neck. Watkins crumbled, unconscious, his coffee spilling on his starched white shirt and gray suit. Jake tried to catch him to ease the blow. He missed and Watkins's head slammed hard on the concrete floor. Jake looked at Lee and held his arms up as if to say, 'I tried.'

Lee grabbed the keys still clutched in Watkins's hand and opened the trunk and disabled the emergency latch. They roughly tossed him, handcuffed behind his back, into an oversized dark duffel bag and then into the trunk along with his briefcase and coffee cup. The entire affair took less than a minute.

With Jake driving, Lee told the other men to follow the Audi to the harbor. Gene Overland was waiting at the private dock entrance. He pushed a two wheeled cart to the car for their luggage and the big duffel bag.

"Let's go. Engines are warmed up!" ordered Overland. Jake and Rooster loaded their baggage while Lee and Alex buried the cars in the parking lot, quickly swapping license plates off the Audi.

Within 90 minutes they were at sea and drifting in rolling waves.

"Wake 'em up," Alex told the others. "Keep your hoods on and make sure his hood is taped on."

When Watkins came to, Alex grabbed his face and shouted over the wind, "Mr. Watkins. We took you from your garage this morning. No one knows you are missing. Yer at sea and will spend eternity at sea unless you tell me what I want to know."

"Take this hood off me – untie my hands, you bastard, you will pay . . ."

Alex slapped Watkins on the side of his head and he crumbled to the ground. "Yer in no position to threaten me. You may survive this only if I permit you to and you've already pissed me off. Do I make myself clear?"

"What do you want to know? Who are you? What do you want of me?"

"We have plenty of time – from the beginning to end tell me about the purchase of Blackstone."

"What do you want to know?"

"Never known a lawyer who couldn't fill a few hours talk'n. Start at the beginning and finish with yesterday before you went to sleep."

"That's all attorney-client privilege. I can't tell you anything."

"You can tell me everything – I'm your only client now."

"Ralph, you and Loren help the attorney out of his suit."

Jake and Rooster quickly undressed Watkins and tied his feet to a long line. Watkins kicked and screamed curses.

"Okay me mates, to Davy Jones's Locker he goes, head first."

Jake and Rooster slowly lowered Watkins over the bow headfirst. The frothy ocean waves came over his head and then receded. Each time the waves receded Alex would shout, "How about now Mr. Watkins, care to talk?"

Each time he came up he coughed and sputtered trying to clear the salt water from his nose and throat. His eyes were wide with certain fear he would drown at the next dunking, each of which seemed longer than the last. He would have chosen to talk, however, he couldn't bring words out before being lowered into the salty brine. The waves bounced him against the boat. His right leg was slashed by the idled propeller blade.

"Pull him up enough for another hit. . . of fresh air," sang Alex as he called to mind the classic Quick Silver Messenger song.

"Bets are down me boys how long can he hold out, one beer, two beers, three or four? This is for dinner on me tonight." Alex looked at his watch and spun the wrist band once around.

"Pussy like him ain't goin' as long as it takes me to toss down four beers. I say two."

"I'm in for one."

"Me too…one will do it."

Alex looked over the side, "Mr. Watkins, you let me know if you wish to…how do you lawyers say it, waive the privilege?"

"Beers all around, mateys."

"Back in the drink with Mr. Watkins."

He made it for two beers before he begged to be released. He rolled, naked and cold unto his hands and knees, wearing only his hood. Alex motioned for Jake to start the recorder.

Monday, October 29th

CIA Headquarters
Langley, Virginia

"SO, DIRECTOR RANKIN THAT IS the evidence we have so far. I would hope to see the FBI act on this." Director Lang finished a very succinct version of the events known to date and looked at his boss.

CIA Director Rankin turned to the FBI Liaison Special Agent Johnson. "Andrew, what do you think you can do?"

"Director, I will have to take this back to headquarters, however, let me remind you, the FBI has already captured Cody Franklin's assassins. It seems to me that the CIA loss of Ali shah Masood was a serious setback in any investigation. Besides, I haven't heard of what crime al Fulani is being accused."

Director Lang came out of his chair, "Do you want me to lay this out for you slower and in simpler terms?"

Director Rankin held his hand up to stop Lang, "Agent Johnson, I see your point, you are right. We are premature. If we get more we will be in touch. Thank you for coming."

Director Rankin stood and shook Agent Johnson's hand vigorously, patted him on the back and showed him to the door while the others remain seated. Rocky in a hushed tone, shared with Young and Mitchell, the story of Agent Johnson's embarrassing departure from Afghanistan.

When the door closed, Lang turned to his boss, "What was that all about? That's the dickhead agent who got his ass tossed out of Afghanistan. He's become a thorn..."

Director Rankin held his hand up, "I have no interest in being a party to the FBI's bureaucratic inefficiency. We did the president's bidding and shared our information with them. It's all recorded and that is the end of that!"

"What are we to do now?"

"My good friend, Director Walter McMillan at the Secret Service, will be most interested and cooperative. They want their revenge and they have domestic law enforcement authority along with their counterparts in Homeland Security.

"I'll call him and set up a meeting this morning. I'll give him the heads-up on the White House visitor…this Jean Paul Duvoire fellow – they can keep a close watch on him and also to get his help in Aspen.

"Director Lang, I would like for you and your agents to take a vacation. Take some time off. Would you agree Aspen is a fine vacation destination? I've heard some of the slopes are already open. You all deserve a break."

"Yes, Sir, that would be a good place to take a break."

Monday, October 29th

National Guard Headquarters
Fargo, North Dakota

MAJOR SMITH SCRUNCHED IN HIS crowded command module surrounded by monitor screens, computers, and flight controls. He was sweating both from the cramped quarters and the tension of the mission. He was on the controlling end of a MQ-1 Predator unmanned aerial vehicle. His drone flew at 25,000 feet over the Shawal Valley in Pakistan. The major knew his target was al Zawahri and the pressure to achieve success was monumental. As he maneuvered the drone, he monitored radio traffic from the naval officer tracking the electronic device left in the commode by al Thani and from the ground unit en route to the area. Real time satellite photos appeared on one of his four laptop screens. The major jockeyed the drone towards the target with a twenty minute estimated time of arrival.

In Washington, President Franklin and General Highcamp watched screens identical to the ones in Fargo. They listened to the radio chatter and chose to remain largely uninvolved. The president could already savor the sweet taste of revenge.

Ten minutes out and the real time satellite display showed a convoy of SUVs and heavy trucks parked in a column in front of the compound, "Damn, they're pulling out," the major said to himself. He wiped his moist hand on his flight suit.

A naval officer on the USS Valley Forge floating off the coast of Pakistan in the Arabian Sea reported what the major could see for himself, "Multiple trucks are pulling in front of the compound."

"I'm still 8 minutes out…do you have any other assets in the area?"

"Negative. You're the whole show Major," responded the naval officer.

"Mr. President, do you want us to see if the convoy leaves Pakistan? Are we clear to authorize an attack on Pakistani soil?" General Highcamp asked.

"Damn right you are General and let's not miss this time!" the president waved his cane towards the screen.

The general keyed the encrypted radio mike, "Major, the president says fire away when you acquire the target and Major, the president says put it in – dead center."

The major was too busy to respond, typing commands, and manning two joysticks the right one with firing controls. "I have the convoy in sight. Have they loaded into the convoy yet?"

"Negative, Major, hit the compound now with everything you have."

"Affirmative, I am fixing the laser on the target now and will commence to fire on the next go around in about thirty seconds."

"Five, four, three, two, one, fire," the Major said to no one in particular as he fired his Hellfire missiles into the mud brick compound.

The president jumped to his feet and let out a Rebel yell that his forefathers in the Confederate Army would have admired. When he calmed, he turned to face his chief of staff, "Notify the Pakistani Ambassador of the drone's attack."

"General Highcamp, order the Navy to make their contribution."

Within minutes of the order, the US Navy boat launched five tomahawk missiles each carrying over 1,000 pounds of explosives speeding at over 500 MPH towards what remained of the compound.

"Notify the Pakistani Ambassador that we have fired missiles at al Qaeda targets in his country. And notify our ambassador to prepare for riots around our embassy."

Major Smith kept his drone over the smoldering compound and kept his live video feed coming into his computer.

"General, where are those ground troops?" President Franklin asked in a steady voice.

"Mr. President, they are minutes away in helicopters. They are just waiting for the Navy's missiles to strike."

"Yes, yes of course they are. When will we know if al Zawahri was in the compound?"

"Mr. President, we know he was in the compound, however, we'd be lucky to find his shadow after all the firepower we hit that compound with. Sir, the ground troops will clean up any al Qaeda still living and make a quick assessment for body parts but it would be too dangerous for them to stay. We are well within the Pakistani border and they have a garrison of soldiers who will be able to get to the site within an hour. We do not want to have to engage them and we can't predict whose side they will take."

"No, no of course not…do we have DNA specialists standing by?" the president asked.

"Sir, the specialists are on the carrier and the ground troops will scoop up anything they can find that might have once been human."

The president and military officers watched as the Navy missiles struck the compound and what remained of the convoy. Minutes later, the screen showed Apache helicopters arrive with machine guns and missiles firing at the rubble. Blackhawks landed and Special Forces carefully approached the hellish scene. The last of the soldiers in the stack could be seen to comb the ground and occasionally stoop to pick up body parts –an arm here and a leg there– and put them into large body bags.

Monday, October 29th

Castle Creek Chalet
Aspen, Colorado

"WELCOME BACK, HOW WAS YOUR journey?" Omar asked. He set the nearly completed crossword puzzle on the table top.

"Successful, although not pleasant," al Fulani replied.

"How is that?"

"The mercenaries picked up Ali. They brought him to the Alhambra where I met with him. They're convinced that they were not followed."

"What was so unpleasant?"

"Ali did have a tracker implanted in his body. The mercenaries took great pains to make certain that the tracker didn't function while Ali was transported. Undoubtedly, they were watching Ali and hoping that he would lead them to a bigger prize."

"Or else they would not have taken the risk of releasing him?" Omar asked.

"Exactly, they believed there were larger prizes to be had if they watched him return to his friends."

"What did Ali tell them?"

"Ali said he gave them nothing, however, the CIA may have used methods so that Ali may not even be conscious that he betrayed us. However, I believe Ali when he told me he gave them nothing. He sincerely believes that he did us no harm."

"Where is Ali?"

"Dead…I had the transmitter removed and his body sent to my father. I hope that his death puts this matter to rest."

Monday, October 29th

Como Lake
St. Paul, Minnesota

DOC HAD DRIVEN BACK INTO St. Paul to pick up a change of clothes and a few supplies at the office. The supplies weren't ready so he drove over to Como Park rather than wait at the office where others would be full of questions about what he was doing…not to mention where he ran the chance of an encounter with Sharon Risling, the employee who had filed complaints against him. He'd wait at the park with the ducks and geese who seldom filed their complaints about humans. He parked across from the Pavilion and walked to the shore with two loaves of bread he had bought from the convenience store on the ride to the lake. He was immediately surrounded by mallard ducks and Canadian geese all of which were demanding a share of the loaves. "Like feeding the five thousand," Doc said to himself and his gathering flock. It felt good to be so popular. The lake glistened in the sunlight. The sky's reflection made the brown urban lake water truly the land of sky blue waters. Doc soaked it all in amid the cacophony of honks and quacks. He was thinking the Hamm's bear would come skiing across the lake when his cell phone rang. It was the Assistant U.S. Attorney who was handling the murder-for-hire case he had testified at earlier in the month.

"Where the hell are you? What's the racket?"

"I'm at the lake feeding the hungry. Wait a minute…I'll walk back to my car." Doc moved up the little hill back to the parking lot followed by the ducks and geese some of whom were now pecking at his legs. "You fat little bastard," Doc shouted when one goose reached up and pecked his ass.

"What'd I do?" the Assistant U.S. Attorney asked.

"Not you, the damn geese are attacking me. Now that's gratitude. OK, I'm back in the car. What'd you need?"

"On that murder-for-hire case, I just wanted to tell you the defendant's attorney called and said he will plead. I wanted your input on what sentence we should offer him."

"I'll leave that entirely to your judgment. I just catch 'em. I don't like to get involved in what is fair punishment. It's not personal for me so whatever you think is justified will suit me just fine."

"I thought that is what you would say. I wanted to be sure to ask out of respect to you. Say, are you going to Hannah's retirement party this Friday?"

"No, retirement parties depress me. Everyone asks if I'm going to be the next to retire and it makes me feel old."

"You are old. What do you expect? You should go. I mean to the party. Everyone always asks where you are. You and Hannah were old partners."

"See, they just want me to be there so they can ask when I'm going to go."

"Suit yourself you old cranky bastard."

"Now, I have a legal question for you, a hypothetical question."

"Go ahead."

"You have the FBI's case on the attack on the president's family?"

"Actually, there are four of us working on it – can't get into the details. It's in secret grand jury proceedings which is a secret itself. What's your question?"

"Do you think these guys really did it?"

"I have never seen a more solid case against a group of defendants in my long illustrious career."

"Here's my question. If an agent had some information about your case that indicated someone else did the crime or at least maybe participated in the crime, would that agent have to bring that to your office to be disclosed to the defendants?"

“Of course you would. If you have information that would exculpate the defendants, you should bring it to me forthwith.”

“First, this is hypothetical. If the information is mostly speculation, would it still be something requiring disclosure?”

“No, just because you have some fairy-tale theory without any evidence doesn’t mean the government has to bring it forth for disclosure. We’ll just leave it at that.”

“Thanks for the advice.”

“I’m looking at my email and just received one from the defense attorney. He wants to schedule a pro-offer interview tomorrow morning, early. Can you make it?”

“Sure. Do you have any idea what he’s going to talk about?”

“The only thing his attorney told me at the last hearing was that it was big –something real big.”

Tuesday, October 30th

Prime Minister's Residence
Jerusalem, Israel

AMBASSADOR HAMILTON HAD BEEN SUMMONED for an immediate meeting. A political appointee with no diplomatic experience, he was ill equipped to face the problems about to be laid at his feet. He wanted to bring the State Department officials who usually carried the day, however, the prime minister insisted on meeting without staff.

Prime Minister Har-el stood over the Ambassador. "When we last met, Mr. Hamilton, you assured me of the support of your country. I believe you were either lying to me intentionally or you are being lied to by the president. Are you lying to me? The president has ordered all U.S. troops out of the Middle East. That directly contradicts the understanding we had when the president agreed to attack Iraq and Iran."

"I protest your claim that I would lie to you!"

"That is no claim, Mr. Hamilton – that is an accusation – do you deny that you are lying?"

"Of course, I am denying that and I resent the accusation and protest this sort of treatment."

Har-el frowned and continued in his heavily accented English, "How do you Americans say it, 'cut the bullshit,' Mr. Hamilton. America and its few allies have been withdrawing from the Middle East at a pace that would otherwise be considered a retreat from defeat. My generals inform me that supplies and necessary parts and materials to keep our aircraft have been delayed with juvenile excuses by your military liaison officers. We must have those parts and soon to protect our borders. The Arabs have squeezed our oil supplies and we will be into our reserves soon. Yesterday, two ships were sunk in our ports of Haifa and Ashdod. That will prevent more oil and supplies from reaching us. Then, without any warning, the United States fires missiles into Pakistan, an Arab nation with nuclear warheads."

"Let me assure you, my government is solidly behind..."

"Enough lies! Mr. Hamilton! Enough! Our Intelligence sources in our neighboring Arab nations report that their entire military forces have been put on highest alert and they are beginning to move forces toward our borders. How do you explain that?" Har-el rubbed the scars on his face – they itched when he was agitated.

"Mr. Prime Minister, just yesterday I received a briefing from the CIA officer at our embassy. She showed me the latest satellite surveillance photos of your neighbors along with the analysis of the region. Our analysts have seen no significant military buildups. None."

"Your Intelligence Officers rely too much on technology, satellite photos and communications intercept. Believe me the Arabs are on to your game. What do your sources in those Arab nations report?"

"We have few such sources I am told and they have not alerted us to any problems."

"Well, Mr. Hamilton, we do have sources in those nations, many sources, and their reports all point to an invasion of Israel, and soon. What is your nation's response going to be to such attacks?"

Hamilton wished again that he could have brought staff with him to get through this grilling. "All I can do is to assure you that America stands behind you 100%. That is the message the president sends."

"Ah, the president sends this message. I believe I need to hear it from him personally... David, put me through to Washington."

"Do as you wish," Hamilton replied.

"Let me remind you, if we are attacked, we have the weapons to reduce the Arabs' desert sand to glass. That includes the oil fields upon which your nation and security are dependent. We will not hesitate to use those weapons if it means our survival. I believe you should carry that message back to your president. If America is so beaten down they will not come to our aid then be forthright with that information and we will plan accordingly. In fact, absent evidence to the contrary, Israel will assume that to be the case and prepare for all out war."

The prime minister wasted no effort to pretend civility, he simply left the conference room without a word. Ambassador Hamilton was left seated in the oversized stuffed chair, briefcase on his lap, looking like a child in time-out. It took several moments before he realized the meeting was over and he was to leave. He hadn't felt so insignificant since he'd wet his pants and forgot his notes at his first piano recital.

Tuesday, October 30th

United States Attorney's Office
Minneapolis, Minnesota

FINALLY, IT WAS DOC'S TURN to speak. The two attorneys had battled for an hour over the minutia of the plea agreement. Then suddenly, they agreed and the prosecutor told Doc he could ask the defendant questions.

"Normally, I'd have questions about the plan to murder the ATF Agent, but frankly, you've got my curiosity stirred. What is the big surprise your attorney promised?"

The rotund man rubbed his shaved head as though that might help him get an answer out. He found talking to the cops distasteful, although that wouldn't have been the word he would use.

"I'm not much liking to snitch like this. My people were dealing in explosives."

"That's it?" Doc asked. He dropped his pen on the table.

"No, that's not it...there's more."

"Well, spit it out, man."

"We sold a lot of explosives to some Arabs. You know, like some Muslim terrorists. A lot of explosives."

"Start at the beginning, where did you get the explosives, how much, what kinds, dynamite, C-4, nuclear – start at the beginning."

"I wasn't involved in the deal."

"Then why are you wasting my time?" Doc stood to leave.

"I can give you my 'brother' who did the deal. He'll talk to you, but you can't prosecute him."

Doc looked at the prosecutor and shrugged.

The two attorneys scrimmaged for a time and finally settled on an agreement which would allow Doc to talk to the source. Of course, it afforded the man little legal protection, however, it did move the matter off the starting gate.

Doc skipped lunch with the prosecutor and drove to St. Paul's East Side, a working man's neighborhood with fewer workers every month. He listened to the radio as the newscaster reported great successes in controlling the raging fires in the West and South. Power grids had been altered and electricity restored to vast areas. Aerial spraying had exterminated the locusts, although prices of produce would remain high. It seemed the country was recovering.

The homes on the East Side, once the pride of the family, were now largely rented and run-down. He pulled curbside in front of a two-story stucco house. A rusty Cadillac rested in the gravel driveway. He briefly called in his location to the dispatcher then walked slowly to the door. It had a front porch where once neighbors stopped by to visit. Now the windows were cracked, the front screen door missing and a sign posted on the front door warned all that the owner was armed and ready to deal out death to the unwelcomed. He knocked then pounded several times. Doc was about to walk away when the door swung open.

"Whadaya want?" a skinny woman croaked. She wore stained gray sweatpants and a Grateful Dead t-shirt. Doc thought she looked vaguely familiar.

"Looking for Stubs, you know where he is?"

"Who'er you?"

"The cops. Get Stubs. He wants to see me. Go get him."

A giant of a man pushed her aside with a hand missing three fingers.

"You must be Stubs. You're expecting me?"

"Get in here before my neighbors see me talk'n to the cops. Woman, get us a beer."

"One each," Doc added as he followed the hulk to what used to be the dining room but now center-pieced a partially assembled Harley Flathead. They sat on the ends of wooden boxes. The woman had a bottle of beer in Doc's hand before he was even seated.

"I'm here...."

"I know why you're here. I don't like doing this but if it helps my 'brother,' I will. 'Sides they was just a bunch of A-Rabs anyway." Stubs tipped the bottle back and demanded another.

"Nice tats."

Stubs turned his palms up to face Doc. A red and black swastika on the inside of his left arm and a SS death head on his right arm. He grabbed the bottle from the woman and screwed the cap off, tossing it among the motorcycle parts. "What'd want to know?"

"Well, your 'brother' was a bit light on details. He said you boys sold some explosives to as you put it 'some A-Rabs'. Tell me about that."

"And this will help him? He'll get time off his sentence?"

"That's the deal."

"Damn, I hate doin' this. It was last summer, early in June – none of this can be used against me, right?"

"That's my understanding."

"I seen you somewhere before, haven't I?"

"Couldn't say. You were saying, 'last summer...'"

"Ya, one of my 'brothers' and me were jacking some smokes from trucks. You know, few hundred cartons at a time. I'd met this Arab dude, owns a smoke shop on the lower east side. He'd buy all we could give him. Like through the back door, you know."

Doc took a swig from the bottle and lit a smoke. It was trying his patience getting this dolt to tell his story. "Then what happened. Tell me about the explosives."

"I'm getting there man, what's your rush?"

"The explosives...."

"So, I got to know this dude pretty well. I connected him to a couple of girls I know, working girls, and he seemed to like that. You know, two at once. Then one day, we'd brought him a big score, you know, and he asks me if I know where he can get some explosives, you know, really serious stuff. I asked him why and he said he wanted to get rid of some competition. What do I care, Arab killing another Arab? So, I told him I'd ask around."

"Did you find some explosives?"

"Ya, but I ain't telling you where. That'd hurt another 'brother.'

"You keep saying 'brother,' these ain't your real blood brothers are they?"

"Hell, no, closer than that. I'm talking Aryan Brothers, man. Brothers for life."

"That's what I thought. So did you get the man some explosives?"

"We did, a lot..."

It took Doc two more beers, four more smokes, and dozens of questions to get to the story. It finally came out, least as much as Stubs was willing to share.

The beer was loosening Stubs's tongue or perhaps jogging his memory. "I got another bomber, 'cept they was just asking for explosives they never bought any."

"Who are they?"

"They's some animal rights dudes. One of the brothers met them at this anarchy meeting...

"Anarchists have meetings?"

"What you talking about?"

"Who were the animal huggers looking for explosives?"

"Don't know, one of the 'brothers' just came to me a few weeks back cuz he know I connected the A-Rabs. Dudes wanted to blow up some lab at a university or something. We already had too much heat man with the arrests and all. I told him 'No.'"

"Anything else?"

"I 'member where I seen you."

"Where was that?"

"Me and the woman were having a domestic on the Interstate a few weeks back, remember, you dickhead stopped and put me on the ground? She got away and I had to walk back here. I swore I'd wring your scrawny neck for that."

Doc hoisted his beer then tipped it back, dropping the bottle on the motorcycle parts. "I say let bygones be bygones." He stood and waited for a response.

Stubs sat and wondered what that meant. Doc turned and slowly showed himself out, listening for rushing footsteps as he walked. He didn't hear a sound but did have to step over a ten foot long python. The snake worked its tongue vigorously trying to determine if the newcomer were friend, foe, or food.

As much as he would have preferred a shower and fresh clothes, Doc pressed on with the leads Stubs had stubbornly dished out. He called IRS Special Agent Jim Hanks.

"Listen, I'm trying to track down a man, Middle Eastern descent, owned a smoke shop in the lower east side, down on Payne Avenue by the old strip joint. I don't have a name, the witness just called him Smokes. You guys are supposedly looking to arrest him."

"You're talking about Abbas Ali Jaafar. We have an arrest warrant for him for tax evasion. Do you know where he is?"

"No, I was hoping you might."

"My best guess would be Lebanon or Syria. He has family in both nations. Who'd you get your information from if I might ask?"

"Dude named Stubs…."

"You mean Odin Rossman? I interviewed Odin. Does he still have the Harley in the dining room and that big-assed python?"

"Yup, and likely will 'til he gets evicted. Why did you interview Stubs?" Doc asked.

"Smokes, as you call him, or Jaafar to us, made a large payment to Stubs. I'm thinking maybe ten…twelve grand and I talked to Stubs about it."

"What'd he say it was for?"

"Said he sold Smokes a car although he had no documentation whatsoever."

"When was that?"

"In June or July of this year – it was outside the period for the tax case, however, I was trying to track Jaafar down and so was looking for any leads."

"Why was that lead important?"

"I didn't interview Stubs until September. By then, Jaafar had vanished so I looked for some trail that might lead me to him. There were deposits about that time from a company named Gemstar. In fact, Gemstar issued a check to Jaafar in the same amount that he then turned around and paid Stubs. Gemstar is some offshore corporate entity. Jaafar had regular checks coming from that company."

"Jaafar, Jaafar….I've seen that name somewhere. Anything else on him?"

"He had a lot of money, spent a bunch in the casino and on women. I don't know what you're looking for," Hanks replied.

"I'm not sure right now. Jim, I'll get back to you when I sort this out. Thanks for putting a name on Smokes."

Doc was sometimes embarrassed about forgetting little things, his keys, appointments, names of relatives. This was one of those times – Gemstar, Jaafar, Stubs. He should know those names. He called the next best thing to his memory, Amy, the intelligence analyst, and explained what he'd just learned from Stubs and Hanks.

"I know that I've had information like this before. Can you look it up on the computer?"

"I did as you were telling me the story."

"That's irritating when you're always a step or two ahead of me. What did you find?"

"Back in August, you wrote an intel report about an informant who told you a guy named Jaafar was looking to buy some explosives, a lot of it..."

"I remember, I tried to identify Jaafar. You were on vacation and so I asked Sharon Risling to do the work. She couldn't identify him from any public records."

"I'm looking at a history of her searches right now. It was on August 13th, she tried making queries, but she spelled the name wrong and that's why Jaafar wasn't identified. I'm looking at records now of real estate transactions, Jaafar is all over the computer. She should have found this back in August."

"And maybe the president's son would be alive!"

Tuesday, October 30th

Brothers Estate
St. Croix River Valley
Taylors Falls, Minnesota

DOC HAD BEEN ON THE land line with Stone for over two hours, taking a few dozen of pages of notes, none of which would ever see the light of day. Perhaps most startling was Darrin Watkins's tortured revelation that a company named Gemstar had purchased a portion of Blackstone. Watkins had identified a couple of men from the Middle East as the only corporate officers known to him. He denied knowingly setting up the assassination.

Watkins had arranged for FARC to supply much needed cash in the United States for political payoffs and contributions. This arrangement solved two problems, Watkins had his hand on $200,000,000 in cash which had been collected from narcotics sales. They were narcotics owned by FARC and sent to the U.S. where they were sold for cash. The cash was accumulated and delivered via courier service to Watkins's law firm. When Watkins sent the profits from the stock deals to Venezuela, FARC got its narcotics profits back into Colombia without interference from Customs officials.

"Alex you men have done a great service to your country, once again. What about your boat guest?"

"He's in the driver's seat of his car which is parked in the garage…by now probably waking up smell'n a booze and with a hell of a hangover. We partied hard with him. I have it all on tape, his words only, and believe me he don't have a clue who we are."

"What do you think he will do?"

"I believe he'll continue with his normal daily activities, tryin' to get his bearings, tryin' to decide if I was a bad dream, he'll be confused for a few days."

"Can you guys get back here?"

"Maybe not until tomorrow, we have to make certain we left no loose ends. I don't believe Watkins will call the police, but we want to keep an eye on things for a day. If he doesn't call today, he won't and this will not ever be an issue. It means he feels between a rock and a hard place – like when a drug dealer gets robbed of his drugs, who's he going to call?"

"That tape will never be admissible against him. We can use the information for leads. Put the tape in a safe place," Doc said.

"It's done already, give my sister a hug and tell Fancy we miss her cooking."

"Jaafar, Jaafar, I know I saw that name recently," Doc said to the pug on his lap. Doc rose from the high back chair. It creaked and knocked against the paneled wall.

He moved to the cardboard boxes next to the desk. He lowered himself to the floor where he sat cross-legged and rummaged through the evidence bags. Of course, it was in the last bag, a crumpled piece of paper seized from the South Minneapolis home of Armando Gomez. Scribbled on the paper was the name 'Abbas Jaafar' followed by a two telephone numbers. The paper had been taken from the trash by Doc.

"Here it is, Gumpy, do you realize what this means?"

The pug cocked his head and raised his ears.

Tuesday, October 30th

Sarajevo, Bosnia

THE THREE MEN DISPATCHED BY Blackstone's Mr. Olness, had watched Maurice Smith for three days. On the first day, they'd seen a giant of a man, scarred and menacing, visit Smith's apartment. He stayed for three hours, and when he'd left, Maurice ran to a nearby tavern where he drank until he passed out. They didn't see how he got home.

On the second day, Maurice stayed home from work. Later in the afternoon they followed him to a small shop occupied by a travel agency. They learned after Maurice had departed the shop that he purchased a one way ticket to London and continuing to New York. He paid in cash.

Maurice's supervisor, Mr. Olness, informed his men that Mr. Smith was not traveling on Blackstone business and his employee had not requested any leave of absence. It was then that the order was issued to grab Maurice. That decision was more difficult than actually abducting the frail accountant. He didn't even struggle when the men tossed him into the rear of the Mercedes sedan.

They arrived at the dilapidated building behind the White Mosque as calls to prayer were announced from the slender stone minaret. The accountant wasn't tortured or threatened – there was no need to – he'd already messed his pants and eagerly complied with every order.

He told his abductors about his discovery of the phantom Blackstone mercenaries and yes he did have a complete list back at the office. No, he'd told no one except Mr. Olness. The mysterious visitor he'd had two days ago? Yes, and of course he'd told him, also. That sealed Mr. Smith's fate. True to his nature, he offered no resistance to the garrote which ended his uneventful life at the same time prayers ended in the White Mosque.

Tuesday, October 30th

White House Press Room
Washington, D.C.

PETEY MAHONEY, WHITE HOUSE PRESS Secretary, stood at the podium, "Two Irishmen, Patrick Murphy and Shawn O'Brian, grew up together and were lifelong friends. Sadly, Patrick developed cancer and was dying. While on his deathbed, Patrick called to his buddy, Shawn, 'O'Brian, come 'ere. I 'ave a request for ye.' Shawn moved to his friend's bedside and knelt.

" 'Shawny ole boy, we've been friends all our lives, and now I'm leaving 'ere. I 'ave one last request fir ye to do.'

"O'Brian fought back tears, 'Anything, Patrick, anything ye wish. It's done.'

" 'Well, under me bed is a box containing a bottle of the finest whiskey in all of Ireland. Bottled the year I was born it was. After I die and they plant me in the ground, I want you to pour that fine whiskey over my grave so it might soak into me bones and I'll be able to enjoy it for all eternity.'

"O'Brian was overcome by the beauty and in the true Irish spirit of his friend's request, he asked, 'Aye, 'tis a fine thing you ask of me, and I will pour the whiskey. But, might I strain it through me kidneys first?' "

When the laughter subsided, he began his prepared statement.

"On October 29th, Allied Forces conducted what may be the last of the combat missions in the Middle East Conflict. With Pakistani officials' knowledge and consent, forces attacked a compound which is believed to have housed Ayman al Zawahri and his key advisors and lieutenants. The compound was destroyed and there were no enemy survivors. Allied Forces sustained no casualties.

"As this conflict comes to an end, it is fitting that that last battle should result in the deaths of those responsible for the 911 attacks and the most recent attacks on our soil. Our fight is over in the Middle East and it is time to bring our loyal fighting forces home to safeguard our own soil.

"The president will announce this week a deployment of military forces throughout our great nation. They will be deployed to guard our infrastructure and prevent future acts of violence.

"We will provide copies of the video showing the attack on the compound. Again, we will not likely find al Zawahri's remains, however, I am confident we'll never again see his videotapes threatening to destroy America.

"The president wishes to thank all Americans for their support in this fight against terrorism and prays for the safe return of all of our troops.

"That is all I have Ladies and Gentlemen, if we get an update on the few DNA samples collected at the scene, I will get back to you promptly." Petey turned from the podium ignoring the shouted questions and left the stage.

Tuesday, October 30th

Willard Hotel
Washington, D.C.

"ROCKY," ED MITCHELL SHOUTED OVER the hotel telephone, "The tracking unit called and Ali's transmitter is hitting the satellite again!"

Rocky rolled over trying to wake up, "Where is it?"

"Electronic guys put it inside the White House!"

"Damn it to hell, won't this ever end? Did you tell Director Lang?"

"Not yet."

"OK, get a hold of that Secret Service agent who we are supposed to be working with."

"I already left a message for him."

"Then relax, there's nothing else to be done. I'll guaran-fucking-tee you Ali ain't in the White House, relax Ed. It's likely that Jean Paul fellow the director warned the Secret Service about. The bad guys are just rubbing our noses in their dung."

Rocky lay back down, thinking maybe he could sleep again when his cell phone rang, "Yeah, what do you need now, Stone?"

"I just want you to know, those local cops have more evidence that it was Blackstone mercenaries who attacked the first lady and that some Arabs arranged it.

"Also that accountant in Bosnia identified the missing Blackstone employees, all Special Forces operators, all from outside the United States. He even kept photocopies of the ledgers that show names of the employees, kept 'em to protect his own ass. He's going to meet with our man on Thursday and give him a list of the mercs gone rogue."

"Listen, Stone, I believe you are on to something. We should meet to talk in person, are you still in Minnesota?"

"I'm in Washington for a couple of days on business."

"No shit, me too. How about Union Station at noon?"

"Noon it is. I'll find you." Rocky hung up and called Ed's room.

"Ed, I have to meet a snitch at noon at Union Station, what time we flying out?"

"Director said 1600 hours from our jet port."

"I'll meet you at the jet port, what's the latest on al Fulani?"

"Remember Gene Bauer? He retired about four years ago, retired to Aspen? He has been watching al Fulani as a favor to us. He says the Arab is staying at the Castle Creek Chalet, owned by some Saudi billionaire. He says there's a bunch of Middle Eastern men at the place."

"Anything else I should know?"

"Yeah, Director's got a deal with Secret Service to bring a bunch of their commo and computer geeks to Aspen see if they can pick up any chatter. They'll be set up by the time we get there."

At exactly 1200 hours, Rocky felt a tap on his shoulder as he stood at the second floor railing scanning the Union Station's courtyard below for Alex Stone.

"How ya do'n Rocky?" He turned to face Stone.

Rocky extended his hand. "Doing great, how 'bout some lunch?"

"Hot dogs would suit me fine. We can talk while we walk to the dog stand on the first floor."

"What you got on this Blackstone group?" Rocky asked.

As they walked and ate their way through seven hot dogs, Stone told Rocky about the nexus between the Blackstone mercenaries and the Middle Eastern owned corporations and trusts. He left out any comments about the tortured lawyer being the source of this information. He concluded with his conviction that the Blackstone mercenaries were responsible for the assassination and many of the events such as the refinery explosion, power outages, fires, and railroad bridges collapses.

"Why don't the local agents take this to the FBI and how do you fit into this?"

"I stumbled into these cops when Blackstone sent me to Minnesota. I was able to give them some information link'n the men who they think did the assassination with Blackstone. I don't understand the FBI thing, but I believe the cops have been told that the FBI already solved this."

By two o'clock, Rocky had squeezed out as much information as he could. "Alex, I need to catch a flight to Colorado. The CIA has no jurisdiction or authority over any of these matters. We have given all of our information to the FBI and it's really up to them. That being said, if this whole affair moves out of the United States, would you be willing to do some work for the CIA?"

"What kind of work?" Alex checked his watch and spun the band once around his wrist.

"The kind you and your partners do best."

"We can arrange something I'm sure."

"We will stay in touch. Can you have that local cop call me?"

"Today?"

"Later tonight."

Tuesday, October 30th

Annabelle Inn
Aspen, Colorado

SIX ROWS OF METAL TABLES were stacked with communication and computer equipment. Eight technicians manned the array of sophisticated almost futuristic, devises. They were supporting a larger operation of surveillance agents and command staff.

U.S.S.S. Special Agent Art Hinkle was the lead agent in the command post which was hastily established in the Inn's Executive Suite. Hinkle told the hotel manager that the president would be arriving in Aspen in a few weeks and the agents were simply the forward team. The manager seemed satisfied.

Hinkle sipped Gatorade to rehydrate in the dryness of the mountain air. A marathoner, he was unhappy to have his training regimen interrupted although he was accustomed to the last minute assignments. He concentrated on the radio traffic between several agents on surveillance and the command post.

"There are three men on the balcony, appear to be in Western clothes, but are likely Middle Eastern descent."

"All three have laptops."

"We have captured their wireless laptop signals and will stay with them."

"We have four cell phones in use. All Arabic, we will record."

"C.P. can you get some translators either on site or patch us to a remote?"

"Same for the computers."

"The transmissions are not in English."

Hinkle keyed the microphone, "I'll check on this although the Service has few available without going to a private contractor."

"We have three men out on foot walking towards town."

"Stay with them."

"Hinkle, there is a spook on the phone for you, says four CIA officers are in town and would like to meet with you."

"Tell them we will send one of our agents to bring them to us."

Tuesday, October 30th

Brothers Estate
St. Croix River Valley
Taylors Falls, Minnesota

DOC CALLED ROCKY AT PRECISELY 10:00 p.m. After the introductions, Doc asked, "What can I do for you?"

"As I understand the situation from Stone, you think the FBI has arrested the wrong persons for the attack on the first lady and her son."

"That sounds too simple for what I believe has happened. I don't know for sure that they have arrested the wrong persons. However, I'm reasonably sure that at the very least there were others involved in the attack. I am dead sure that Blackstone mercenaries were in Minnesota when the attack occurred and there is some solid circumstantial evidence linking those mercenaries to the attack."

"Why don't you just take it to the FBI or the U.S. Attorney?"

"I will when we have enough convincing evidence. Until then, it would be treated with disbelief not to mention there may be requirements to make the information public."

"Why would they make it public?"

"The persons arrested by the FBI have been formally charged. If I bring information forward that another person may have actually done the crime, the U.S. Attorney would have to release that possible exculpable information to the defense attorneys who you can be sure would release it to the media. That would absolutely destroy any possibility of catching the killers or the puppet masters."

"So what are you going to do?"

"What they pay me to do. I will continue to pursue the leads as best I can wherever they take me. I think Alex told you that Blackstone is owned by Arab investors who try to conceal their ownership."

"Yeah, he told me and I know he has told you about his capture of a terrorist named Ali."

"He did. You know, all this foreign intrigue crap ain't my deal, but when I saw al Zawahri promising to visit biblical plagues on America and then I see plagues being delivered including the death of the president's son, even I can connect the dots. And those dots point to the Arabs who run Blackstone being behind the assassination."

"I think you are on the right track."

"Quite frankly, if I am, then this whole investigation is way over my head."

"I wouldn't sell yourself short. You seem to have put this together so far. I don't doubt you would pursue the bastard to hell if given the opportunity. I am in Colorado with the Secret Service. Unofficially, I am here following up on the Ali matter. Actually, on the record I'm here on a vacation. Ali was supposed to have possessed knowledge of secret plans to attack America. If you are right on your theory of the attacks then I think Ali may have unwittingly led us to the Arab conspirators and they are here in Aspen right under our collective noses. Can you join us here tomorrow?"

"I can arrange that, however, I also will be there kinda unofficial. I'll call you when I arrive."

Wednesday, October 31st

Brothers Estate
St. Croix River Valley
Taylors Falls, Minnesota

DOC DIALED HIS FBI PARTNER, "Pat, would you like to fly to Colorado with me tomorrow?"

"Skiing?"

"Nope, work. I have some new leads on the assassination and it's time for us to get together to continue this investigation. I have taken it as far as our agency can."

"Tonight, I am flying to Washington. I'm at the airport now. Tomorrow the president, himself, is presenting us with awards for capturing the assassins. So, no, I can't fly to Colorado with you."

"Listen up, this is more important, I'll give you the abbreviated version. . ."

Twenty minutes later, Pat demanded, "Why the hell didn't you bring me in earlier?"

"Because your bosses would have never let you pursue this when they were convinced you already had your killers."

"I can't just fly off to Colorado. I have to get permission from my SAIC and they have to teletype the regional and national offices, the Denver SAIC and he has to assign a local agent. It's not as simple as just catching a flight."

"Well, I'm leaving tomorrow on the red-eye. You do what you need to do."

Thursday, November 1st

Annabelle Inn
Aspen, Colorado

"HINKLE, I HAVE A MINNESOTA cop on the telephone. He's with two FBI agents and says you are expecting them."

"Tell them Donna Lyons will pick them up. Find out where they are and tell Donna."

"Roger that."

The radio in the C.P. chattered as six Arabs in three separate groups moved about, "Stop talking over each other. Let's split our radio channels. Earl, you guys go to channel 13, Anne, take your people to channel 2, I will take mine to channel 6."

"We have two wireless computers running."

"No cell activity."

"Hinkle, all your guests are waiting for you downstairs."

"Roger, I'll be down shortly."

While they waited, Lyons took Doc aside. "I talked to a liaison agent in Canada. He went to Vancouver to follow up on the flight from St. Paul to Vancouver the day the president's son was attacked. What he found was the commercial charter was paid for with cash by a Bermuda corporation, Holdingford Ltd. The corporate officers for Holdingford are the same as Gemstar. Does that mean anything to you? They have no office in the U.S. or Canada. He did a little more snooping with the RCMPs and found that two days after they arrived in Vancouver, they flew to Mexico City."

They were interrupted when Hinkle arrived downstairs, he saw that the agents had already introduced themselves and were engaged in conversation. "Donna, did you bring these agents up to date?"

"I did, we were just waiting for you."

"We have been following the Arabs around Aspen, they are acting like tourists. We are capturing cell phone and wireless computer transmissions. All are in some Arabic dialect. Few, are in English. The CIA is translating through computer links so it is taking awhile to get back to us…although we're not intercepting much of interest."

A young man standing between Doc and Pat raised his hand to interrupt, "I am Special Agent Ortiz from the Denver FBI Office and I have a couple of questions."

"Go ahead," Hinkle said.

"What in the hell is the CIA, the Secret Service and some state cop doing conducting a domestic terrorist investigation? Does the State Department know you are intercepting communications of diplomats? Do you have court orders for these intercepts? And why has the FBI been kept in the dark on this?"

Director Lang blushed with anger. "I personally briefed your national office on this matter two days ago. They apparently are not interested enough to get involved. Yes, the State Department was briefed yesterday when we first learned that some of them were diplomats. The CIA is here as consultants and not conducting any investigations. And I'll let the others speak for themselves."

Doc spoke first. "While I am a state cop as you put it, I am also a sworn deputized federal agent assigned to the FBI's Anti-Terrorist Task Force and we are wasting our valuable time even explaining this to you."

Hinkle interrupted, "We are intercepting these communications under the emergency powers of the Patriot Act. The Secret Service is involved because based upon what these agents have told us, I think the FBI stopped their investigation of the assassinations too soon."

Ortiz raised his voice, "I think you all are off base and probably violating a dozen policies and even committing a few felonies with these intercepts. That's the message I will take back to my SAIC in Denver."

Director Lang suppressed his anger and spoke softly and definitively, "I hear there's a storm moving in. Perhaps you should get an early start back to Denver."

Friday, November 2nd

White House Oval Office
Washington, D.C.

THE PRESIDENT STOOD BEFORE THE floor to ceiling window. He leaned slightly towards his cane. The others continued to argue as he soaked up the sunshine letting his mind wander away from the meeting to his wife. She was getting better physically by the day although her mental condition was not improving. He asked himself what more he could do for her. What specialists could he bring in? He wondered what it really mattered to be thought of as the most powerful man on earth.

"Mr. President, Sir."

The president looked at the clouds forming great thunderheads. "Yes, I have made my decision. We will stay the course I laid out a week ago." He turned and faced his staff members.

CIA Director Rankin took one more stab at trying to alter the decision. "Sir, I plead with you to let our agents follow through with this Blackstone matter and try to determine who the puppet masters are."

"We have been through this over and over. What does the FBI have on this Blackstone matter?"

"Nothing of substance," F.B.I. Director Marashov said. "I just don't see the point in pursuing these allegations. We have rock solid cases on your son's assassins. We have suspects in custody for each of the significant events."

"What about the frogs?" asked the Homeland Security Secretary Richard Wilkins.

"I don't see the frogs as significant. We've killed the algae in the Potomac River. The fires in the Rockies, we still don't know that those were started by al Qaeda. The rest we pretty much have a handle on."

The president interrupted, "General, what are you being told about the al Qaeda activity?"

"Mr. President, first of all I haven't had an opportunity to share with you. DNA tests confirmed that we killed al Zawahri in the raid."

"Outstanding, just damn outstanding."

The general continued, "Acting on the special information that your chief of staff continues to provide, we've pretty much emasculated the al Qaeda and Taliban leadership. Pakistan continues to open their borders for us and we're using Special Forces and missiles to strike them down. We should have this operation wrapped up in weeks. I don't know who your source is, however, the information thus far has been spot on."

The president pounded the floor with his cane. "I just don't see any reason to pursue this Blackstone matter. I particularly don't want any more wiretaps on diplomats in this country. That will come back to harm us if it is ever uncovered. Right now, I believe that each of you can go before Congress and hold your heads high. The results speak for themselves."

The president moved slowly back to his chair and sat stiffly facing the others. In less than two weeks, he'd aged more than ten years. "We have killed al Zawahri and his command. We have won agreements with the factions in Iraq and Afghanistan to a peaceful coalition government. We have arrested killers of my son and my wife is recovering. These have been horrifying days, however, we have united as a nation and can claim many victories. We should all thank our God for these victories. The terrorists have little to be thankful for. Lastly, I want to commend you all for the excellent work your agencies and forces have done. We will stay the course."

Friday, November 2nd

Annabelle Inn
Aspen, Colorado

DIRECTOR LANG POURED HIMSELF ANOTHER cognac as he waited for Doc to return from the bathroom, "Feeling better?"

"I'm not used to eatin' so well…runs right through me, sorry."

"I understand, please continue with your story…"

Doc wrapped up his story after much questioning by the Director, particularly about what evidence existed against the men from the chalet.

Director Lang looked at his watch and raised his eyebrows. "I don't have much time. Please, tell me how you connect these men here in Aspen with the Blackstone affair."

"I'm afraid I can't tell you the source, however, I'm confident that it is accurate considering how it was collected. The source has named two of the players in the Blackstone purchase. Both men are with the group you are watching. That, and as I understand the situation, your men were chasing a man named Ali who somehow you've connected with Blackstone."

"That is true," Director Lang said as he checked his watch again then moved to the window. Snowflakes, big and fluffy, blew up against the glass pane. He didn't speak for an uncomfortably long time then turned to face the seated Doc.

"The CIA has finished its business here in Colorado. I believe we can agree that the FBI has to run with this, if they choose to do so and our presence will distract them. I've been told that FBI executives have already informed the Senate Intelligence Committee that the CIA is spying in the United States on foreign diplomats, all of which is true."

"You know the FBI is not going to pursue this. They are not going to expose themselves to Congressional criticism. They have announced that the assassins have been caught and that's the end of the story," Doc said.

"I agree that they clearly will drop this. I thank you for bringing this matter as far as you have, yet I must remove my agents from this affair and I am certain that the Secret Service agents will be leaving, also. Agent, when do you retire?"

"I am eligible to go anytime I choose."

"I could use a man like you if you ever want to live abroad and work as a subcontractor."

"I'll think about it."

"We are leaving in an hour for Denver hopefully ahead of the storm and before the roads close down. Here is my cell phone number, call me if you wish to accept my offer."

Doc stepped over to the director and extended his hand. "You may be hearing from me."

"I look forward to that and I most certainly appreciate you spending these last few hours briefing me on the details of your investigation.

"One more thing before I depart. Might I suggest that this evening, you and your partner put surveillance, a very overt surveillance on the Middle Easterners?"

"Why?"

"I believe that doing so may have some desirable results. My translators tell me that there may be some action tonight."

When Doc had left, Director Lang picked up his private secure cell phone and dialed, "My friend we need to meet soon…"

Friday, November 2nd

Castle Creek Chalet
Aspen, Colorado

"WHAT'S THE PROBLEM?" OMAR ASKED of the ashen al Fulani.

"We are under surveillance my brother, extensive surveillance!"

"How do you know this?"

"You remember our Mexican housekeepers have been instructed to report any rumors of men watching us. They believe it is for fear of kidnappings. One of the housekeepers has learned from her sister that at least 20 police officers have taken up residence at the Annabelle Inn. They have been there since Tuesday. They have refused housekeeping the entire time.

"When I learned of this I asked Jean Claude and his men to step up their vigilance. They tell me that there is a car with men watching our chalet through binoculars."

"This chalet has served us well, however, it is time to return to our homelands where we can better monitor the invasion of Israel. Quickly, tell the others to prepare to depart immediately. Have the pilots prepare to leave. Is the weather favorable to fly?" Omar asked.

"No, we will leave that to the pilots, if not we can drive to Denver and fly commercial."

"Have Jean Claude attempt to identify who these men are, what agency, FBI? Make it clear that we want no problems created with these men," Omar said.

....

Doc and Pat sat low in their rented Ford Taurus parked about 500 yards from the Chalet. The snowfall was getting heavier and the wind increasingly strong. At times the men couldn't even see the Chalet. There was no activity, likely due to the weather.

"This makes no sense, sitting out here in the storm," Pat said for the third time.

"The Secret Service is pulling out and you and I will be out of here tomorrow. Let's just wait awhile to see what happens."

"What happens will be nothing, absolutely nothing. That's what we'll see," Pat said as he pushed lower in his seat.

"Let's just give it awhile longer," Doc said as he rolled his window down and lit a Camel.

"One more hour…I have a life out there I want to catch up with."

"You will – now pull up a little closer, I can't even see the place with all of this snow."

"Fine, but I won't be returning to Minnesota with you. I have been ordered to Washington. Apparently our director has gotten a pretty good tongue lashing from the president. The president believes his family's assassins are in jail and wants this matter brought to an immediate halt." Pat put the car in drive and eased it up another 150 yards.

"Keep going."

"Why?"

"Because when you moved so did a car parked a couple of hundred yards to the rear."

Pat drove to the end of the block and turned right.

"They are back about a block and a half, but they made the turn with you. Take another turn."

Pat continued two more blocks before he turned left and crossed the bridge spanning the Castle Creek.

"They are further back although they definitely made the turn with us. Take it out of town for awhile."

"It's probably the Secret Service or some local cop. A citizen probably called 911 on us."

Ten minutes later the Taurus had threaded its way up the mountain switchbacks.

Doc's cell phone rang twice. "Hello."

It was his mother, sobbing.

"Ma, I can hardly understand anything you are saying. I understand you are unhappy at the home."

She continued to cry and beg for her son to come and get her from the nursing home. "I had a dream – I was at your funeral. And it was packed with cops and that chubby priest friend of yours was standing over your grave."

"Look ma, I'm really busy now. I'll call you back in a half-hour then we can talk and make some plans – half an hour ma. Bye"

"When you make this next switchback, stop and let me out."

"What the hell?"

"Just drive ahead and make a u-turn. Wait a couple of minutes for them to catch up and then come back and get me."

"Why don't we just stop here and wait for them?"

"Because they won't come that close to our car – just do it. Stop here, wait a few minutes and come back for me."

Doc jumped out and moved quickly to the rocky ledge. He rolled a couple of large boulders across the road.

Within minutes, the Cadillac Escalade with lights off, came around the curve, slowly to about 10 mph to make the sharp turn and braked at the rocks. From out of the ledge, Doc approached the Escalade front passenger side, badge in hand and held out in front of his chest. His right hand on his pistol gripped tightly behind his back.

"Police officer! Roll your window down, now! Roll it down!"

The window came down, "What is wrong officer? What is wrong?" asked the man with a thick French accent.

Doc stepped closer, seeing the driver and passenger posing no threat, "Let me see your hands." They complied and Doc came one step closer.

The rear passenger window exploded as the hollow-point smashed through the glass striking Doc's head. He collapsed onto the road and rolled into the shallow ditch next to the cliff.

Pat drove the Taurus toward the Escalade just as Doc fell. The Escalade shot forward towards Pat. The Taurus was in reverse although there was nowhere to go as the Escalade pushed the Taurus over the edge of the mountain road.

Saturday, November 3rd

Georgetown, Washington, D. C.

DARRIN WATKINS WAS NEITHER A foolish nor a brave man. After his abduction, he installed a security system, including video cameras throughout the house and garage. He'd purchased a handgun and even taken lessons. He grew eyes in the back of his head and was more paranoid than a crack dealer on Pennsylvania Avenue. His schedule was altered to assure no more ambushes.

But a summons from al Fulani was not to be ignored. He dressed in his best suit and in addition to the royal red tie, he strapped the .45 onto his belt before he left through the back door and drove off to the early morning meeting at an office not two miles away.

al Fulani was still dressed in his casual ski wear and Watkins felt a bit overdressed when he was ushered into the cluttered office. al Fulani was standing at the massive window and ignored the attorney for a few uncomfortable moments.

"Mr. Watkins, I have heard some disturbing rumors. I hope they are not true," al Fulani said without turning to face his guest.

"What have you heard? I'm sure there's an explanation." Watkins moved next to al Fulani. When the Kuwaiti faced Watkins, his hopes of talking his way out of any problem faded like the moon al Fulani had watched sink over the Potomac.

When al Fulani – with his cold reptilian eyes – stared into Watkins's face, he likewise knew there was a problem that no amount of conversation would remedy.

Saturday, November 3rd

44 Wall Street,
New York City

WHEN DARRIN WATKINS CALLED THE office, Bernie Silverstein was putting the finishing touches on a monetary arbitrage that would by his calculations net him a few million – and all without using his own money. It wasn't unusual for a client to call on the weekend.

"Bernie, I'm with our client from Kuwait and he has some financial needs that must be taken care of immediately."

"Yes, of course, what can I do for him?"

"This must be done in person."

"Yes, I'm at the office now. Where are the two of you? Here in New York?"

"Yes, in New York City. Six, can we meet you at six?"

"Of course, I can wait – it's eight now and I've got to work here until about two so, I'll run over to my condo for a few hours and then come back at six."

"Thank you, and our client insists on taking you out for dinner when we finish our tasks."

Sunday, November 4th

Orleans Café
Outskirts of Rennes, France

THE ORLEANS CAFÉ IS LOCATED some twenty kilometers from the city of Rennes nestled in the Paimpont forest. Enormous century old oak and beech trees bordered the picketed white fence surrounding the café's patio. It seated only thirty some customers and was always crowded. Except Sunday when it was closed by the owners, Julen Auffray and his wife, Madrilène, ardent Catholics, who shunned labor on the Sabbath – the Lord's day.

Director Lang was seated under the protection of a large beech tree. It was his favorite table which allowed him to keep his back to the tree. Every seat was filled this Sunday. Many couples enjoyed a bottle of French wine and the sunshine. All of the guests were there by invitation of Director Lang. An accordion player meandered through the tables softly playing romantic folk tunes.

When Lang saw al Fulani walk under the striped canopy through the 10 foot hedges, he stood and waved to get his attention. al Fulani passed the *maitre d'* and joined Director Lang. They exchanged a warm embrace and kisses to the cheek.

"My friend, how good to see you and thank you for joining me on such little notice."

"I am pleased to see you again. Because of the short notice, I must tell you I have only a limited time to spend with you."

Director Lang held up his hand, "I understand, although surely we can have an early dinner while we talk." He waved for their waiter.

"We are unfortunately rushed, what special can you serve promptly?" Lang asked.

"The chef has prepared roast pork which has been cooking on the wood fire for two days with new potatoes and truffles – I would recommend a Bordeaux wine."

"Director, I will have to decline lunch, perhaps we could get about business."

"Yes, of course, sorry Pierre, I'll order later." The squat man with a white apron dragging on the cobblestones backed away.

"Our concern is the military build-up around Israel. We are withdrawing our troops from the Middle East which has the Israelis very concerned and preparing to battle. I fear they will attack first and your country should know that it is a likely possibility and soon. My friend, I must warn you that I know the Israelis have plans to respond to any major attack by bombing the oil fields and that includes your nation. I wish to see no harm come to my friends."

"We thank you for the warning, however, I know of no plans to attack Israel, in fact, I hear rumors of another round of peace talks."

"Are you certain of this?"

"I assure you, there are no plans, as Deputy Minister of Defense I would know."

"That is a relief to hear this from you."

"Is that all you wanted to discuss?"

"Yes, yes, Director Rankin is pushing for all of us to meet with our sources so he can brief the White House and the president can reassure the Israelis."

"I'm pleased I have been able to help, now, if that is all, I…"

"Yes, Yes, I understand. How is your family, your father?"

"He is old and sickly."

"Your half-brother Ali?"

"I haven't been in contact with him for months. Now Director, I must go."

"No, no, no...you must not stand up – please remain in your seat."

"Why?" al Fulani asked as he began to rise from his chair.

"Sit Down!" Lang barked. "If you stand before I am done, you will be dead before you take a step."

al Fulani plopped back into his chair, "What is this about?"

"Turn slowly in your chair. Pay close attention to the only two men still seated in this café. I believe you know one of these men?"

al Fulani turned slowly, realizing that all of the diners and wait staff were gone. The accordion music continued to play a sad tune by Eric Montbel and clouds now hid the sun. As he focused on the two men seated across the café, the larger of the two turned slowly in his chair to face al Fulani.

"Omar, that viper," he whispered, the color gone from his face, he turned back to Director Lang. "What is this about? I am a diplomat and your treatment of me will adversely affect the relationship between our countries."

"No, it will not. However, you need to know this before you decide to stand. Your half-brother talked to us while he was our captive. He told us he could lead us to you and he did. We didn't believe you would kill him but you did. No matter, he told us of your purchase of the American company Blackstone and we know of your plans to use the Blackstone mercenaries."

"I know nothing of what you speak about. I think you are a drunk who should retire."

"Well, we can agree on that my friend. Nonetheless, we were able to watch you all meeting in Aspen. I believe you call yourselves the Council. We also were able to access Abulhassen Mumtaz's computer hard drive and it seems that he exercised poor judgment in storing some battle plans to attack Israel."

"This has nothing to do with me. What do you want from me?"

"It is best to not begin this new relationship with lies and mistrust. Let me remind you, Ali talked."

"What do you want?"

"The truth, I know that your little group, this Council, is behind the attacks in America. We will dismantle much of what you have done. I want to know the entire affair. I want to hear it from your lips."

"I don't think I can help you, Director Lang."

"Let me finish, first your people will not destroy America. We will prevail. The agent with Omar is making the same offer to him. If you elect to help us, remain seated and we will talk this afternoon, then you will return to your people and continue to furnish information. If you elect not to help, simply stand and leave. I will give you a minute to decide."

Alex and Jake were hidden in the hayloft of the stone barn across the narrow footpath from the café. Both had scoped and silenced rifles trained on the heads of the two Arabs. Rooster and Lee trained their spotting scopes on the CIA officers seated with the Arabs, waiting for a signal. Alex checked the time on his watch and spun the band once around his wrist. Finally Rooster whispered, "Take Omar!"

al Fulani turned at the soft report of gunfire followed by a brief guttural groan. He saw Omar standing although without the top of his head.

"I assume Omar elected to leave – a pity for his three wives – what is your decision? You see I, too, have little time to chat."

al Fulani was as silent and frozen as a sphinx.

Friday, November, 9th

Brothers Estate
St. Croix River Valley
Taylors Falls, Minnesota

"GUMPY, YOU'RE TWO INCHES SHORTER and ten pounds fatter! Still ugly though. Who the hell is looking after you?" Tony Brothers asked as he entered the kitchen.

"Hello, Tony," Fancy answered from the kitchen pantry. "I'm looking after him – chasing after him is more like it. Got the appetite of a bear and the brains of a bird! How have you been," she asked with a smile and a hug.

"What took you knuckleheads so long?" bellowed Doc's voice from the deck. "Get out here and tell me what's going on…you young guys trying to cut the old man out of this investigation?"

The agents shuffled through the kitchen past the aroma of fresh baked banana bread and out into the sunshine. Doc was rocking in a wooden rocker looking impatient.

"That's not likely to happen," Pat replied. "I just got back from Washington. After days of trying to explain your unusual investigative methods, I think I can keep you from being indicted or at least out of prison."

"I doubt it…more like you picked up another trophy for your mantle – the usual methods."

"Seriously, the brass is really, really pissed at us."

"Screw them," Doc added as he scratched his bandaged head.

"How's your head? What's left of it anyway."

Tony piped in, "Passed clean through his head, didn't hit anything, no harm."

"My other ear is mostly gone now so it'll make my barber's life easier. All in all, I'm a better person for the experience. And you?"

"Good, good…if that pine tree hadn't stopped the Taurus, I'd rolled down the mountain all the way back to Aspen, but no, I'm fine."

"So it's true – you saved my life – just want you to know my will has been reworked and Gumpy is yours as soon as I pass. I hope that makes us even."

"I saves your life and you sic the hound from hell on me…better throw in your house and the '48 Cadillac convertible."

"A done deal but until then, are you still an agent or did the brass take your badge?"

"On Tuesday, they made me turn in my gun and badge. By Thursday, Director Marashov himself gave them back and told me to go back to Minnesota."

"What the hell happened, you threatened him with those old J. Edgar in drag photos?"

"They said they couldn't tell me much, although it seems someone is talking and old man you were spot on."

Tony, Pat and Doc settled in the cedar Adirondack rockers facing the sun. The leaves had all fallen and now lay ankle deep on the ground and covered with a light dusting of snow. They caught up on the news when they were joined by Father O'Reilly. He had been spending a few days with Doc at the estate. After introductions, the conversation turned to the events of the past few weeks and plans for the future.

"I had dinner with Donna last night," Tony said. "She said she would stop by today."

"Dinner? Does that mean that there is more than a professional relationship going on here?" Doc asked.

"We're just friends," Tony replied. "Did I tell you that Lora has applied for a job with the Texas Rangers? Seems she re-kindled some love interest down in the Lone Star State." He quickly added, trying to change the subject.

The priest spoke up. "Nikkei is back on the streets. The girls say she is using heavily again and walking Lake Street. As it turns out, the Catholic Charities Shelter needed a couple of cooks and I got Blondie and Fancy starting a job there next week. They both are going to begin some serious counseling to see if they can turn their lives around."

"Pat, I was thinking maybe we could get those girls some money for what they have done," Doc said. He took a long pull on the stub of a cigar.

"Doc, I'll ask, but right now I don't have an investigation to even associate the payment with, but I'll see what I can do."

Donna, dressed in her finest tailored black suit, opened the patio door and was greeted with a wolf whistle from Doc. He got up and gave her a hearty hug. "I see you're still employed. Please have a seat. Pug, get your big hind end off that chair and let this lady have a seat."

The wind picked up and the leaves began to swirl up from the ground and onto the deck. A few sprinkles began to fall from an isolated dark cloud. Not enough reason to go back inside, however, Doc leaned over to the deck heater and turned it to high.

"Tell us what news you bring back from the Beltway?" Doc asked.

"Well, we executed search warrants on the Blackstone corporate headquarters. We looked for the employment records for the soldiers we had identified. They don't exist as Blackstone employees."

Doc leaned forward from his chair, "You mean none of the soldiers identified by Stone and his men as Blackstone mercenaries are currently employed at the company?"

"No, I mean the company has no record of them ever having been employed. Most of the employees we found were ex-cops or soldiers and almost all from the United States."

"Son-of-a-bitch, excuse me Father, that just can't be."

"There's more. The executives we interviewed claimed to know nothing about employees from Mexico or South America. They said those soldiers wouldn't meet their high standards, they wouldn't hire them. Not only that but we were told that new owners would be taking over within the month. The company has been sold to some investors from Europe."

"Sounds like some damage control going on."

"Here's another curious event. We asked our liaison in Europe to find and interview Maurice Smith."

"Who is Smith?" Tony interrupted.

"Remember, he is the Blackstone accountant that Alex said found the phantom employees and reported it to his boss. He was transferred out of the Middle East to Bosnia."

"That's right, and we asked for one of our agents in Europe to interview him. He is nowhere to be found. His apartment had been ransacked and he hasn't been at work for days. He has just disappeared," Donna finished her story.

"Looks like that has turned into a dead end," Doc said.

"That would be a fair assessment. We have sealed the search warrant affidavits so at least we didn't have to disclose any information to Blackstone. I spoke with one of their executives, a Mr. Olness, and it was really strange, he didn't even seem curious why we were executing a warrant. I mean most execs would be ranting and raving and would have lawyers all over us, however, it was almost as though they expected this. This Olness guy told me that he was being transferred to Iraq by the new management."

The priest brought a tray with refreshments. "Fancy says she is cooking wild rice soup and fried walleye. Says she found a stash of walleye in the freezer. Be ready in about a half-hour. I'll call you when she gives the word."

Doc grabbed one of the egg rolls and with his mouth full asked, "What about the Washington attorney, Watkins?"

"I went back with another agent to interview him…a rude angry man. He claimed attorney-client privilege on the Blackstone matters and claimed the fifth regarding any involvement with arranging a trip to Minneapolis by the first lady and Cody."

"I'd give my right testicle and a million bucks to get that asshole before the grand jury."

"You'd still need another million to get this bastard to talk – won't happen. Turns out the son-of-a-bitch killed himself a day after we talked to him. When he didn't show up for work one of the law firm interns was sent to his house and found him in his car in the garage. Car stopped running when it ran out of gas and Watkins stopped running when he ran out of O2," finished Donna.

"So that's a dead end?"

"I had one more lead we picked up from bank records. Watkins was doing business with a guy named Bernie Silverstein who's a financial consultant in New York City – really moving a ton of money."

"Did you interview him?"

"I went to New York City and to his office. The police bomb squad was still investigating the explosion that killed Bernie and pretty much all of his records."

"More damage control." Doc shook his head at the efficiency of the terrorists.

"Pat, what about from the FBI?" Donna asked.

"Like I was telling Tony and Doc before you got here, I flew from Colorado to D. C. and they took my badge and gun for a day then called me back in and basically said to forget the whole deal. I don't think they plan to investigate anything beyond what you all know. We have rounded up a bunch of terrorists who are suspects in all of the so called plague attacks. I've been told that the evidence against them is overwhelming. On the other hand, the brass has to have some more cards than they are showing because they reinstated me so fast without explanation. In so many words, they told me to get back to work and forget about chasing leads on cases that have been solved."

Donna turned to Doc, "What about you, Mister. What are your plans here?"

"I'm sort of on leave to recuperate from losing my head in Colorado. My SAIC has given me a couple of months to recover then he wants this operation shut down. I'll spend the time writing reports and getting the case files in order, nothing exciting. The employee who filed a complaint against me was fired after she attacked another employee for using the last of the copier paper and not replacing it.

"I'm thinking seriously about retiring. Ma is moving in with my brother. He is a bachelor and is pleased to have the company. I got an offer to do some work overseas and maybe I'll take that if I can convince Kelly to adopt Gumpy. Although, I think he would like Paris. I can picture him and me strolling down the *Champ de Mars* and Gump stops to lift his leg on Mr. Effiel's tower." Doc said as he rubbed Pug's velvety black ears. Gumpy softly snored and snorted as he lay contently on Doc's lap.

"Dinners on," sang out the priest in a finely pitched alto voice.

After the meal, Doc asked Pat to join him while he walked the dog. They strolled down the pine-lined gravel driveway. Off in the distance a neighbor burned piles of leaves and the earthy fumes drifted in the light breeze. Doc handed Pat a cigar. They strolled quietly enjoying the cool night air.

"I wanted to talk to you about a couple of things. First, I owe you my life, as tattered as that may be. Thanks. Second, I wanted to tell you what has happened since we parted ways in Colorado.

"I've had a few conversations with the CIA's Director Lang about the men we were following in Colorado. Lang said that he believes you and I pushed them to move out of the United States which is what the CIA wanted so they would have more discretion to act outside of the American judicial system. Anyway, after I got shot, the whole damn lot of them scattered out of the U.S. The CIA was still reviewing and translating the wire tap and computer trapped information as this was unfolding. I think we could all agree that the taps and computer intercepts were not going to stand up in court. The judge would have thrown out all of that evidence and we would've had nothing. So the CIA was pleased when they all fled.

"It turns out the group we found in Colorado calls themselves the Islamic Council and they were a part of the recent attacks. It isn't clear of their exact role in the attacks. However, the CIA had enough evidence intercepted from one of the computers to show that the Council caused the attacks to force the president out of the Middle East and to allow the Muslim nations to attack Israel.

"The CIA caught up to a couple of the Council members in France. Now, I'm reading between the lines, but it sounds like they killed one of the Council and the second guy agreed to be an informant. You know how those CIA guys talk in code like they'll tell you they offed the guy although they never really say they offed him."

"What are they going to do with the guy that's talking?" Pat asked as he, like Bill Clinton, exhaled – without inhaling – the smoke against the light breeze.

"They are working with the Israelis, who apparently have a great deal of freedom to deal with these matters. I don't think they are constrained by a legal system or scrutinized by the media the way we are. Lang says that he is confident that between his agency and the Israelis they will take care of the threat."

"If this Islamic Council is responsible for all of the attacks, then that means that the defendants my agency arrested are innocent. If that is the case, don't we, you and I, have to bring that information to the Department of Justice? It has to be disclosed."

"I asked Lang about that. He says that his guys told him that while those men who the FBI arrested were not the actors in the actual attacks, they are all bona fide al Qaeda who were in this country plotting their own attacks. I know it's a fine distinction. They'll be convicted of the crime they were conspiring to commit although not the exact crime."

"That's a stretch, Doc."

"Lang says that if we press this issue now, it could jeopardize what they are doing and he asked me to just stand down on the investigation. Let it play out in their playground. Pat, I'm inclined to do just that, however, I want you to make the final decision."

"Does Lang know what the president's position on this is? After all they murdered his son."

"Again, I have to do some interpretation here. I think Lang believes the Council has some dirt on the president and some other politicians. Consequently, the president wants the Council members laid to rest, so to speak. Lang assures me that we will never be questioned about how this went down. He said some guilty will escape justice, some innocents will pay, maybe with their lives. Most importantly, the Council can be brought to their knees with no further harm to the United States."

"That's a lot to digest. There's so much we don't know, we've both taken oaths to uphold the U. S. Constitution."

"Lang made a comment that stuck in my mind. He said that terrorist attacks are acts of war and that our legal system is not set up to deal with this type of behavior. He said that it doesn't work to try to deal with these people as though it's just another crime. I think he is correct and it is right for us to do what he asks."

"Man, I'll defer to you on this one."

"Men are not hanged for stealing horses, but that horses may not be stolen."

"Hanging Judge Roy Bean?"

"Nope, that great British statesman, George Savile. Evidently, the royals had some problems with the horses being stolen."

They walked down to the river in silence…stopping to listen to the rushing water spray over the rocks. They had much to think about.

Saturday, November 10th

Prime Minister's Residence
Jerusalem, Israel

DIRECTOR LANG STOOD WHEN THE prime minister entered the room, "Mr. Prime Minister, it is good to visit with you again – even at this late hour."

"Old friends should visit more often. We have much news to catch up on," Har-el said. He gave Lang a hearty bear hug.

"First if I may, let me share the events that brought me here." Over the next two hours Lang detailed all of the events ending with the meeting outside of Paris during which Omar met his death. Lang took a sip of his cognac leaned back into the high topped leather chair and put the Cuban cigar to his lips.

"Lastly, this brings me to the purpose of the visit. I am not here officially representing the United States. That must be agreed to in order for me to continue." He paused to allow Har-el to respond.

"I do not like to agree to such matters without knowing your purpose."

"My purpose is to prevent the annihilation of the Jewish State of Israel."

"I will agree with the understanding that depending on the nature of your information, we can stop this and there will be no record of this meeting ever taking place."

"Agreed. I personally interrogated the Kuwaiti Deputy Minister of Defense al Fulani in France. Only I have a recording of that interrogation. He told me of an Islamic Council which is comprised of Islamic business leaders and government officials from 12 nations. They have amassed billions of dollars and a private army with the approval of their respective governments. Their goal is to push all American influences out of their nations, form a union of Islamic states and expel the Jews from Israel.

"I have an outline of the Council's plan to invade Israel. Their plan assumes that the United States will not intervene. I believe that my nation will not come to your aid for reasons I will explain later. I will give you that outline in return for your assurances."

"What assurance?"

"I will give to you a list of twelve men who are the Islamic Council. One, Omar, the Egyptian is dead and al Fulani, the Kuwaiti, is more or less under my control. I would like your assurances that your Mossad will either capture and interrogate or kill each of these men."

"Why don't you act on this yourself? Why doesn't America take care of these matters?"

"There are several reasons. The Council has made political contributions to many of our leaders. They were made illegally and would end the careers of those politicians if made public. That, according to al Fulani, includes the president himself. They have these men by the short hairs. You are well aware of the political fighting between parties. The Council has hired private detectives to gather dirt on the influential. They will use that to control our leaders when it comes to threats against the Council. I'd be required to report such activity to the president and congress. They would leak such information to their own political advantage and that would be the end of that. You're not burdened with these obstacles.

"I must warn you, also, that some of the computers connected to your tanks and aircraft may have been compromised. Our military experienced substantial problems in Iraq. In part, that failure pushed the president to pull troops from the area out of fear that we would suffer major defeats which would emboldened the terrorists to step up attacks. The Pentagon is investigating, very secretly. I am told by friends that your military hardware is likely compromised."

The prime minister walked stiffly to the bar hidden in the cedar credenza. He poured two crystal goblets and returned to Director Lang, "You have my assurance. We will take care of these problems."

He held his glass to toast, "*L'chei-im. Zol Zein.*"

Thursday, November 22nd

Orleans Café
Rennes, France.

IT WAS A CRYSTAL CLEAR day. The autumn sun warmed the guest seated in the patio of the Orleans Café. A hint of a breeze carried the earthy aroma of the decaying leaves from the nearby forest floor. It mixed with the smell of garlic, onions, and cooking sauces venting from the kitchen.

Michael Lang soaked this all in as he sipped from a glass of Port and watched the young and old lovers seated all around him. He was startled when Alon-ha Koheim, the Mossad director greeted him. "I'm sorry, I did not mean to sneak up on you," he offered.

"No, no, I was just lost in my thoughts. Come join me." He gestured to the seat next to him. "I have a fine bottle of Port waiting for you. Please refresh yourself."

Koheim joined him and accepted the proffered glass of port. "It's been a few years since we have been able to enjoy each other's company outside of formal meetings. Reminds me of the years when we were young and took the time. Those were the good times. No?"

"Yes, indeed. Those were the good times. I am thinking of buying this café and retiring."

"You may buy this café, but you will never retire. You and I both know that."

"Maybe you are right. What news do you have for me? Let's get this business done before our meal. Claude has prepared lamb for us."

"Not the sacrificial lamb, I hope. I have welcomed news for you. As you requested, we have, 'visited with' you might say, two of the Council members. One is still alive and tells us that there are two shipments of nerve gas delivered to your country. This is the gas that President Bush claimed Saddam Hussein had hidden. Saddam moved it to Syria before the invasion. They are waiting for orders to disperse the gas should your president back down on his deal to abandon the Middle East and Israel. Your president sold us out."

"A fact for which I personally am ashamed. I pray we will be able to work around that."

"We will. I have all the details of the whereabouts of the gas in this envelope. One of the Council members has apparently fled to your country. He is a diplomat and we will not pursue him onto your sovereign land. Do you have any suggestions?"

"Well, nothing officially will be done by our government. However, I did meet a police officer while in Colorado who may just fit that bill. Let me think about that."

"Now there may be an unintended consequence of bringing down the Council."

Director Lang raised his eyebrows, "And might that be?"

"The Council's demise comes with a price. One of their goals was to preserve existing sheikdoms and governments. They wanted stability and economic independence. They wished for Shariah Law and to be free from the Islamic terrorists. There's a difference you know."

"I would agree."

"The Council has spies inside the radical elements, like the Islamic Brotherhood. These extremists are going to overthrow the existing rulers."

"Like Tunisia, Moammer Gadhafi in Libya, and President Mubarak in Egypt," Director Lang said knowing he could extend the list threefold.

"Exactly, it is unfolding as we speak. These radicals are using the Imams to turn millions into the streets. They call it democracy, however, it will not be anything like your nation. The end result will be a Taliban-like rule over the oil producing nations. The Council had implemented a plan to bring these radicals to their knees. Now, with the impending death of the Council…"

"The radicals will prevail," the director rightly concluded.

"Given how close the Council has come to wiping Israel from the map, even though we may be creating a worse situation, I don't see that we have any other choice."

"Let's just leave it like that. I wish you well as you continue to pursue the Council members."

"I wish you well with your new café."

"I propose a toast to a new beginning."

Alon-ha Koheim raised his glass, "To the promised land. Next year in Jerusalem!"

Thanksgiving Day

White House
Washington, D. C.

THE PRESIDENT AND THE CHIEF of staff slipped away from the first lady and their guests at the Thanksgiving Dinner. They repaired to the president's office and lit up Cuban cigars to be enjoyed with their brandy. For ten minutes they said nothing, they just relished the moment. The chief broke the silence, "The Joint Chiefs have finished their plans to re-engage in Iraq. The missile attack by the Iranians on our warship in the Straits will be the provocation to return."

"Do we have enough proof that the attacks were by the Iranians?" asked the president.

"With the help of our Israeli friends, there is enough evidence. More than we had when we went into Iraq."

"Has the Israeli Prime Minister calmed down?"

"No, we can expect him to make demands in return for his silence."

"The FBI Director assures me that the cargo with the nerve gas containers is under control. There is no reason to believe that there may be more," the president said changing the subject.

"Can we trust him to keep that matter off the front page?" asked the chief.

"He sees the wisdom in that," President Franklin replied.

"What about his agent in Minnesota and that cop that got shot? Are they under wraps?"

"The director promises to keep a close eye on both of them. He put the fear of God in his agent and thinks the cop won't create a problem. Even if he did speak out, who is going to believe him against the FBI? Nobody," the chief answered his own question.

"We have to learn from these attacks. We have to get a grip on our borders. We must be more careful about acceping contributions. We have to have better regulations on the stock market. We can't have foreign investors with the ability to get defense contracts. We can't have them able to control our stock market. We have to for the sake of my son's death be more vigilant defending our nation. If we don't, his death will have been in vain. I made him that promise the day I buried him." The president stopped, tears streamed down his cheeks. He took a gulp of his brandy to regain his composure.

The chief pulled a note from his breast pocket. He read it to the president. "It's from the Israeli Prime Minister. He wishes you a blessed Thanksgiving and has invited you to visit him in Jerusalem next year."

President Franklin exhaled smoke from his fine cigar. "Next year in Jerusalem – I think I will go."

CPSIA information can be obtained at www.ICGtesting.com
Printed in the USA
LVOW131659091112

306667LV00003B/138/P